COMMUNION

F.D. Gross

BOOK THREE OF THE WOLFGANG TRILOGY

Communion
F. D. Gross

Edited by Deborah DeNicola
Internal artwork by Diana Gross
Maps and lineages by F. D. Gross
ISBN: 978-1-5356-1758-1

For Greg,
Your time on earth wasn't long enough…

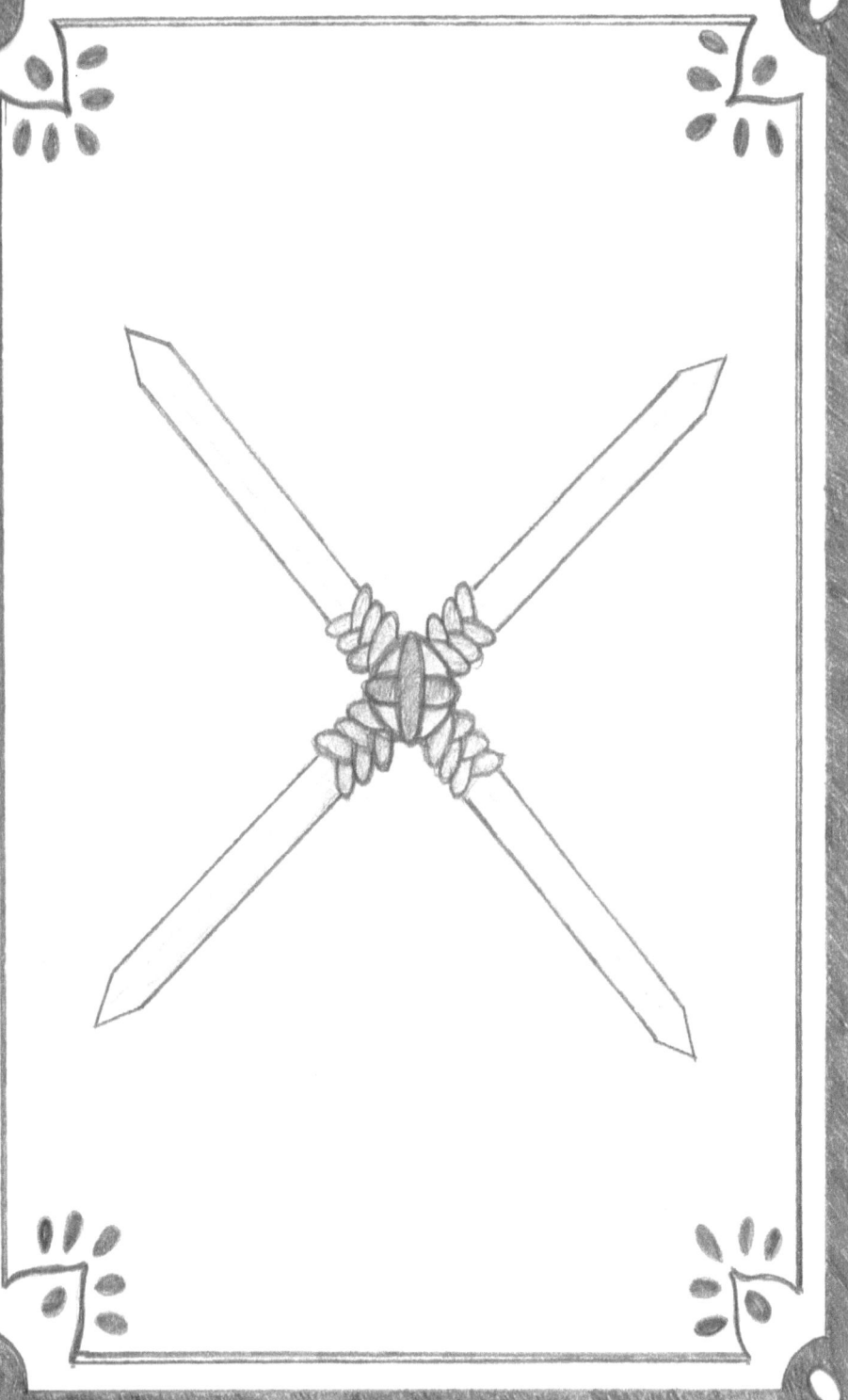

PORSON

MELD

SUNSTONE

AGONT

FRILL

DECAMERON FOREST

GAULDUST

THE GREAT

CARPELLA ROAD-RIVER

THE CORDOVA MOUNTAINS

WALTERS

DAY SIXTEEN

PROLOGUE

DORIAN

MOANING RISES FROM THE DARKNESS.

I hear it all around me. In the walls. In the floors. In the ceiling.

"Hello? Who's there?"

No one answers except the silence of the dank cold in which I lay. Hard stone pressing against my face, I taste it on my lips and tongue. These things I shouldn't feel, yet here I am, *feeling*. I thought for certain the last time would be the end. Something sharp, piercing my skin.

A loud, plangent clang echoes from somewhere beyond—a hallway perhaps— louder than I can stand. It shakes my soul awake, passing through my layers of skin, fascia, and bone. It drills into my core, churning my stomach like rusty gears. My body aches with a pain I cannot subdue. The memories over-whelm me, flooding my thoughts with tears and convoluted images.

Mother.

I can smell her hair. The peonies decorating the strands woven around her head.

She is cowering behind me as I stand defiant, protecting her, calming her, yet I am batted away like a useless doll.

"Watch, boy. Remember this day as the day your mother lost her humanity," says the masked demon in the red robes. Stag horns protrude from the top of his head; fangs appear under the mask as he leans in to give her the eternal kiss...

A sharp pain ignites my stomach again as I writhe in agony.

It's been sixteen days since my nightmare began, the day I was abducted by vampires, the ones called the Carnalreesee, and I fear this incarceration won't be over anytime soon. My fingertips still ache from the scratch marks etched into the coffin lid.

"Wakey, wakey..." echoes a voice from somewhere that sounds like a hallway. It triggers the moaning again that seems to come from all directions at once, even from the floor I lie on. The words I hear are like a thousand souls trapped in a prison, begging for forgiveness and release.

"Help me."

"Please, I'm trapped."

"The pain, oh the pain..."

I attempt to open my eyes, but the flickering flame is too much at first. The light is unbearable as my eyes adjust. A burning torch drips embers beyond a set of metal bars.

Slowly my body comes around. *What is this place? Whose voices were those?* The loud metallic sound from before left a dull ache throbbing in the temples of my skull. I am cold, yet sweating, as I know I have succumbed to some fever. My hands and feet burn with an insatiable itch. Dry and cracked, I examine my bandaged hands, scabbed over from the wounds in each palm. Now irritated, they weep with infection. I squeeze my hands in frustration and immediately the pain returns, searing deep into my muscle and bone like a hot knife. It travels up my wrists and through my elbows and suddenly I remember the iron spikes driven through my hands and feet as if it were just happening.

Shaking, I crawl to the bars glistening in the torchlight and press my face against the condensation, straining my eyes to see down the hallway. There is nothing and no one. Just the gray solitude of stones layered thick upon one another. Shadows dance along the walls depicting faces of torment and pain. *Are those people?*

Again the sharp sound of metal echoes from somewhere deep in the corridor causing my head to pulsate.

Whatever is making the sound is coming closer.

"Wakey, wakey…" comes the watery voice again.

I strain my eyes in the dark. *Those are definitely faces moving.* "Hey! Can you see me? Help me!"

I remember the last time I saw my father, Tenor. The way he screamed my name as the Carnalreesee stole me away from the depths of Egleaseon's ruins. It was painful to hear. The unforgettable love a father holds for his son. That terrible feeling of abandonment.

I remember the horrible ride through the countryside. Every bump. Splinters in my face, bruises on my head. The moments the

Carnalreesee stopped along the way, removing the lid from my coffin for fresh air. Day in, day out. I never saw the sun.

"Why are you doing this to me?" I cried one day, knowing very well they wouldn't tell me. Every day they fed on my blood to satiate their hunger. Why they never made me drink their blood, I do not know. They made me watch as they turned Joachim and my poor mother into vampires, but never me. I was spared. I was their prize. I was the one thing they came for and there was no escape.

I remember the beatings, the terrible power they possessed. They did it to exact revenge for their fallen comrades, to strike back against the lineage that has hunted and destroyed their kind for centuries.

I remember the hand that went with the beatings. The long bony fingers that tormented me, tainted me, made me flinch out of their pure enjoyment.

A metallic bang jolts me out of my nightmare.

"Good evening, Dorian. Have a good sleep?"

I stagger back from the bars terrified, doing all I can to distance myself from the one creature I've come to associate pain with.

Martyr the vampire.

He stands behind the thick metal bars like a hungry animal, eyeing me intently as if I were his next meal. Dressed in an onyx coat and white ascot, black polished boots rise from the floor to greet his knees. Red hair bounces around his shoulders like wild fire, curly and disheveled as if blown in a windstorm. With a chiseled alabaster face, ruby blood drips from his chin in an endless dribble. His eyes seem non-existent, sunken within the hollows of his high cheekbones. His lips recede from his gums like an exuberant jester having played a terrible trick. He parts his red-stained teeth and takes a swallow from the goblet in his long fingered hand.

"Ahhhh, now that is refreshing. Blood of wasted youth." He pauses, finishing the last of it and turns towards me, frowning. "Such a long face you have."

I say nothing as I cower against the wall, my fingers tracing the many bites running up and down my neck. I stopped counting days ago.

Martyr slams the goblet against the bars and lets it fall to the floor with a cacophonous rattle. "Dumb boy. So much trouble for a stupid little boy." He practically spits the words as he leans his head through the bars. "I could come in there. Comfort you if you'd like."

I shudder at the thought of his backhand against my skin. The burning sting I recall so many times.

"Do you remember our times together, Dorian?" Martyr's body fades into a mist as he passes through the bars unimpeded. The moaning from before rises in the hall, agitated by his actions. "I just want a little bit more of your blood. So much power flows through those veins. Blood of the son. It's intoxicating." He moves in quick, grabbing the side of my face with his long bony fingers, filling my senses with the scent of burning leaves. There is nothing I can do for I have no energy. He shoves my head aside to bite into the many raw holes along my neck.

"*Fool!* What are you doing?"

Martyr retracts from my neck, hissing, vanishing in an instant and reappearing behind the bars he was moments ago.

"You forget, Martyr, we are not to harm the boy any longer. He must regain his strength." The voice speaking now comes from a tall menacing figure dressed in metallic red armor that reflects in the torchlight. Straight black hair hangs about his face as he stares down at Martyr now leaning against the bars. A two handed, red-pommel sword rests at his waist.

"Damn you, Vargus, and your stupid rules. No one ever gets to have any fun around here because of *you*," says Martyr with an air of sarcasm.

In a furious rage, Vargus draws his massive sword and whirls it above his head, stopping it just before Martyr's heart.

Martyr laughs as he grips the blade with both hands and guides the weapon above his forehead. Giving it a squeeze, blood trickles from his hands and onto his face, turning his pale white skin a messy red. The moaning, coming from everywhere, seems to react to this behavior. Martyr maniacally laughs. "Vargus, you're always so dramatic!"

A smirk spreads across Vargus' lips. He wipes the blood from his blade on Martyr's coat and slides it back into its scabbard with ease. Turning to face me, Vargus' expression is just as empty and lifeless as my surroundings. "Dorian, his holiness summons you." Raising his hand, the lock on the gate clicks and the door opens with a groan. "If you will follow me."

His holiness?

With no choice but to obey, I collect what little strength I have left from the floor and step into the dim orange light of the dungeon hall, wondering. I am strategically forced to walk in the middle of two vampires. Vargus leads the way as Martyr follows closely behind me. I can hear him breathing and sniggering, lusting in the background for the blood he nearly had a taste of. I shudder at the thought of his fangs digging into my shoulder, sucking the precious lifeblood from me like so many times before. I stagger as vertigo passes over me. Using my hand to brace myself against the wall, I realize what I thought to be faces moments earlier are actual skulls. As I gaze at the floor, they are the same. Empty eye sockets and missing jaw bones stare up at me. Entire skeletons form the solid foundation of this godforsaken place.

Vargus stops and turns to face me with his expression cold and indifferent. "I can carry you." His towering figure stares down at me with his piercing yellow eyes.

"No. I can manage," I say, holding out my hand and shaking my head.

With a grunt, and a judgmental gaze towards Martyr, he continues on without saying a word.

"I didn't do anything," mumbles Martyr behind me as we move forward, listening to the wails and moans of this strange dungeon, a place I have no doubt come to dread in the little time I've spent awake here.

We pass sweeping corridors of wafting candle smoke and high archways decorated with black stones and painted portraits of the heavenly order bowing before some omnipotent being. Who or what that being is, only God knows, for surely it is not

He, but some imposter, some false idol that the vampires look to. It is a black-robed figure aglow in a halo of red.

Remembering the six Carnalreesee appearing at Wolfgang Manor in their holy robes and masks condemns my memory to pain. The blasphemy and evil plots of the vampire show no boundaries. My abduction, the turning of my mother, and their impersonation of The Holy Order.

As I limp along the cold bones of this accursed place, I notice the skeletons in the walls becoming less and less frequent as the three of us exit the dark chamber through heavy wooden doors. Passing through a macabre archway made of decaying corpses, the voices I heard earlier seem delighted at my arrival. All at once, I am bombarded with the moaning of the damned, disembodied words reaching my ears as wisps of light pass through the stretched skin of decaying bodies.

"Release us."

"Save me."

"God, please forgive me…"

My pace quickens as I bump into the back of Vargus, nearly grabbing him in fright as a scared boy would to his brave father. There is no reaction as he continues forward, never stopping, never breaking his stride.

"All of these trapped souls. Isn't it marvelous?" Martyr whispers into my ear from behind me. There is slight glee in his voice. "Just think, all of this potential in the dark cathedral. Spirit energy at our beck and call. Listen to their *woes*. Listen to their *cries*. It's what makes this place so strong, more so than ever before! It is built upon the bones of acolytes, devotees to the cause. They didn't die in vain—well, not all of them."

I feel Martyr's bony hand clasp over my shoulder as he leans to point something out in front of me.

"There. Look. Some of them still live."

Following his gesture, I stare in horror at what lies before me. A creature—no—a thing. Still living and breathing. *Barely.* It reaches towards us as we pass, grasping at the air. Sinewy tendons hold it imprisoned in the wall like a grotesque living portrait.

"What is it?" I ask through trembling lips, but my answer is Martyr laughing to himself. *What sort of place is this? God, where are You?*

We come to the base of a staircase that spirals upward into oblivion. A cylindrical well mortared with black stones. Giant cathedral windows rise vertically along the walls of more trapped acolytes squirming in their cocoons. Stained glass illuminates the floor with dim hues of red, orange, and purple. An open window sends a chilly breeze through the stairwell corridor, stirring Vargus' hair and blowing out some of the candles lining the inner well. Thousands of candles glitter in the pale light of night as we ascend each blackened stone. Young boys in white priestly garb make their way up and down the many steps, frantically tending to extinguished wicks and disheveled red curtains. Not all of the windows have been opened and as we pass, I can tell the boys are trying their hardest not to look at me. Yet one particular boy stares at me, his eyes never leave mine as we exchange glances of sadness and pity. I catch him looking at the many holes running along my neck and arms and suddenly he pulls the sleeve down on his robe, hiding what I've already noticed. The same feeding marks.

Quickly he goes back to tending the curtains as we continue our ascent, Martyr behind me giving his unwanted tour of this terrible hell.

"Those are our balcony boys. They tend to the cathedral's every whim, day and night. They are the prodigies of our acolytes, ones destined to serve in the light of God." Martyr laughs at his own joke as I watch another pair of servant boys' robes turn red and purple as they draw the curtains of another window. Round and round we go, ever upward and never resting. With my feet sore and legs heavy, I wonder if the pilgrimage through this *dark* cathedral is my penance for being human. This is my first glimpse into the vampire world and all it holds. Why they do the things they do. Was it really their existence to simply drink the blood of the living, or was there some higher purpose, a cause to their plague over the land? My father never really showed me much about the outside, only how to fight.

Vargus stops suddenly and I realize we have reached the top. Directly behind him rests a massive double-door made from a dark red wood. Trimmed in iron hasps and studs, they stand twice the size of Vargus in height. Martyr moves to pass first into the room, but Vargus blocks his way.

"Are you joking? What the hell is this? Out of my way you half-wit!" says Martyr, but Vargus hardly flinches.

He stands firm and stoic as he looks down at the disheveled mess of Martyr. "His holiness says you are needed elsewhere. New arrivals have come into the chapel. See to their recruitment as acolytes." Vargus pauses. "By the way, all of the edicts are currently out searching."

A look of curiosity pours over Martyr's face. "Searching? Searching for what?"

Vargus lets out a groan. "For *him*. Marcus Cornelius."

It is the first time I see the blue in Martyr's eyes as his face contorts into realization. His receding lips elongate into a wider smile. He backs down the stairs, with deranged laughter. "Well now, that makes things interesting."

Forced to go first as I enter the chamber, a blast of warm air greets my face. Massive in size, its pillars reach higher than I can see, disappearing into inky blackness. I hear Vargus close the door behind me with an echoing thump. Immediately my thoughts are of confusion as the smell of cooked meats and breads fills the air. To the right of the room sits a masterly crafted table carved from red wood as if it were bleeding. Polished to a fine sheen, atop its gorgeously mantled sides rests a feast fit for a king. Plates of roasted chicken. Skewers of pork rib. Baskets filled with fluffy white rolls. Bowls piled with steaming carrots and peas. The colors are enticing and my first reaction is to move towards sustenance, but something stays my foot as my stomach growls in protest.

"Ahh, the young wolf is awake," slithers a voice from the back of the room. Gloom covers the rear of the chamber like a thick blanket.

That voice. Where have I heard it before?

"Your holiness. I have brought the boy as you requested," says Vargus behind me. The light in the room makes him more massive and intimidating with his blood armor and blood sword.

"Yes, thank you, Vargus," says the voice from the shadow. "Dorian, I trust you weren't treated *too* poorly. I know you've had quite a journey." Flames burst to life suddenly as a balcony boy tends to the many candles surrounding the figure who was once in shadow. It is a man, sitting atop a throne hunched over, dressed in robes of white and a hat in the fashion of religious regalia. His balding makes him all forehead despite the long white braid draping down his back. A second balcony boy sits to his left, holding a white cloth stained red to his neck. The boy seems lost and lethargic.

I am at a loss for words as I stare at the one man who stands as the pinnacle symbol of the Church, the one who my family has served and trusted for so many generations. Archbishop Faeradon. The second highest ranking official of The Holy Order. I remember him from the many sermons held at Albestan church in Roland and the stories my father told.

"Archbishop? What's happening? I don't understand…" My hands shake yet I force words I thought I would never say. "Archbishop, you are the head of The Holy Order and church. You're its leader!"

Vargus steps forward, raising a hand.

"That won't be necessary, Vargus. The boy is tired and stressed and no doubt famished." Faeradon stands motioning to the massively long table. "Please, won't you join me?" As he moves to the table, he calls over his shoulder. "That is all, Vargus." The balcony boys hastily follow after Faeradon tending to his every need.

"Join you? Are you mad?" For the first time, I notice Faeradon in a different light. The fact that he looks exactly the same as I have always remembered him. Immaculate porcelain skin. The same creases on his forehead and the crow's feet around his eyes. After all this time, he hasn't aged in the least. Something doesn't feel right, yet I cannot place it. How is it he is here, where ever here is— and the Carnalreesee stand as his servants? They obey him. Had the church come to some strange arrangement or resolution?

My stomach aches and I can't help but stare at the food spread before me. It is overwhelming and my glands salivate.

"Yes, yes, eat my boy! There is plenty. You need to gain your strength!" says Faeradon with jubilation.

Indignant, I glare at him before tearing into the succulent meal. Focusing on filling my stomach with the nutrients it needs, I pause every so often to notice Faeradon staring at me intently with his piercing blue eyes.

"I know you must be wondering after all this time why the Carnalreesee have done the things they've done to you and brought you here now before me. In time, you will see what is to be offered here. A chance at a new life. A good life, even more grand than the one you were taken from…" there is a pause in Faeradon's word, "when the master returns."

When the master returns? Does he mean Cardinal Glass, the first in The Holy Order? Was he too in on this dark pact with the vampire? I continue gorging feverishly, eating as much as I can to gain my strength back. I think of my father and what he would do in a situation like this, if he was captured and held prisoner by menacing foes. *If only I had my sword! I could destroy these monsters and their accomplices. They would taste the fury of the Wolfgang house. Taste the power of the prodigal son.*

As I pack my gullet with food, an idea fills my head and suddenly a plan begins unfolding. A counter measure that will call for patience. I have no idea what their plans are, but I must bide my time. Keep gaining strength until the time is right. And then... Yes, I will do this. For the honor of my bloodline, the honor of my mother and father. Yes, the house of Wolfgang will live within me, through me, and never end.

I will make you proud, father.

"Already the color is returning to your face," says Faeradon, standing up from the table. I notice he hasn't eaten a single morsel from the feast. "In time you will get to know the corridors of this holy place. Know that it is safe. There is no need to fear anymore, Dorian."

Faeradon moves to stand beside me, running his bejeweled fingers along the smooth table's edge only to stop over my hand reaching for a dinner roll. His frozen touch sends an uneasy feeling through my shivering body. As he takes my bandaged hand into both of his, he begins unwrapping it delicately, fingering the wound site in a caressing way. "I must apologize. They did such a poor job the first time," he says with a smile. "In time you will heal. In time, all things heal." Gingerly he kisses my hand and I pull away in horror. The balcony boys become excited by Faeradon's actions, giggling and glancing at one another. His hand moves up my arm and comes to rest on my shoulder as fear holds me to the chair. His breath smells of copper and cloves as he whispers in my ear. "Do not fear, Dorian, for fear makes the blood sour. Summon your courage, muster your strength. In time the master will come," says Faeradon, cradling my face in his hand, "and we have all the time in the world."

DAY SEVENTEEN

CHAPTER
I

WOLFGANG

My head aches something terrible as I'm tossed about the back of the wagon, bumping shoulders with Kronklich.

It's been two days since we left Walters and the cold hasn't let up. In fact, it's gotten worse. With a blanket spread over us, I shiver at the thought of sitting in Councilor's seat, the large man driving the wagon. Such constitution he possesses. Such *determination*. It's as if his resolution is stronger than mine now. But why and for what? His revenge was fulfilled. The vampire that killed his daughter is dead. I made sure of that. It's not like *his* son was kidnapped by a horde of vampires.

Still, Councilor presses us ever forward, driving down the treacherous terrain of the Cordova Mountains at a grueling pace, rarely stopping to light a fire due to the monsters. It is for his horses—Abel and Jasmine—that we stop so they don't freeze.

Blinking my eye, a frozen tear cracks just above the cloth over my face. I pull it tighter around my ears and nose, doing my best to cover the scars on my cheek. *How long has it been since I drove the wooden stake through my loving wife's heart? Two weeks? Three weeks?*

"You know, it's been seventeen days since we've left Roland," says Kronklich, as if reading my thoughts. Snow collects in his unshaven face as he glances at me thoughtfully.

Yes, seventeen days of hell. I look at Kronklich in wonderment. *How does he do that?*

"Us gallivanting around the countryside, searching for Dorian in the freezing cold. It's no wonder—" Kronklich clenches his teeth as he adjusts his leg "—that we haven't seen a bloody soul since we left civilization." It is clear the grievous wound caused by Constable's black hook still irritates him. He places a hand on my shoulder. "Tenor, I hope you know, not all is lost. We will find Dorian. He is like a son to me. Hope is our most intriguing quality." He smiles.

Hope. What a strange and convoluted subject. After all the things we've been through, I can hardly relate to hope as a good thing. And what was a *good thing*? For starters, I suppose having lots of money would be one. And eating three square meals of the finest foods a day could be another. But those simple ideas were all available to me at one time. I had the life of a rich noble. The whims and wants in life were at my beck and call. But for me, these things were minor at best. It is my family that I cherish most. Always has been. And it is for this sole purpose my tale of woe continues.

My family was taken from me on that fateful night seventeen days ago by the Carnalreesee, the night creatures known as vampires. Not just any vampires, though. *The* vampires who served their late master, Lord Egleaseon. With four of them now dead, it is the final two who continue this game of cat and mouse, forcing me on this chase through desolate wastelands. My heart sinks at what fate awaits Dorian.

Still to this day, I criticize myself over that fateful night, wondering how things could have been different, wondering *if* things could have been different. Diana would still be alive and by my side. Dorian would be free from the evil of the Carnalreesee.

But I left Wolfgang Manor for the Danbury Hovel earlier that day, to purge another vampire infestation and consequently, left my family unprotected. I know now things couldn't have been different. The answer as to why this happened is clear to me. Clear as the dismal day we currently ride in, jostling around the back of a wagon with Kronklich at my side, freezing in the cold and Councilor serving as our guide behind the reins of this treacherous terrain.

To put it simply, it was planned from the start. All of it. From receiving the yellow envelope with the red seal, to the attack on Wolfgang Manor. The journey to Egleaseon's ruins was treacherous and the chase through the Cordova Mountains was perilous. The Carnalreesee had a plan all along and it was led by that which I least expected. The Holy Order. Bronin, priest of Albestan church, was proof of that. He acted on his selfish desires and aiding the mastermind behind it all, Faeradon, the Archbishop. I remember reading his name scrawled at the bottom of the message delivered to Scepter by crow in Walters that read: "the boy has arrived." He was speaking of one place. Sunstone.

And so that is where we go.

The sound of rushing water stalls my thoughts as the wagon banks a sharp left, forcing all the supplies in the back to shift. Peering over the side, I see the misty spray of the washed-out Carpella Road, now a river of coppery water, spume over boulders and debris accumulated over the last week since the beginning of the winter solstice. Myth says the mountains weep during the winter season due to the gloom and death of living things, but the reality is that many of the Cordova Mountains are active volcanoes, generating heat from vents at the highest peaks. The melted snows bring on the floods at its lowest points and the washouts of copper minerals along its plethora of quarries turns the water red. Broken branches and dead animals float down its churning waters, reminding me of the Faust River and what awaits those who attempt to forge its depths.

I hear Councilor's reins cracking over the wind. "Hya!" and again the wagon shifts away from the menacing water vein. Without a doubt the path Councilor has chartered is a danger-ous one. With our descent down his *secret passage*, following large "s" shaped switchbacks that cut deep into the ravines, I wonder about our safety—overall.

"Are you sure we aren't going to die a horrible death?" I shout over my shoulder. The howling wind is relentless.

"I'm pretty sure," shouts back Councilor. His head is wrapped tight in a black cowl with a heavy layered cloth covering half his face and neck. "We have about a ninety percent survival rate that we will make it out of this storm. I'm sure of it."

Councilor's deep voice dies off as I see him focus back on the hidden path only he can see. His hand often runs the length of the massive black scythe strategically placed to the left of him, ready to strike in a moment's notice.

Sinking back down to shield my body from the snow and wind, I rub at my irritated eye, wishing we could stop for fire. But I know stopping in these parts of Decameron Forest could spell death for two reasons. One is the snow trapping us in with the wagon and the horses, effectively burying us alive. And two, the monsters never stop roaming in the freezing cold. Atters and lechers lurk around every corner and crevice breeched.

No, we cannot stop.

Another bump and the wagon lurches like a seesaw. My bottom collides with the wood floor sending more aches through my already abused body. Wondering how many bruises I've accumulated after all this time, my eye comes to rest on the cargo of sacks and boxes sliding back and forth around my boots. One in particular, the large box shaped like a coffin, continues to be the center of my attention. Having loaded it on the wagon at the beginning of the trip, Councilor insisted that we take it. I remember his exact words as he patted the crate: "One can never be too prepared when hunting monsters." What exactly that meant, I'm not sure, but as I stare at it now, its perplexing existence continues to consume me.

"I would let it go if I were you," says Kronklich. His body is turned away from me and his hat is over his face. How could he possibly see what I'm doing?

"Let it go you say," I respond with indignation. "Not so easy when we've been staring at it for the last two days." I look over my shoulder at Councilor, but I'm certain he can't hear me over the wind. "Here he is, insistent upon taking this heavy laden cargo, but not once has he opened it." I hold my hand out to it. "There's a lock thicker than my wrist on there and he is always looking at it as if we are going to do something to it." I shake my head in frustration and look away. The snow-covered forest lingers in the distance like a heavy cloud waiting to consume us. Slowly it passes us by as we continue zig-zagging through switchbacks.

Kronklich mumbles from under his thick coat. "I'm sure he has his reasons, Tenor. Maybe it's his secret weapon."

"Hysterical, James, really—"

The wagon suddenly comes to a jarring halt as Councilor's voice moans over the wind. "Whoa!"

Immediately I am on high alert. It would still be another couple of hours before we stopped for fire.

Collecting myself from the back of the wagon, I stand up, my knees stiff as I stomp the circulation back into my legs. With my hand firmly grasped over Enivid tucked beneath my long coat, I spring over the side, landing in the snow and slush. I feel Diana channeling through me for I now know her power resides within the blade, ever since her father, Old Man Dora re-forged the holy weapon of destruction.

"What is it?" I call after Councilor who has already covered a great distance in front of the wagon. He is crouching in the snow, using his scythe to balance his massive frame from tipping over. He moves the snow with his one free hand as I approach cautiously.

My eye scans the surrounding woods for ambush. Ice crows are notorious for inhabiting the frozen trees of Decameron Forest and forever they plague my mind. My body flinches at the thought of them again, when Kronklich and I were surrounded by white feathers and blood, desperate to survive. I did all I could to protect Kronklich as they pecked at his body. Palming the hole where my eye should be, a pain surges through my head as I recall the moment those goddamn fiends took my eye, forever crippling my perception. Seeing the world through one eye takes getting used to. Now I see things in half its light. A world—my world, incomplete.

"Remains of a human, from the looks of it," says Councilor standing up. His breath puffs around him in great clouds. "There's nothing left. The atters and ice crows got to it. Whoever it was must have died from starvation or freezing to death."

"Or both," I say, standing beside the pile of blood-speckled bones. "Whoever it was, they didn't have much." Scattering the remains of a backpack and shredded cloth with my boot, I look back to the wagon to see Kronklich hasn't bothered to move. Good. Better for him to rest now anyway.

"In two days' time, if everything goes well and the weather holds, we should reach Galdaust. We'll be able to properly rest there and tend to the horses. Abel and Jasmine won't last much longer in this high snow." He turns around looking back towards the wagon and again I can't help but assume he's checking on the large rectangle box that's been haunting me this entire trip. Slowly he starts trudging back through the snow. "We should keep going. There isn't much light left."

Off in the distance, I notice tiny black figures moving about the base of the trees. Glowing white eyes stare back as they move up the trunks and perch in the branches. The group of atters wait patiently as I make my way back to the wagon, thinking about the giant wool blanket Kronklich and I were sharing. There's no use staying out here wondering any longer about what we should be doing. The mission for now is simple. Reach Galdaust to re-stock and re-supply. Then it's off to the great white city of Sunstone. I hope Councilor is right, that it's two more days to Galdaust. Despite the horses needing attention, despite Councilor's obsession with his—dare I say coffin—I know the three of us need a hot meal and a thorough night's rest.

Leaping over the side of the wagon, it rocks back and forth as I land beside Kronklich.

Just as I left him.

Pulling the wool blanket up to my neck, I settle back down for another session of shaking and bouncing along the secret trail, watching the lock slap against the long rectangular box with an ominous thump.

DAY EIGHTEEN

CHAPTER
II

It is a strange feeling. Diana no longer visits me in my dreams. In fact, my dreams have ceased all together. Why? I'm not sure. But I have an idea.

There is not a day that goes by that I do not think of her. I miss her nightly visits, where my body is assaulted by her hands and kisses, but they too have perished. In philosophy, it is said time heals all things, but I know differently. I will never heal. Ever are my thoughts filled with Diana's essence and beauty. Her long locks of raven hair, her eyes full of black magic. She haunts me every day, following me wherever I go. Even now as I lay in the back of the wagon listening to Kronklich and Councilor conversing with one another, I have visions of her. The disarming smile she always gives me. The words 'curse you Tenor' resonating deep within me. I smile to myself as the cold surrounds my body. I am impervious to it, at least for a while, as I think about her.

Holding Enivid against my chest is my way of keeping her close. I feel her warmth channeling through the weapon used for killing vampires. Four blades extending from a center handle wrapped in leather. This weapon of death I now associate with love.

Last night's reprieve was short. With imminent threats lurking in the woods, we chanced a fire for only a few hours. The horses need to survive if we are to survive. It was in that small window of time I was able to sleep. But like most nights, since the encounter with Stellamane in his ruins, the visits I receive from Diana have ceased. I recall the dream where she freed me from Stellamane's enslavement, how she protected me from the skeleton king and fought for my soul. As I slept in an old ruin of an old king, the dream was so vivid; I still have a hard time determining if it was real or not.

God be damned. I miss my D.

The neighing of horses brings me back to the present. Bleary-eyed and hungry, I stare up through the canopy of rotting leaves and snow to see a blue sky. It's been days since I last saw real color. The low branches bend from the crisp wind blowing down the west slopes of the Cordova Mountains. Again, I listen to the conversation taking place between Kronklich and Councilor. For past days, the cold has been enough to prevent useless chatter. But now, with the sun thwarting the dismal sky, the winter air is somewhat tolerable, possibly enjoyable, if the circumstances were different.

"… And so by the time I left home, I knew exactly what it was I was going to do with myself…"

I hear the sadness in Kronklich's voice as he speaks to Councilor, telling him about the past—his past. From his brief moment of silence, I know what comes next.

"… until my parents were killed." There is another drawn out pause. The wagon shifts in weight and I can tell Councilor is uncomfortable. The direction of Kronklich's words is a path I seldom hear. "My parents, bless their souls, were slain by vampires, to which I'm sure you can relate. A random attack on a random town. Porson, to be exact." The sound of crows caws in the distant. "So you see my good man, fate deals us a terrible hand at times, and is anything but selective. As I always say, it doesn't matter what happens in the end, really. Things are because they are; we can only do what we can do." I hear the leather reins creak as if tightened in a fist. "Keep up the good fight, never waiver, and give quarter to those deserving. Understand?"

For a moment I wonder if therapy is in session. Is Kronklich lecturing Councilor? A strange thought without a doubt.

"It is these principles that have allowed me to live thus far, and as much as it pains me to say it, one can never be too aware, for ignorance breeds failure…"

"It is your principles that afforded you that wound in your leg," responds Councilor's deep voice sarcastically. "Sometimes if you think too much on any one thing, you can get yourself killed…"

"On the contrary," counters Kronklich. "Most, if not all scenarios and situations can be thought through and executed in the mind, consequently achieving victory before a sword is ever drawn."

"You know, I have half a mind that says you're bat-shit crazy. What do you think of that?"

"A fair assumption, indeed, but you will find that I am right in the end, about the end."

"About the end? You mean death."

"Quite so. The tiniest window is opened in that moment before dying, where purpose, *your* purpose, is realized and fulfilled."

"What? That doesn't even make sense."

"It absolutely does."

"You're insane."

"Am I truly? One must ask the inner-self such a question."

I stop myself from laughing as I continue listening. The sun is nearly exposed from the clouds and I wonder about the sound coming from afar. I no longer hear crows but— is that bird song?

Another drawn out silence lingers long enough for me to focus on the wheels spinning from the wagon and the horses' hooves thudding on the saturated ground.

"So you never did say what you are," comes Councilors deep voice again.

"Quite right you are, my good man. T'would be silly of me to say I was any one thing…"

Rubbing my face, I try to wake myself up. I can only imagine where this conversation is going.

"A cook. A facilitator. A coachman. A doctor. Did I ever mention undertaker?"

Kronklich goes on and on. I can't tell by Councilor's silence whether he is either bored or entertained. I acquiesce to myself to think the latter for who doesn't like a good Kronklich story?

The tone of his voice is always genuine and never once has he proven himself false.

"Really, you've been all those things? I take it your family was well off then?"

"It depends, really, on what you consider wealthy is. My mother worked very hard as a book binder. She was a charitable woman always give, give, giving, and my father, well, he was a master of anatomy, a doctor, Atreyu Valonius Kronklich."

"That's some name."

"Yes it is. Have you heard of him?"

"Er—no."

The sound of rushing water fills my ears as I roll around in the back of the cart. I'm thoroughly surprised how warm the weather is despite yesterday's chill even if we are descending out of the mountains.

"So that explains your eligibility for education, but where did you go to study so many professions? Seems you have learned everything."

Kronklich laughs out loud. "Surely I haven't learned everything, but I have learned a great deal. I owe most of the knowledge to the Five Cities Academy within the Sunstone province. It was there that I too learned to become a physician much like my father. He was very proud of me and even more proud that I excelled in mathematics more so than he."

"So you know numbers?"

"Quite so."

"How many gold dauntess do you have left if you have one thousand gold and take away five thousand and sixty two silvers?"

Without delay, Kronklich responds with his exact answer. "Four hundred and ninety three gold with eight silver left over."

There is a moment of silence again as I imagine Councilor trying to count the amount in his head and then there is a grunt. "Is that right?"

Kronklich's voice couldn't sound more confident "Of course it is."

Unable to rest any longer, I prop myself up on some of the supply sacks and gaze at the rushing washout of the Carpella Road.

"Ah. Look who's up!" says Kronklich with an air of excitement. "I take it you slept well, Tenor?"

Staring at the grin on Kronklich's face, I can't help but frown at his genuine concern for my well-being. "I would have slept better if you two would have watched the road instead of giving each other philosophical lessons."

"Lessons. Clearly not. We were merely indulging in stories of each other's pasts. Our good friend Councilor, here, was just about to tell me his, weren't you?" Kronklich gazes at the side of Councilor's hooded face.

Seems Councilor has no intention of indulging in anything at the moment.

"Come, come, man. I have given you my story. Now it's time to hear yours. Don't be shy. Let's have it. Tell us how your love for murder—I mean, espionage, came to be?" There is a large grin on Kronklich's face. With his hair combed back into a ponytail and top hat lowered over his brow, I wonder how he is able to stay so serious for such occasions despite the imminent danger Councilor poses for the both of us. Councilor is nearly triple our size.

"An assassin doesn't divulge his secrets of the dark arts."

"*The dark arts.* You make it sound so foreboding."

"That's because it is." Councilor turns his head to face Kronklich. It's impossible to see his eyes hidden in the shadow of his hood. "It's a life I excelled in, but something I didn't choose.

"I see," responds Kronklich with an air of regret. "Well there's no need to discuss it if you don't want to—"

"I don't want to," interrupts Councilor. His head turns back to face the front. "Besides, we have a problem."

It is only now I realize, distracted by the intensity of the conversation, the wagon has stopped moving. Sloped downward on a decline, the wheels of the wagon are skillfully chalked in rocks as the three of us stare at what lies ahead: the breaking waters of the Carpella Road.

CHAPTER
III

"Nowhere to go except straight through," says Councilor pointing ahead.

I stare at the red churning waters, spitting and spraying among the rocks. It sends my mind into a tailspin of regret for there is no doubt we have come to a roadblock. All this time we've driven by the red water, trusting Councilor on his "secret" trail but we've never had to go through it.

Although the water looks shallow enough to forge across, it's what's below the surface that worries me. What sort of refuse lives down there? I see carcasses of once living things floating down the rapids, swirling in pools of coppery blood, spinning round and round the jagged gray rocks of the mountain's base until they release on to their next destination. Atters, deer, sometimes cadavers of humans. They float their way down, becoming caught on the rocks like snagged debris. How many of these corpses are lechers waiting to spring to life?

I wonder about the Carpella Road and whether or not the locals refer to it as the Carpella River when the floodwaters come.

Jumping off the wagon, I stand beside the river, gazing at its mesmerizing effects. Seeing the reddish water reminds me of the blood Scepter stole from me using the extraction dagger. How he shipped it off like some package to Sunstone and again I can't help but think of Dorian and his potential fate. They have my blood and they have him.

Suddenly that feeling of anxiety rises inside me; we should be moving quickly instead of wasting our time here on the bank of a bloody river, staring at rocks.

I grab the reins from Councilor and begin advancing across the river.

"Tenor! Wait!" shouts Councilor. He brings up the rear, his massive frame splashing through the churning tide. But he never makes it to my side. Instead, he lingers towards the back of the wagon, staying close to his crate, his black box of mystery.

Something moves underneath the water.

Kronklich comes splashing to my side, crossbow at the ready. "What is it?"

"Kronklich? Why aren't you in the wagon?" I grit my teeth in agitation. "You should be resting your leg."

"What, and miss out on all the excitement? T'would be a shame!"

Lechers burst from the shallows of the river, arms reaching upward for air, groping for living flesh. A low gurgling escapes their mouths as they converge on us. Muck drips from their half torn faces and patches of rotting hair. Kronklich fires off a shot, piercing one through the head. It falls helplessly back into the water with a splash.

"Besides," continues Kronklich loading another bolt, "I'm a bit rusty. Need to get the kinks out!"

Arms stretched out, the wailing from the lechers grows louder.

"It's great you two are having a nice chat," says Councilor from the rear of the wagon, "but if you haven't noticed, we're surrounded." He raises his black scythe over head and slices it through the air, cleaving a pair of lechers in half.

The undead's numbers continue to increase as if disturbing the very water summons more. One appears before me and I drive Enivid through its forehead. Pushing the lifeless corpse aside, I sever the head of another. "Protect the horses at all cost!" I yell, watching Kronklich fire another bolt into the back of a lecher's head, its hands falling short of Jasmine.

Kronklich and I draw closer to one another, yet I notice Councilor still lingering by the box. *What the hell is he doing? His size alone will help even the odds.* I watch as he glides his scythe back and forth like a farmer harvesting crops. In a matter of seconds, he is covered in blood and gore.

I sever a lecher's arm as it latches onto Kronklich in the middle of reloading. Kronklich follows through by caving in its forehead with the butt end of his crossbow, sending bits of bone and brain into the water. Two more fill the gap and Kronklich starts swinging wildly using the crossbow like a club.

There's too many of them.

"We need higher ground!" I yell, slicing left and right. A rotten hand splashes into the water, then a severed leg. It is all I can do to keep them away from the horses as they gnash with their teeth and claw with their fingers.

Kronklich spins one of them around and shoves it into a group, buying himself some time. Gripping the side of the railing, he jumps back into the wagon with one motion and bashes the brains of another lecher.

"Councilor! We could really use your help here!" I plead, body-checking another and decapitating it.

Councilor barrels through the water like a bear, splashing to my aid, meeting me shoulder to shoulder. "Need a hand?"

I glance at the devastation left in his wake. He must have killed twenty of them already.

Together, the two of us, along with Kronklich's vantage point, begin turning the tide in our favor. We cleave, stab, and shoot our way to balance.

"Where do you think they're coming from?" asks Councilor as he skewers two lechers at one.

"Where do you think?" I say sarcastically. "Egleaseon's evil is everywhere. The very water we stand in is cursed. Nothing is safe in these mountains. Not anymore."

As I finish my last words, the sound of croaking rises from the depth of the river and suddenly my hope turns for the worst. I know that sound. Sounds of the Faust River and the beasts that dwell within it.

With a splash to my right, I see two frog-like creatures soaring towards me. Gellies. Part frog, part fish, these wretches have a mouth that runs along the center of their face. From top to bottom, a full rack of razor-sharp teeth snap open and shut ready to devour. With eyes to either side of a gaping maw, their only disadvantage is their sight. They can't see straight ahead.

Sidestepping out of its line of vision, I bring Enivid down with a force severing the scaly head. Like the lechers, gellies triumph in numbers, so if there is one, there is bound to be hundreds.

There is a splash from the other side of the wagon. Kronklich dodges one gellie as another comes soaring straight at him. He launches a bolt into its belly sending the creature spinning away into the water.

"See, nothing to worry about," chimes Kronklich while setting another bolt. But as he looks up, another group of them attack him from all angles, flinging themselves at him, attempting to topple him from the wagon. The crossbow is knocked from his hands.

"Watch out!" I warn as the gellies spring for his face. He ducks while snapping the flap of his coat outward to reveal two small mini bow guns. At the ready, he shoots a gellie pointblank and follows through, swinging his arms about and taking aim at me. His expression is serious and so I dodge just in time as he fires a bolt straight into the face of lecher. With mouth open ready to bite, the creature slinks back into the water and floats away.

Grabbing the reins of the horses, I lead them through the channel until they understand what is happening. Brave horses. "We need to get out of the water!" I shout, my heart racing as if it's about to burst. A lecher grabs the side of Jasmine and she head butts it, sending it splashing back into the burgundy water.

Stowing his scythe across his back, Councilor brings up the rear of the wagon, pushing with his arms while gritting his teeth.

Kronklich continues his barrage of arrows as the wagon slowly traverses the river, grinding over rocks and tilting from the current. Within moments, we make it to the other side, sucking the air as if it were our last. I smash a gellie underneath my boot as I survey the bank of the river for stragglers. Soon the croaking and the moaning dies off and we are once again left alone in silence and peace wondering how long it will take to freeze to death.

"We need fire," I say, stowing Enivid away, while I lead Abel and Jasmine further up the bank.

"You know we can't do that," says Councilor, looking over his box, making sure the latches and locks are still in place. "Not here. We're too close to the river."

"If we don't get heat soon, we're as good as dead. Sound good to you?"

"We'll be fine. It's just a little ways up."

Hopping into the back of the wagon, I give Kronklich a warning glance, wondering how his leg is holding up. But he doesn't notice me at first. Too busy with his new toys, I can only guess where he acquired such weapons to begin with.

"Neat little gadgets, aren't they?" comments Kronklich. "They come in handy at the right moments."

Yes, perfect for an assassin.

I glare at the back of Councilor's head as he cracks the reins to get us on our way. We almost died because of that stupid box. I watch Kronklich rummage around through one of the bags as I wrap a blanket around myself, attempting to counter the cold as best I can.

"Well, I must say. This calls for a celebration. " Having found what he was looking for, he removes a small tin from the bag and places it under his nose while taking a long drawn out sniff. "Ahhh. Tea anyone?"

DAY NINETEEN

CHAPTER IV

MOST OF THE MORNING AND early afternoon passes by in a dull haze as I watch the Decameron Forest slowly dissipate from a giant frozen forest into a smattering of thawing trees. No longer do we encounter dense patches of wood or harrowing switchbacks through mountainous crag lands. We enter into somewhat of a rolling countryside of white hills and broken streams. The Carpella River lingers in the distance, the sound of its breaking waters ever present, and for the first time, the tracks of the Iron Carriage come into view. Memory of the runaway death train lingers in my mind, the horrible crash on the mountainside that would forever change the course of our actions. I put it behind me now, the same as the lechers and gellies and atters that can rip your toes off in the night. This open woodland—dare I say prairie—is unlike the dark forest. Innocence seems to linger here. For a time anyway.

And here I am again wondering about the black box in the back of the wagon. Reminded of its presence each time Councilor glances over his shoulder. For a moment I think he is checking on us out of concern, but I know deep down the truth. His obsession with weapons, as Kronklich points out, is far from it. No. There is something else in the box. This I am sure of. And tonight, I will find out.

Towards the end of the day, late afternoon, the presence of civilization begins to show, however dull and miniscule it might be. The outskirts of Gauldust linger in the distance like a dull brown shoe. The sight of small gray smoke stacks is a small reprieve, despite the depravity this small highway junction town may have to offer.

Chickens and cattle scatter as we ride in on the only thoroughfare. The road is a blessing for this town, it being the only evidence of the modern world. Homes made of wood and roofs poorly thatched make up the majority of this quaint yet tired excuse of a hovel. It is more like a village, so far removed from the province of Sunstone. It is the last frontier west of the Cordova Mountains.

One well sits in the middle of town serving as the only watering hole the people and their livestock use to survive. As we drive past, locals stare at us while waiting in line with buckets to claim their nightly rations. With a first glance of the town, one could easily associate poverty to the locals. Scantily dressed in nothing more than rags to keep warm, most are thin as the rails of the Iron Carriage. *I wonder what they eat in these parts.*

Councilor guides us through Gauldust as if he knows exactly where we are going. The smell of cooking meat sends my primal instincts into rage. Kronklich props himself up on an elbow as he too seems to be affected by the smells.

It is nearly nightfall when the carriage finally stops in front of an old beat-up inn. Glowing in the early dusk by torchlight, the wagon lowers and rises as Councilor dismounts from the riding perch. "This is where we'll stay the night. Decent lodgings and the food is a step up from eating dried apples and stale bread."

Hospitality at the Moss Inn is a welcome luxury as we sit and eat our fill of a rich dinner by the fireplace. I watch Councilor speak with others as I pull a chicken leg from the plate at our table. I wonder about his connection to this town and any other things I might not know about him. After all, he is a Black Blade assassin, a contract killer working for anyone willing to pay the right price.

Kronklich is in and out of consciousness as we finish our meals, and it is at this time, Councilor sits down at our table, observing his surroundings, always watching as if someone were conspiring to kill him.

"There is some business I must tend to in town tonight," says Councilor in his deep barrel-like voice. His massive frame blocks the light from the fireplace. "You two should head back up to the rooms. Get a proper night's sleep."

I stare at Councilor across the table from the rim of my mug as he scoops up left over mashed potatoes with his finger. *So there it is. What sort of business is he going to conduct? What contacts did he have here in Gauldust? Did he really have a mark in this rundown town or was there something else? Some other kind of business?* My trust factor is still at an all-time low with Councilor. Ever since the revelation I received from Scepter, the vampire I killed in Walters, my paranoia about his actions hasn't dwindled. *He conspired with a vampire to use me.*

"Yes, you're right. We both need to rest tonight. See you in the morning then," I say, rising from the table, retrieving a groggy Kronklich. But I have no intention of sleeping. Once Councilor is gone, other plans will come to fruition.

Climbing the rickety steps to the second floor, I pack Kronklich away in his room for the night, ensuring he is comfortable and has the supplies he needs. Heading back down the stairs, I spot Councilor's black cape leaving through the front door of the inn. *Just what are you up to?*

Instead of going after him, I wait awhile sipping on barley wine by the fire until I feel enough time has passed.

Stepping out into the frigid night, a light snow flutters from the sky. It has grown colder, much like the past few nights, but I counter it, buckling all of the bronze straps of my thick leather coat. With Enivid close to me, my body stays warm. Energy channels through me every time I think of her.

Thank you, Diana.

Moving around to the back of the inn, I make way to our wagon tucked away in the far corner of the stable, nodding to the caretaker, who is anything but alert as he dozes in and out of consciousness, a tankard lying empty at his feet. *So much for doing your job.* With carrots in my hand, a treat for Abel and Jasmine, it takes me a moment to realize the wagon is gone and I curse under my breath. *So much for prying open the lock on the box.*

I dash into the night, following tracks left in the snow. They lead to the well in the middle of town and I wonder what sort of business requires the use of our wagon. My optimism dissolves seeing the multiple tracks going in all directions.

"Dammit."

Leaning against the side of the well, rubbing my gloved hands together, the desolate sounds of the night sets my nerves on edge. My breath comes out in puffs of steam. A light wind whistles through town and *what's that?* The faint sound of goats and chickens lingers in the distance. *One of the barns perhaps?*

With no one walking about the town at night, it's easy to go undetected as I slip past glowing candlelight coming from resident's windows. There is no town watch as far as I can tell and if there were, there was a good chance I saw them drinking the night away at the Moss Inn. *Where the hell did you go?*

My hunt for Councilor seems to go on forever. Retracing my steps twice, I have lost all hope in finding the expert assassin, realizing my efforts have been in vain.

On my way back to the inn, I recognize the sounds of farm animals again and pay them no mind until the high pitch squealing of a pig raises the hairs on my arms. I take off running, heading for the sound toward a group of barn-like structures. Moving from one building to the next, I peek through dirt-speckled windows and hay-filled doorways only to see darkness. Nearby, I retrieve a small oil lantern hanging from a doorframe and spark it to life. Slowly, cautiously, I maneuver among sleeping goats and cooing chickens as my light disturbs their slumber. The neighing of horses alerts me to a stable nearby and so I double back, moving on to another barn, shading the lantern with my hand. Still no sign of a pigpen.

Desperately I move through the dark, wondering if what I heard was simply my mind playing tricks on me. But the thought is soon discarded when I see the wagon—*our wagon*—in the distance with Abel and Jasmine at the lead and no Councilor in sight.

My first instinct is to approach in haste but I stop myself. What if it isn't Councilor who brought the wagon here? What if it was stolen and there was a thief waiting to slit my throat? I decide it would be better to gain a different perspective. Climbing a ladder I passed moments ago, I realize I can gain a higher vantage point by lobbing into the loft through an open window on the second floor. Reducing the glow of the lantern, I creep to the edge of the railing and squint through the dark, trying to see something, anything that would give away the culprit.

And then I nearly drop the lantern. My hand instinctively moves to Enivid on my belt.

Strewn about the barn floor is a massacre of pigs. Slaughtered with their necks ripped open. Blood mixed with mud everywhere. In the center of the carnage, a young girl is bent at the knees, finishing off another. I can hear her slurping the last of the pig's blood with her mouth until the pig gives a final snort before falling over.

My eye widens in horror as the girl in the purple gown and long dark hair pulls away from the pig's neck, gasping for air and wiping her mouth with the sleeve of her dress. Frantically she searches around in the dark for more animals and more blood. A solitary candle on a barrel serves as the only light in the barn. But I know she doesn't need it. *That* candle is for someone else. *She* is a vampire and like all vampires, they see in the dark.

I cannot allow her to exist.

Slowly, methodically, I maneuver down the scaffolding from the loft, placing my boots in soft straw to cover my sound. With the vampire girl focused on the next kill, the blood lust which consumes *all* vampires, ending her life will be a simple task.

Burnt leaves and cloves fill my nostrils as I approach from behind, her awareness thwarted by hunger, and as I rush forward, a massive shadow moves in front of me. Loud ringing fills the inside of the barn as my holy weapon, Enivid, clashes with the black metal of a scythe. A figure the size of a bear, covered in black cloak and hood, shoves me back with such force, I nearly crash to the floor. The figure braces its weapon before it like a shield.

"Stop, Tenor! Not like this!"

I can never forget Councilor's voice. The vampire girl clings to him like a bat, startled and confused, her purple eyes peering from underneath his bulging biceps. Seeing her closer now, she is an adolescent girl maybe thirteen or fourteen years of age. *Those eyes. Where have I seen those eyes before?*

Councilor pushes the girl back behind him.

"What are you doing, Councilor?" I say in disbelief. I knew he couldn't be trusted, but this was going too far. "Get away from her!"

"No, Tenor. I can't. Not like this," he says again in a calmer tone, pleading almost.

The girl peeks out from behind him once more and again that feeling of familiarity tingles inside me. My memory—a jumbled mess of twirling vines—struggles to untie this mystery knot of a girl, who she is, and what she is doing here. Suddenly my memory is triggered like a bolt in my heart.

The night I stirred awake in Councilors cottage. The keyhole in the forbidden door. Those purple eyes. The whispering voice.

"You can't kill her, Tenor. We have to save her."

Now there was no doubt what was inside the box this whole time.

Councilor's daughter, Winter.

CHAPTER
V

DORIAN

"So you're the one everyone's talking about. The secret boy who came in the other night. Is it true what the others are saying? That you're the heir to the Wolfgang house, the son of Lord Wolfgang?"

The question catches me off guard as the name of my house lingers in the air like a distant memory. I stare at Charles, the boy who is currently my ward these past few days, wanting to say something to him, but no words form from my lips. I'm not sure if telling him who I am would be the best thing right now, or if it even mattered. All this time and Charles said nothing about it.

"If you are him, I've never been in the presence of nobility before."

I look away, not giving an answer, and continue the work of preparing the Dark Cathedral's grand spiral staircase for the evening, the main task appointed to me among other tasks, ever since arriving in Sunstone. The job is quite simple, really. It entails drawing many red curtains from stained glass windows lining the stairwell and unfastening the numerous latches lining glass panes. The work is tedious and there are so many.

Already my fingers hurt as I undo the next one, standing in a bath of faceted multi-colors. Having been given new clothes to wear, I don the same robes as the rest of the balcony boys, the familiar white cloth with yellow embroidered trim.

Finishing with the last latch, I wait for Charles to finish his side and together we thrust the heavy framed windows open, swinging them open to full capacity before catching on the brackets that even the strongest winds can't blow back. I suck in a deep breath. A cool breeze blasts through the open window, coupling with the last rays of sunset. The beams warm my face and I cherish the moment. Living with vampires these past weeks has deprived me of this simple privilege taken for granted. It is the only thing I look forward to when waking in the cramped bunks where I sleep. Three others share a room with me.

Charles gazes at me timidly as I step onto the ledge to look at the vast buildings of white that make up the great city of Sunstone. The so-called holy city of purity. From what I've experienced so far, I have my doubts this place is anything but pure. Stretching before me for what seems like miles, the white wash stonewalls fade to orange in the dying light in every direction I look. Glancing up and down the tower's exterior, it is truly amazing how high the spire reaches. It seems to extend into the very clouds.

For a moment, I think of jumping. I am so tired and beaten, it would be easy to end it here and now, a quick leap, a quick escape, and never would the Carnalreesee have whatever it is they want from me. But thoughts of my father force me to step back. I hear the tension in Charles' breath as he exhales. I can't abandon my father now. I know he's out there somewhere, trying to get to me. I don't know how to explain it, but I just sense it, as if something inside were pulling at my guts, letting me know somehow everything will be all right. I need to remain strong, figure out a way to escape. Of this I am certain, for it's in my blood. The resolve of the Wolfgangs.

Charles is staring at me again like he always does. Staring at the holes along my arms and neck. "I thought you were going to jump," he says, the brown curls atop his head fluttering about in the wind. "I'm glad you didn't. So many I've known have ended themselves in that way. It's nice to have company. Someone new to talk to. A noble, at that." He smiles.

"Thanks," I say, not sure if he is being sincere, or saying the natural proper response. "I won't be going like that."

"That's comforting." Charles looks around worriedly. "Come on, let's keep going. They don't like it when we stop." He makes his way down to the next set of windows and I follow. He gathers a bunch of thick fabric in his hands and begins drawing back his side of the curtains while looking at me inquisitively.

"Why do you keep staring at me? If you look any harder, I might burst into flames." It's not just Charles who does this, but the other boys when they are around me.

"Sorry. It's just that your arms and neck. The holes. They are going away. Healing." Charles looks away tying back his cord.

"Isn't that supposed to be a good thing?" I ask, not sure what Charles' direction is.

"You tell me." He stops suddenly and pulls the sleeves up his arms to show me hundreds of bite marks. Puffy and red, he scratches at them. "Mine aren't going away. That makes you different from the rest of us. You're special in some way. Why do they want you?"

Is that jealousy in his tone? I do my best to simmer the mood. "I'm not special. At least, I don't think I'm special." Again, I avoid telling him anything more than he needs to know. Nothing about my usurpers, Martyr and Vargus, and certainly not Faeradon. I begin unlatching the locks on the panes.

"Well, I guess it doesn't matter, right? We're all part of the same cause, aren't we? Doing the same thing?"

"Yes," I answer, not having a clue as to what he means. "How did you come into the service of the church?" I ask, changing the subject quickly.

"My parents. They are acolytes of the cathedral. Have been for quite some time I suppose. Haven't seen them in years."

"Years?"

"Yes, they left some time ago on a pilgrimage to the western shores to recruit more followers from the ships that come in. I suppose missionaries have the toughest jobs of them all."

I remember the conversation with Martyr when we walked the lower halls of the Dark Cathedral's prison cells days ago. He said the souls trapped in the walls were devoted acolytes. Could it be the two were related? If so, Charles is oblivious to it, and it is quite possible he will never see his parents again. I realize even more so now that escaping this oblivion is of the utmost importance. The Carnalreesee draining these poor servant boys each day has clouded their ability to think and reason. They are being controlled, and I want no part of it.

We work for a time more, drawing more curtains, lighting candles, brushing steps with wicker brooms and unlatching more windows until we finally reach the bottom of the stairwell, where most of the other boys have gathered. The last rays of sunlight have altogether vanished on the horizon. The many colors have been replaced with the monotone yellow of flame.

Again I feel eyes staring at me and try to ignore the feeling of being different from the others as they converse amongst one another. One of the boys, big, heavy and fat, comes forth, corralling the younger ones into a closer group.

"Dinner is being served. Come on then. Let's regain our strength and feed our bellies with the good food the masters have provided us."

At the same time, figures in red tunics and polished black boots appear from doorways hidden in the shadows of the cathedral. With dark hoods covering their faces, they seem to materialize out of the very air itself. In that moment, the great hall becomes a loud conglomeration of noise and conversations, balcony boys and the ones that have come to be known as edicts. Collectively they pass one another toward unknown destinations, keeping to themselves or casually holding conversations in pairs. And at the same time, like every night, bats fly from the interior black corridors, the places where we are not allowed to go. They fly through the great spiraling stairwell towards the holy chamber where Faeradon awaits or out the open windows we conveniently prepared. Only God truly knows their purpose. I say a prayer to the innocent victims who will fall prey tonight.

I lose sight of Charles in the masses and use the chance to slip away from prying eyes. Passing into a hall full of flickering torches, I sigh with relief as I see no one who will stop me to ask questions.

Staying close to the wall like a slinking shadow, I use every opportunity to duck behind stone pillars and wooden pews as edicts pass. Utterly lost with no direction, I marvel at the beauty all around me. The Dark Cathedral. One word describes how I feel about it. Eloquence. Ornate sconces trimmed in metal roses and twisting leaves blaze in cold stone walkways. Angels and demons carved into dark wooden archways decorate anything resembling an exit. The entirety of the place is immaculate and no traces of blood can be found. No wax drippings droop from the chandeliers high up in the rafters. It's as if spirits were tending to every minute detail this holy place harbored at one time, the ghosts of the past paying their dues to services provided by the church long ago. The way it stands, that's what this place reminds me of. A great big medieval church with all the fixings. And just like Albestan church in Roland, there is an organ, although much larger. Roped off, forbidden to be played, it lingers in the shadows like a great feral beast waiting to be woken from it's slumber. In fact, since the days I've been allowed to walk around this terribly beautiful prison, there has been no music. No hymns. No chants. It's as if the very essence of sound has been drained away like the balcony boys' blood.

A bat swoops past my face, screeching down the hall with a maddening purpose. Startled, I duck low, rolling across a tattered worn rug and tucking behind a set of polished black pews. Still as a statue, breath locked away in lungs, I am centered in what seems to be a chapel. An altar at the far end of the room houses two high backed chairs draped in black and red cloth. Behind it, immense stain glass windows now blacked out from the night, rise high into the rafters. There is a walkway where the worn rug traverses along a center aisle. I notice multiple exits from this place of unholy gathering. Belongings of individuals line the seats as I cautiously pass along the center, glancing left and right at leather satchels and overcoats normally worn outside. *Where are all the attendees?*

Making my way to the back, voices drift up from one particular archway that begins with a flight of stairs leading down into a spiral of flickering light. There is sobbing and shouting and—laughing. *Not that way.*

I retrace my steps, moving to a massive set of wooden portcullis-shaped doors. Pushing with all of my strength, I manage a groan from one of them and continue my way into a wind-blown foyer where shadows dance among walls of armored suits. Lined in neatly fashioned rows, there are six in total facing one another across the hall as if assigned sentry duty. There at the other end of the entryway lies another set of thick oak doors waiting to be opened.

My heart flutters.

Beyond that threshold stands my freedom, my chance to escape this decrepit prison of pain and torture. My chance to find my father.

The air is thick with energy. Sweat trickles from my temple as I advance one step at a time. Tarnished and full of blemishes, the plated armor displays embrace long pole axes within their gauntlet hands. A mouse scurries away from the base of one of them and I inhale with anticipation. I am nearly there. My hand reaches for the iron ring hanging from the door.

The metal is cool under my fingers. My ears prickle. The sound of creaking metal startles me and my body fills with tension. Someone—something, is watching me.

A dark shadow moves towards my face and immediately I duck. A poleaxe embeds itself into the door freeing wood chips from their foundation. Pushing with my legs and rolling onto my back, another flash of metal comes crashing down, crumbling stone beneath its weight, inches from where I just stood.

Death lingers in the air like a foul stench. Six suits of armor come to life shattering my perception of reality.

This is not possible.

Kicking up loose pebbles, I scramble out of the way as deadly weapons swing at me from all directions. The suits of armor creak and groan as their blades come down in a furious storm, one after another, preventing me from escaping into the night.

I am forced back and they move forward, dragging their halberds of doom behind them, scraping and sparking in the darkness. Although they are slow, they are precise with their movements, leaving me only the advantage of speed. Quickly, I make my way back to the chapel and attempt to close the great oak door with all of my might, but my strength fails and the door doesn't move an inch. Having lost so much blood from the vampires feasting on me throughout the journey through the Cordova Mountains, my strength still suffers after all these days in recovery. I watch as the suits of armor advance and they're nearly upon me. Again I brace the door using my back and legs and summon all the strength I can muster, grunting under the pressure. A deep groan escapes the hinges as wood scrapes ground. The door slams shut just as the first poleaxe strikes the other side, vibrating the wood with a muffled thump.

The dull *thunk* of metal on wood doesn't last long before it ceases all together. With ear to the door, I hear the haunted knights moving back to their designated posts, their weapons dragging, their armor creaking.

So much for going that way. What the hell were those things?

I slow my breathing as best I can as I lean against the strong wood.

Despite my coughing, I'm hearing words again. I pick up on the voices I heard earlier and decide to investigate, regardless of my traversing deeper into the bowels of the cathedral. It's not the way I should be going, but what choice do I have? If I were to leave the chapel another way, my discovery would almost be certain.

Mentally preparing myself for the worst, I begin descending each step quietly, listening to the disturbing moans and cynical laughter. The voices seem familiar as I travel deeper down and my wits are set on edge. Reaching the end of the stairs, I cling to the wall as if it were my life source. As I peek around the corner, pushing disheveled hair from my eye, nothing prepares me for what I see next. I catch my yelp before it escapes my throat.

Martyr and Vargus walk among human victims chained to walls, bloodied and stripped of their earthly possessions. The two vampires admire their catch as they inspect them head to toe, their hands folded behind their backs as if strolling through the woods. Some of the victims are still alive, squirming and indignant, pleading for their lives, while others simply cry.

Currently, Vargus, with his long black hair flowing down his back, addresses Martyr as they turn back in my direction. "We did what we had to in the mountains to survive. Nothing more. I will not hear another word about it."

"Listen to you!" says Martyr in the most irritated way; his red hair bounces about in the torch light like burning fire. "If it wasn't for the kid's blood we would *both* be dead. Don't you see the potential in the strength of his life source? We could become the masters, the two of us!"

Vargus slaps Martyr to the ground with his large meaty hand and shouts at him. "You dare betray the master?"

Martyr looks up from the floor, blood dripping from his grin.

"You are *not* to feed upon the boy again. He is to remain *untouched*. He must regain his strength for the *Master. Not you.* Do I make myself clear?"

More whimpering comes from the victims shackled to the walls. I realize these must be the same kind of acolytes Vargus spoke of the other day before my audience with Faeradon, and with all of their possessions left behind, abandoned in the chapel, I can only wonder what sort of fate waits for them.

I should never have come down here.

I turn, intending to slip away undetected, but the sound of Martyr's rancid voice freezes my tracks.

"Leaving so soon?"

Before I can blink, Martyr appears before me, a gust of wind following behind his body. He grabs a fistful of my hair, nearly tearing it from the roots. "Seems we have an audience."

"Let me go!" I scream. I rake his face with my nails, drawing lines of blood across his cheeks. Martyr wipes away the crimson liquid with his free hand and licks his fingers clean. The wounds instantly vanish.

"Stupid boy…" Martyr raises an open hand to throttle me, but Vargus intervenes.

"Martyr!"

"What? I wasn't going to *hit* him." Martyr's sunken eyes glow a furious blue as he smiles. "Honestly."

Vargus shoots him a warning glare.

"What is it that you want with me?" I ask, looking into Martyr's ice-cold eyes. "What are you going to do? Who is the master?"

Martyr laughs, pulling me by my hair again.

"Remember what I said, Martyr."

Martyr looks back at Vargus with a wide grin and a grunt. "You're such an asshole!" He gives my head a hardy shake. "Come on, boy!" He hollers, beginning to drag me down the tower steps I hadn't noticed before.

"Ow! You're hurting me!"

"Quit your whining. You sound like a little girl."

"Listen to me! Please. Don't keep me locked up in this darkness. I'll go mad. If you want me to get better, I need to be in sunlight!"

Martyr laughs. "Don't worry about that. You'll get your chance, boy! We'll *all* get our chance for a little bit of sunshine!"

DAY TWENTY

CHAPTER
VI

WOLFGANG

I FEEL AS IF I was thrown into the icy depths of the Faust River last night.

My thoughts are a mess trying to process the dark secret unveiled to me in the most absurd of places. And to think, this whole time my intuition, my *paranoia,* was justified!

Having ridden along the Carpella road, no longer a river of burgundy slush, it was decided that we should get out of town as quickly as possible due to our current circumstance. There was no discussion about our next destination, only that we needed to get away from Gauldust. Harboring a vampire was far from something acceptable in any society.

It is about midday when the wagon comes to a stop. With the horses tired and spent, it is a good time to make camp. I find myself staring at the black box while we rest, my thoughts still hovering around the insanity of Councilor's intent. *There is a vampire in that box. Councilor's daughter.*

Back against a tree, facing Kronklich's welcomed fire, I shake the sleep from my tired brain.

"I'm going to ask you one time, and one time only," I say, standing up, emphasizing my frustration. "That time we were left for dead in the Decameron Forest, how did you know how to find us?" I give Councilor the sternest of looks, my cheeks red and puffy and irritated from my unshaven scruff.

With his large frame sitting cross-legged opposite the fire, he says nothing in response. He doesn't even look at me.

"Answer me goddammit!" I yell, brandishing a knife from my belt.

"I hardly think resorting to violence will help our current situation," says Kronklich in a smooth tone. He grabs two skewers from the fire, each with their own piece of meat, and hands one to me, exchanging it for the skinning knife, and one to Councilor. "You both should eat. Bad moods grow in empty stomachs."

"I'm not hungry," says Councilor, a look of sadness over his face.

"Nor am I," I say, handing the skewer back to Kronklich. I move over towards the wagon, running my hand over the black box that serves as Winter's protective coffin. All I have to do is open the lid and Councilor's precious little girl evaporates. He watches me for a second, then stands as if to retaliate.

"He told me," begins Councilor.

"Who told you?" I ask, as if not knowing the truth already.

"Scepter. He told me there was a force in the woods that could help avenge my daughter, get back at the one who turned her into what she is. He said there was a way to save her. Blood of the father." He pauses a moment, staring at the black box. "That force was you. That's why I saved you and nursed you back to health. So you would kill Cresthaven for me and get this." Councilor produces a small red vial from the folds of his cloak, hiding it from the sun.

The blood I extracted from Cresthaven.

Immediately my mind rushes back to a series of horrific visions, as if they were happening in this very moment.

A sharp stabbing pain in my side. Bronin, the diabolical priest, whispering in my ear, 'I'm sorry, Tenor.'

A sharp stabbing pain in my side. Scepter, the vampire, smiling in my face, 'can't have you dying on me yet!'

I grip the side of the wagon, stabilizing myself from falling. Councilor's voice drifts back to me...

"Getting the blood of her killer was the first step." Councilor moves over to Winter's box and rests his elbows on the lid, placing his face in his hands. "Don't you see? I would do anything to save her. I would do *anything* to bring her *back.*"

"But there is no coming *back*," I say, completely drained of emotion. "What were you thinking? No one comes back from transforming into a vampire. Not even my wife." I move away from the coffin in frustration and resume my seat by the fire, leaning against the tree, realizing I'm exhausted.

"But there has to be a way," presses Councilor. "You're the vampire hunter. You of all people should know."

"Look. I already told you…" I say with agitation, but then stop myself short. *Was there a way?* I think about the Hand of God, the holy artifact that was melded into the Bawaka, forged by Diana's father, Old Man Dora, to make Enivid. The Hand of God possessed the power to revert vampires back into humans. *Could Enivid do the same in its altered form?*

I look up at Kronklich, whom I know is thinking the same thing, and then over to Councilor.

"There might be a way," I say softly.

Peonies were Diana's favorite flower and one of the more prominent things I remember about her. I recall the way her hair smelled of them when I held her from behind, lacing our fingers together, and the way she weaved them in and out of her braids. Even now, as we resume our trek along the Great Carpella Road, bobbing up and down rolling slopes, there seems to be an aura of them around me, filling my senses, forcing me to remember. I smile to myself. *I will never forget.*

Night descends quickly.

For most of the day, silence was our companion of choice. Neither Councilor or myself wanted to talk after our conversation earlier. Even Kronklich remained silent for a time until he chimed in about how time seemed to flow more quickly as we descended deeper into the valley of Sunstone.

Now, with dusk lingering on the cusp, there is a pendulum of dread swaying over Kronklich and Councilor's heads. Perhaps it's a timetable for what's to come. I see the growing anxiety on their faces. They are worried for Winter as am I. My plan of action isn't the most *conventional*, but we all agreed it must be done. For her sake and ours.

The road takes us on a long bending curve, and eventually lands us in a copse of scattered trees and patches of snow. Gazing up into the branches of towering birch, my hand subconsciously rests over Enivid, its warm leather handle comforting my lingering thoughts. *Will it work?* I glance down at the fine craftsmanship of Dora's final masterpiece. Once the sacred heirloom weapon of the Wolfgang house, the Bawaka, and once the holy artifact, the Hand of God, it is now something completely else. Transformed. An instrument of destruction. It is this aspect that worries me. I ask myself again. *Will it work?*

Dora mentioned the Hand of God was melded into the handle of the weapon. Fingering the leather straps curiously, I begin unwrapping. The oiled strips slowly uncoil exposing a gray and bronze finish which in turn transverses into four steel blades protruding from the center. Nothing prepares me for what I find next.

My heart flutters.

Emblazoned in the center of the handle rests a peony flower, the very symbol of Diana. His daughter. My dead wife. That which was most sacred to him, to me, has been melted into this holy weapon of destruction.

My fingers tremble across the intricate grooves and smooth polished finish as my eye begins to water. *I never knew. He never told me.*

"This is as good of a spot as we're going to get," says Councilor, bringing the wagon to a jarring halt.

Rubbing my eye, I stow Enivid for now.

"Plenty of cover. We're far enough from the road where no one will see us."

The road was desolate all day, but the precaution is still necessary.

We make camp with what little light is left and soon Kronklich's fire brings new color to our evening. As he sets up tins for boiling soup, Councilor and I lift Winter's coffin from the wagon and set it near a cluster of trees, far enough away from open flames but still with enough light to see. A light breeze blows through the wood while Councilor unlocks the latch. Slowly he helps Winter out of the box as if she were a delicate mannequin, her skin like porcelain. Upon seeing me, she instantly reacts, cowering behind Councilor as if I were a demon from her nightmare. *In many ways I am.*

"It's him father! The man from yesterday. He's here to kill me!" Still wearing her purple dress from the night before, she tucks her long black hair behind her ear revealing chiseled features of sunken cheekbones and purplish lips. She would need to feed more if she were to restore any semblance of human color. Hopefully, after tonight, she will never have to drink blood again.

"Calm down, Winter," assures Councilor's deep voice. He turns her around to face him. "He's not here to kill you. He's here to *help* you."

Her purple eyes gaze toward me and my mind travels back to the time I saw her. Behind the locked door in Councilor's cottage. A night of silence filled with the begging voice of a girl. Then there was the time behind Councilor's cottage when I practiced throwing Enivid. Those eyes I felt staring at me from the window. All this time it was her.

She gives me a knowing look as if confirming my thoughts and I immediately break my gaze away. *She is reading my mind. Had her powers grown so quickly?* This worries me.

"Alright. Let's get on with this," I say, not wanting to wait a second longer. The danger, the *risk*, is too great.

"What about the soup, Tenor?" asks Kronklich. "We all could use a bit of warming up, wouldn't you say? Get to know the girl a little?"

"There's no time for that." I point at Winter. Her frail frame seems to hover in the air like a ghost. "She's a *vampire*. Every second that passes is a danger to us if she's not in that box."

Councilor pulls his daughter close to him. "She's not a danger. I've taught her to control her urges."

I don't have time to sit here and explain the urges of vampires. Their need to feed. Every second that passes as we argue about it prolongs my quest to save Dorian.

"Enough talk," I say, unbuckling the straps of my leather coat. My hand brushes over Enivid. "Do you want my help or not?"

Kronklich stands, putting his bowl down.

Councilor hugs his daughter tight and kisses her forehead. "Everything will be alright, sweet angel. I promise."

But as the words leave Councilor's mouth I can't help but feel a sense of dread at the task laid out before me. There's no way of knowing what will happen. Enivid was made to destroy vampires.

With Councilor and Kronklich to either side of Winter, I have her face away from me as they grip her arms. Methodically, I unlace the back of her dress, exposing her alabaster skin and smooth shoulder blades. So delicate. So *innocent*. I can't help but think about the time at Albestan church, when I cut off Isabella's head, sending her vampire blood to splatter across the walls. At the time, there was no choice. No options. But now—now was a chance.

"It's ok," whimpers Winter. "I understand what must be done. I hate this curse. Everything about it. I want to feel better. I want it to go away. Please—help me." She bows her head, exposing her upper back and shoulders even more. "I'm ready."

I nod to Kronklich and Councilor then focus hard on Winter. I try not to think of anything else. "Hold her tight," I say, squeezing the handle of Enivid. "No matter what happens, no matter what she says, *do not* let her go. Do you understand?" For a brief moment, my eye betrays my comrades' faces. Pure terror. *"Do you understand?"* I ask again.

They nod and grip her tighter, forcing a small cry from her.

"I'm sorry, angel," says Councilor closing his eyes.

Raising Enivid before me, I gently press its peony center into her spine, and immediately the sound of sizzling meat fills the vicinity. Burning flesh tingles my nostrils as Winter screams in writhing agony. A horrifying scream, a banshee shriek, ethereal in nature. One cannot describe the experience a father goes through, having to listen to his child suffer, unable to do anything about it.

Winter's body shakes under my resolve. "Please! Stop! It hurts! It's too much!" Her head thrashes back and forth like a viper, wanting nothing to do with the terrible instrument pressed against her back. *Is it working?* I press harder and then she vomits. Smoke and ash exudes from her skin, twirling away from her body like wisps of smoke.

"Stop it! You're killing her!" screams Councilor, shielding her body with his own, forcing myself and Kronklich back like rag dolls. Enivid tears away from her skin like a hot cattle iron, leaving behind the smoldering charred brand of a peony flower.

Heart thumping and breath panting, I stagger away from the gruesome scene, dropping Enivid without a care and listening to Councilor console his daughter as best he can. "I'm sorry angel, I'm so sorry!"

A hand touches my shoulder and I startle, not knowing Kronklich has followed me.

"You alright, Tenor? Now, now. Let's come away. Let him be alone with his daughter." I feel Kronklich tugging at my arm, motioning me to the fire. I didn't realize it, but my entire body is numb, either from the cold—or fear, I'm not sure.

Hunching over the flames, I glance back at them with envy, wishing Diana and Dorian were here with me right now. "It didn't work, James. I wasn't sure if it was going to work. Did I do the right thing?"

"Of course you did," says Kronklich, poking a stick into the embers. "You did what you thought was right. T'is all that matters."

I watch Councilor help Winter stagger away into the night, disappearing amongst the trees. She will need to recover. She will need to feed.

"I hope you're right, James. I hope you're right…"

DAY TWENTY-ONE

CHAPTER VII

GUILT.

It weighs on me like a heavy stone.

All morning I think about Winter and my inability to save her condemned soul last night. The journey northwest along the Carpella Road is a dreary ride through scattered trees and dripping rain. All I can do is dwell on what happened. The reality is sharp and overwhelming.

Such sadness. Such suffering—I wonder what sort of awful things went through her head as I flayed her skin from her body, the flesh bubbling up like cooked meat.

Hate?

Revenge?

Would she resent me for what I did? Attempt to sink her fangs into me? I don't want to imagine any of it, yet she is young and will never forgive me. This I know.

I battle with my thoughts, wondering if I should have killed her in the barn where I found her sucking pig's blood. I could've put an end to her suffering. But something inside me lingers, telling me otherwise. What is this strange notion I feel right now? Possibility? Hope?

Hope died within me days ago.

"I wanted to say thank you for last night," says Councilor's voice. He is looking ahead of the wagon driving the horses. "We may have caused my daughter unbearable pain, but we had to try. We can't blame ourselves."

"Yes. T'is no one's fault," says Kronklich, pulling wet bags out of his tea kettle.

"You shouldn't be thanking me," I say, turning over to my side, "I almost killed an innocent girl, vampire or not."

"Don't be so hard on yourself," says Kronklich. "What you did was a noble act. Your intention was real and focused. That counts for something." Kronklich pours hot tea into a cup. "Besides, there's more work to be done. We mustn't stop trying." He raises a finger. "Scepter knew something. He had all the pieces to the puzzle in his pocket and only gave *one* to Councilor. A tiny morsel if you will. The vial of blood Councilor possesses might be the answer to all of our questions." He raises his cup of tea with a salute as the moving wagon jars back and forth spilling some on him. "That'll warm the spirits."

Maybe Kronklich's right.

My brain is tired. I try to focus on something else for now as the black box bounces around the wagon with each bump on the road. I stare at it knowing Winter waits inside just beyond my grasp. A vampire. Sleeping in an immortal capsule. A prisoner caught somewhere between the realm of the living and the dead. Rejuvenating.

It is unnatural. Unclean.

I wonder what my father would say in a time like this. I smirk to myself. I know exactly what he would say. Unlike him, my feelings are mixed and disturbed. Vampires are the sworn enemy of the Wolfgang House but here I am, *escorting* one along the heartland road straight toward what is supposed to be the holiest city in all of Ashton. Bealeon would twist in his grave twice over if he were here to witness this.

But no matter how much I try to fill my thoughts with other notions, my mind is set in turmoil with Kronklich's words.

Vials of blood. Pieces to a puzzle.

The Carnalreesee have my blood and Councilor has Cresthaven's blood. What was so special about either of them? I remember the words Scepter said to me in his final moments. "Your son will be the vessel of our salvation." There was such excitement in his delivery. It was chilling to listen to. Were the Carnalreesee going to use Dorian in some bizarre ritual like the time I found him in the catacombs of Egleaseon's ruin? Would they bind his hands and feet, drive nails through his flesh and extract his blood? I begged Scepter to release my son. To use me instead of him, but Scepter simply laughed. "You cannot offer what is not yours to give." The words reverberate in my thoughts like poison. I remember my blood. The blood extracted from my body.

Blood of the Father.

Blood of the Son.

The Carnalreesee have a sinister plan, but to what end, I do not know.

Turning my head toward Kronklich, I am filled with frustration. "You say the vial of Cresthaven blood is the key to saving

Winter from her curse. How? Where does that leave us? We don't have a clue what it means or how it works. We don't even have a heading. And what about Dorian? He is the main reason we are going to the white city in the first place."

Kronklich sips from his tea quietly, never looking up. "I have not forgotten about your son, Tenor. My sights have never waned from our main task. We must save him at all cost. The truth—what I mean to say—is the vial of blood might be the answer to both Winter *and* Dorian›s dilemma." His gaze meets mine. There is sincerity there and I feel foolish for doubting him for a second.

Councilor interrupts. "We do have a direction."

I look at him quizzically. "How is it that you always have the answer at the right moment?"

"Never mind that. You said The Holy Order is corrupt in Sunstone, right?"

"Without a doubt," I reply. "Bronin's betrayal was proof of that. Blending in with the ranks, serving as a priest. He damn near killed me." Bronin's name leaves a bad taste in my mouth.

"Then we will need a plan entering the city. If The Holy Order is holding your son prisoner, then the most likely place they are keeping him…"

"… is in the Grand Cathedral at the heart of the city," Kronklich finishes Councilor's sentence for him. He leans back stretching his leg. "How long has it been since we've been there Tenor?"

"Eons." My memory of the place does me no justice.

Councilor snaps the reins and the horses move a little faster. "They will be expecting us," he says, focusing on the road. "We will need to figure out a way to get in the Grand Cathedral without being noticed. There's no telling how many vampires are holed up in there." Councilor bends at the waist stretching his back.

"Do you think the whole of Sunstone is corrupt? All of its citizens— vampires? It's children little *vampirions*? Or has the veil been pulled over their eyes as well?" Kronklich's strikes a valid point.

"There is no way to know for sure," I answer, looking out in front of the horses. "We will need to proceed with caution."

"Well, I say we're in luck," says Councilor, watching the snowy road. "It just so happens we might be able to sink two bodies with one stone."

"I beg your pardon?" asks Kronklich suddenly.

"Er—I meant kill two crows with one stone."

Always the resourceful Councilor. "More secrets?" I ask.

"No, not really. I have this contact on the outskirts of the city. A master scholar known for his world exploration and science journals. He could help us I'm sure. I have this feeling that if anyone knows anything about the intent of the Carnalre-esee, *he* is the one to speak to.»

"You seem to know a lot of people from all over," says Kronklich with a hint of sarcasm.

"You have to in my line of work. Most cases, having the right or wrong information could be the difference between life and death." Councilor looks back at the both of us, his eyes hidden within the folds of his hood. His teeth grin large and white. "Listen. It is as good of a start as any if you ask me. My contact is the only one I feel that will be able to help us and possibly tell us more about this blood of the father business."

The wagon hits a bump in the road and Councilor looks ahead.

Kronklich smiles. "Does this contact of yours have a name or shall we call him the shadow?"

"Funny," says Councilor over his shoulder. "His name is Marcus Cornelius."

It is a strange thing watching a vampire in action, knowing you can't kill it.

I have a hard time separating the two aspects of Winter's predicament: One, that she is a blood-sucking fiend of the night, and two, she is the loving daughter of Councilor.

A screech comes from somewhere off in the distance. The familiar sound of death.

We ride along in the wagon watching Winter move beyond the limits of our torch light, ducking in and out of shadows as she hunts for all manner of creatures. Atters. Owls. Even small mice are unable to escape the wrath of her vampiric powers. She is like a graceful cat passing through the night. A shade of death sucking the last essence out of life. She is doing what all vampires do—drink blood and regenerate. What I did to her, using Envid in an attempt to free her soul, must have done damage far beyond my understanding. And so she continues to drink. Killing indiscriminately.

Morality.

What was right and what was wrong? The questions spin in my thoughts as I try to consolidate my own reasoning. Draining the blood of animals in the forest to sustain her own life was something I could understand. Something I could cope with. But my thoughts linger to the other of end of reasoning, the part that has to do with humans. We are out in the middle of nowhere, where no one will find us or see us or judge us for aiding in such blasphemous acts. What will happen when we go to the city? Sunstone is either brimming with vampires or fresh human blood. Will Winter be able to control her urges? In most cases when dealing with vampires, they are ready to kill, ready to strike at any given moment. The blood lust consumes them. How will it not be the same for Winter? What will happen when Councilor isn't around to control her?

I shiver from the cold and the thought while listening to the dying screams of living animals all around us. Who's to say she wouldn't lose control right here, right now, and kill us all?

You're dwelling Tenor. Stop dwelling.

I try to think of other things, like the good that could come of harboring a vampire.

Watching her from the distance reminds me of Joachim, my old butler, the one the Carnalreesee led me to believe responsible for the disappearance of my son. The way he moved about the underground ruins of Egleaseon's abode when I first saw him. Hunting. Tasting the rocks. Smelling the air. He was like a rabid dog tracking down Dorian, seeking out his blood. Joachim didn't know it at the time, but he had become a vampire, despite maintaining his humanistic thoughts and his eagerness to help me. The way I met him at the underground river trying to eat meat like a human was proof of his innocence. The poor bastard. He was dealt a bad hand all through life. Many years ago, his mother turned vampire and I was forced to kill her. I took pity on him, providing as much of a life as I could for him, a life of servitude to a noble house. And still in the end, he died protecting those he loved, my wife, my son, even me. Joachim was a good man.

Maybe there were good things to come from vampires after all. Harmony in the dissonance of vampires and humans. Like in all things, maybe culture was the answer. Was it right under our noses? Care. Love. Thought. Maybe that's all it took.

The night grows longer as the wagon rattles along. Not once do we stop as Winter continues to slaughter beyond our torchlight. *How much blood does a little girl need?* The thought is absurd knowing the situation we are in, yet at the same time, I remember her limited skill in the barn slaughtering all those pigs. She seemed such a helpless creature. Innocent. The way she looked at me, cowering behind her father's enormous build while blood trickled from her fanged teeth. It proved to me the girl was lost. Could she learn to get along in life in her new state? Could Councilor really teach her morality?

My thoughts come back to the present momentarily. Something is wrong. The sounds of the dying in the distance; they have stopped with no Winter in sight. Did something happen to her? Had she abandoned us? As I look over at Councilor, he does not seem the least bit concerned over the matter. Since he is a Black Blade, his training may make him stoic in the face of catastrophe, yet she was still his daughter, and like any decent father, he must worry about his child.

All is quiet. With the sound of the wheels creaking along their axles, the scattered wood becomes convincingly darker in presence. A light wind jostles the leaves as we descend further into the valley and soon, we are no longer surrounded by trees. There is no cover for a vampire to hide.

"Aren't you the least bit concerned?" I ask over a long period of silence.

"Concerned with what?" Councilor never turns from watching the road.

"Winter. It's been a while since we've last seen her."

"No."

"No? That's all you can say? Take a look around, Councilor. There are no trees. There are no animals. I think your daughter ran off."

Councilor lets out an exaggerated snort. "Is that what you think?"

Why is he laughing at me?

"Trust me Tenor, she is out there. You just can't *see* her." He nudges Abel and Jasmine along the road with the tethered rein. "Look at it from her perspective. All this time, the poor girl has been locked up in that godforsaken box. You can't blame her for wanting to explore. This is a new world for her."

Councilor falls silent as Kronkilich picks up the conversation. "He's right, you know. Winter needs to learn to control her powers, her urges, especially if we are to reach Sunstone soon.

What better time than now. Could be bloody awful if she's not ready. All those humans or vampires in Sunstone…" Kronklich takes a deep breath and extends his arms around him. "Out here, she is free with no want of care or worry. During the day we saw very few people along the road and even less since nightfall. I assure you Tenor, there is very little for you to worry about at the moment."

How was it that Kronklich shared the same insight as Councilor?

As he finishes the last of his words, the wagon violently shakes. Winter appears, clinging to the side of the wood-plank railing with her purple eyes ablaze and torn dress littered with leaves. Her long nails dig into the wood as she surveys the three of us like playmates. "What did I miss? I could hear you talking about me over there beyond the hills."

Caught off guard by her appearance, my hand instinctively passes over Enivid.

She looks at us waiting for an answer.

"Ah, there you are my sweet," says Councilor leaning his head back. I see him smile from underneath the big bush of his beard. "Have you found us dinner?"

"Of course, father, just as you asked." Winter's voice is soft and sweet like honey from a jar. She reaches into a satchel strapped over her shoulder and drops four little creatures onto the floor of the wagon. Smooth black skin, white washed eyes. None of their rat-like tails move which indicates they are dead. "Fresh atters from the woods."

My stomach churns at the sight of their twisted broken necks.

"There, you see," says Kronklich with a smile. He pats my hand as if consoling a child. "No need for concern. The girl has brought us dinner! Such a good lass."

Moments later, under an overcast sky, Councilor pulls the wagon off to the side of the road to make temporary camp. Strategically angled to block the wind, the three of us huddle around the fire to cook the grimy meal of squirrel. Winter, cautiously staying away, lingers near her father, who is stoically staring off into the night like a hawk.

"T'is an interesting taste this atter meat. A bit nutty in my opinion," says Kronklich, not the least bit concerned that a vampire caught this supplement to our meal.

"Aren't you at all worried by the potential ingestion of poisonous meat?" I ask. "You weren't like this that one time we ate soup from the gypsy camp." I hold a singed piece of atter leg before me. The meat underneath the blackened skin is surprisingly light in color.

"That was a completely different situation. We never saw the source of that meat." Kronklich points to Winter. "Fortunately, our hunter is right there, hovering close to our ring of warmth and comfort. Many thanks to you, Winter." He bows his head, tipping his top hat, but she doesn't notice. Kronklich slurps the remaining meat from his bone with a satisfying chew. "Oh yes. And there was the fact of rushing off into the night from Gauldust without properly restocking that might have put us in this predicament." Kronklich looks up playfully.

"We've already gone over this, Kronklich. Someone would have discovered the slaughtered pigpen. Paranoia would have spread from those simple minded people and the first fingers would have been pointed at us. Imagine. What a coincidence it was that a group of strangers arrived that same day from the east. No one passes through the mountains during the snow months." Taking a deep breath, I bite into the atter meat, the flaky skin crackling between my teeth. I try to ignore the grimy taste, something between rubbing oil and dirt. "Trust me. Better to leave when we did than risk getting held up by crazed villagers. We all know what that's like."

"You make an excellent argument," agrees Kronklich. I see him hiding his smile.

"You think it's a joke?"

"Not at all. It's just, the look on your face. It's quite horrendous."

"You would make this face too if you knew what this meal reminds me of."

"Here." Kronklich reaches into one of his coat pockets and tosses me a small folded paper packet. "Sprinkle a little of that on it."

"What's this? Holding out on me?"

"Never, Tenor. Just watching out for your health."

"My health? Do you see what we're *eating*?"

"As much fun as this conversation is, you seem to forget we need to hurry and eat. Out here in the open we are sitting ducks.

All manner of evil can spot us a mile away with this fire." Having already finished two of the atters, Councilor stands shaking the flakes of charred skin from his black jerkin.

My stomach churns as I take another bite. "How much further is it before we reach Sunstone?"

"As long as we don't wander from the road, get caught in a blizzard, or get devoured by a horde of flesh eating lechers, I'd say three days. Give or take."

"Try to make it three days or less. I'm not sure how much longer my stomach can handle eating this *delicacy*." I notice Winter look away from me with an expression of disdain. So she *was* listening.

Kronklich looks up from gnawing on his bone with surprise. "That's the spirit, Tenor! Who knows when we'll have the chance to eat atter meat again."

"That's not what I—" I stop myself, sighing deeply. "Oh never mind."

DAY TWENTY-TWO

CHAPTER VIII

DORIAN

I'M A FOOL FOR THINKING I could escape this place.

Even now as I sit here in the dark, listening to the woes of man's suffering, I contemplate my actions days ago. How many days has it been since Martyr dragged me down those treacherous stairs with those long twisted fingers? Two? Three? I'm not sure. It's impossible to tell how long a day is.

If I had stuck to my duties with Charles, I wouldn't be in this predicament. Solitary confinement. Chained to a wall like those poor naked people below the chapel. Those acolytes. But then where would I really be? Free? Anything *but* free.

I check over my body. My hands. My feet. The bite marks. They are getting better by the day. My skin slowly changing back to its fleshy plush state.

If the Carnalreesee were so set on me recovering my strength, why in God's hell did they enslave me down here in this part of the cathedral? This cesspool of scurrying rats, bile, and piss?

The smell down here is terrible, where ever *here* is. No one has come to see me. No edict. No Martyr. No Vargus. The only thing certain is that in my waking hours of limited light—the source coming from somewhere down the hall—a new tray filled with meats, cheeses, and breads waits for me. A feast for a king.

Sliding my body across the floor towards the barred gate, I shoo rats away from nibbling on the cheese as I tear into a chicken breast, wondering why—despite these horrible conditions—I am so hungry all the time. Had the Carnalreesee taken that much blood from me over these past weeks? My body so deprived of nutrients?

I can only imagine what I look like at this point. My arms and legs seem thinner, but there are no mirrors down here to know my true state, let alone anywhere in the cathedral. I touch my face, feeling the gaunt sunken curves that are my cheeks and run my fingers through my hair, the spot where Martyr pulled at the roots. So tender. So greasy.

I sit in my little world of isolation, eating my meal with the rats while listening to the sounds of the prison all around me. In one direction, somber cries echo their way down the hall. In the other, prayers of those who still choose to believe. Thanks be to God *this*. Please forgive them father *that*. It is quite incredible to listen to actually, knowing the condition, we—the prisoners—are in. And after the prayers come and go, the torturing then begins. The edicts or the vampires, I'm not quite sure for I never see them come and go, revel in bringing pain to those unfortunates that are not me. We are all chosen for something, but my place, is apparently special. The screaming will start and not let up for some time. It is terrible to listen to and I can only imagine what our jailers are doing.

Taking a long pull from a skin of water, I nearly spittle over myself as a loud echoing bang makes it way down the vast corridor. The rattle of chains. The clinking of keys. Someone is coming.

Straining my neck to see, I try to catch a glimpse of the visitor who always comes around this part of the day. But as always, the angle of my cell and the chains restricting me prevent me from seeing anything. My view consists of a stone wall.

The footsteps fade for a moment, then come back, followed by a groan from a metal gate. Chewing on a piece of bread, I wonder about the new activity taking place. Usually the sounds are far away, distant, as if I were a forgotten animal nobody ever came to see. But then I hear boots clicking on stone coming closer, and my first instinct is to back away. Collecting my chains in both fists, I retreat to my wall of comfort—what I like to call it—and there I wait, not knowing what to expect.

Not one, but two figures appear on the other side of the gate, pointing to me and speaking in low voices.

"Dorian Wolfgang," says one of them from underneath its red cowl, "The masters wish to accommodate your request." Dangling the keys before them, the edict selects a specific one and jams it into the lock, rattling it once and turning the mechanism with a click.

"What request?" My throat is ragged from not speaking for days.

Both edicts enter the prison cell, kicking aside a rat while stepping over the food.

"We are to escort you to your new room. A burn chamber."

I gaze at them startled, not knowing if this is a good or bad thing. Grabbing me by the shoulders, they lift me off the ground with ease and tether a chain through both shackles at my wrists. They pull me along like a beast, forcing me to leave my tiny world of isolation behind.

"What is a burn chamber?" I ask pathetically as we pass cells of emaciated prisoners and crazed-eyed victims, but receive no answer. The edicts are stoic in their task and refrain from saying anything until we reach what is supposedly the burn chamber. Nothing is unique about it, and in fact, it looks exactly the same as my last quarters. The only remote difference is—as they unlock the chain from my shackles—they simply leave me free to roam the cell without restriction.

With the slamming of the gate and the click of a key, in a matter of seconds they are gone and I am again left alone. Staring around the empty chamber, I wonder what the reason is for putting me in such a place. *This was my request?* I am thankful to be free of my chains, but the strangeness of the whole outcome baffles me until, looking out from my prison bars, I see that my view has changed drastically, and not necessarily for the better. A man, shackled to a wall, crouches on bent knees directly across from my cell. With one arm secured tightly against the prison cell wall, his other faculties remain on short leashes. Words mumble from under his trembling lips in almost a whisper, as he calls forth prayer to God, telling himself, "They know not what they do, Lord. Please forgive them. Please forgive them."

With only a dirtied cloth around his waist, he is stripped of all his clothes. His skin is so pale it carries a purplish tint. Head bowed forward and eyes closed, chin-length hair falls in his face.

"Father. Please forgive them."

I notice other things about his cell. A system of pulleys and chains range up to the top of the entire chamber on a wood frame. It is the strangest contraption I've ever seen and as my eyes wonder about, I notice the copious amount of blood splattered across the floor, varying from one location to another. A torture chamber perhaps? It would certainly explain the sounds coming from this direction every day at the same time.

The one thing that brings me comfort is the single solitary beam of light thwarting the darkness. It is only a few feet from where the holy man is bound. My chamber has a similar beam, coming from a slat high up in the wall. Holding my hand up to the light, I turn it over so the warmth lands in my palm. *Sunlight. It is actual sunlight.*

"You must forgive them, my son."

I turn at the sound of the man across from my cell. Was he talking to me?

"You must forgive them, my son, for they know not what they do."

Gripping the bars with both hands, I bring my face closer, trying to get a better view of the tortured man I've been listening to these past few days. Expecting to see his body racked and bruised beyond help, his appearance is anything but. Despite his nakedness, his body shows no signs of abuse. Only that he is rail thin.

"They know very well what they do," I say as clearly as I can, fighting through the hoarseness of my throat.

"They do not," he says more confidently than before. His head lifts in my direction but his hair lingers on his face. "They are still God's children, condemned to a life they did not choose. They must be saved. They must be spared."

There is something familiar about him but I can't place it. His voice? His looks? "If they are God's children, then why do they kill innocent people and drink their blood?"

"It is the Master of Evil who has corrupted them. Do not blame them. You must forgive them."

"I will do no such thing!" I say, raising my voice. I loosen my grip on the bars realizing my knuckles are turning white. "We have hunted the *Master*, as you so call him, for centuries. My entire family has dedicated their life to hunting the *Master* and all those who serve him. Vampires. Carnalreesee. Call them what you will. They are all the same in my eyes! Demons that must be destroyed. I will never forgive them. They destroyed everything I've ever loved! My friends. My mother. The Wolfgangs will never bend their knees to this so-called Master!"

"Wolfgangs?"

The man suddenly comes to life with a new vigor, pushing the hair from his face as he lifts his head. "Did you say Wolfgang's? Come closer so that I may see you better."

My fury subsides at his words and find myself obliging his request. Moving closer, so that I am aligned with his position directly across from the prison bars, I angle my head.

"My God, it can't be," says the half-naked man. "Hair and face like your father, eyes like your mother. You have grown so much, my son."

I'm confused at his words. "You speak as if you know me."

"Of course, I know you. I never forget the faces of those I baptize. Right here in this very church, this cathedral, years ago when you were a child. Dorian Wolfgang, son of Tenor Wolfgang." The man drops his head, cradling his face with his one semi-free hand. The chains and pulleys jangle. "If you are here, then I fear the worst has finally come."

"The worst? What do you mean, what do you know?"

"Too much." The man begins to cry and I feel bad for not knowing who this man is. Again the familiarity is there, but I can't place it.

"Who are you?"

The man stops crying and looks up, a sad look plaguing his face. "I am Cardinal Glass, our Lord's grace and commander of the church."

Cardinal Glass. What I know of him is vague, except that he is *the* head of The Holy Order. Although he's known me since I was a child, my only recollection of him was when I attended mass at Albestan Church. Once or twice the Cardinal made the pilgrimage to our little town, Roland, to pay homage while touring the surrounding regions. Seldom did I pay attention at these events. I was always focused on the physical work of the church, weapons and the killing of vampires, just like my father did, just like my father expected.

"You must tell me, Dorian. Is your father alive?"

The last time I saw my father is clear as day. Shouting my name, attempting to rescue me from the Carnalreesee using every ounce of his might, body, and soul. His voice and the passion behind it.

"Yes, he's alive."

"Have you been bitten?"

The question catches me off guard and I look down at my arms. My hand reaches for my neck. "Yes, but they are healing. I never drank the blood." I recall the time when the Carnalreesee, wearing their horrible masks, forced Joachim to drink their blood after biting him. The agony and pain he went through. The way he writhed on the ground. I shiver at the memory.

"Then there is still hope. Maybe not for me but for you most certainly—"

A gate down the hall creaks open and closes, cutting Cardinal Glass off from finishing his words. I watch the same two edicts from before approach us, one carrying the set of keys, the other, an oversized wooden club in one hand and a goblet in the other. I try to get a better angle as I watch them stop before the Cardinal's cell door and twist the lock. As the two of them enter, Cardinal Glass looks at me solemnly and closes his eyes.

"How about today, Glass? Feeling thirsty?"

There is no response from the Cardinal as he continues to keep his eyes shut.

"No?" The edict holding the keys takes the goblet from the other and steps aside. The one with the oversized club steps forward and bludgeons the Cardinal, over and over, smashing his face and cracking his knees.

The Cardinal cries out in pain, bending over at the waist and vomiting blood. It drips down his neck, over his ribs and onto the floor.

"It's a shame you don't shatter like *glass*," says the edict with the goblet. "This would have been over a long time ago."

The edict steps forward, offering the goblet to the Cardinal as an offering of salvation, yet the Cardinal turns his head. "I will never drink that." He begins saying a prayer under his breath between bloody lips.

The edict holding the goblet sighs and splashes the deep red liquid in the Cardinal's face.

"Stop!" I shout uselessly from my cell. "Leave him alone!"

The two edicts toss the goblet and club aside as they maneuver about the chamber, adjusting the chains and pulleys hanging from the ceiling. It isn't until the Cardinal's body starts moving that I realize the purpose of the mechanism. As the edicts pull and release the chains, the shackles bound at his wrists and feet become taught with tension.

The Cardinal says nothing as they manipulate his body like a marionette, pulling one of his arms towards the beam of light.

What on earth are they doing?

It's as if they were puppet masters controlling his every move, forcing him into a strange macabre dance while I am the audience. As his arm comes to rest under the beam of sunlight, the reaction is instantaneous. Cardinal Glass screams with unbearable pain, tossing his head back and forth, both edicts struggling to hold the chains firm.

The light burns the Cardinal's arm as if set on fire, and within seconds, flames erupt from the wound, turning the skin black and filling the chamber with smoke. I choke on the fumes as the edicts stand their ground, both of them sinisterly smiling, sweat dripping from their foreheads.

Cardinal Glass continues screaming until the tension breaks, sending the two edicts to the floor.

Words cannot describe the horror on the Cardinal's face as he watches his arm disintegrate into a mixture of fire and ash.

A burnt stump of a shoulder is all that remains.

DAY TWENTY-THREE

CHAPTER
IX

I COME TO IN THE early morning light.

As the sunlight slowly makes its way down the wall, my eyes have a hard time adjusting to the surroundings. Neck stiff as a board, I slap myself awake, still groggy from sleeping on the floor. Again food has arrived, a massive plate of roast beef and whole potatoes roasted with hints of rosemary and chives. It is amazing how my hosts treat me so poorly, yet feed me so well. I'm convinced all they really want from me is the healthy state of my body, not the well-being of my mind.

Within the darkness, I strain my eyes to see across the way where I can barely make out Cardinal Glass slumped against the wall, his chin resting against his chest. I don't want to look, but curious human behavior demands my eyes explore the devastation of his body. His shoulder, arm, and hand have all come back, completely reformed to their original state as if nothing ever happened.

Impossible.

I know about the regenerative qualities vampires possess, but such was the case for *vampires,* not humans. Could it be? Was it possible? I look at Cardinal Glass in abject horror.

"I know what you're thinking," echoes Cardinal Glass's voice from across the hall. He is staring at me, eyes aglow in blue. It is a look I will never forget. Disgust. Treachery. Not towards me, but for himself. "It is so, I'm afraid," he begins slowly, painfully, acknowledging my disbelief. "They did this to me. Faeradon, the Archbishop, and the Carnalreesee. They are the ones who changed me, bit my neck and drank from me. Forced their blood down my throat. The change was terrible. My insides twisted and tangled like snakes until my body died. That day I journeyed to the very depths of hell."

Cardinal Glass attempts to stand but nearly falls over, forgetting he is still shackled to the wall and floor like an animal on display. He rubs at his new shoulder and arm while sitting cross-legged on the floor.

"You're a vampire," I blurt out. It is obvious, but I'm stunned nonetheless.

"Yes, unfortunately."

"Yet you refuse to drink blood."

"I am a man of God. I will not drink that filth even if it means my own death."

"How are you still alive then?"

"My faith in God nourishes me now."

I look at Cardinal Glass in disbelief. "Why would they make you a vampire instead of killing you?"

"To mock God, I suppose. To spread fear into the hearts of humans by showing the highest order of the church was made into the very embodiment of evil. In a way, they have killed me, but my will lives on."

"If that is the case, why do they have you locked away in chains while I remain free to roam my cell?"

"Most likely so I don't kill myself. Refusing to drink blood won't outright destroy me. If I could, I would bathe myself in God's light." He points to the narrow beam slowly creeping its way down the wall.

What he says makes sense, yet I am at a complete loss for words.

I stare at him from across the way and sink to the floor using the bars as support.

"What happened here?" I ask, trying to gain some sort of insight and understanding. The cell is dark and damp in the dismal light, the perfect mood for how I am feeling at the moment.

The Cardinal stares at the floor as he speaks. "A man came to join The Holy Order many years ago by the name Faeradon Alagast, a promising acolyte of faith who bore all the intention of making the world a better place. As he was already advanced in his elder years, none considered him a threat at the time, just an old man of faith seeking his place in the Church. He excelled in practice and wisdom and so climbed the ranks of the Church very quickly. His charisma was unmatched and before long, had won the favor of all the bishops. At the time, I had not yet joined the enclave of The Holy Order. But when I did, it was I who came to the understanding of who he might possibly be. His look. His credentials. Everything he offered hinted of his influence from the east and his dealings with Egleaseon." Weary from the strain of speaking, the Cardinal pauses to catch his breath before he continues. "The knowledge he possessed of ancient artifacts. History of the world. The rise and fall of the past as if he had actually been there." "You know, it was he who tipped your father and the priest Bronin about the Hand of God and its whereabouts." He scratches at his neck and continues. "It was strange that a man of the cloth had such great interest in ancient artifacts. Most of The Holy Order looked on them as sacrilegious. Power shouldn't come from things. Power comes from faith. I was one of those doubters."

"Wait a minute. Are you saying Faeradon intentionally lead my father and Bronin to find the Hand of God? If that is true then Faeradon knew exactly what he was doing." I take a moment, soaking in the realization. "Faeradon is responsible for Egleaseon's death. It was intentional."

"Yes, it is true."

"It doesn't make any sense! Why would a vampire want to destroy his own kind? Power perhaps?"

"This I am not sure of, my son."

There is crying from somewhere down the hall, but Cardinal Glass ignores it, absorbed in his tale.

"For years I tried to uncover Faeradon's hidden past by inquest and errands, but I always came up short or was led astray. Knowing I was pushing the fold, eventually I dug too deep and triggered the insurgence, which unleashed his horde of vampires to overtake the Grand Cathedral. It was then the city of Sunstone fell into darkness. That was nearly three months ago."

So that was it. The reason why the monster's activity increased, spreading over the countryside like wildfire. Vampires, willdermen, lechers, bogarts. The countless others. It all made sense now.

"Faeradon and the Carnalreesee soon took all of Sunstone, dabbing their bloody fingers in everything. The priests and the clergy, the balcony boys and the acolytes. None of them can be trusted. They kept up the charade, acting as if the holy order were fine and that the people's beloved Cardinal had stepped down. The citizens of Sunstone are now the condemned. The vampires, under the guise of The Holy Order, now corrupt the heart of the city like a spreading disease. If the citizens of the city don't know it now, they will soon, for a great master plan is at work from what I understand."

"But why Sunstone?" I ask, completely engrossed. "Other than seeing The Holy Order fall, what is this master plan?"

Cardinal Glass takes a deep breath. "Deep within the heart of the city, this very cathedral, lies the sunstone in the bowels of the catacombs. It is a stone of great power which is said to harbor the energy of the sun, the purest form ever contained on this earth. My guess is they want to use its power to somehow gain the ability to walk in the daylight." Cardinal Glass closes his eyes and slowly breathes. "Imagine. This world would be lost if they achieved such a thing."

"If that is the case," I ask, somewhat frustrated, "then what are they waiting for?"

"They have been searching for a man named Marcus Cornelius, a well-known scholar and historian who understands the nature of the sunstone. He alone may be the only one who knows how to harness the sunstone's power."

"But something doesn't make sense," I say, somewhat confused by this trifle predicament. "Why do they need the sunstone's power if the edicts can walk in the daylight?"

"Because the edicts are not vampires. They are but servants to them, familiars trying to gain favor from their masters."

As my brain fills to the brim with information, I cannot stop thinking about the one thing truly bothering me. The reason why I was kidnapped.

Again there are voices down the hall and our natural instinct is to stop talking. Standing up, I grip the gate and bring my face close to the bars, trying to speak in a hushed tone. "All of this is so much to take in! I am filled with this sense of dread. You have to help me, Cardinal. Please!"

Cardinal Glass shakes his head in defeat, "I cannot help you, my son. If your arrival is to mean something, then let it mean *you* are here to *help* us."

"What? What are you talking about?" I look at his pathetic form across the way, his head resting in his hands, but he doesn't show any sign of strength. His very essence has been stripped from his body. Literally. Judging by the position of the light, in another few hours, the edicts will come to hold him down and burn his body again. I wonder what part they will choose this time.

Another wail down the hall hammers home the reality I am living in. Desperate and provoked by what's to come, my fear of the unknown triggers even more anxiety. I try again. "If you can't help me, Cardinal, at least tell me why they chose me."

"This I do not know, my son." There is a certain pity in his vampire eyes and yet I know he is telling the truth. "All I can say, Dorian, is that you have some part to play in all of this. That is why you must get out of here and find a way to harvest the sunstone's power."

DAY TWENTY-FOUR

CHAPTER
X

WOLFGANG

Sunstone.

The Holy City of White.

The Great Mother of Pearls.

It has been called many things over the centuries but none so much as the Guiding Light in which to see. Such names have given it power, as in all things named, and as it is written in the chronicles of old, it stands impenetrable and magnificent and frightening, a fortress of stone and mortar, towering over its peripheral spawned cities of Porson, Meld, Agont, and Frill, like a great sentinel watching over its commonwealth, which in turn feeds commerce, bleeding from all of them the very life force which has risen to corrupt men in their states of existence.

Dauntess.

Coin of the realm.

Gold, silver, copper, sharing a place among the overflowing coffers of the great capital city that is Sunstone.

And none shall oppose Sunstone. For if the word of God were to slip from the tongues of even the lowest of men, then his majesty's wrath, in all of his prowess and ability to thwart the darkness, would crush the naysayers and evil doers, setting them as the kindling for the great Conflagration and its storm of fire.

It is said the very grounds on which Sunstone stands, was blessed by God himself, back in the time when earthly dwelling was fickle and the land was full of monsters and darkness. The sky was parted by a great storm and poured blistering rain to sear away the damned. The tears were relentless, scalding flesh from bone, washing the sins of beast away. Eventually everything dried, leaving behind one solitary tear. And that tear crystallized, forming the sacred sunstone, the source of power that now emanates from the Grand Cathedral and its surrounding fields of green.

This place...

This is the place of my woe and suffering. This is where Dorian was taken.

Holy City Sunstone.

The Bright stone.

The Burning sun.

How many names could one city have? And of its inhabitants, who of The Holy Order was still here in the name of God? Where did Faeradon the Archbishop's loyalties reside? Was he a perpetrator or was he still of The Holy Order? What of Cardinal Glass and his priests? His fathers and clerics? Were they all diminished or had they been subjected to the dark horrors of the Carnalreesee? These questions pollute my mind as we enter the great city, much like the red-brown sludge passing through the waterways underfoot, the city's state-of-the-art aqueducts.

Having traveled for three grueling days of rationed bread, roasted atter, and little sleep, our bodies are tired and rank. A good wash and decent meal is in order, but Councilor has a plan we must stick to, no matter the cost.

We are in enemy territory now.

All is white.

All is calm.

But I know evil lurks here. Waiting behind the smiling faces of children and their mothers holding their hands. The men driving their buggies, leering at our beaten wagon with splintered and peeling paint, a lopsided bump for every turn of the wheel and our disheveled appearance as we pass, three travelers wrapped in black cloaks with blankets atop. If we are not careful, our presence will be detected. To be found by the wrong crowd, this would be our greatest folly. Our current situation calls for absolute stealth, but entering at nightfall is too risky. If—in fact—vampires ruled the roost here, our chances would be better during the day for the sun is our only ally. According to Councilor, there was another ally, a man by the name of Marcus Cornelius, an astute man of knowledge, an artificer, and researcher extraordinaire. This is where we are headed. Reaching his estate is paramount.

"Such a massive city. Bloody light hurts my eyes!" Kronklich shields his face with his hand. "Look at all the white-washed walls and roofs. Where's their sense of style?"

"Sunstone was never made to be glamorous," I reply. "Just symbolic with its color of purity."

"Symbolic, hardly. More like pretentious, if you ask me. The blearing white is everywhere. The alabaster stones scream, *'Look at me!'*" Kronklich shakes his head in distaste as if it really mattered. "The light is sure to cause a headache. So where are we to find this Cornelius fellow anyway?"

"Shush, you fool," retaliates Councilor, snapping his formidable passive aggressive stare. "Why don't you just announce to the vampires what we're here for."

In the distance, men dressed in red tunics and black boots roam the streets; it is the signature garb of The Holy Order in Sunstone for clergymen from the cathedral. It is strange they are carrying wood-cutting axes with them, which gives us more reason to stay away from them all together.

"Vampires?" asks Kronklich. "T'is daylight. Just trying to speed things along my good man. No need to get excited."

"Excited. Hmph!" Councilor turns to face front with a grunt. "If you call being mobbed by vampire servants excitement. How about you let me handle things for a while. Sit back and relax."

But relaxation is far from my mind. With Enivid snug within the folds of my coat, I am ready to use it at a moment's notice. There will be no rest for any of us today except Winter, conveniently hidden away in her coffin, tucked under the blankets.

Sunstone spans an entire flat of plains that opens into wide sweeping circular sects, each growing smaller as you move toward the heart of the city where the Grand Cathedral waits.

But we go nowhere near there now. We stick to the outer urban crop circles, turning down shaded alleys and backtracking up avenues. I know what Councilor's intent is. He is covering our tracks and rightfully so. There is no telling what we might encounter in this heart of darkness.

My stomach turns at the thought of food. Cooking fires hover like fog of war over the city as we roll along pristine cobble stones and formidable bridges; it is a good sign that humans still inhabit the city.

After what seems like hours, we finally come to the end of a drive where a section of thirty-foot wall rises high as a fortress.

"This is one of the outer section walls," says Councilor, guiding the horses to the north. "Not much further."

In the distance, the rise of a massive structure is illuminated under the sun, a tower of incredible height, piercing the epicenter of Sunstone like a holy lance cast down from God. My heart churns at the sight of it. *That's where they're keeping Dorian.* I feel it in my gut. At my side. Diana's warmth channels from Enivid, egging me to go now. Storm the front doors of that unholy place and take back what is yours. *Patience my love. Patience. We must bide our time. We can't go in blindly.*

The irony of it drives me to impatience and anger. If all the citizens were not vampires and not working for the Carnalreesee, then how could they not suspect anything odd going on within the city walls? Were the Carnalreesee keeping their influence hidden from the public? I imagine dark tendrils spreading throughout the city like snakes slithering their way behind every wall and under every stone. Although the outside shell of the cathedral appears to be innocent, uniform with its standard white stones and paint, there was something *unnatural* about it. *It's height and the way it leans in the shimmering glow.*

The last time I saw the tower was over twenty years ago with my father Bealeon. So many times we took pilgrimages to Sunstone on the inquest for vampires. The people of the land called upon the church for guidance, and so then, relied on the Wolfgang House. We had to climb the many steps to reach the holy vestibule where Cardinal Glass and the Archbishop Faeradon greeted us. I remember the stairs and looking beyond the stained glass windows to the see the white buildings below. The great stink of the city hitting your nostrils like a poisonous cloud. Never could you see the clouds from such a height. But now, its height was beyond measure. Higher than the sky itself it seems. Was it fatigue playing tricks on my mind or the glare of the sun peeking its way through the overcast sky?

The image of it vanishes suddenly as the wagon passes under two archways which lead to a main service road. Following this road, the trotting of horse hooves echoes in the alleyway as we emerge from another eclipse of shadowy buildings. Not far in the distance, waits a modest looking house, equipped with a stained white roof and curled-leaf balconies, which in turn abuts to the thirty-foot tall perimeter wall looming as a back drop. A smattering of birch trees surrounds the grounds while dry swooping vines dangle from its roof and creep up the stonework walls. The house, once a brilliant sheen of white, is now a dull yellowish tint, tainted from rain and vegetation. Dozens of water-stained windows plaster the front of the small country mansion. I look upon it in awe as it reminds me somewhat of Old Man Dora's home. With an atrium in the front full of dried dead shrubbery, we stay in the tiny garden path that remains snow-free.

The thin road snakes back and forth in long swooping arches until it reaches the front of the house complete with a circular drive and moss-covered fountain. Mineral stains run the length of the large porous vase sitting in its center suggesting water plumed from it some time ago. It is now a simple birdbath for local finches, who scatter as our wagon rattles across the leafy drive, and the clopping horse hooves add to our announcement that we have arrived.

"So this is the place?" asks Kronklich with an air of excitement. "T'is quite the size! Never thought of it to be owned by a teacher."

"He's not a teacher. He is a researcher and artificer," says Councilor with a scowling look.

"All the same. Tell me Councilor, is this Marcus Cornelius fellow nobility?"

The same thought goes through my head as I gaze up at the dizzying heights of balustrade roof and pergola entryway. Such an extravagant place. Marcus must be an aristocrat.

"At one point he might have been," says Councilor as he busies himself with the horses. "But not anymore. He doesn't delve into such trifles any longer. Religion and politics. He was right to get out of them."

By Councilor's response, I know where he is going with this. His feelings on organizations and how they should be run are vastly different than those of the nobles and higher classes. He is a Black Blade. An assassin. And he has his own set of rules.

"Marcus is a man of science searching out the needs of people, helping where he can, when he can. Like a doctor of information." Councilor pulls a long drink from his water skin. "All sects of order respect him very much. The church, the government, even the Black Blade society hold him in high regard."

"T'is strange I have not heard of this man, myself having attended the Five Cities Academy in Porson. Tell me," says Kronklich as he gingerly descends the wagon steps. "He must not come from around here so I must ask. Where *is* he from?"

Piling more blankets in the back to secure Winter, I keep a cautious eye on our surroundings through the chirping of birds. The courtyard. The mansion facade. Councilor and Kronklich seem to forget we are in dangerous territory as they carry on with their tangential conversation.

"You're absolutely right. The man comes from the east, beyond the Cordova Mountain range and even further than Katal."

Katal. Now that was a place I hadn't heard or thought of in a long time. Immediately I think of the gypsies from Widow and their shops and caravans we encountered in the Decameron Forest. How their ways were not our ways. Strange things were out beyond the reaches of Katal and the lands of murk. Strange plants and animals, species never discovered before. They say the monsters out there are much different than here and that entire cities and towns have vanished under the swamps. But aside from how different the land was from Ashton, one thing always stayed the same: vampires. They flourished even more so in the east than in the west, and there was always talk of the Wolfgang House going on expeditions into the east. To rid the world further of vampires.

"Katal?" asks Kronklich with surprise. "That is certainly a long way from here. I've only ever read about in books. They say it is a realm of madness."

I notice Councilor eye Kronklich inquisitively. "Is that all they say?" Unpacking a few satchels, a couple of sacks, and his massive scythe, he hefts the bulky items over one shoulder while glancing over the wagon one final time. "How about the Black Blades?"

"What are you saying? Is that their point of origin? I was always curious of where they started."

"It is," says Councilor ascending the moss-covered stairs. "The ways of thinking in Katal are much different than the ways of Ashton."

"I would say so," responds Kronklich, clicking his cane up the steps. "You kill people in exchange for money. I say your philosophies are slightly different than ours."

"Yes. I suppose so."

As the three of us reach the top landing of the steps, it is Councilor who lifts the knocker with his large meaty hand. He raps the door three times followed by a pause and then again a fourth.

Birds chirp.

Horses snort.

Councilor knocks again.

"Maybe he is out back gardening?" Kronklich suggests, shrugging his shoulders and smiling.

Normally I would have found it funny, but my answer is a dry frown. Another moment passes before I start wondering if this Marcus Cornelius is real. And as Councilor turns around—most likely to share a similar thought—there is a loud pop from the other side, followed by a bolt sliding in its casing. The large door with a gargoyle emblem opens inwardly, forcing a short vacuum of air from the outside to gush past me, pushing my hair onto my shoulders as if I were drawn into a void of oblivion.

A tall lanky figure stands in the doorway greeting us; the confused look on his face speaks more than a thousand words. "Good afternoon, gentlemen. Is there something I can help you with?"

Although the man is tall and thin, three of him could fit inside Councilor easily. Councilor steps forward consuming the doorway with his bulk. "Yes, we are here to see Marcus Cornelius. He is expecting us."

Whether he is lying or not, I'm not sure. I go along with Councilor's lead regardless, wondering what exactly his plan was going to be now that we were on the front steps of the most renowned scientist in all of Sunstone.

"That's unfortunate," says the man, his thin golden hair tied neatly behind his head.

I can't see Councilor's face, but the agitation in his voice says it all. "What are you getting on about?"

The man leering in the doorway inhales an exaggerated breath. "Marcus Cornelius is not here."

CHAPTER
XI

"What do you mean he's not here?"

Stepping to the side, I anticipate the rage boiling on Councilor's face; his skin turns redder than a volcano.

"I must humbly apologize, sir. The good doctor is not in. For some reason he has left on sabbatical to the east. Something along the lines of *urgent*. However, I am Asher Vandrake, Marcus's attendant and estate caretaker at your service." The man standing in the doorway wears a long white trench coat, which drapes from his shoulders to the floor as he bows courteously, one hand at his midriff, the other behind his back. Straps and buckles line the front of his torso with various instruments hanging loosely from belt loops. Magnifying prism. Monocole. A compass with ink. His instruments suggest something in the profession of an analyst. With chiseled chin and high cheekbones, the man's gray eyes remind me surprisingly of Joachim, my former butler. As he comes up from his bow, he smiles at the three of us with his thin lips. "A pleasure to make your acquaintance."

Immediately my guard goes up over this Asher Vandrake. His soft words and venomous tone, responding with such tact and precision. It's as if he had been practicing these lines all day.

"Well that's a shame," says Councilor, pushing back his hood to reveal his face and big bushy beard. I notice Asher shift his stance as if uncomfortable. "Usually my business with Marcus is a solid juncture. I find it strange he just up and left. It's not the Marcus I know."

Asher Vandrake narrows his eyes. "The good doctor is wanted by many people in the world, *sir*, not just the needs of local citizens. But be that as it may, it is my solemn duty to accommodate those he breaks appointments with, especially if the company is held in such high regard." Asher turns to me, smiling even sicklier. "Lord Wolfgang, it is an honor and privilege to meet you in the flesh. Your reputation precedes you. Allow me to assist you anyway I can."

At least he knows who I am, yet his flattery, by no means, reduces the weariness he provokes in me. Too many times I've seen opportunists like this at work. This man is no different. There is something off about Asher Vandrake and I can see Kronklich has the complete opposite thoughts about his character.

"Well if you are offering assistance," says Kronklich brightly, "Might we come in for a spot of tea? T'is awfully cold out here."

The inside of the Cornelius estate is not what I expect.

Lush plants. Polished wood banisters. Our steps echo off the black and white checkered marble floors of the foyer. Vegetation hangs from every window and balcony, filling the air with rich earthen scents reminiscent of a deep forest. Large chandeliers hang from thick brass chains; they sway slightly from the breeze coming from the doorway. The combination of metallic hues and organic green creates a stark contrast to Asher Vandrake's attire. His polished buckled boots click along the floor in unison with ours as he leads us beyond an open set of double doors and into a much larger portion of the house.

If the earthen smell was mild in the foyer, here, in this large room spanning upwards two stories, the scent is ten times stronger. We are greeted with the sounds of cascading water, trickling from a sky light in the ceiling. An atrium of sorts. The three of us gaze at our surroundings, mesmerized, breath taken by the unmistakable beauty of flowers, butterflies, and moths. They flutter up the center, reflecting the sunlight in their wings as they pass from leaf to leaf, and instantly I'm reminded of Diana. My hand fingers the metal grooves of Envid tucked neatly under my coat. It is impossible to realize the full extent of this room from where we stand for as we traverse forward, Asher leads us quickly along a windowed hallway and into a smaller side room where the view to the outside is white and a fireplace roars in the far recesses of the corner.

"Do make yourselves comfortable," says Asher motioning with a hand. "I will have the staff prepare some tea."

"Er—, bergamot, my good man," says Kronklich, "—if you have it." His cheeks redden as he removes his hat, as if embarrassed by his sudden and out of place request.

"Yes," responds Asher sharply, a raised eyebrow creasing his forehead. "Bergamot, for the gentlemen. Anything else?" He turns on the spot seemingly agitated and exits the room, closing the door behind him softly.

Immediately, I begin my assault on Councilor as he stands near the fire warming his backside, gazing out the window at the wagon. "You call *this* a plan? Coming to see this Marcus Cornelius?" My tension rises with the thought of each wasted second spent sitting on plush couches and sipping tea. My words seep through clenched teeth. "The man is not even home!"

"Calm down, Tenor," counters Councilor, dropping his belongings on an antique couch. Wisps of vapor twirl off of his scythe as he leans it against the wall near the fireplace. "Don't give up on this venture just yet. There's more to meet the eye here" and he points to his eyeball to drive the point home. "Marcus Cornelius may not be here, but his massive book collection, *is*."

"Oh wonderful, a library!" says Kronklich excitedly. His slouched demeanor perks up from the chair ever so slightly.

"Not just any library. The library of a master researcher and artificer."

"And you expect to find the answers we are looking for in a book? What are we going to do? Have Asher point out the book on vampire children and how to change them?"

"I didn't say that," says Councilor in defense.

"That *would* make things terribly easy," says Kronklich rubbing his hands together.

The door to the room opens and in walks Asher Vandrake followed by a cart pushed by a servant dressed in black and white. The color scheme must be significant to the household.

"Tea for our distinguished guests," says Asher, directing the servant in our direction. The servant wastes no time in preparing cups and saucers, pulling the lid from the sugar bowl, and scooping healthy amounts of dark herbs from a small rectangular bin.

"Please, sit," suggests Asher. It is evident my standing near the window makes him nervous. I glance at the pile of blankets in the back of the wagon before picking out a spot on the long couch near Kronklich. Sitting rigidly, my back never rests against the cushion.

"So tell me," begins Asher, sitting himself opposite of Kronklich. "What sort of errand has brought you three here? Surely some intimate quest perhaps? Or rather, a less pressing matter?"

My eye wanders to Councilor gazing at the floor and then back to Asher who watches me intently, staring at the patch where my other eye used to be. Opening my mouth to answer, Councilor suddenly interjects, his deep voice cutting me off.

"No pressing matters, I assure you. We've come on professional standards, unfortunately, and the subject matter is strictly confidential. We were hoping to benefit from Marcus's supreme knowledge. Our particular situation is—*sensitive*."

"I see," says Asher coolly, taking a sip from his plain tea. "Well that is understandable. Certainly we've had our fair share of well-to-do people coming here, seeking claims for such personal audiences with Marcus. However, if that *is* the case, I don't see how I will be of much help to you. Fortune smiles poorly." Frowning, he sets his tea on the small table and relaxes into his chair. Holding up his monocle, he breathes hot air onto it and rubs it with the sleeve of his coat.

Councilor holds his hands out in contemplation. "You may not be able to help us directly… but access to your library will work just fine."

Asher pauses in his cleaning, a look of surprise spreads across his face. "The library?"

"It's not a problem is it? We can conduct our own research and won't be long. Just a day or two."

"Er—a day or two?"

"You did offer to assist us. Isn't that right, Lord Wolfgang?"

I watch as Councilor is nearly unable to hold back his smile. Keeping my eye locked on Asher, I nod my consent.

Asher sighs. "Very well. Whatever my master's colleagues' request, it will be carried out as if they were the masters themselves."

"Splendid!" says Kronklich, holding his cup up in salute.

The look on Asher's face is something between wearing soiled garments and smelling a dead body. "I will not dishonor his request." He rises from his chair abruptly and turns to Councilor. "Shall I have your horses and wagon drawn to the stable then?"

My thoughts go on high alert. *Winter.*

Councilor smiles, clapping his hands together and putting his gloves back on. "No need my good man. I'll be taking care of that."

CHAPTER
XII

EVEN WITH ASHER VANDRAKE'S WILLINGNESS to accommodate us, my mind continues to wonder about his demeanor and intentions, that certain weird feeling I'm getting from him. The way he looks back at us as we ascend the grand staircase, leading us to the large library encompassing the entire third floor. Pushing the thought from my mind for now, I become enamored with the books upon books upon books… So many books, in so many directions, with so many varying heights. Books lining shelves. Books stacked on one another. As we reach the top step, the rows seem endless. Kronklich's head swivels around like a top, looking left and right so many times. How was anyone to find anything specific in this mess of a study?

"Quite the collection of books you have here," I say, unable to hide my distress. How exactly did Councilor think this was a good idea? We could be here for weeks, let alone days, trying to find anything remotely tangential to vampire lore. If vampire lore was even here.

Asher takes a deep satisfied breath. "The biggest collection of its kind, second to none—except, of course, that of the Grand Cathedral."

Mention of the cathedral sets me thinking about Dorian again. *I wonder if there is a book on the Carnalreesee and blood extraction daggers. That would make things simpler.*

"Hello up there," lofts Councilor's hearty voice from below. His heavy footfalls follow shortly after.

"Up here, sir," says Asher, cupping his hand to his mouth. He turns back to us in his practiced etiquette. "You will find all that you need on this floor and more. Whatever it is you are looking for, I assure you won't find it anywhere else. Dr. Cornelius's library is—*extensive*—to say the least. We have documented accounts in all subjects and an overabundance of science journals and memoirs that date back hundreds of years." He pauses a moment, waiting for the reaction he must expect from all of his guests when told this information. I simply yawn.

His glory diffused, Asher continues his monologue. "You will find the library is divided into four sections, A through F over there," he points across the massive cavity overlooking the lower floors, "G through L there, M through R quite so, and finally," he motions behind him, "S through Z."

"That's where we'll be looking first," says Councilor, reaching the top of the stairs, cheeks flushed from the exercise. I wonder how long of a walk it will be to take a piss around here.

"I take it then all is in order?" asks Asher, pulling out a timepiece from one of his many pockets. He clicks the locket open. "Dinner will be served at seven o' clock in the dining hall should you become famished. Fresh water will be brought right here to the pedestal table should you thirst."

At the thought of food, my stomach growls fiercely. *Finally, some civilized food.*

"In the meantime, your rooms will be prepared on the second floor. Shall I have your things sent for?"

"No," Councilor answers quickly. "I mean, no, it's all right. No need to fuss over us anymore then you already have. Thank you, Asher."

Asher narrows his eyes and nods his head gently before turning on the spot and leaving us to our faculties. "Very well then."

Despite my original weariness of Asher, his accommodations and willingness to help seems to diffuse my guard somewhat as again my attention is drawn back to the impossible task of searching through these stacks.

"Already have a heading?" asks Kronklich, pointing to the S through Z section.

"No, not really. I just said that to get the guy off our shoulders. Hell knows we need a history lesson on this place."

"So what exactly are we looking for?" I ask in a hushed tone, glancing at a nearby towering stack of neatly piled papers.

"Anything relating to the extraction of blood procedures I'm guessing," says Councilor. He looks around and seems to realize for the first time how enormous this place is.

"So then the medical journals section, my expertise," says Kronklich with an air of excitement.

Back in his days of the Five Cities Academy, Kronklich studied all sorts of academia, one area of which was in the field of medicines. I feel that if anyone was going to discover what we are looking for, it was going to be Kronklich. Although I had my fair share of time spent at the academy, a vast majority of my upbringing was saturated in the eternal struggle of my family. Seldom did my father Bealeon push for anything except skills in combat, a life dedicated to fighting monsters. It was my mother, Deloris, who supported the learning of anything else.

"Alright. Good. It's a start," says Councilor, handing Kronklich a few candlesticks. "This might take a while."

Cheerily, Kronklich sets off for the S through Z section, setting a match to his wick, bathing the aisles in a yellow glow.

Councilor stretches his bulging muscles and pushes his elbows back. "Well. Guess we better split up. We'll cover more ground that way."

I want to say I am as enthusiastic about this as they are, but my nerves get the best of me. Heading off in the direction of A through F, I try to convince myself that our time spent here researching won't be a waste. My thoughts fill with Dorian and Diana as I pass the many aisles of stuffy journals and golden bound books, and begin searching through the "B" section, hoping that something could be found relating to "blood."

Blood.

I never want to read about it ever again.

After hours of skimming over countless pages relating to animal blood, human blood, loss of blood and its effects on the body, blood content, blood anatomy and physiology, blood contamination and blood effects on circulation, the only remote subject relating to what we are looking for was anemia, the condition where blood lacks the amount of healthy red blood cells which leaves the patient in a state of tired weakness.

Daydreaming from staring at words too long, my mind wanders on this topic and I envision vampires sucking the blood from human victims. Thoughts of the nightmare I had once about Diana biting my neck come back to me. It forces a shiver through my body. If a victim was afflicted by a vampire, there would certainly be a loss in blood. But how did that relate to the extraction of Cresthaven's blood? What was so special about the vampire's blood?

An announcement from down below startles me out of my wandering mind. Wiping salivation from my mouth, I answer the call for dinner and make my way through the many aisles, keeping my candle close to light my way. Two more lights emerge from the dark shadowy areas of the library, Kronklich from behind a stack of books, rubbing his stiff leg and shaking his head in confirming failure, answering my question before I even ask, and Councilor, climbing down a ladder, a mess of books on the floor as if thrown there on purpose.

The three of us in a daze, we convene at the head of the stairs and make our way down in silence, confirming that we know just as much now as we did before.

Nothing.

The sun has already set and Cornelius's estate transforms into a dim orange glow of melting candles and shiny brass. We spend the next hour feasting over lamb shank and pea soup in a glorious dining hall filled with silver chandeliers and servants ready to attend our every need, until eventually, the tiredness sets in.

"I hope dinner was to your liking," announces Asher Vandrake from across the room. His slimy appearance is quite sudden as he stands in the large archway monitoring us like a predator does his prey.

"Very much so," answers Kronklich in his usual boisterous tone. "Although we might do well with another tea and some morning black for Lord Wolfgang. I fear the night will run longer than we expect."

I don't think there is anything that can ruin the man's mood.

"Consider it done. And what about for you, sir?"

Councilor holds out his hand, shaking his head. "None for me. Thanks."

"Then I bid you gentlemen a good night's end. Other house attendants will be roaming about should you need anything else." Asher bends a low exaggerated bow and exits the hall.

"Well that was a bit much for me," says Councilor rising from the table, cracking his neck one way and then another.

"Is it time already?" asks Kronklich, the disappointment on his face transparent as crystal.

"No, no. You lads enjoy. I have business to attend to," he says, leaning over the table towards us, his eyebrows raised. "My night will surely be longer than yours."

As I watch him leave, there is no doubt he is referring to Winter. How were they going to go about the night in search of food now that we were in Sunstone? My thoughts and hope go with him as his over-sized frame disappears through the archway.

A few minutes later and the beverages arrive. Kronklich and I sit in silence for a bit, enjoying each other's company, admiring the finery of the Cornelius estate. And how fine it is indeed. Lush carpentry. Glass goblets of varying colors. Such art is an uncommon thing and very hard to find. Even the culinary ware was of sterling silver, another indication of aristocracy. It is strange I've never heard of him up until now, especially since he is so well established.

"It is quite possible that over the past couple of years we've might have missed the formal introduction of Marcus Cornelius into high society due to the overabundance of work we've attended to," says Kronklich taking a sip of his tea.

"Yes, killing vampires is time consuming." I am reminded of the last time we were on a hunt, how we were drawn away from my home on purpose so the Carnalreesee could kidnap my son. How work can consume your life. I still hate myself for not possessing foresight of their plan. How could I have known?

"And there is the fact he is from Katal, the far east. If the man is anything like Councilor described, then he is a man of great importance. More so now than ever."

Gulping down the rest of our beverages, we set off again for the long climb back to the library, our determination diligent and full of purpose. I'm not going to retire just yet. Kronklich feels the same. And with Councilor leaving to attend to his nightly business, there was no doubt we had to pull his weight.

Turning more pages. Thumbing through indexes. My eye soon aches with fatigue, and shortly thereafter, my back and hands join in the rebellion. Burning through more candles, I have a cordial brought up by one of the servants to help with the brain fog settling over my mind. Tension in my temples, I relax into one of the recliner chairs allowing the drink to pass through me, warming me while perusing through another book.

I wake to someone nudging me; a terrible ache shoots through my neck.

"Come now, Tenor. T'is late. Tomorrow is another day." Kronklich's reassuring words.

Still with no sign of Councilor returning, we journey to our rooms, the wax burning my hand as we go, my mind numbing. I am unable to think of anything but sleep.

Thankful to reach my room without stumbling over myself, I make no motion to change or remove my armor. Instead, my head sinks into the pillow with grim satisfaction knowing tomorrow will be the same thing, a routine of books upon books upon books...

And I dread every second of it.

DAY TWENTY-FIVE

CHAPTER
XIII

DORIAN

So many days of darkness.

So many bouts with consciousness.

The nightmares keep coming. The nightmares of terrors in the abyss with sharp teeth and razor claws and milk white skin. Purple veins and blue eyes. Nails dragging across skin. They come for me. All of them.

There is a burning itch just underneath my skin. Is it my wounds healing or something else?

I startle from my daze to screams and crying from unseen faces down the hall. In a panic, breathing heavily, I survey my surroundings, the same ones I've been committed to all this time. Stone walls. Iron bars. Will it ever change? How long will they keep me down here before I lose my sanity? They keep stuffing me with plates of food as if I were live stock…

So many times I've watched Cardinal Glass lose his body parts. Both arms, a leg, and yet each morning—*I think it's morning*—he is restored anew. A fresh arm. A fresh leg. But now with the beam of light, I can see well past the middle section of his cell. It was hours ago that edicts came for their routine work: wooden sticks, a cup of blood, pulleys and chains; they chose his right leg today. Cardinal Glass lies in a heap of skin, bone, and wrangled hair, still breathing, his mass moving up and down. I wonder how much pain he is in. It's incredible to know he is a vampire, yet at the same time it is terribly frightening. His resolve to resist blood each day is horrible to watch. He literally starves himself yet he doesn't die. How long will it be till his body gives out? It is certain his faith in God is strong, but the same question keeps coming to me, even though I know it is sacrilegious to think it. Why would God allow such evil to happen? Glass *is* the cardinal of The Holy Order.

I still have no idea how many days have come and gone since my imprisonment at the Dark Cathedral. I no longer call it by its true name for it is anything but 'Grand'. And as I sit here in my prison cell with my plate of food, my shit pot in the corner, and my furry friends scurrying about my legs, I find myself unable to concentrate on anything except two things: what the Carnalreesee are planning to do with me and how to get the hell out of this dungeon.

Escape is futile. I already tried pulling on the bars, but any sane man would have laughed at that. My attempt at coercing the edicts while they tortured Cardinal Glass went unnoticed; they were too overjoyed with beating him to a pulp. I remember the cardinal telling me I needed to escape this place, to try and help everyone imprisoned down here. But my options were thinner than the ice over the pond back home. Walking on its surface would crack it, and I would drown.

An echoing bang in the distance.

Footsteps approaching.

I pull myself away from the bars and huddle near the wall, my natural reaction, wondering why the edicts are coming back so soon. Hadn't they done enough to Cardinal Glass? If he was awake right now, he wouldn't be able to stand.

Looking on, waiting for the two clergymen to appear, something entirely different emerges from the shadows. A figure carrying a lantern, dressed in a white robe and hood. It moves along the corridor, bathing everything in an orange glow. A leather satchel hangs loosely from its shoulder.

Not what I was expecting.

I stand and move to meet the figure that has stopped before my cell gate. We stand inches away from one another, not saying a word. Then, as if on cue, a high-pitched voice emerges from underneath the cowl. I imagine blues eyes glowing at me from underneath, but it is too dark.

"What were you thinking," comes the stranger's voice, but the tone is familiar.

The figure pulls back its hood revealing its face in the lantern light and I am appalled by what I see. Charles glares at me through the bars. One side of his face is pink and puffy, while the other has two fresh holes pierced in his cheek. Streaks of dried blood run from the scabbed wound down to his neck. Bruises cover his throat in the shape of a hand.

"My God… what did they do to you, Charles?"

"They? No. *Him*."

No words can express how I feel. I babble over my words. "I'm so sorry, Charles. This is all my fault…"

"Believe me when I say it could have been worse." His brown curly hair shimmers in the lantern light. "You were my charge and you escaped. What did you think was going to happen?"

A moan from down the hall wails its way to our ears. Charles looks around cautiously and then back at me.

"I'm so sorry…" I say again. "I wasn't thinking."

"I don't blame you for trying," says Charles. Holding out his arm from the folds of his robe, a set of keys dangle from his hand.

"What are you doing?"

Charles inserts one of the keys into the lock. "Setting you free."

There is a click and the gate swings inward on its hinges, groaning with resistance. Moving forward, Charles removes the satchel from his shoulder. "I couldn't find any weapons, so I filled the bag with as many supplies as I could. Bread. Cheese. Water. Enough to hold you over until you find some help."

I look at him, still stunned from his actions and motives. He hands me the bag.

"How did you get past the edicts?"

"Something happened in the city, a discovery of some sort. Most of them were called away from the cathedral."

A discovery? What sort of event would call away more than half the edicts in the Dark Cathedral?

"Quick. We must leave now if you are to have a chance. Follow me." Replacing his hood, Charles stoops low in his gait as if to mask who he is as he exits the cell. "Come. Hurry now."

As he leaves, I try to ask questions, but already he is ahead of me, moving quicker than ever before. I exit the cell and stop before Cardinal Glass's cell, placing my hands on the bars in sympathy, knowing well he won't wake for some time. He will never know what really happened here. What will they do to him after they discover I'm gone? The thought sickens me, but there is no choice in the matter. I will have to do what I can and come back for him, one way or another.

I follow after Charles in a frantic game of tag, moving quickly through the dungeon, passing victims chained to walls. "There are so many!" I shout up ahead. "How will we get them all out?" But my words go unanswered as I try to keep up with Charles's insane pace. "Charles!" I shout again down the hall until finally he freezes.

Pressing himself against a wall, Charles waits for me to catch up. "You can't save them, Dorian. Not now." He peers around a corner and waves his lantern around to see in the darkness. "You need to first get out and find help. It's the only chance you have."

We press on, Charles leading us deeper and deeper beyond the dungeon, descending steps of broken railings and walls of crumbled stone. The entire way down, Cardinal Glass's warning repeats over in my head, his warning not to trust anyone in the Dark Cathedral. I stare at the back of Charles wondering the same thing. Could I trust him?

Having no clue where we are, I notice the steps eventually stop, ending in an arched doorway made of slick stone. It glistens in the lantern light as we pass through, the sound of rushing water greeting us on the other side.

"Not much further," Charles says louder over the rushing water which now stands to our left. "Follow the aqueducts until you can't go any further. At the end of the tunnel, there is a gate." He hands me a rusty key, evidence of its exposure to water for many years. "There will be your escape to freedom. Let whomever you can know what happened here."

Glancing over the side, I see water rushing from somewhere beyond the dark. Large water wheels churn in the flowing current like giant menacing beasts. And from that darkness, moans from the deep travel upwards. A death call traveling on the wind like a bird's song. What was going to be down there... except the only possible place left we haven't gone?

The catacombs.

Looking back to where the water runs, I see it siphons into a duct large enough for a man to fit through. Daylight fills the narrow tunnel full of stench and mold. There's no telling how deep the water is.

"Charles," I begin to say, still not fully understanding the situation. "Why are you helping me? You could come with me. We could escape together!"

With his hood fallen back from all the running, Charles pushes damp hair from his eyes. "Because, if anyone is going to help us—*save us*—it can only be you. I am scarred and tainted. I don't have the strength like you to fight them." Charles's expression turns sour and dark, one of utter loss. "They would find me, and next time will be worse."

I smile at Charles and grip his shoulder. "I'm coming back for you."

I leave him there, standing in the water gushing through the tunnel, and make haste, splashing into the icy depths of the aqueduct, running around a bend until I am out of sight. But instead of continuing on, I stop and wait, resting against a wall, catching my breath, listening for Charles's vanishing footsteps, and then I proceed back, retracing my steps.

Although weaponless and short of any guidance, my resolve is steadfast. Who would I go to for help outside in the city? I realize now, if not more than before, that my chance to make a difference is now, when the Carnalreesee are least expectant. Cardinal Glass said the sun stone was down here, somewhere, and I know deep in my heart, there is no other choice I can make except one.

I am a Wolfgang.

Grabbing a lantern off the wall, I follow the rushing water back into the darkness, back toward the moaning souls, descending deeper into the bowels of the Dark Cathedral and its foundation of bones. Not knowing my fate, not knowing if there was a chance at stopping the Carnalreesee with whatever plan they had, I was going to take it.

My father would do the same.

CHAPTER
XIV

WOLFGANG

WHAT WERE WE NOT GETTING? What were we not seeing?

Yesterday we searched well into the night. For hours we searched this morning.

And still, nothing.

Not a morsel.

Not a hint or an inkling of a lead.

I wanted to ask Asher Vandrake if there were any areas we missed, some extra books in another section of the estate, another library perhaps, but he was nowhere to be found. When I asked a servant where he was, they simply said he stepped out early this morning and had not returned yet.

Sighing to myself, I knew there were just too many damn books.

The dead weight in my stomach tells me we are missing something. As if it was right under our noses.

The daunting expression on Kronklich's face after his tea this morning said it all. At this rate, we were going to be here for a very long time. And that wasn't going to work for me. Dorian was a prisoner. Most likely held in that forsaken cathedral fortress, subjected to whatever horrors went on in there. Although searching for the mysteries that entailed the blood of Cresthaven and whatever secrets it held to unlock, Winter's condition would just have to wait.

At least Councilor has his daughter. I need my son.

"Come on," says Councilor slapping me on the shoulder. "There's something I want to show you."

I wonder how things went last night for him and Winter as I rise from my table, every inch of it covered in open paperbacks and hard bound tomes. How was he able to get her fed in the city, let alone sneak away from Marcus Cornelius's estate without being questioned? But it is a silly thought. He is a Black Blade.

"Where are we going?" I ask as we move down a couple of center aisles and turn suddenly to the left to approach the far northern wall. Standing before a massive bookcase stuffed to the brim with gilded books, he stares at the wall in contemplation with chin in hand, the most confused look I've ever seen on his face.

I look at him, then the bookcase and back again. "What? What is it?"

Councilor clicks his tongue against teeth. "Don't you see it?"

"See what?"

"The rectangular outline."

I stare, dumbfounded at the absurdity of his claim. There are dozens of rectangles. Large ones. Small ones. All in the shape of books. "I don't see anything."

Councilor steps forward, holding out his arms. "Right here." He points to a section where two shelves come together to form an 'L' and he continues moving along the wall, outlining the L shape with his fingers as if in a frame.

At first I don't see it, but then, the realization sets in. Soon I find myself staring at a book shelf shaped like a small door.

"See it now?"

Not waiting a second more we set our bodies against it, trying to push and shove our way through. But the combined force of our weight does nothing to dislodge the secret door. Councilor starts pulling books from the shelves and putting them right back. "I've seen these types of secret passages before. There has to be a catch, a mechanism of some sort."

I join him, pulling books down frantically from the wall, throwing them on the ground, not a care in the world except for what may lie on the other side of this facade.

Running out of books, I dare not look at Councilor in defeat as I methodically continue pulling and setting, pulling and setting. Just as I think my luck is up, my hand pulls another book and there is a solid click. Immediately, the small bookcase dislodges, and becomes loose.

Councilor steps back as I push cautiously on the swiveling door revealing a small passage leading to another room. A musty smell exudes from within as I look back at Councilor who now has Kronklich standing next to him with a pile of books in his arms and an astonished look on his face. "Well that's certainly progress!"

Marcus Cornelius's private library. Who would have thought?

An entirely new catalogue of books, old and weathered, surrounds us in a tiny space consisting of old furniture and dust. A dark-red wooden desk covered in blemishes sits near the center of the room against a bookcase; a soft leather chair creased with age sits tucked behind it. Next to them both, a side table covered in loose parchment, yellowed and dusty, rests quietly, waiting for its owner to organize the chaos on its surface. Inkwells, half empty, line the outer edges of the desk, encrusted by inches of white melted wax. Quills and writing plume in a resident bin sit fastened to the side of the desk like an archer's quiver ready to pull arrows.

My eye wanders the small antechamber full of mystery and wonder, the moldy leather smell overwhelming my senses. A cluster of spider sacks hangs loosely within a slick shiny web in the nearby corner. It's creator, a black and silver spider, scurries away from the flame in Kronklich's hand. Scraping the old wax out of a freestanding candelabra, he sets the candle in the stand, adding a little more light to this very dark room.

"Cozy," says Kronklich, kneeling before one of the bookcases in front of the desk. He runs a hand over the spines removing layers of timeless dust. "I say, this place could use a cleaning. Maybe an incense or two."

This was it. What we were looking for. A means to cross the broken bridge.

As I pour over the multi-colored books spanning deep wide shelves, I notice Councilor's massive form inadequately moving about in the tiny space.

"Good old Marcus. I knew he wouldn't let us down. I told you he was a researcher, a master in knowledge. I'm sure we'll find something relating to Cresthaven's blood in here. I just know it!" Councilor sets to searching the room waving his candle around like a torch. His excitement is just as heartfelt as mine. "Gods be damned. Look how old some of these books are! Classic…"

Classic wasn't quite how I would describe it. They were more ancient than anything. Brittle and in advanced states of decay, I wonder how many more times they can be moved before falling apart in your hands. For a while, we mull over the books, systematically searching memoirs and journals relating to Marcus's personal experiences, his beliefs, cultural influences, realizing this man was quite an academic scholar, a man, who after a few murmuring praises by Kronklich, was someone we definitely wanted to meet. However, despite the captivation and intrigue his prose provided, we found nothing pertaining to vampire lore.

Moving to a new section, I pull a faded blue journal from one of the shelves behind the desk and cautiously ease myself in to the soft chair, wondering if the old wood and crumpled cushion will support my weight. With no words to indicate a title on the worm eaten cover, I begin flipping through its delicate pages gently in fear of tearing the sacred volume. What I find inside is astonishing.

Despite the old man's constitution, he never seems to age. For many years now I've observed up close and from afar, the Archbishop, a man of God, having come to Sunstone from beyond the eastern mountains, stays the same. His skin never cracks, the crow's feet around his eyes never spread. It's as if the holy man discovered the secret to never aging… alas, this concludes my assumptions.

Hungrily skimming through more pages, I run out of entries and come to the last record located halfway through the journal:

It is only a matter of time before Glass is overthrown by that monstrosity, Faeradon. He will come to power and his influence will spread like a plague. I cannot sit idle any longer, knowing what I know. There is work to be done and so I must go east.

Closing the book with a soft thud, I start realizing this Marcus Cornelius is more than just a purveyor of history and art, or a researcher and artificer as so Councilor conveniently put. This man is a journalist—dare I say investigator. Seems he is onto something and skipped town quite hastily. Looks like Asher Vandrake was telling the truth after all.

The memoir is an astonishing find and as I hand it over to Councilor to formulate a second opinion, another book on a nearby shelf catches my eye. Bound in yellowish-gold and weathered from extensive use, it is much smaller than the journal I just read from. It is what's written on the spine that catches my attention and immediately I pluck it from its home. Dust billows around my face. As I read the words, my heart begins to thump harder and harder at the title inscription: *Centuries; A History of Ancient Artifacts and Heritages*. Maybe there was something in here about the Cresthavens. Without saying another word, and with Kronklich across the room busy reading his own stack of papers and Councilor meticulously picking through Marcus' diary, I begin to investigate, sliding my finger down the table of contents, until my finger comes to rest on one subject I never thought of looking up, not until now, now that it was smacking me in the face: *The Hand of God*.

Quickly I skim the pages:

The Hand of God - The Bringer of Hope; The Curse of Humankind

It was once said there existed an artifact so powerful and so destructive, that its name was forgotten and its existence was hidden from the world on purpose so that none would ever find it. The Hand of God. Impossible to destroy by fire, by earth, or by sea, it was taken, hidden away to an undisclosed location thousands of years ago by the Vestige, during the age of the first vampires. Lost to the passage of time, its legacy of destroying vampires was legendary and its intrigue was upheld in the hearts of all men. After much inquisition throughout many lands and research through hundreds of ancient texts, I discovered the mighty and horrible truth about The Hand of God.

But first... reader be warned: The knowledge contained within these pages is sacred information and should never fall into the wrong hands. If the Hand of God were ever to surface again, take heed! Do not linger. Do what must be done. Seal it in a chest, throw it in the deepest ocean, and forget it for an eternity. This you must do, or face the dire consequences.

The properties of the Hand of God consist of two metal rods, bound together by thorn wire, which was created in order to be handled by human hands, for at its center is a stone which burns brighter and hotter than the sun. A crystal called the sun stone. A stone derived directly from the sun itself. It is said that it harbors purity and goodness, the very essence of God, and it is this stone that gives it its true power.

Used in ancient times as a weapon against the vampire, its qualities go beyond the simplicity of destroying a vampire. In fact, its sole purpose was to carry out the service of God, the act of purification, not destruction. Simply touching the artifact will revert the vampire back to its original human form, removing the curse in its entirety, back to the time the vampire was created. Aside from true death, The Hand of God is the only means which can cure vampirism. Per translated ancient texts, no tonic or restorative will abate the dark poison which renders humans into vampires.

Now one might ask: How could such a relic be so dangerous to the human race? Believe me, I asked myself the same question, for how could a symbol of God be associated with wickedness. But after further study, and many hours of lost sleep, I discovered the horrible truth about this ancient weapon. The reason why it was abandoned and forgotten long ago.

The truth is this.

The Law of Equipoise.

Taking the immortality of one subject and transferring it to another. The Hand of God channels through the blood of its wielder. It serves as the conduit which burdens the user. There is no simpler way I can explain it except this: The one who wields the Hand of God can live forever.

My blood freezes from the words written on the page and I am unable to move. The confusion. The fear. The reality of the situation begins settling over me like an icy river. What did I just read? There is shouting coming from somewhere in the background, but my mind is set in turmoil. I keep reading unable to pull away from the cryptic words:

So you see, this artifact can never be surfaced. It would mean one man would come to bear all the power of the world. What would be deemed as righteousness would also be a curse.

The words dripping from the pages sends me into a catatonic state. Those words have been said to me before. 'You too bear a curse.' The words of Constable just before I killed him. I find my hand moving over to my side, feeling the warm metal resting softly against my hip. The weapon of ancient power. The weapon of immortality.

"Tenor!"

Feeling my body shaking violently, all at once I am pulled back to reality. Kronklich is shouting in my ear.

"Tenor! The enemy is upon us! We need to go, now!" Kronklich draws the sword from his cane and hurries out of Marcus Cornelius' private library.

Still in a daze from what I just read, there is no time to analyze the journal's contents further. Shouting and the sound of breaking furniture echoes in the distance. The smell of smoke lingers in the air.

Closing up the journal, I stow the decrepit book inside my coat, under my breastplate, and draw Enivid from my hip. Glancing over the room one last time, I dash out of the hidden library, ready for the fiends who seem to have found us.

CHAPTER
XV

THERE IS NO DOUBT THAT whoever or whatever was looking for us, found us.

Exiting the secret library is like passing through a portal of time. Moments ago peace and tranquility surrounded us in a dim glow of reading light. Now, raging fire spreads up the columns of the house in the distance. Long curling snakes of yellow and orange. Smoke fills the inside of the estate scorching the air which is hard to breathe.

Chasing after Kronklich through the third floor library, I hear shouts and screams of people fighting downstairs. Sounds of steel clashing and wood breaking. As the fire spreads to the ceiling, it won't be long until the entire place transforms into a fiery inferno. Images of my home and Cresthaven Manor enter my thoughts all over again. The burning heat a reminder of things lost and things cleansed. But why would they burn a library? There is so much information here. And yet, even as my heart pounds against my chest, I remember the hard firmness wedged behind my breast plate. The book. Was it the object of their desire?

Reaching the first step of the stairwell, the sight below spreads before us like a chaotic vortex, the waterfall spilling from the skylight splashing down into an atrium of blood, plants, and people. Among the whirlpool of destruction, Councilor stands in the thick of it, wielding his scythe around him like death, a farmer harvesting wheat from a golden field. His giant black mass is surrounded by other figures dressed in red tunics and black boots. Edicts. Clergy men from the church, the ones we saw earlier in the streets. They wield weapons of persuasion. Short swords and jagged daggers. One of them carries a wood chopping axe, similar to the one I saw in the streets yesterday, and hacks away with confidence, yet misses with each strike. But Councilor is not alone. There is another figure, all in black, much shorter in comparison to Councilor. Masked in a black cloak and hood, it moves about in quick stocky bursts. There is something in its hand I've never seen before. A short black stub of iron and wood. There is a flash of light, a loud bang, and one of the edict's head explodes off its shoulders. Blood and brain spray about the atrium in a foray of gore.

"What the hell was that?" I shout, plugging my ringing ears as Kronklich charges down the steps, hobbling as fast as he can.

"That my boy is the Calvary!" The joy in Kronklich's delivery reminds me of the old days when all that mattered was hunting and destroying the enemy.

Calvary?

I follow after Kronklich, my hand raising Enivid above my head. Already I taste the power of it flowing to my core, the adrenaline of battle rising in my chest and shoulders. Whether these edicts are working for the vampires or not, it does not matter, for I cannot let things matter anymore. Too long my foe has hindered my progression to find my son. Too long I have done the work of others. Morality died many days ago when I was forced to slay my wife. No more is the time for hesitation. No more is the time for mercy.

Stop the enemy at all costs.

With swift precision, I throw Enivid.

The four pointed blade whirls down the stairwell in a deadly arc cutting through the first two edicts before they have a chance to meet with Kronklich at the bottom. The blades spur through them passing judgment, separating their arms from their torsos. Blood is added to the darkening pool of water. Holding their stump of an arm, they cower along the floor, howling in pain.

Another edict fills in the gap, stepping over the bodies as if they didn't exist, thrashing with its axe wildly. Kronklich steps to the side once, dodging the menacing swing and flicks his blade forward, piercing the man's wrist, forcing him to drop the clumsy weapon. Following up with two whirling circular strokes, Kronklich carves into his chest like a diced sausage, finishing with a piercing thrust through the throat. The edict drops the axe, clutching its throat as it drowns in its blood.

Dividing our forces, Kronklich maneuvers towards Councilor while I move to help the mystery figure taking on two edicts at one time. A head shorter than me, the figure moves about the floor, crushing plants underfoot in its destructive path. Although its movements are awkward and rigid, there is a flash of finesse to its tactics. Wielding a thick black double-edged axe, the phantom figure moves like a shadow in the midst of fire and smoke. Bringing its axe to meet an edict's sword, it catches the flat of the blade in the head of the axe. With a twist, the blade shears in half. A swift crack to its face with the handle and the edict crashes to the floor. The cloaked figure again flashes its strange stocky weapon at the approaching enemy a foot away. It squeezes the trigger and again a blast of fire and smoke ejects from the barrel. The edict's spine explodes in a spray of bone fragments and blood. A look of shock and terror begets the edict's dying face as it slumps to the floor, clutching at the air.

The mystery figure faces me with a dark cowl covering its face, yet all I see is gleaming white teeth, smiling.

"Well, well! If it isn't Freakshow!"

It takes a moment to comprehend and connect the meaning of the words. *Oh no… Reyes the Baker.*

"Nicholas."

"I knew I'd be seeing you soon—"

A sword rushes by my face and I block.

A dagger rises behind Nicholas and he reacts, lodging the axe into the edict's forehead.

"—but not like this."

I wipe blood from my face as Nicholas pulls back his hood revealing his sinister black eyebrows and cold blue eyes. His hair, short-cropped and glistening. I remember our encounter in Walters all too well.

"How did you—what are you—?" The questions come rolling off my tongue, but go unanswered as he shakes his head violently.

"Goddammit, Freakshow. Now's not the time for chit-chat! We've got more killings to do! Look!" Nicholas points with one of his stubby hands towards the foyer of the estate. More edicts come pouring through the burning doorway. An unlimited supply of fodder.

How are there so many of them? Was the whole Order coming here?

"Put your backs up to fountain! Come on now!" With a throaty growl, Nicholas braces his double-edged axe before him like a shield and cuts into the first edict that approaches.

Boots splashing in the fountain water, I quickly survey our surroundings and see the odds are greatly in the Holy Order's favor, three to one.

"Tenor! We need to get out of here. The place is going to come down!" shouts Councilor over the raucous noise of battle. As he continues to fight the impossible onslaught of the enemy, I am only able to depict two more words that make any sense. But it is enough for me to understand. "Winter—wagon!"

An edict charges forward, splashing bloody water in my face. Ducking low and gripping Enivid tightly, I ram one of its blades through the edict's stomach, pushing him forward with all my might. His breath in my face, I come eye to eye with my adversary, the whites of his eyes sinking into the dark depressions of his face. I can see now the edicts could easily be mistaken as vampires walking in the daylight.

Teeth clenched. Muscles taut. The edict drops his weapon while falling to the blood stained ground.

As if reading my mind, Kronklich clears a gap for me, cutting down another edict and keeping yet another busy. "Go now, Tenor!" His top hat bouncing amongst the enemy. "I will get our things!"

Collecting myself, I make for the back of the estate, passing the burning stairs and falling debris. Shielding my mouth and nose with my coat, I charge forward into a hazy mist of smoke, towards the dismal light waiting for me on the other side.

A flash of light. A glint of steel. Suddenly there is a dagger headed straight for my head. Rearing back before the needle penetrates my neck, I wield Enivid around me in a great arc to counter the assault, hoping to catch my assailant off guard. Only twirling wisps of smoke lingers.

Where am I? The kitchen? One of the great hallways? It's impossible to tell by the smoke.

"The book, Lord Wolfgang. Give me the book."

A tall lengthy shadow materializes out of the smoke. Slowly and surely, the figure becomes clearer as it approaches. Long white coat and black boots. Long stringy blonde hair. Asher Vandrake appears like a smoky apparition, poising a wickedly long dagger. In a smooth calm tone, his voice slithers through me like a snake. "I know you have it, Wolfgang. I won't ask again."

"I don't have anything," I say, gripping Enivid in both hands. A piece of the building crumbles in the background; fiery debris adds to the already growing piles.

"Oh really," says Asher smiling coyly. He lunges forward, first going low, then high, landing his dagger inches away from my one good eye. The only thing between the dagger and my face is Enivid. Bloodshot irises stare at me with determination and purpose. Asher's height is an advantage over mine. "You will soon join the ranks of the dead. This I assure you." He pushes harder on the blade and I feel my feet slipping underneath. How is he so strong? What sort of edge does he have?

"Now, Wolfgang! Give me the damn book!"

I see long black nails creep over the top of his shoulder. Following those fingers, I notice a head of long black hair and purple eyes cresting from around the outline of his back like two moons. Without warning, the smooth porcelain face of Winter emerges over Asher. A look of ghostly terror spreads across his face as two fangs clamp down over his neck. The strike is precise and clean. Asher wails in pain, instantly shying away and thrusting the dagger into Winter's forearm. The effect is instantaneous as both Winter and Asher retract at the same time, Asher gripping his bloody shoulder in shock, and Winter holding her bloody arm to her mouth, savoring their commingled blood. Her eyes, now burning red with desire, stare at him like a wild animal, her body, ready to pounce.

"Bloody hell! What is this?" Asher staggers back, his own blood flowing freely down his white coat. He bolts from the room, vanishing into rays of light shining through the smoke.

I can see Winter is ready to go after him with no regard to the outside.

"Winter! No!" I shout, tackling her to the ground, doing my best to stop her from leaving. I struggle against her as she tries to resist me and soon I realize I am in as much danger as she is. The blood lust is taking her over.

"Stop Winter! The sunlight!" I shout, using all of my strength to stop her frenzy, but she is lusting and I will be her next victim. She strikes my abdomen and I am sent reeling back, coughing in the thickening smoke. I feel her eyes on me, red and glowing and just as she lunges, a large mass swoops in front of me. Councilor. He blocks her advance, catching her in his arms.

"Winter, no! No!" Councilor shakes her violently, whipping her head back and forth.

In the same moment, Kronklich and Nicholas barrel through the smoke suddenly, Nicholas eyes searching for the enemy, his black axe dripping with blood.

"Come on, gentlemen! We mustn't dawdle, lest we are buried in this wrath of fire and smoke!" Kronklich helps me up while Councilor wraps Winter in his cloak and lifts her over her shoulder. She kicks and screams and hisses from underneath the fabric.

"Quick, this way," says Kronklich waving his sword before him, clearing the smoke with his other hand. Nicholas brings up the rear as we exit the manor in haste, just before the stables collapse into a billowing cloud of embers and smoke.

CHAPTER XVI

"I THOUGHT EVERYTHING WAS UNDER control, Councilor. I thought *she* was under control!" I can't begin to explain the anger I'm feeling at the moment, escaping a near death experience only to nearly be killed again—and by a vampire of all things.

We are all breathing hard as the wagon speeds away from Marcus Cornelius' estate, its lingering existence in the distance, a branch of flames and smoke extending over the white buildings.

The look on Councilor's face is one of defeat and remorse. Breathing heavier than the rest of us, he sits at the rear of the wagon with his back against Winter's coffin, his arms outstretched. A trail of blood drips from his forehead along the scar on his cheek and into his black bristly beard.

"Things *were* under control…" begins Councilor, "… until she tasted human blood. It's the only thing that caused the lust. I've been able to control her up until now." He looks sternly into my gaze. "Nothing has changed, Tenor. She will be fine. I promise."

Nostrils flaring, I turn away angry and frustrated, focusing my attention elsewhere. I'm not so sure Councilor can keep his promise.

With Kronklich driving the wagon and Nicholas giving directions just behind him, the back alley walls and cobble stones pass by in a blur of white.

And what the hell was Nicholas doing here?

"Left here," says Nicholas over Kronklich's shoulder, surveying the road up ahead. "We should be good along this route for the next mile or so. Don't falter unless absolutely necessary." Seemingly satisfied with his directions, he pats Kronklich on the shoulder and lowers himself back into the wagon, turning around to face Councilor and myself.

"So I take it the edicts came looking for your lot at Cornelius's place." He surveys a passing wagon conspicuously. "There's no doubt the city will be on high alert now. Every edict and guard on patrol will be looking for you—" he shakes his hand rapidly in the air, "—us." He slumps back with a sigh and methodically begins cleaning the blood off his axe. "I understand them coming after your lot, especially you," he points his finger at me, "the vampire hunter in a city run by vampires. But what I can't wrap my head around is why go to great lengths to burn Cornelius's place down? I think they were after something more. A book most likely."

"The same book we were looking for," says Councilor, looking from Nicholas to me. "Although I can't say much for the book anymore."

I avoid his gaze knowing very well where the book is. Sitting tightly packed against my chest and breastplate. I take deep, labored breaths, feeling its pressure against my ribs.

So the vampires were after the book. Asher Vandrake confirmed that, a human servant working for the Carnalreesee. And yet I am still reluctant to let the group know that I have it. I feel guilty. Having read what I read earlier, the whole secret about The Hand of God and what it's made of, I wonder how they would take it if they knew what it does. Hell, I'm not even sure I know if it's true or not. Immortality? How could I know for sure? Did it mean I could live and live without ever growing old? Possibly. But at the same time, I know there is a chance of dying. My face, my hand, and my eye are proof of that. If parts of my body could be mauled beyond recognition then—oh yes, death was imminent, always watching, always waiting. There was no mistaking it. How would they take it knowing that I would outlive them all, watch them die and have to bury them? What would Kronklich say? What would Dorian say? And then there was the fact the book mentioned there was no cure for vampirism except to revert the vampire to human. Now that the Hand of God and the Bawaka were altered into something else, Enivid, the possibility was no more. Scarring Winter's back was proof enough.

No. It's best not to say anything at the moment. I need to keep the book a secret for now.

The wagon takes a sharp turn suddenly and Nicholas is at the ready. The strange weapon he used earlier appears in his hand in a quick draw from under his cloak—*fascinating*. That weapon, with a simple squeeze of the trigger, is capable of blowing a hole in a man the size of my fist. One blast of fire and smoke from its short cylindrical barrel would send any mortal to oblivion. I wonder how it would fair against the undead.

As quickly as he draws the weapon, he lowers it just as fast, giving me a look of knowing, that I want to ask him a million questions.

"Go ahead, Freakshow. Ask away."

Nicholas's outward mannerism hasn't changed the least since the last time I saw him. I do my best to ignore his antics while watching his hands remove two pouches from his belt.

"The last time I saw you, you were in Walters at the Knotted Rope."

"Yes, that's right."

"And well…" I try to find the right words to express my consternation. "What the hell are you doing here and how did you find us? Don't you have a bakery to run?"

Nicholas laughs as he pours a fine black powder from one of the pouches into his weapons. "Well, it's a bit tricky. You see…"

"I sent for him," interrupts Councilor.

"Yes, you sent for me alright, and would have been here a lot sooner if not for Gauldust. The whole town was up in arms about vampires. Said there was an attack. You wouldn't happen to know anything about that now would you? I lost a whole day because of it."

Councilor smiles. "But you couldn't have arrived at a better time."

I look at Councilor with a want of knowing, ignoring the blunder in Gauldust.

"You sent for him. A baker. He is one of your contacts?"

"He is more than just a baker. He is a force to reckon with. He is a Black Blade."

"Ex-Black Blade. More like retired," finishes Nicholas with a smirk. Packing the powder with a strange instrument, he proceeds with removing small metal balls from the other pouch. "I gave up that profession long ago. I'm not as agile as I used to be."

"Once a Black Blade, always a Black Blade. You know the rules," says Councilor.

"Yeah, yeah. I know the damn *rules.*"

"You're a Black Blade?" I ask, completely astonished. The supposed baker of Walters was a trained contracted killer. Who would have thought? It certainly explains the terrible food he served.

"And don't you worry," continues Nicholas packing the small pieces of metal in the cylinders, the same as the powder, "Hector's watching over the shop while I'm gone. I have faith in him."

"That's how you knew who I was," I say, thinking back to when I first met him. I feel somewhat betrayed.

"Of course. A Black Blade needs to know the lay of his land. Everyone and everything in it."

"You played me for a fool."

"*You* sound like you're whining, Freakshow. Think of me as your guardian angel." Holding his two exotic looking weapons up to the light, he blows in the barrels and sets to wiping them down with a rag. "Kind of like the sound of that. Better yet, your guardian *death* angel."

"He owes me a favor," says Councilor, adjusting himself against Winter's black box. "You know how that goes," he says pointedly at me. "I need someone to watch my daughter in the event I am no longer around. What I'm doing—what we're all doing—is a dangerous exploit. There's no guarantee of success. Now that we've lost our means to finding a cure at Marcus' place, there is only one other place I know of that might give us a chance. That scumbag, Asher Vandrake said so himself, not realizing he gave it away. The Grand Cathedral. There is a library even bigger than the one we were looking through, a laboratory and research facility that hasn't been used for hundreds of years. The Holy Order thought it sacrilegious to use such things of science, so it was sealed off. Caved in the doors and everything. If there's a cure to vampirism, it has to be there."

I flinch at the mention of this.

Councilor looks to me. "Which means I'm going with you. We have a common cause, you and I. You save your son. I save my daughter."

"Well, it's good to know we have a plan then. I thought I was going to carry all of you on my back!" Nicholas smiles, holstering one of his weapons.

Yes. A plan within a plan. Unbelievable.

I stare at the two Black Blades wondering. Such a bizarre turn of events. Is this fortune or some terrible luck of the draw? Would these two assassins spell my ultimate doom, or give me the leverage I need to save Dorian? My hope, my faith, lies in the latter.

A sheer jolt of the wagon sends Nicholas into a paranoid rage. With both of his short cylinders of doom at the ready, he leers from the wagon's side at passersby, staring down, pointing at children and judging mothers.

"What are those things anyway?" I ask, unable to curb my curiosity any longer. "Those weapons certainly get the job done."

Nicholas laughs out loud while settling back into the wagon. "I knew you couldn't resist, Freakshow. These…" he holds the small weapons up, "… are called *Last Resort*. Capable of putting holes the size of your fist in your face. I've severed hands and arms with these beauties."

I recall the edict losing his head earlier. They certainly can do more than that.

"In ancient times they were called many things. Flint locks. Powder pistols. But now, I like to call them something else. Short barreled muskets. Has a certain ring to it. Pack 'em with powder and shot, and they're good to go. You just have to pull back this thing here, called the pin, and poof, whoever, whatever is on the other end of *Last Resort,* is dead." Smug with his description, he twirls the gun in the air with bravado.

"You said 'ancient times.' What do you mean? Where did you find such weapons?"

"Marcus Cornelius, of course." Nicholas looks at me as if I should already know this.

"So you've met him too then?"

"Well, yes, we all have… the Black Blades that is. These pistols are ancient artifacts. He found them back during the time of the Vestige."

"The what?"

Nicholas and Councilor look at each other, that questionable look that borders on secrecy. "Let's just say Marcus is a man of vast knowledge."

"I hate to interrupt, gentlemen," says Kronklich leaning back, "But we might have a bit of a problem."

Looking ahead, I see what Kronklich is referring to as Nicholas curses under his breath. A roadblock has been set fully equipped with city guards on foot carrying spears. Edicts on horseback join their cause patrolling back and forth along the main street. A long line of citizens and merchants forms in front of it. Guards are roughly searching and questioning the people.

Nicholas stands up and moves to the front. "Here, let me drive. Take this," he says, handing Kronklich the short-barreled musket. A look of surprise besets Kronklich's face. "Any problems, point and shoot."

Kronklich's expression is one of both joy and terror.

"What? It's just like your crossbow except it makes a bigger sound. Got it?"

Kronklich nods his head rapidly, handling the weapon as if it were venomous snake.

Nicholas cracks the reins with a *Hyah!* and the wagon takes a hard right sending cobblestone and dirt scattering across the roadway. The look on his face is intense, his blue eyes piercing like a hawk's.

"Where are we headed?" I shout over the wind and the thundering of hooves.

"Some place no one will find us. Somewhere safe."

For a time we pass through empty back alleys, proceeding with caution around corners with Councilor watching our flank and Kronklich and I watching the sides. Clearing another perimeter wall, rolling along undetected through a gigantic archway, I keep watch over the time of day. With the gray haze of city smoke blocking out any potential for sufficient light, I can tell the day is waning to a close. Soon we will worry about more than just guards and edicts. A new enemy will be roaming the streets and sky and I know if we are to stand a chance at evading the horrors of the vampire, we will need to find this 'safe place' soon.

In the distance there is shouting and neighing of horses and suddenly Councilor slaps his hand against the side of the wagon. "We've been spotted! Edicts on horseback!"

"Shit!" grumbles Nicholas, turning behind a building. But instead of sending the horses into a full galloping panic, he gently encourages them on, as if nothing were happening.

"What are you doing?" I say over his shoulder, adrenaline rising. The edicts' shouts become louder. Closer.

"Patience, Freakshow… we're almost there."

"What are you talking about—" I begin—until a huge crowd of wagons and people on foot pass by the road, heading in the direction of the approaching edicts, congregating into a massive crowd of sellers and buyers. The crowd would slow the edicts down significantly.

After the last person clears the way, Nicholas clicks his tongue and nudges Abel and Jasmine to proceed at a canter. The clip-clop of hooves reverberates off the alley walls as we disappear into the growing dusk, the long dark shadows of the buildings serving as our cover. A little further down and Nicholas turns the wagon again, forcing us into complete darkness. The sky disappears above us and I can only assume we entered a tunnel of some sort.

Unable to see my hand in front of my face, I worry for our safety until a spark, ignited by Nicholas, illuminates his face in a dim glow. Within seconds, he lights a brilliant torch and holds it high over his head, swiping it back and forth, surveying his surroundings.

Nicholas nods his head. "And here we are. Don't worry. They won't find us here."

"What is this place?" I ask. There isn't much to see except a few barrels, a couple of hay stacks, and a long row of wooden doors and shuttered windows. Long arched columns line the wide expanse of the tunnel in a symmetrical layout.

Councilor speaks up. "This, my friends, is an Elysium, one of the few left of its kind."

CHAPTER XVII

DORIAN

Darkness spreads before me like a thick soupy abyss. It swallows the light of my lantern with fierce hunger. Soaked to the bone from traversing the aqueducts, the tunnel system seems to go on forever like a network of viscous veins. Everything corrupted and impure from the cathedral washes its way down here, dripping from cracks in the ceiling, saturating my hair with an oily slickness. The smell is atrocious as I splash through rat-infested waters, pushing aside crates of rotten food and up-ended barrels. Ever moving forward, the light from my lantern pierces the darkness like a hammer-driven wedge. Every step from my right foot shifts the angles of light one way, then back causing the shadows to dance erratically. Anxiety level high, I hold my breath around each corner, wondering what sort of abomination waits for me.

Ducking under large water wheels churning above the black deluge, I wonder how much time has elapsed since deciding to take matters into my own hands, the decision that may cost me my life. For now, daylight lives outside the walls of the Dark Cathedral, but for how long, I'm not sure. The sun is my ally and time is my foe. But my ally will be going to sleep soon.

Armed with nothing but a lantern and a satchel of food, I travel into the darkening twilight, descending deeper into a spatial abyss of loose rock and rutted holes. The air becomes thicker with each step, making it harder to breathe.

Swaying my lantern back and forth, skeletons in the walls greet me like long lost cousins, their smiling faces like reminders of what's to come should I fail. There is no doubt I've reached the catacombs, the lowest portion of the cathedral's foundation, and once here, I wonder about the generations buried within its confinements.

Skulls stare at me from every direction as I pass sweeping halls full of open passageways. The catacombs are a giant cavernous network of tombs, like great dragons of the earth, capable of swallowing thousands of bodies. I realize becoming lost down here would be an easy task if one's sense of direction were turned around. Already I feel overwhelming odds against me. The graves I pass, one after another, all the same, and with no definitive markings. Where this sun stone might be, I have no clue, so I gather up my courage and keep pressing forward, trying my best to ignore the moaning echoes from the darkened passages.

After what seems like hours of searching, I take refuge behind a decrepit tomb covered in silvery threads. Feet aching, stomach growling, I devour some cheese and bread wondering if my plan at making a difference will actually work. There is nothing down here except the dead, and they are agitated. Not once, but twice, I found ensnared acolytes trapped in the walls, their wails loud and obnoxious, their skin barely intact, tearing with the slightest movement.

"Please sir. Set me free. I just want to be free," one said earlier.

"It's been so long since I've seen light. Are you my salvation?" asked another.

The comments and questions were both ominous and foreboding. A certain sadness was all I could feel for them. I wanted to grab them by their arms and pull, but how would that save them? Their limbs would have torn out of their sockets. They are a part of this place, have been for God knows how long. Poor souls. They are trapped—like flies in a spider's web, long forgotten by their predator.

"What I wouldn't give to taste food again," comes a voice directly next to me. A skull in the wall moves its mouth up and down, unable to make any other sort of movements. I back up against the tomb with a fright. Seems there is nowhere down here where I can be free of acolytes.

"That must be cheese," says the skull again. "It looks like cheese."

The skull keeps mumbling out loud as if it were talking to itself.

"Quiet," I say, raising a shaking finger to my lips, unable to think of anything else to say.

"It's been a long time since I've seen—well—anything, let alone a person. I will not be quiet."

"But you must," I say breathlessly, looking over my shoulder, wondering if anything else down here might have heard us. "It's a matter of life and death."

"Then there's nothing for me to worry about," says the skull.

The sounds of creaking and tapping pull me from my conversation with the skull as I absentmindedly chew. Peering around the corner of the tomb, dust trickles down its side as I squint to see the strange blue light hovering in the distance. Watching it come closer, I hold my breath, hoping not to make a sound.

A skeletal figure comes into view holding a lantern between its bony fingers. Blue light glows from inside the metal housing of the lantern, casting streaks of purple and pink along the many skulls lining the walls and floors.

"What is that thing?" I ask in a whisper, hoping the skull has an answer.

"A caretaker," says the skull loudly. I put my hand over its mouth as if it will make a difference.

"Shhhhh!" I say in a harsh rasp. "It will hear you!"

"You should be more worried about the beacon in your hand."

Quickly, I shutter the light.

The skeleton jerks about the passage way as if looking for something, walking slowly in its strange animated gait. I notice teeth missing from its jaw as it stops feet away from my hiding spot and looks about suspiciously with its hollow eye sockets.

Suddenly, the caretaker rushes to a wall nearby and with one hand grabs the head of an acolyte encrusted in the wall. The caretaker leans in, howling in its face. With a sharp twist of the wrist, he rips the head from the wall like plucking a potato from the dirt. A dark red liquid spurts from the newly opened wound in the wall, spraying onto the bones of the caretaker's body. The spray reduces to a trickle down the uneven floor as the caretaker continues roaming the corridor away from me.

I sigh with relief.

"That is what happens to those who show any lack of devotion to the cathedral," says the skull. "The caretakers serve as monitors to our Lord."

"You mean God?"

"Oh no. Not at all. Faeradon."

What sort of dark place this cathedral has become I cannot say, but my taste of it first-hand suddenly turns the food I just swallowed into an unappetizing lump in my belly.

"I would like to thank you for the reprieve however short it was. It was nice to see what life was like again." The skull's mouth stops moving.

Making sure the caretaker is gone, I stand up, gathering my things while the coast is clear. "Thank you, er, sir." Not sure what to call it, I hear it mumbling to itself as I make haste and travel in the opposite direction of the caretaker.

I feel the deeper I descend, the more blue lights I see. Still not completely convinced of what a caretaker is, I shake at the thought of one of them touching me. Cold dead fingers groping at my skin, the screech of its hollow voice deafening my ears. But what makes traversing the catacombs even more difficult is not so much the frequency of walking skeletons and their eerie blue lights, but the narrowing of the corridors. Tighter they become in the maze-like structure, the stones in the walls seeming to jump right out at me as I go, glancing around bends, unsure if using my lantern is even safe anymore.

Still with no signs of anything resembling a sun stone, my hope dwindles even more. I begin second guessing myself and my intent and at one point, turn around hesitantly. The hairs on the back of my neck rise. Something is following me. A blue light in the distance.

Spinning about on my heels, I begin walking frantically, almost jogging, as I skim along the walls with my hands, scraping dirt from between skulls and stones. A rock jutting out of place clips my shoulder, the pain hardly registers as I come to an intersection of sorts. Three corridors lie before me, but my intuition's gone numb.

"No, no, no," I say under my breath, looking down each daunting passageway, none of them better than the other. Moans come from the left hall while growls come from the center one. My blood pressure rises as I stand here, indecisive, sweating, and as the growls get louder. I barrel down the right passage, bouncing off walls recklessly, cursing myself for becoming so paranoid. This is a test. Where is my bravery? This isn't how a Wolfgang should act.

Unexpectedly, a wall of skulls and bones encased in dirt explodes beside me, throwing me against the opposite side as some unearthly creature, moaning and gurgling from its decaying mouth gropes at me, pinning me against the wall with its crumbling arms. An overwhelming stench bellows from its windy throat as it snaps rotten teeth at me, trying to bite the living flesh from my face and neck.

I scream, unable to control myself as I bat at its face, stripping its papery skin with my fingers. "Get away from me! Get off me!"

Dropping to my knees, the walking corpse loses its balance and topples over, leaving me an opening to escape from. Looking beyond its shoulder, I see a skeletal figure with a blue light charging its way down the corridor.

"Oh God, no, no, no…" I stutter, collecting myself and running in the opposite direction. Down corridor after corridor, I run for my life, passing open passageways and ancient tombs. In the distance, another wall breaks apart and more wretched creatures pour out of the hole like spiders and ants. They see me and I turn right, barreling down another random hallway. Now I am getting good and lost and my nerves are exploding.

Running.

Breathing.

I don't know what else to do.

Panting.

Breathing.

Something grabs my leg and I fall to the ground, knocking the wind from my lungs. I see a bony hand holding me fast as another one breaks through the floor grasping my ankle. Kicking at the corpse-like appendages, they break apart like brittle sticks and just as I stand to escape, another creature bursts through the wall nearly tackling me. Heart thumping in my chest and temporarily free, I find myself running down the hall again, my only concern to get away. With the lantern held high, I frantically search ahead, hoping the passage is clear but… there it is again, a blue light materializing out of the dark.

Oh no. Oh god no.

Searching the ground for something to swing, I reach for a long shafted bone and ready it like a club. *It is no sword, but it will have to do.*

With fierce resolve, I alternate swings between bone and lantern, bashing the undead creatures as they come at me from one direction. The caretaker makes its way towards me on my flank with an army of undead behind it.

I crush a skull here.

I shatter a pelvis there.

The undead swarm me, forcing me into a corner and blocking off the caretaker's advance.

With a dirt wall and scattering spiders to my back, the dead moan with grisly satisfaction, trying to get at any part of me they can. I smash another head and feel the pressure against the wall on my back. The dead surge, forcing me to sink low, scraping along the wall in the process.

Battered, bruised, and covered in dust, I am nearly consumed by bodies as they trample about me. They try to bend down at the waist but there are too many of them. My hands frantically search the wall for salvation. Feeling an empty space behind me, I back into a hole in the wall, a catacomb chamber bed, and scatter old clothes and bones like unwanted debris. The walking corpses snap at my feet and reach with their hands as I retract as far and deep as the grave will allow me to go. Kicking and hollering, I push back at one of the dead who clambers into the crawl space with me, yearning for my guts, clawing at my robes and shoe.

One kick.

Two kicks.

The creature releases and suddenly I have nowhere left to go. Another creature climbs into the tiny space with me and this time, using the bone I used for a club, I jam it into the creature's mouth, uselessly trying to choke it. It bites down with a jarring force, snapping the bone in half and proceeds in its attempt to maul me. Again I kick with as much strength as I can, then swing the lantern with all my might, smashing its face and detaching its jaw. The blow stalls the dead long enough for me to kick the ceiling, trying my best to loosen the stones.

With the lantern in pieces, and the wick ready to go out any second, I take a deep breath and thrust my foot into another creature's skull, grinding it into the wall. The force dislodges some of the stones and the stale air fills with rumbling. Within seconds, the hole collapses with pebbles and stones and old tattered remains, separating myself from the dead and the last tendrils of light.

CHAPTER XVIII

WOLFGANG

THE ENTRANCE TO THE ELYSIUM is anything but ordinary. A hallway full of paintings as far as the eye can see. A long tunnel wide enough to fit two carriages side by side. Large sconces line the entry corridor on both sides, covered in dust and filth from disuse. How long has it been since someone was here? Only a member of the Black Blades would know the answer to such a question.

Nicholas guides the horses and wagon into a nearby stall hidden inside the headquarters. He dismounts and waves his torch back and forth inspecting the place, motioning with his hand. "Come. This way. There's a lot of ground to cover. We'll have to secure hay and water later tonight."

As I survey the surroundings, admiring the paintings of beautiful landscapes, mountains and forests, colors vibrant and full of life, I notice Councilor undoing the locks and latches on Winter's box.

"Is that necessary?" I ask, still wary from her earlier attack on me.

"Yes, it's necessary. I can't just leave her locked up and alone. Besides, dusk has settled. She will need to feed. Maybe we can find some rats around this place."

Subconsciously, my hand goes to my neck as if I had been bitten. The memory of Winter jumping on me lingers like all the other bad dreams from the past. Sharp fangs piercing my skin. The cold breath of decay on my neck.

As we continue walking, I can't help but admire the enormity of the Black Blade's secret headquarters. We pass one passageway ignoring it and continue on as if there were a dozen more to see. "How many of these Elysiums did you say were left?" I ask, trying to keep my mind off Winter.

"I didn't give a number," says Nicholas. "There used to be one in every major city across Ashton, but those days are long gone. Most of them were found and rooted out by the local authorities. To tell you the truth, I wasn't sure if this one was still intact." Nicholas waves his hand about, motioning us to follow him again. "But I'm glad that it is, because if it wasn't, we all would be dead right now. There is no doubt the vampires have a hold over the city now. The city guard and The Holy Order's edicts are now theirs." Nicholas lets out a short laugh. "I'd say we have a crisis on our hands."

We continue walking with Nicholas lighting the sconces, the cobwebs igniting instantly then fizzling out, until finally we reach what seems to be the end of the tunnel. Large wooden oak doors reinforced with steel stand before us defiantly. Their half-moon shaped arches give the sense this place used to be something else before it was ever an Elysium. Old dusty statues of armored figures stand guard holding scythes in their hands at both ends of the doors, watching and waiting for those who would dare challenge entry. Layered in dangling spiders and silky threads, I banish all thought of these sentinels coming alive. It wouldn't be possible, would it? The darkness still plays tricks on my mind, memories of Egleaseon's castle haunting me still to this day. Would I ever be rid of that foul place's stigma?

"I know I have a key somewhere here—" says Nicholas, patting himself down. "Ah, here we go."

Within moments, the weathered doors of the Elysium open outward, an extra security precaution in the event of a raid. From the looks of it, it would take more than a battering ram to breach its strong construction.

We enter into a giant chamber. Open. A void of darkness. The sound of chirping and flapping wings echoes through the air as we all crouch to our hands and knees. A swarm of bats pass over our heads while Nicholas shouts above the noise, "Not to worry! They'll clear out soon!"

Apparently, the local bat population moved in during the Black Blade's absence.

"Wait here," says Nicholas, his short stature and torch getting smaller and smaller as he moves deeper into the chamber, lighting more sconces and candles.

What I now deduce as an old sewer system long since abandoned, the main room of the Elysium is a sanctuary of medieval design. Tall brick columns stand firm and beams of oak run along the support rafters high above. The five of us spread out to observe the surroundings while I turn to look at Winter every so often, my paranoia setting in. First I notice every available inch of wall space is covered in black weapons and black armor, the trade mark of the Black Blade. Full sets of leather armor to single pieces of plate for shoulders and forearms. Vast collections of swords and bows line one wall while an assortment of axes, spears, and crossbows line another. Kronklich immediately gains interest in a particular crossbow on the wall. From the spiders crawling all over it, it's obviously lingered on this wall for some time without apparent use. Winter hangs back not far from him, stepping into the hearth of a dormant fire place and leaning in, looking up the ventilation shaft as if inspecting it, the wood that once burned now long gone.

As I move to the center of the room, the floor slants downward with each step, leveling out into a recessed base. Sitting atop the surface like an ancient being is a giant oak table with dozens of maps spread across its surface. The whole place is reminiscent of an old medieval war room. I recognize another map, much larger than the rest, hanging low along one of the back walls strategically placed between the swords, a complete map of Sunstone with its boroughs and perimeter walls, circling outwards from the center focal point, the Grand Cathedral. Great webs of dust hang like curtains along the low bearing archways. Multiple openings pass into other areas of darkness. Passageways I cannot see, but I do hear the chattering of rodents in the distance. It will take some time to explore this place. Doors, shelves, wood. There are more than enough supplies to hold us over for the time being, but for how long, I'm not sure.

Kronklich lets out a low whistle as he runs a finger along the war table. "When was the last time this place was used?" Two inches of dust flutters to the floor.

"Years," responds Nicholas. His voice is far away as I realize he is no longer in the chamber with us.

I squint through the dim light. "Nicholas?"

From within the shadows, his torch approaches from a distance. Smiling, he holds out his hand bunched into a fist. "Guess what it is?"

"What are you doing? This isn't time for games."

"This isn't a game, Freakshow. Look…"

Opening his palm, small silver balls roll around in his meaty paw.

"Silver bullets. A project I was working on when this place was operational. You see," he points with his finger at my chest, "You're not the only one thinking ahead in these dark times. I knew they would come in handy one day, and here we are, preparing to take on a horde of vampires. It may not kill them, but it sure as hell will slow them down." Shaking the ammunition around in his hand, he stows the bullets in his pouch and moves over to the giant map table, gripping the edge with both hands.

"What good are silver bullets to us if we're down here cowering from the enemy?" Again my emotions for Dorian start to surface. *Again* I feel we are wasting time. "We need to act now before the entire city catches wind of our actions. Asher Vandrake is still out there, alive. I just know it. I knew that bastard couldn't be trusted."

"Do you think great battles are won on empty stomachs? How can you assault a place if you don't have a plan." Nicholas stares at the map intensely. "Don't forget, we are all human here."

I'm not so sure about that. The book, Centuries, pops back into my head.

"So you have a plan then?" I ask.

Councilor's large frame strides across the room joining our conversation. "Without a doubt."

"Yes, as a matter of fact," adds Nicholas. He shuffles through the mess of maps on the table until he finds what he's looking for. Laying it out for all to see, he gestures with both hands, smiling with satisfaction. Even Kronklich comes over to get a better look.

"Schematics to the Grand Cathedral," says Nicholas. "Every floor. Every hallway. Every chamber. We have the entire layout of the place and know exactly where the old library and laboratory are. See this right here?" Nicholas flattens down the paper, dragging his finger to a specific spot just outside the foundation of the cathedral. "This is our meal ticket. A way in. The aqueducts."

Looking at the map in astonishment, I still can't help being skeptical. This is exactly how my trip to Egleaseon's castle started. "This can't be real. How is this possible to have the designs of the entire cathedral in the palm of your hand? Literally."

"Years of scouting and cartography," says Councilor. "This is the life blood of the Black Blades. How we are able to accomplish so much without being seen. We have hundreds of these drawings from all over the city. Banks. Churches. Markets. It's all here." He motions to the numerous baskets and desks bunched up near the fireplace.

"Well t'is certainly an operation you have going on here!" Kronklich's excitement is clear as day.

"Like I said, if there is a cure to be found for my little girl…" I see Councilor glance up at Winter with affection, "… then it will be found inside this cathedral."

Studying the map, I see somehow this crazy plan might actually *be* a plan, and the only approach to go on. "So what is it you propose then? We just show up to the aqueducts and let ourselves in? You saw the patrols out there. The city is crawling with edicts and spies. We will never be able to get close enough in broad daylight."

"No, you're right. That is why we have to do it at night. Tomorrow night." Nicholas sits back into one of the hard wood chairs, folding his arms over his chest with satisfaction. "Right now, we should be focusing on eating and resting. There should be enough supplies on the wagon for us to conjure something for dinner."

"Not to worry, lads." Kronklich stands up and moves across the room. "I'm sure I can make something out of whatever we have. Maybe there are some old spices lying around I can use."

"Good man," says Nicholas. "Councilor and I will work on getting hay and water for the horses." Still wrapped in his standard Black Blade Society garb, he replaces the hood over his head, hiding his face; only his stark blue eyes stand out. "And by the way, there are more than enough rooms to go around in this place. Have your pick." Leaving with Councilor, he calls over his shoulder from the entryway. "But don't mind the rats."

It isn't until later that I finally get some time to myself. After another surprisingly amazing meal created by Kronklich, we all sat and ate together (minus Councilor and Winter) allowing Nicholas to expand more on his journey to Gauldust from Walters, more than what the wagon ride offered us. And he told how he and Councilor became affiliates of one another. Despite the hiccup in Gauldust delaying him a day, it was the next few days along the road to Sunstone that seemed to tax his time the greatest.

"Monsters, monsters, and more monsters," is all Nicholas said. They plagued the roads to and from the surrounding mountain villages and with the appearance of willdermen on this side of the Cordova Mountains, he was concerned for the people (most likely more for him and his bakery shop). As for him meeting Councilor, they only knew each other from the Black Blade Society and explained that once one enters into the society, there was no getting out of it. All members were sworn to secrecy of each other and if ever they did work outside of their contracted way of life, any calling relating to their secret work would take precedence over all other things. The breads and the muffins would have to wait.

We talked for more than an hour until eventually Councilor, in his typical bitter mood, and Winter, looking a bit pink in the cheeks, returned. Not much was said in their presence thereafter and it didn't take much convincing for us to decide we should all turn in for the night.

Tired beyond exhaustion, I close the door to my room, sliding the bolt into place for added measure. For even though my body yearns for the soft bed across the room next to the fireplace, my mind is restless, racing in different directions, especially toward the book nestled against my breastbone.

With careful consideration, I remove the gold bound book along with Enivid, placing them on the desk with a half dozen lit candles. The room is quiet and comfortably warm as I take off my leather long-coat and drop it in front of the hearth in a steaming pile of dampness; its buckles glimmering in the firelight. Each piece of armor creaks as I remove them one by one. First my bracers, then the grieves, and finally, my breastplate. It's been so long since I've slept without them, I feel out of place with my body. Light and fluttery. The density of the world finally giving me a break. Unbuckling my boots, these too I set by the fire to warm and dry and finally slump down into the chair, pouring myself a glass of water from the glued leather decanter.

With my throat no longer parched, I turn to face the book, staring at the cover, *Centuries - A History of Ancient Artifacts and Heritages*, and wonder what other secrets wait for me. Opening to the first couple of pages, I skim through the table of contents, thinking about what to expect from this ancient text, when suddenly the candles in front of me flicker. Glancing about the room, I do not recall feeling a draft when I took off my armor, and instinctively, my eye passes over the handle to the door.

Nothing.

Turning back to the book, there is a creak in the floor boards and the candles waver again, two of them extinguishing from a gust of unseen force. Dragging Enivid off the desk, I turn to face the enemy that somehow infiltrated my room. How could the Carnalreesee have found us here, tucked away underground? A place that doesn't exist. What about the others, were they being assaulted as well?

But instead of finding an evil that wants me dead more than anything, there is a different kind of evil standing before me.

Long dark strands of Winter's hair fall forward around her shoulders and face, outlining her purple eyes and thin jaw line. With her pink-colored skin having returned to the pearl white of ghost, she stands timidly before me an arms-length away without saying a word. She is staring at me—fascinated perhaps? Scared? I'm not sure.

"Do not fret, vampire hunter. I am *not* your enemy. I swear it. I want just as much as you do for everything to be good. I'd like to make things right again."

My mind travels back to her in the burning house of the Cornelius estate, how she lunged at me ready to take my blood. Her frenzied lust. Her red eyes.

"How could you possibly know what I want?" I ask, gripping the handles of Enivid tighter.

Winter steps forward, gingerly, cautiously. "I was just trying to help. That man was going to kill you. He was after something. A book—I believe he said. Please, Tenor. I'm begging for your forgiveness." She tries to approach again.

"Don't."

A sad look begets her face, but only for a moment. Within a split second, she shadow moves before me, grabbing my hand and bending her knees. I am startled beyond belief as I can do nothing to counter her speed. "Please forgive me." She kisses the back of my hand. "I know you are a good man. You are helping my father search for a cure."

I look at the book on the table and then back to Winter. Her touch is ice cold and I pull away. The look on her face is that of hurt, but she smiles anyway. Her eyes are large and consuming. "I will make it up to you. I promise," she says.

I turn away, unable to look her in the eyes. The emotion passing through me is too much to bear. A single tear trickles down my cheek from my eye, now a lake of sorrow.

Turning back to tell her something she won't want to hear, she is already gone. Like the wind outside, she is a shadow vanished in the night.

Quickly, trying to get myself under control, I do all I can to banish Winter from my thoughts. In some strange semblance, she reminds me of Diana when she was younger. I can't let emotion break me down. Not here. Not like this. My emotions will have to wait. Wait until all of this is over…

Taking a sip of water off the desk, I shake my head and run my hand through my dirty hair. Passing it over my face, I adjust the patch covering my empty eyehole.

Focus Tenor. Focus.

Concentrating on the book for a while, I soon find myself engrossed within its pages. Rereading the part about the Hand of God sets my mind into turmoil as I try to reason with the meanings of its words. '*The one who wields the Hand of God will live forever*'. How was it possible? How could I really believe such a thing? Maybe I should tell the others. Maybe they could make more sense of this insane proclamation. But then what would it do to our morale? How could I tell Councilor there is no cure for his daughter because the crazed writings of a researcher says so? As much as I want to say something to them about any of this, I know deep down inside, now is not the time. No. It will have to wait until all of this has passed.

Flipping through more chapters, it is the last chapter, *Houses and Heritages*, that I turn to. What sort of chronology was Marcus keeping track of? His own bloodline from Katal? His family tree perhaps?

My thirst to understand the man hits me even harder. But as my one eye hovers over the pages of the chapter, my mind becomes a whirlwind of confusion. Instead of reading timelines and family trees of Marcus's history, I read something entirely different. Three prominent names of three notorious vampires, one of which I had no idea existed until recent events. Egleaseon, Stellamane, and Faeradon.

My body begins to sweat as I read on, tracing the lines with my fingers, the blood lines connecting from one vampire to the next, the years and generation gaps in between. Incredible. All this time, Marcus wasn't only keeping track of his people and those related to him. He was keeping track of everyone's time lines. Noble Houses and Vampires. As I keep turning the pages, a wave of chill passes over me as I realize something I didn't think of before, my hand stopping at the ledger on the top of the page.

The Wolfgang House.

Looking down the line, my finger traces along Zandor Bealeon, down to Bealeon Tenor, continuing on to Tenor Alvadine. There, I see Diana's name next to mine and instantly my heart melts at the sight of her name. Again I feel the tears welling in my one eye as I travel across the page to her family line, her father Dora and her mother Katelyn.

One of my tears lands on the page and as I go to wipe it away, I see the lines that connect me to Diana, and then down to Dorian. But as I rub my finger over his name as if this was the only way I would ever be able to touch him ever again, I notice a second line branching down from our union. Where a name should be outlined in a box, only question marks remain. Next to it, etched in what could only be Marcus's handwriting was the word "son".

For a moment, I don't understand. I look back on my family, not realizing the true meaning of that which lies before me. I read it again. And then…

A sorrow like never before fills me with dread. A dread so sinister the words I try to say to myself never come. I stutter as my lip trembles and my drool drips onto the desk. I bang my fist on the table extinguishing the candles as they roll onto the floor. Enivid clatters against the ground. Over and over, I strike the wood surface until my hand starts to bleed. "No," I say, striking it again. "No," I shout, crying into my balled up bloodied fist.

I kiss my hand and place it over the page of the book smearing some of my blood.

Diana was pregnant when I killed her. She—*we*—were going to have another son.

Slamming the book shut, all I can do is stare at the cover as I try to get a grip over myself. Why didn't she tell me? I pull at the hair on my head. Looking at Enivid on the floor, I want to throw it across the room. *Diana, my love, why didn't you tell me?*

Picking Enivid up, I stare at it a moment, feeling the warmth radiating from within and instead of directing my anger at the reasons why I was never told about my son, a new, impossible notion fills my head. More bewilderment. More confusion. It forces the anger inside me to melt into oblivion.

How on earth did Marcus Cornelius know any of this?

CHAPTER XIX

DORIAN

I am buried alive.

Paranoia sets in as anxiety spreads through every cell of my body. Claustrophobia, my old friend, visits me.

In a great rush of nightmare, the memory of Martyr's coffin comes to me all over again. All those days spent with the Carnalreesee, trapped in a box, sucking my blood and laughing with joy. Banging on wooden walls. Scraping with fingertips. Trying to find the loose nails that would set me free. Freedom never came until we reached this godforsaken cathedral. And now here I am, again. In the same predicament. Buried thousands of feet under the most unholy place in all of Ashton.

I feel my breath rate increase.

Inhale. Exhale.

Dust tickles my lungs. I cough.

Inhale. Exhale.

I want to control the sound rising in my throat, but can't. I shout and scream for help, unable to see a thing, yet it does nothing for my soul. Fear has a new meaning for me right now.

Tears and mucus stream down my face as panic overtakes me. *Keep calm, Dorian. Keep calm.* But it's no use. My arms are pinned to my sides and there is little room for me to do anything. Dirt trickles on my face. There is an itch I can't scratch. I hear granules of sand slipping through cracks like an hourglass. This whole place is going to collapse at any moment.

I grope my surroundings, reaching for something but only find rocks and bones. Again I try, scraping the ground with my palms, digging my fingers in the dirt.

My hand touches something. Something metal and cold. Hard. *Something familiar? A sword pommel?* Gripping the handle firmly, I make the only movement I can at the moment, thrusting down toward my feet, using the sword like a giant chisel, chipping small pieces of dirt, little by little.

Thrust. Rotate. Thrust. Again.

I do this many times over until eventually I am able to move both arms. Gripping the blade with both hands, I maneuver the sword across my chest and begin chipping the stone and debris into small fragments.

Thin beams of light seep through cracks as I hack away with micro stabs, the light staining my world crimson. Hands covered in scrapes and cuts, it's impossible to tell the difference between the dirt and my blood.

With enough room to move my legs, I realize the rocks and debris are draining from somewhere, like a quicksand trap.

Frantically, I kick out the inside of my almost permanent tomb. More sand shifts. Now the debris around me is clearing out a bit and more light illuminates my surroundings.

A hole filled with red light the size of my fist clears away and immediately I set to pushing away large chunks of rock, one piece at a time. The more I move, the more my world is filled with the sea of red. A skeletal hand from my tomb passes through the draining hole, then a rib bone, then a sternum. I use the sword to hollow out the rest of the hole into a larger opening, something I can pass through. For a moment it works; already I can taste the new stale air. Then, a rumble in the distance. Suddenly I am sliding out of the catacomb grave trying to stop myself.

As I tumble down the slope like a runaway barrel, my vision spins around and around, creating lines of swirling red, until my body slams into a pile of boulders, my head cracking against hard stone. Delirious with all equilibrium thrown to the high winds, my feeble attempt at discerning my surroundings in this chaos leaves me in a sickening state of nausea. I cough and spit, rubbing my forehead, glancing upward. *Did I really fall from up there?* The hole I escaped from seems miles away.

Shaking my head to clear the cobwebs, I glance around my surroundings to get a better understanding of where I am exactly.

A subterranean cave. Full of rock-like spears hanging from the ceiling. Stalactites—*isn't that what they're called?* I remember from my tutoring lessons in geology and science, how natural rock can form from dripping water. I am in awe, my boy wonderment at full scale.

From my limited vision, the cavern is vastly wide and expands to heights unseen. Echoing off the cavern walls are the faint sounds of chirping and flapping wings, leaving me with the dreadful assumption that bats are present. Standing in my pile of rubble, I squish something beneath my supporting hand. Warm and gooey, I look down to see a colony of swaying eyeballs among plant-like stalks. The eyes of the stalks move unblinkingly in unison as if they are a red sea of grass. I watch my every move carefully as I step down from the rocky bed and out into the light. The passage forward seems to snake through countless stalagmites—the bottom teeth of the cave—and I can only wonder as to what might be waiting for me down here.

Swallowing to moisten my parched throat, I grip the rusty sword in my hand, the red light showing all the imperfections of cracks and chips in the metal work. *At least I am not weaponless any longer.*

Rummaging through my satchel and thanking myself for not losing it, I pull the water skin out from within and savor the mineral liquid. *Thank you, Charles,* I say silently as I collect myself to explore this strange place.

For a short distance, I traverse through uneven plains of rock and bat droppings, straining my vision in the dim red light. Where was the source of light coming from? Every so often, something taps my head from high above forcing me to wonder if it's bat excrement instead of water. Pressing on, trying to stay focused, I think about the sun stone and how I will go about finding it. So far my search has nearly led me to my death, and I fear that I might have created my own doom in the hunt for something impossible to reach. How deep are the catacombs? Am I even still in them?

Passing through stone pillars shaped like the jaws of a monster, the glowing light seems to intensify. A colony of bats swoops down screeching from an opening nearby, close to colliding with my head. Ducking behind a rocky outcrop set back in the slanting slope, my heart races as I peer over the side. Wide-eyed, I stare at the massive formation growing out of the ground, a crystal-like pillar spreading upward at the center of the cavern like a cancerous growth. It begins wide at the foundation and thins as it reaches high into the ceiling. I wonder how far the crystal rises into the cathedral. Recalling what Cardinal Glass said, a question comes to mind: was this red pulsating rock *the* foundation of Sunstone and the Dark Cathedral?

Something moves about in the sea of red glow. Blue lights float like ghostly anomalies. Water drips on my face again forcing me to flinch. Wiping it away, I catch the heavy scent of metal. Looking up into the depths of the ceiling, I realize the water is dark in coloration, almost opaque. Blood.

The plaintive sound of moaning reaches my ears as I move from one hiding place to the next, ducking in and out of holes, passing between realms of black and red shadows. The closer I get to the center of the crystalline mass, the more I realize the floating blue objects are the lanterns of caretakers. Even here—*wherever here is*—the caretakers roam around the giant red crystal sentinels, screaming at the acolytes embedded in the rock floor of the cave. Yet something about them is different. The pieces of armor they wear and the multiple swords and axes sticking out of their bodies like pin cushions tell a different story. It's as if others had come here before, ready to fight, but failed. Who came to claim the sun stone and died? Did others know of the church's corruption? Did they attempt the very thing I was about to do myself?

Looking about the ground, acolytes saturate the floor in every direction. Their emaciated skin is pulled taut over skeletal frames. These are condemned souls bound in their individual hells. Heads twitching back and forth, their pleas for release are all too familiar. Like before in the halls of the damned, they are in their own personal purgatory and will never escape.

With three caretakers hovering over their flock like shepherds over their supply of souls, the odds still make me cringe. These ethereal beings, impossibly real, are menacing to look at. Their hollow expressions. Their teeth clicking together in bony percussion. I can only imagine what would happen to me if one of them were to touch my skin.

There is no doubt in my mind now that the giant crystal in the center of the chamber is the sun stone. For some reason I envisioned it to be much smaller in size, but now with the attention it seems to draw from everything down here: the bats, the eye stalks, the caretakers, the acolytes, I know my salvation, and the salvation of others, lies within that crystal. It is the weapon I need, the secret tool that will eradicate the Carnalreesee and Faeradon, one way or another.

Squeezing the rusted sword tightly in my hand, I emerge from behind the rock with stealth, edging myself slowly towards the center of the cavern, attempting my best to avoid the caretakers. Maneuvering between stones shaped like broken teeth and bowed archways, I realize the closer I get, the more acolytes I encounter trapped in the ground. Some of them stare up at me. Their eyes following my every movement, begging for mercy for me to release them. Liquid seeps from their eyes and mouths as if their blood were somehow being siphoned from every available orifice. Their mouths move in silent agony. I wish I could help them, save them, but there is no help for them. There are so many of them stacked together, it is impossible not to step on one. I feel terrible for doing it, but what choice is there?

Stepping over another cursed soul, one of them suddenly grabs my leg, its arm still intact, begging loudly to be released. "Please sir. Please. My son. Have you seen my son?" Unable to tell if the acolyte is male or female, I try to shake free from its grasp. "No. Please. You must tell me. My son, Charles. He is my everything."

I am taken off guard, shocked from its words.

"Let me go!" I say in a harsh whisper. "You're going to get me killed!"

But the acolyte doesn't hear me. Was this really one of Charles' parents? The ones he told me about who went on the supposed pilgrimage?

Looking out from the crevice, I see a caretaker making its way towards me. What the hell am I going to do? The palm of my hand is drenched in sweat making the sword slick in my hand.

"Don't leave me here, please!" begs the acolyte again.

"I said, let me go!" I shout, this time with no regard for my surroundings. With a swift kick, I break its hand off while stumbling over myself, unable to come to terms with the idea that this is one of Charles' parents.

The acolyte's voice wails across the chamber.

Not good, I think to myself, cringing.

On instinct, I duck as the caretaker that was some distance away swings its whistling lantern over my head, missing me by inches. Tucking and rolling over acolytes' faces, the caretaker comes for me with a ferocity unlike before, its mouth open and ready to scream. This place is its domain, and I am its trespasser.

Again it swings, clanging the metal lantern on the ground, forcing the blue light to flicker inside. Its hollow eye sockets seem to size me up as it recovers upright, poised for its next strike.

With sword in hand, I thrust the rusty blade into its rib cage, impaling nothing but air.

Not good.

I barely clear the sword from its torso as it attempts to smash me over the head with its club-like arm. Stepping to the side, I smack the flat part of the blade against its leg, sending its appendage skittering across the floor. The caretaker wobbles. With another quick strike, the tip of my blade connects with the hand holding the lantern, forcing it to drop from its fingertips. Metal and glass shatter across the cave floor releasing the blue flickering light within. An unearthly howl escapes the caretaker's mouth as the blue light fades into nothingness.

Bones collapse to the floor scattering across the rocks and skulls.

So they can be destroyed.

Within seconds, the other caretakers are upon me. Sweat beading my brow, I rush to the closest one, bringing my sword up to meet the lantern it so eagerly wields ready to take my soul.

The caretaker is slow and jerky in its delivery of attacks.

With sword in hand, I sense my confidence building, thinking at least the odds are somewhat better for me now. The sword is what I trained under, unlike the Bawaka, the weapon my father Tenor uses, or the spear my grandfather Bealeon used. I recall those moments of training now, the times of preparation with my father. With an upward slice, my blade makes contact with the caretaker's clavicle and shoulder, severing its lantern arm from the rest of its body. The lantern twirls through the air and smashes against the ground causing the blue light inside to explode into gaseous mist. The skeleton crumples to the floor.

Thank you father.

Making my way to the center of the chamber where the sun stone waits, I taunt the remaining caretaker to follow me, tapping my blade across the ground. "Hey, over here!"

But my summoning affects others as well. The surrounding bats stir from my shouting and begin gathering into large groups, spiraling around in long trailing arcs above the cave floor. The volume of chirping and screeching increases and I soon find myself taking cover. Ducking into a hole, the conglomeration of leathery wings and teeth swoops past the opening with deadly intent, the vampire bats ready to suck my blood.

Having lost sight of the caretaker, I wait in suspense, panting in my temporary sanctuary until the swarm passes.

The air clears and the shrill cry of the bats dies down. All seems quiet as I inch my way to the opening. Peering along the ridge of the rocky lip, there is movement to my left as a pair of bats scurry across the ground.

From my peripheral, a hand reaches for my face and I use the sword to block the caretaker's advance. Its bony hand wraps around the blade without care and pulls me out of the hole as if finding a prized rabbit.

Unable to wrench the sword free, I am forced to stare into the empty sockets of a black abyss. The skeleton raises its lantern towards my face, filling my world with the unholy blue light.

This is it. I'm going to die. Right here. Right now.

I avert my eyes and notice the pommel of a sword protruding from the caretaker's chest. Reaching in a last attempt, my hand locks around the handle and draws the weathered blade. With the lantern inches from my face, I drive the sword through its glass, releasing the blue glow I've seen expended so many times before. The mist, freed from its prison, hovers around my head like a cloud, filling my thoughts with screaming victims tortured and abused. It's as if the voices are trying to penetrate my brain, make what's mine, theirs.

"Noooo!" I shout in defiance, shaking my head violently, trying to break free from the entrancing fog.

The caretaker falls to the ground and I fall with it, instantly regaining control over my thoughts. The last of it's screams echo through the deep canals of my ears.

Frantic, and breathing heavily, I look around wondering where the next horrible menace will come from. But the air is still. The taste is stale.

Regaining my hold on reality, I stagger away from the pile of bones that nearly claimed my life and towards the giant pulsating crystal.

Standing so close to the sun stone fills me with a strange sensation, a sensation of hope and purpose. The feeling is incredible. All at once I come to understand the meaning behind this stone, not—by any sense—in an intellectual way, but in the way of feeling.

Approaching the crystal is like walking up to a giant underground tree; the red stones breaking through the surface serve as the roots of the trunk. I see my reflection staring back at me in its massively impressive smooth face. The light inside pulsates with every step. I feel the eyes of the acolytes watching me with anticipation, their silence a thousand words of warning. What was it about this stone that so many people died over it—because of it?

Standing before the geode in a wave of wonder, I find myself second-guessing what I'm about to do. How else would I be able to use it— if not for this?

Squeezing the sword tightly in my hand, I raise the blade and swing, slicing down into the stone like a miner digging for precious stone. And precious it is. This is a God stone. Part of me feels guilty for defiling such an artifact. What right did I have to crack the God stone?

As I follow through with the first strike, it does nothing to the red surface. Again I hammer the crystalline stone with all the strength I possess and nothing happens. Was I not determined enough? I think about the people who have suffered in this world due to the monsters and their conflicts. I think about my mother, and Joachim, their suffering and unnecessary pain. The great lengths my father is going through to find me. All of it wears on my mind like a heavy stone and yet here I am finally able to do something.

Gripping the sword with two hands, I let out grunts as I swing the blade again, and again, and again, and…

The surface cracks. Thin bright lines spread in jagged directions and a piece of the red stone falls away.

A brilliant light shines through. Almost blinding. Underneath the red crystalline surface, another surface exists. Chipping more away, I realize the sun stone is in fact not red, but searing white. It's as if the red was a protective coating over the precious God stone.

Holding my hand out to it, I feel the heat generating from within. So much power. Such concentrated energy. I look around in excitement unable to contain myself. This was it. The weapon I will use to decimate the enemy.

Using the tip of the sword, I stab into the fractured stone, wedging the blade as deep as it will go. Pulling down on the sword like a lever, I feel the old blade's integrity bending. "Come on," I plead with the metal. There is a creek, a groan, and the sword snaps.

I fall back onto my knees, blade clattering to the ground in two pieces. The sun stone lands on the floor in front of me. No larger than an apple, it radiates with the same brilliance as the parent stone. Scooping it up into my hands, it burns my skin on contact. Crying out in pain, I am shocked, yet awed at the same time.

Quickly I remove the satchel over my shoulder and dump out all of its contents; food, water, doing my best to gather up the stone. With it safely in the bag, I close the flap and secure the latch realizing I have just accomplished the impossible. It is a strange feeling knowing a piece of God resides inside this bag.

The sound of clapping echoes from behind me.

"Bravo. Bravo. I must say, that worked out quite nicely, Charles."

My blood freezes at the sound of the voice that haunts my dreams. Slowly turning around, my confidence melts away with every second that passes.

Martyr and Charles stand in the distance observing me. Martyr is smiling, rubbing Charles' shoulders while Charles remains stone cold, his face blank and emotionless.

"Seems like time is no longer on your side," says Martyr, his blue eyes turning red. "You've run out of daylight, Dorian. Such a pity."

DAY TWENTY-SIX

CHAPTER XX

WOLFGANG

IF I HADN'T GONE TO the Danbury Hovel, none of this would have happened.

Diana would still be alive. My unborn son would still be alive. Dorian wouldn't be a captive of those terrible creatures, feasting on his blood for nourishment, sustaining their lives to uphold sinister acts.

Damn them. Damn me.

My thoughts are withering, draining, as the others try to talk to me throughout the day. Every time someone approaches me, they ask if I am all right. *How could they know? I am not alright. I am anything but right.*

My eye is bloodshot from a terrible night of sleep. I blink several times hoping to clear it up as I wonder what it would have been like—the four of us together. My beautiful wife. Two healthy sons. Driving into town. Visiting the market. Watching them play with one another. Sparring with each another. All the while Diana disarming me with her smile. That smile that could set the world on fire. I shudder at the thought of how things should have been.

Unable to touch my food, I feel heated staring, burning a hole in me from across the table. I know Kronklich is watching me, concerned for me, but he says nothing at the moment as he's chewing his food. He is a good friend. Really, the only one that has ever truly understood my dilemma. My heart breaks at the suffering physical pain that debilitates me on a daily basis.

"Come, come, now Tenor. You must eat. Gather your strength and wits for what's to come. Whatever thoughts plague you now must pass on, or please, I beg you, divulge them onto me, my friend. We are partners." Kronklich now stands beside me, gripping my shoulder with a firm grasp.

I notice Councilor and Nicholas in the distance, pointing at places on the map plastered against the wall, shaking their heads every so often, arguing about something.

Kronklich continues, "If you keep it locked up inside, then all is already lost. It is during these dark times that we need each other most. Make the best of the situation and our companions. Because when all is said and done, and only few are standing, it doesn't matter what happens in the end. Things are because they are, and that's all we can do."

I look up at Kronklich, his mustache and hair clean and groomed. "Things are because they are? Such a bold and meaningless statement." I raise my eyes to follow the natural beam of light coming through the large open hole in the ceiling, conveniently lighting up the entire war chamber. As Nicholas explained, it is the only source of natural light this underground ruin will ever see. Old aqueduct shafts stocked with strategically placed mirrors bend and aim the light from outside to the underground. Genius? Perhaps. Flawed? Almost certainly. If one were to discover the true drain grate that led down here, this whole underground Elysium would be uprooted and burned... just like the rest. Luckily for us, that time hasn't come... yet.

"Are we not attuned to our own destinies, James?" I question his bold statement further, poking at the fried bits of ham, bacon, and ground cornmeal.

"Of course we are, Tenor. That's not what I meant by any means." Kronklich returns to his chair and pours himself another cup of tea, motioning me to join him. I decline with a wave of my hand, shaking my head and sipping my morning black. "What I meant by it is simply this..." He takes a hard swallow and deep breath. "We cannot control or change what happens to us on the outside, however, by all means we can react to our surroundings. As long as we try our best, give things a shot, and never give up, well then," he raises his cup, "It doesn't matter what happens in the end. Things are because they are, and that's all we can do." He smiles at me as if he just imparted the secret to immortality.

Immortality. If only he knew what I knew.

I stare off into the distance, past his ear at one of the far walls full of axes and daggers. "You know, sometimes your logic is way beyond my comprehension."

Kronklich smiles. Seemingly satisfied with his explanation, he merrily returns to his meal, cutting his meat into small square pieces with knife and fork.

The day creeps on as if we were all living in the sea. Slower than slow, like sea slugs sliding along a coral reef.

With my anticipation of what's to come this night, I can't help but mull over the inner workings of the Grand Cathedral once again. Running my finger up and down the map still splayed out on the giant war room table, I find myself committing to memory every aspect of the compound. There are so many corridors and places that fill the floor plan of this monstrosity; I try to make sense of this once medieval castle now turned diabolical church. More and more, I think about Egleaseon's castle and how much it reminds me of this cathedral, despite it being the home of The Holy Order, the ones I trusted once, the ones I worked for... *once*. Vampires and their minions roam its halls now.

There is a library and a dining hall, an aqueduct and a dungeon. There's even an underground catacomb. I shiver at the thought of its infinite blackness and my recent horrible descent into the bowels of Egleaseon's dark, fetid place. The skeletons and bones lining its walls, the stench associated with its rotting corpses and the creatures that lurked behind its rickety doors. The undead that shambled through its rat infested waters. But aside from those daunting places, there are other places, new places, such as the sealed off laboratory and research facility, the holy chapel and the entry hall. Then there's the great stairwell labeled Heaven's Door. I stare at it for some time. It is this tower, the one I saw rising into the clouds two days ago, that peaks my interest. *Yes. Here.* My finger slides up to the top of the tower. *The Chamber of the Cardinal. The ritual chamber. This is where they're holding Dorian.*

"Stare at that any longer and the only eye you have left will pop out of your head." Nicholas' breath is strong, a mixture of onions and garlic, as he stands behind me, peering down at my meanderings. "You should be resting. Won't do you any good if your nerves are shot."

Peering up at the beam of light filling the large war chamber helps relinquish my dark thoughts. Even with its brilliant efficiency of mirrors and angles, on an overcast day, it still doesn't provide enough light for the deeper recesses of the chamber and hallways. In the distance, the sound of metal striking wood repeats over and over. Sconces and candelabras illuminate Councilor's silhouette throwing daggers at wooden dummies down one of the corridors. Seems he can't rest either.

"You two are hopeless," says Nicholas, waving Councilor over to the table. "Might as well get this over with. Hey Kronklich. Come on, lets strategize."

Kronklich bustles over to the table with a book in his hand. "Strategy? Now this is certainly my forte. Outwit the witty, I say."

For the next hour, we pour over maps of the city, learning where and where not to go, the pros and cons of drawing attention to ourselves, and with the city sectioned off into six circular sects, the perimeter walls that divide the rich from the poor, the final approach to the Dark Cathedral is straight forward—a pass through the grove of trees at the back of the fortress. "The cathedral is no longer labeled *Grand*," says Nicholas. "A new target deserves a new name."

From there, it was anyone's guess what resistance we might encounter inside the Dark Cathedral. With possessing the schematics as our only advantage, the plan was simple. Find Dorian first, at all costs. "There's a good chance they might be holding him here," says Nicholas, pointing to the area labeled, *Dungeons*. Although my thoughts are different about Dorian's whereabouts, I remain silent. Either way, we would be coming up through the dungeons from the aqueducts.

"Right. And once we find Dorian, we search for Winter's cure," says Councilor resolutely. Everyone nods their head in unison except for myself. I try to avoid his gaze, but it's impossible. He looks at me and I look at him. Slowly I nod my head.

Damn.

Nicholas pushes his chair out to stand and stretch. "Now that we have a plan, the best part has finally arrived." He glances at all of us for a moment and then resumes his speech. "It's time to stock up. The Black Blade Society's weapons are yours to take. Whatever you need in the Elysium is yours."

The four of us, like children in a toymaker's shop, disperse amongst the vast array of weaponry, drool seeping from our mouths like dogs wagging their tails. With Winter out of the picture, resting in her coffin to hide from the day, we set to compare our selections with each other for the upcoming, and most likely, deadly battle.

Knowing I will need nothing more than Enivid at my side, my eye still falls prey to a set of black gleaming daggers, their edges serrated and wavy for precision cuts. I find myself stowing the blades inside my coat.

"You know," says Nicholas from across the room, "I've never taken on a vampire before. Let alone a goddamn horde of them." Picking a select double edged black axe from off the wall, much darker and larger than his current one, he gives it a few good swings followed by a few grunts before returning it, unsatisfied with its performance.

Councilor's deep voice echoes from another part of the chamber. "Then it's a good thing you aren't going. What with your inexperience and you coming out of retirement and all."

I don't need to see Councilor's face to know he is smirking.

"Ha! Laugh it up you big ox." Nicholas selects another axe from the wall and slashes it through the air with better results. "Someone has to make sure your daughter doesn't get into trouble while you're gone." He switches out his old axe for the new one and turns to face the chamber, breathing it in. "Besides, I could really turn this place around. Maybe even have it reinstated, eh?"

Over in Kronklich's den of archery, particularly the cross bow he was playing with earlier, I watch as he fiddles with a contraption, some sort of mechanism that carries multiple bolts at once. Loading it onto the stock barrel, it attaches with a click, and he points it down the hall, the same one Councilor was practicing in. He fires his weapon with precision. Bolt after bolt discharges down the corridor causing the candles to flicker in their wake, until the last one is dispensed. Lowering the black crossbow, I notice it is smaller and more compact than his standard issue. "I think I'm going to like this," says Kronklich, admiring the weapon in the light.

As we spend the next hour rummaging through the stock weapon supplies that could outfit an army, I notice Councilor sticking with his same weapon, his scythe never leaving his back. The only new additions are the endless supply of daggers he stuffs into every part of his body. With a look of, *you can never have too many,* he begins breaking spears in half and sets to whittling their jagged edges into fine points, sharp enough to stake a vampire. We all follow his example, making the same instruments of death while Kronklich disappears into the mess hall to prepare what would be our final meal before setting out tonight.

Steadily carving, keeping my mind busy for the duration, a trunk lands at my feet, startling me from my lingering thoughts on Diana and Dorian.

"Open it," says Nicholas with a grunt. "A little extra something with a kick."

Bending down and undoing the latches, the leather bound chest reveals an entire cache filled to the brim with glass vials and flasks.

"I knew it would come in handy one day. Stole it off a wagon full of holy high rollers."

Holy fire. Fire bomb type weapons used by The Holy Order. Throw it at anything and wherever the glass shatters and touches ignites instantly. Perfect for burning the undead. I remember Bronin using them before and already I know it will be most useful. Such things are hard to come by.

"Thank you, Nicholas. Every bit helps." I hold out my arm to embrace him in a shake and he does the same. For an older, retired Black Blade, his grip is strong.

"All right, Freakshow. Let's not get sentimental about it. It's time to eat."

Nightfall in the Elysium.

The halls are quiet. The flickering flame of torch light crackles in harmony with the roaring fireplace.

With the four of us having finished dinner and our bellies full, we sit in silence for a time, lost in our thoughts, Councilor smoking an abandoned pipe that belonged to a Black Blade long since dead or forgotten. Kronklich moves around the table pouring tea, essence of bergamot, for all of us, for the last time before heading into the den of the enemy. I watch Winter as she shares the table with us, her posture straight as an arrow, her arms and hands placed rigidly on the table. My eye never leaves her as she watches her father smoke, my judgment never moving from the night before. The way she snuck into my room without invite and proceeded to make amends. How *could* she make amends? She is a vampire, and like all vampires has the desire to feed. When would the day come when she shows her true vampiric colors and rips out our throats in the middle of the night? *When?* The question lingers sourly at the back of my thoughts as I watch Kronklich pour the last cup in front of me.

The sound of etching and scribbling comes from Nicholas as he adds the final touches to the action plan, the detailed map that would lead us to our victory if followed correctly.

"There. That should do it." Rubbing his hands clean from charcoal, Nicholas raises his cup in salute to the three of us who would be infiltrating the Dark Cathedral in the hours to come.

"To the three hunters. May your efforts prevail and your targets be found." Taking a long swig, he sets his cup on the table and leans back in his chair, cracking numerous vertebrae.

"I second the motion," says Kronklich. He sips his tea rather than guzzles it.

Councilor does the same and as I raise my cup to my lips, I feel those cold dead eyes staring. Winter is watching me. Is it me or is there a look of hunger on her face?

"Well, best be on our way. If we time it right, we'll be able to slip past the changing of the guard.

All of us stand to go, including Winter, whom I note—of any of us—seems the most eager to leave.

"Where do you think you're going?" asks Councilor in his deep menacing voice.

"With you, Father."

Councilor's brows furrow into a look of consternation. "No you're not. You're staying right here." He points with his finger at the floor.

"But I want to help, Father. Please."

Although all of us are rested and ready for the task ahead, a look of exhaustion seems to permanently shadow Councilor's face.

"No, Winter. It's too dangerous. You will stay here and that's the end of it. Nicholas will look after you."

"But he's going with you. I want to help. I want to come."

"He's only coming to help us find the entrance. That's all."

"Yes, Princess," says Nicholas stepping forward, "I will be back. Maybe I can pick up a tasty dog or cat on the way back. What do you say?"

Winter backs away in a manner that can only mean insult and bends her head low in an animalistic way. "You think... this is a joke? How *could* you, Father? What if you don't come back? What if I never see you again?" Her face once porcelain white now burns with crimson anger. Flushed with a look of agitation and hurt, she looks up through her disheveled hair as tears stream down her smooth cheeks.

"You don't understand, Winter," says Councilor, moving forward to embrace her. "Where we are going is far too dangerous. You are not fully aware of your powers. There are others like you. You might... turn on us."

Winter's eyes widen, full of rage and what seems to me the fury of betrayal. "How... dare you... How could you?" Bursting into a fit of sobs and shouts, Winter stomps from the war chamber in a raging storm, leaving behind her a whirlwind of extinguishing torches and knocked over racks. Her screams echo down the hall as the four of us stare in bewilderment, speechless at what to do.

Councilor moves forward to address the issue, but Nicholas stops him, placing a hand across his chest. "No, don't. It's for the best, Councilor, it's for the best..."

CHAPTER XXI

LIGHTING ARCS ACROSS THE SKY. Tumultuous thunder rumbles through low bearing clouds. The wheels of the wagon rattle along broken cobblestones, matching the sounds of the earth and sky in a harmony of dissonance.

Cold rain pelts our faces as we roll through the streets of Sunstone, once a brilliant white by day, now a terrible black by night. Like a bottomless hole ready to swallow you up, the main city street carries people and carriages to and from their destinations like unwanted debris, flushed into drains. Souls (or the soulless), brave enough to withstand the damp chill of winter's night, splash through the many droves of tiny lakes lining the road's edge. Pot holes and ruts. Carriage wheels and boots. Water gushes along valley gutters emptying into metal grates at the end of roads, the wash expanding to lower portions of the city's limits.

As we travel closer to the center of the city, the elevation changes, rising into steeper climbs and sharper turns. I can't help but stare at the glistening glow of lantern light reflecting in the sheen of water. Everything once pure, now runs downhill, commingling with the sins of those who would follow The Holy Order—a holy order, now corrupt. The Dark Cathedral rises in the distance, a black spear splattered against a backdrop of flashing skyline. It stands as a reminder of our mortal danger. Our destination. Our destiny.

My mind is a somersault of emotions. Between the harsh words exchanged by Winter and Councilor, the harrowing secret of the book buried against my chest, and my constant obsession over Dorian, I begin to shake with anxiety, not the cold. My stomach turns in great knots not knowing what we'll find in the cathedral, but I know I must remain strong above all else.

Water drips from my hood and my nose and the horses make a sharp left, then right.

Like a wraith in the darkness, Nicholas carries us to our final destination in silence driving, encouraging the horses to go faster and faster. Rain pelts the ground with ferocity, the sound of beating hooves muffles to a low thudding, the ground saturated and soft, mixed with the slush of snow. On we go, to the one place we've harbored all this time to prepare for. Nicholas is master at his craft, this I'm assured, despite his hiatus and coming out of retirement. A skilled assassin and a member of the elite Black Blade Society, his knowledge of Sunstone and the streets associated with it come second to none. Even Councilor looks over the side of the wagon, gazing at passing landmarks, obviously unfamiliar to him.

Still—I can't help but think that we are being watched by those that would oppose us, the Carnalreesee lingering in the corner shadows of buildings as we race by. Every so often, I see something move along the awnings of adjacent buildings. Sometimes above. Sometimes below. We are prey stalked by the predator. I feel a presence, their presence of dark oppressing power. The calling inside me warns me of such things. It is, of course, in my blood. It always has been. A son of a Wolfgang. The father of a Wolfgang. A curse? An immortal? Who's to say?

The three of us keep our heads down while Nicholas drives, four black shadows moving through an ocean of deceit and conflict. With weapons strapped to every portion of our bodies, I feel as if we are headed straight into a war zone, where the inevitable event of total annihilation will take place.

Kronklich watches me purposefully as if he knows what I'm thinking and nods, reassuring that our madness is not a single effort by any one of us, but a joint effort of lunatics, we, the culmination of insanity, we, the acting will of men.

"Not much further," shouts Nicholas over the howling wind and rain.

Peering ahead, I notice a thin line of yellow and orange approaching in the distance, my best guess, a roadblock.

"Hang on," says Nicholas, guiding the wagon and horses out of direct sight and into an alley that transforms into a tunnel. As the horses clip-clop down the narrow arched corridor, the sounds bounce off of empty doorsteps and shuttered windows. No torch or lantern lights the way down this desolate passageway and I can only imagine this is part of Nicholas' plan. To remain in darkness—on the path of the assassin.

The tunnel abruptly ends with an abandoned stock of crates and barrels which forces us to stop. With precise maneuvering, Nicholas guides Abel and Jasmine around the barricades and waits in-between the surplus of wood. Still within the arch of the tunnel, we are protected from the rain temporarily. Nicholas adjusts himself in his seat and pulls out a pouch from his belt.

"Now we wait," says Nicholas, drawing a thick dark root from the bag and passing it along. Ebon root. The drug known to enhance senses of the body, boost the energy of the mind, and pump your cells with an energy that never sleeps. This drug can be the fall of man, but in recent days, has saved the life of Kronklich and me. I take the bag hesitantly.

"Each of you take one. God knows we'll need it. And I don't even like God."

Each of us steadily chews the thick tough material, the familiar tingle comes back to me like a bad memory, the time in Egleaseon's ruin when Bronin stabbed me and Kronklich saved me.

"We have to wait for the exact moment..." explains Nicholas as I start to feel the effects of the drug take over me. Suddenly the rain beyond the barrels seems louder, the chewing sounds coming from Councilor's open mouth rise to a level of beyond annoying.

"... for the changing of the guards. As soon as fresh replacements come, we wait till they're out of sight and then we move."

And so wait we do. For what seems like hours, according to Nicholas, only thirty minutes pass. We finally see movement and an exchange between the two sets of guards.

Remembering the schematics, a total of six sect walls impossible to scale, and fortified various outposts, encompasses the entire city of Sunstone. This one before us, is the only thing separating us from entering the grove, the holy garden that surrounds the Dark Cathedral.

"Alright. This is it. Make it hard and fast." Nicholas says raising the reins. "Councilor to the left, Kronklich to the right. Freakshow, tie up any loose ends. If this all goes right and the guards aren't alarmed, we'll have about an hour window to find the aqueducts and allow me to get out of the sect without them noticing."

With fingers sensitive at the tips, I remove Enivid from under my coat. Kronklich and Councilor follow suit removing their weapons the same as Nicholas edges us onto the road and back into the rain. First, approaching at a slow trot, a minute passes before Nicholas flicks the reins and sends the horse into a frothing frenzy.

Like a black owl swooping onto mice, it is we who have the advantage. And as the city guard finally catches wind that something approaches, we—the dark shadow with no lanterns or torches—descend on them. It is too late for them to sound a warning or retreat. We gallop forward at blistering speed, tearing through the enemy, running one guard over with the horses and wagon with an obnoxious tha-thump, while Councilor and Kronklich take the left and right flanks. Even a man dressed in armor and helmet stands no chance against Councilor as he brandishes his black scythe through the night air, removing the man's head in one swipe. Kronklich, on his side does the same, putting to use his newly discovered and cherished weapon, the black crossbow. Repeatedly he fires at the guard, placing a bolt in the man's throat and forehead. The wagon clears the barricade before the guard falls to the ground.

Passing through the gate un-impeded, and seemingly challenged by none, we hastily speed our way through the sect walls under the cover of night, the high solid stones passing us on either side like a fortress gate.

The wagon inclines again as we enter the grove surrounding the Dark Cathedral. With the aid of thick oak trees covering our advance, we veer to the right, passing into an earthen hall of bark and root, the only light to see with coming from the pillar fires that surround the circumference of the fortress. The trees, still bearing enough foliage to hold large amounts of snow, thicken into a dense bramble of wild brush and frozen flowers. Here in the sanctuary of the grove, the rain is nearly non-existent. A strange sensation washed over me the second we passed through the gate, a feeling of suffocation. I do my best to ignore it, sucking in deep breaths with each passing moment. Nicholas guides us effortlessly; pulling out the schematics of the fortress, then brings the wagon to a halt.

"Well, I'd say that went rather well." The grove is filled with the sound of insects and distant rain. Unfolding the paper, Nicholas spreads the map before him, trying to get the best angle of light. "If my calculations are correct, the entrance to the aqueducts should be just beyond that open patch of trees, at the backside of the tower. There should be a store house next to the entrance with a grate."

Never taking my eye off our surroundings, I notice a patch of eye moss swaying off the bark of a nearby oak. It follows our every movement. "We need to hurry. The enemy knows we're here."

"Impossible," snorts Nicholas, waving me off like some child. "Come on, this way."

Collecting the last of our equipment: black wooden stakes and flasks of holy fire, we leave the wagon on foot, concealed in the copse. In single file formation, we stealthily maneuver between trees and large boulders, until eventually we reach the perimeter wall of the stone fortress. From this angle, the top of the Dark Cathedral tower vanishes into a swirling mist of clouds. Following the base around to the backside, we come to a dried up stream covered in snow and sprouting grass. Walking longer than anticipated, we arrive at a square-looking addition to the fortress wall and rest in its shadows.

"Goddammit," says Nicholas under his breath as he crouches to the floor and surveys the schematics again. "According to the goddamn plans, we should have already passed the entrance. Where the hell is it?"

But for the next few moments of searching the wall behind us, with Councilor disappearing around the bend—only to come back shaking his head—the four of us stand dumbfounded, wondering what to do next. Backtracking to infiltrate the front of the cathedral was out of the question. A direct assault on this place would surely spell our doom.

"Well, shit," says Nicholas in a way I haven't heard him speak—in a while. "How is this possible? It's like the goddamn place completely changed. How can a building change?"

I hold my tongue knowing all too well how a place can change, even live and breathe as if it were alive. Egleaseon's ruin was proof of that. One moment there would be an open passage, the next, a solid brick wall.

Nicholas crumples up the paper and throws it over his shoulder. "I can't believe I'm saying this, but, does anyone have any suggestions—?"

Just as he finishes his question, a voice startles us from behind.

"Halt! Who goes there? State your business!" A patrolling guard, obviously having stumbled upon us points a long spear in our direction, ready to throw it at a moment's notice.

Kronklich steps forward. "Our deepest apologies my good man. You see, we were a bit lost and seemed to have made it worse having gone the wrong way. You see—"

"Lost?" The guard never lets up, poising his weapon like a deadly missile. "I'd say you're trespassing with ill intent. How did you get in here?" Standing atop a boulder looking down, he clearly has an advantage in height over us somewhat below. He steps forward to brace his spear for a throw when suddenly his eyes roll into the back of his head. The color drains from his face.

Stepping out from behind the guard, a female figure with long dark hair, dressed in a tattered mauve dress, finishes sucking the blood from the guard's neck with precise efficiency. Within seconds, the sentinel is dead at her feet and she kicks the body off the boulder like a sack of grain.

"Winter!" shouts Councilor and already, I see this getting out of hand.

Winter looks down on us from atop the boulder, her eyes blazing red. Blood drips from her fangs and down the front of her dress as she seems to savor the moment, her temporary bliss of the blood lust overtaking her.

"Winter!" shouts Councilor again. "What are you doing here? I told you to stay behind!"

But she doesn't seem to hear him.

His fury grows with each word and he begins moving towards her, stepping over the dead corpse.

In the blink of an eye, Winter vanishes. Councilor reacts, shouting Winter's name as he runs around the side of the boulder to head her off. The rest of us chase after him, knowing very well what's to come. He won't be able to stop her. He's putting his life in danger.

Making our way around, the four of us stop dead in our tracks. Not one of us wants to advance on Winter.

Panting heavily, her breath comes in short bursts. Winter crouches low in the brush staring at us as if we were her next meal. Her eyes red as clay, she sniffs the air like a wild animal.

Councilor takes a step forward and I grab his arm, stopping him. "Don't. Look."

We watch in horror as Winter smells everything around her. She has caught scent of something. In a sudden burst of energy, she darts from the bushes, breaking branches and scattering leaves. On foot, she runs faster than any dog or horse.

"After her!" I shout, sprinting in her wake. "She wants us to follow!"

Just as I thought. Like the time in Egleaseon's ruin—Joachim—with that crazed look in his eyes, smelling the ground, smelling the air, tasting the blood on the ground.

She's leading us to someone or something.

The four of us, like crazed bloodhounds, crash through the thicket after Winter, weaving in and out of trees like deer in the forest. Blood pumping, adrenaline peaking, I feel the Ebon root working through my blood. The enhancement allows me to move quicker than a fox.

Within moments, the chase is over as Winter comes to a jarring stop. Standing before an outcrop of trees and rocks, a wide gaping hole births from the ground, large enough for a human to pass through. I cover my nose from the stench pouring from within. All manner of insects and reptiles crawl their way through the passage as if emanating the presence of evil: worms, ants, snakes, frogs, roaches, centipedes; they slink, creep, and hop their way through, an organized system of chaos going in and out. Gore encrusted bones cover the ground in a collage of red and brown, a decaying white seeping through the patches of skin and fur. Whatever animals or humans that were disposed of—lie in ruin before the cave entrance as if in an exposed mass grave.

"Well this certainly is *disgusting*," says Kronklich holding the hem of his cloak to his face as he examines the remains closer.

Winter, now having calmed, turns to face us, the red in her eyes gone, replaced with her entrancing and sinister purple.

"Winter," says Councilor trying to catch his breath. "What on earth… I told you to stay behind. Why didn't you listen to me? It's too dangerous to be here."

Winter, now standing fully erect, extends her arms to her father lovingly, nearly collapsing with exhaustion. He catches her in his arms, cradling her like any loving father would.

"I told you. I wanted to help… anyway I could. This…" she points to the hole in the earth crawling with maggots, "… is how they leave and return at night. The vampires. Their blood… is strong. Intoxicating. It calls to me…"

She seems faint again, reaching toward the cave in a yearning gesture.

"No," says Councilor, shaking sense into her. "Snap out of it."

The tactic seems to work as Winter looks into Councilor's eyes again. She hugs him, his bushy black beard swallowing her porcelain face.

Such a touching moment. It's hard for me to look away. Although she is a vampire, I envy Councilor. His daughter is in his arms. Embracing him. I wish I had the same, my family, any of them, right here and now to give me strength. A tear drips down my face and I look away, trying to compose myself.

Dammit. Stay strong Tenor. Stay strong.

Councilor bends down and looks his daughter in the eyes. "Thank you, Winter. You were a big help, my sweet. But it is time for me to go. You must not follow us. Please tell me you won't."

Winter gazes at her father with genuine love and nods her head. Tears pour from her eyes as she embraces him one last time. "I love you, Father."

"And I love you."

Councilor turns to Nicholas while cradling her head with his large hands. "If I don't make it back, care for her. Find a cure. Don't let her endure the days of madness and devilry."

"I swear it," says Nicholas, taking Winter's hand. He peels her away gently while the rest of us gather before the opening of death's cavern. Councilor looks back at her one last time.

Where we're going may very well be our final destination. The point of no return.

"Well, this is it," I say wearily, rubbing my eye from the effect of the Ebon root. "There's no going back now. Until the end…" I nod my head in grim satisfaction.

Kronklich and Councilor nod their heads the same.

"Until the end."

"Until the end…"

CHAPTER XXII

DORIAN

The light hurts my eyes.

Although they are closed. It's too much to bear.

My conscious mind stirs as I swallow back the vomit in my throat. Had it all been a dream—or rather, a *nightmare*? The last thing I remember was the horrible grins of my captors, Martyr and Charles. Staring back at me. Mocking me. Relishing in their moment of triumph. Cardinal Glass warned me and yet…

Betrayal.

I was so close. The power in my grasp. But now I am left empty handed. Stripped down to nothing but my clothes, and even those are *minimal.* The only dignity I'm spared—I'm still wearing my pants. Everything else has been taken. My shirt. My shoes. My satchel. The *sun stone.* Where was it? What did they do with it? I try to move my arms but can't.

Lying at a forty-five-degree angle, I am displayed on some sort of stone slab, shackled at the neck, wrists, and ankles like a specimen waiting to be dissected. The situation is all too familiar to me. The stone slab at Egleaseon's ruins where the Carnalreesee conducted their *ritual*. The iron spikes driven through my hands and feet.

The nightmare returns.

Barely able to open my eyes, I wiggle my bare feet and flex my fingers, confirming they are still free. With scabs still covering the holes from where the long iron spikes were driven through my body, it was only yesterday—I think it was yesterday—the pain started subsiding. The itch, finally gone.

I begin to panic.

My eyes squinting in the light, I see there are torches along the walls, candelabras around my table, and chandeliers hanging from the high ceiling. A slurping sound comes from somewhere in the room and so naturally I turn my head, trying to find the source.

I appear to be in some sort of workshop or laboratory filled with instruments and tools I've never seen before. Long wooden benches tucked into long tables line the walls, and off on one side of the room, a demolished wall lies in ruin. Bookcases and shelves lined with red and blue flasks bring colorful life to the room. A large oversized tome lies sprawled open on a table where I catch my first glimpse of the despicable creature— Faeradon.

Faeradon. With his holy regalia hat and white braid draped over his shoulder, the paling of his skin does nothing to compliment his stark white attire. He is a ghost like phenomenon in the bright light of the room, dust covering himself and his subjects. To either side of him, attending to his every need, sit two balcony boys, one of them in a state of ecstasy as Faeradon, bent low over him, sucks the life blood from the arteries in his wrist. The other boy, his brown curly hair falling about his brow and ears, I recognize as Charles, the one who tricked me into friendship. He sits at the ready, a moment's notice for when Faeradon summons.

With a succulent smack of his lips, Faeradon laps up the trailing blood from his chin and reclines back into his chair, looking towards the ceiling with a sigh of satisfaction. "Ahhhh, there is no sweeter blood than that of the young…" He pushes the boy away, forcing him to slump back into the chair as if he were a useless doll. Charles is quick to clean the spilt blood on the table.

Throat dry, I try to speak, but my voice croaks instead.

Behind Faeradon, within the dark recesses of the room, stands Vargus, his long black hair and red armor gleaming like a ruby, and Martyr, his sunken eyes and fiery hair teased more than usual. The two remaining Carnalreesee stand stoically in silence like statues, watching everything unfold in the chamber.

Straining my neck to see more, I feel eyes staring at me, and I know Faeradon is watching with his icy orbs. His features seem more chiseled and angular in the light, unlike the first time I saw him in the ritual chamber high up in the tower.

But instead of addressing me directly this time, he simply smirks while turning his head toward the exit of the chamber. "Bring him."

Through a set of creaking doors, a figure practically naked, withered away to nothing with hair in its face, enters the chamber dragging chains. Head hanging low, the figure is escorted by two edicts in their red tunics and black polished boots; one of them carries a wooden cudgel. There is no mistake it is Cardinal Glass who has been summoned. Immediately following this entourage of edict and vampire, a fourth figure enters the chamber dressed differently than the rest. A long white coat covers his entire body and strange looking contraptions dangle from straps and pockets, giving him the appearance of a scientist. He holds a hand to his neck as if he were attacked recently, the rest of his blonde hair spattered with blood. He makes his way through the room, placing himself next to Vargus, conveniently out of the way.

"Cardinal Glass," begins Faeradon with his sickening cool voice, "It seems you have served your purpose and fulfilled the task given to you…"

His eyes, a map of red veins, Cardinal Glass glances up at Faeradon. Regardless of his shaking body, his expression is one of disgust.

"There is no longer any need for you to suffer." Faeradon nods to one of the edicts. "He may be set free."

Closing his eyes, Cardinal Glass seems relieved for a moment until his head turns and sees me chained to the slab for the first time. Immediately, he begins shaking his head violently, attempting to reach at me with his thin arms and hands, pulling against the edicts' restraints. "Dorian… no… it is not true! As God is my witness, I swear I didn't know!"

The Edict holding his chain yanks hard, choking him to the ground in one motion.

"Do not say that name here, Cardinal." Faeradon stands, bracing the desk with his long fingernails. "Too long have I had to endure in service to that *wretch*. You and all that serve *Him* will soon forget in time the meaning of God and what He has to offer." He settles back into his chair like a stone. "So pathetic…"

What was I to think? What was I to say? The very one I trusted, the very one that warned me not to trust, was about to be set free. Was I that gullible?

Despite my current condition, chained to a slab, unable to escape, I feel a seething hatred rising up within me. Something I haven't felt since the time Scepter bit my mother, condemning her to a fate far worse than death. All this time, The Holy Order was corrupt, every last one of them, all the way down to their last and most prominent figure. Cardinal Glass. I will never forgive him. Never.

"And now for your reward," says Faeradon, his countenance, one of boredom. "Bring forth the stone."

With a look of duty and pride, Charles moves from Faeradon's side and approaches the edict holding the cudgel, handing him a satchel, the same satchel he had given me with supplies, the same satchel I used to collect the sun stone.

Using a thick pair of gloves, the Edict pulls the gleaming sun stone from the bag and holds it out for all to see. A look of abject horror fills the faces of the vampires while a look of absolution flits across Cardinal Glass's eyes.

"On your feet," says the edict holding the chain. Cardinal Glass does his best to stand in spite of a blow to the back of his legs. Wearily, he sways back and forth awaiting his destiny.

The edict presses the stone against Glass's head and all at once it is illuminated with a brilliant white light. Cardinal Glass screams either from pain or joy and as his cry dwindles down to a drawn-out moan as the light of the stone dims, pulsating with an after glow.

Slowly the edict backs away, loosening the chain while Cardinal Glass examines himself. Holding his arms out before him, he gropes at his skin, feeling its texture and running his hands through his hair and touching his face. Although he is still fragile and frail from malnourishment, the tone of his skin seems restored, the light in his eyes, returned.

He turns to face me again and all he can do is stare with pleading eyes, too weak to speak, his physical humanity wasted beyond salvation. It is a look of begging forgiveness.

Before I have a chance to say anything to the poor man, a giant sword bursts through his abdomen. It travels upward, ripping through his organs and chest sending his body into quivering spasms. Sliding off the tip of Vargus' sword, Cardinal Glass crumples to the floor, his life ending with an empty stare.

My parched throat cracks in horror, "Nooo!" I scream as I gaze into Vargus' deadpan eyes.

"Why?" I cry, realizing my only ally is now dead.

The answer comes not from Vargus—who systematically wipes the blood from his sword with his hand, licking it off—but from Faeradon, who appears to be entertained by the ruthless murder.

"I said he would be set free… I made good on my word." Faeradon smiles and crosses the room, collecting the sun stone resting safely in the satchel again. "And now we know the stone is real. No need to search for Marcus Cornelius any longer. He is worthless to us now."

Faeradon turns to me and glides in my direction, moving up close to caress my chin with his long fingers and nails. "Today is a good day, young wolf. As one vampire perishes, another is born." His breath is poisonous as he passes close to my ear and then stands erect facing his entourage of servants. "Asher Vandrake. Come forth."

Asher Vandrake, with his stringy yellow hair hanging loosely over his shoulders, obediently approaches, still clasping the bloody wound on his neck. "My lord," he says in a low dramatic tone. He nearly bows to the floor in respect.

"Kneel," commands Faeradon, raising his chin before his subjects. Placing his own wrist to his mouth, he tears it open, allowing the blood to flow freely. Holding his dripping hand out in offering, Asher takes it up eagerly, gripping Faeradon's wrist with both hands and clasping down over the wound with his mouth.

Turning to look at me, Faeradon's smile is almost ecstatic, his eyes rolling around in his skull, his body quivering with joy. "Like I said, today is a good day."

Before Asher drinks more than his willed share, Faeradon shoves him away. "Enough!"

With unseen force, Asher is sent sprawling across the floor before his body starts shaking in uncontrollable spasms. I watch his body convulsing, his hands raking across his chest and clutching his stomach.

Again it is the same when the Carnalreesee forced me to watch my best friend suffer in the same manner. Joachim's body wracked with pain. Watching the human body die. Becoming a vampire is a terrible thing. One I wouldn't wish on the most vile of foes.

As Asher Vandrake continues to writhe on the floor like a sick mental patient, Faeradon addresses his servants as if never having been interrupted. "Now that that business is over with, we can focus on the important things." He raises his arms above his head and instantly the balcony boys move to attend his every request. "Twenty six days have come and gone. The twenty seventh approaches. Soon the ritual will begin. But first…" Faeradon turns to me again, placing his hands over my bare chest, "… we must be rid of the *old* Dorian. Make him pure once more." A trail of blood oozes from his fangs and on to my shoulder, cold and slick.

I struggle feebly against my restraints, cutting my wrists and ankles on the rusted metal. I won't go through this again. I can't. The pain then was unbearable. What would happen to me a second time?

"Struggle all you want, young Wolf. There is nowhere for you to go. Your place is here among us…"

Straining one last time against the shackles, I am left defeated. Faeradon is right. What was I to do? "Why?" I ask. "Why are you doing this to me? What's the point?"

"The point? There is no finer point than that of rebirth. Witness!" Faeradon raises my throbbing head off the slab and points to the still figure of Asher Vandrake.

Slowly, the invisible tendrils of life and death are summoned back into the room. Asher's body twitches and rises from the ground. Knowing Faeradon's blood has been mixing with Asher's, I watch in terror the birthing of a vampire.

"Exquisite." Faeradon moves before the newly restored Asher, helping him stand easily with the simple movement of his hand.

Just how powerful is Faeradon? His mannerisms. His elegance. His nightmare reality is now my reality.

"How do you feel?" asks Faeradon.

Asher looks around as if seeing his surroundings for the first time. "Alive."

Faeradon slowly looks in my direction. "You see, Dorian. This is how the natural order of things will succeed the past. No longer will the Order of the Dark Cathedral linger in the shadow of the unknown. You should feel honored. A new power stands to rise here, and you are its catalyst."

Faeradon moves across the room to take his place at the desk again as Vargus approaches him with purpose, a look of discontent riddling his bland facial expression. Words exchange between them too low for me to hear as a look of surprise overtakes Faeradon's face.

"Are you certain?" asks Faeradon.

Vargus nods his head.

"That's impossible." Blood flies from Faeradon's mouth. "Asher, I thought you said they perished!"

A pattern of creasing lines passes over Asher's face. "They did, sire. I personally saw the estate burn to the ground."

"And the book?"

"Nothing could have survived the fire."

"Well, no matter. If they are here, they won't survive the night.

Overhearing their conversation, I can't help but hope what I hear is true. *Could it be?*

"You think you three can handle it?" asks Faeradon, agitated as he holds onto one of the balcony boys. His long nails tap over the exposed skin of his neck, fingering the numerous holes lining it up and down.

The three vampires, Vargus, Martyr, and the newly created Asher, gather around Faeradon in an orderly fashion, nodding their consent.

"Good. Make it quick. I'll need you here to help with the final touches."

I take a deep breath and exhale. I am filled with elation. My father is here in the cathedral! Somehow I know it... he is coming to save me!

My head snaps back painfully as my hair is nearly ripped from my scalp.

"It's a shame we have to wait," whispers Martyr in my ear, his breath of spoiled blood stinging my nose. "I just hate waiting. Waiting is for the dogs." I hear his tongue scrape over his dry lips. "Soon, I suppose. Soon this will all be over..."

CHAPTER
XXIII

WOLFGANG

THE TUNNEL IS A SWOLLEN womb in the earth. Wet with moisture, the three of us descend into its sludge filled depths, slipping along muddy banks and deep-rooted holes.

Leaping over small streams and pockets of water, it is evident this passage may have been a moat at one point in time.

Eye moss squashes under our boots like jelly as we trudge forward, ducking low under curtains of slime, roots, and rotting leaves.

Heart pumping, joints creaking. I am a demon descending into its pit of hell. With Ebon root surging through my bloodstream, there is nothing that will slow me down. If there is something to kill, I will kill it.

I swing my torch back and forth as if assaulting an unseen ghost, surveying the passage ahead as far as the light will reach. Massive roots spring from the earth like an underground forest. Angled at different directions, the trunks form dark canopies above our heads like a mossy pitch of black wood. I hear Kronklich shouting behind me, but it's so hard to heed his warning. I've taken rest longer than I've wanted to. I don't want to take the lighthearted approach anymore. Caution, as far as it concerns me, is gone, eradicated to the four winds. It belongs to a past time I can't afford to repeat. Not anymore.

Kronklich's breath is heavy behind me as he catches up. "Careful, Tenor. Winter was able to find this hidden passage that may lead us to the Dark Cathedral, but it doesn't mean the Carnalreesee are not aware of our presence. These eye stalk things *are* quite repulsive."

"I know they know we're here. Let them come." Leaping over a rock, I use the roots above for leverage. My hand slips on the wet surface and I find myself sliding down a murky slant, splashing into a boggy soup filled with hopping frogs and squirming centipedes. Cold mud seeps into every crevice below my waist, forcing me to intake a sharp breath.

All around me, sounds of the dead begin to surface through the muck, escaping through air pockets and thick bubbles.

"Quick, Tenor! Get out of there!" warns Kronklich just as Councilor reaches his side.

"You've given up on precaution I see," adds Councilor, shaking his head. "You're going to get us all killed at this rate."

Kronklich fires a black bolt into the head of a rising lecher reaching for my arm. The force of the impact snaps the creature's head back with a sickening crunch and then slumps forward, unmoving. Shoving it aside, I use the strength of my legs to wade through the bog at an urchin's pace. "If you don't like it, then stay behind…"

More lechers burst through the mud groaning for the taste of flesh. Their bodies are covered in slime and muck while tree roots protrude from their heads and shoulders as if summoned from the earth itself.

Councilor leaps to the opposite side of the bank and sends his black scythe humming through the air. The lechers' heads are sliced clean off their shoulders with one stroke. "… What, and let you have all the fun?"

I feel something shift around my boots and suddenly I am pulled downward and swept through a small-eroded passageway. Slamming against a wall, I struggle to keep my head above the muck, all the while swishing through a channel of churning dirt and sand, passing lechers reaching for me like a bobbing buoy.

I hear Kronklich and Councilor calling my name in the distance, but their voices are lost over the gurgling water. With a new path opened up, the brown wash mixed with dirt eventually dissipates, draining me into a natural system below the rocky ledges. Lechers approach from every direction, shambling and shifting their sick twisted bodies through twisted roots. Up close, I see more detail than I'd like to. Flesh peeling from muscle and fat. Bloated skin and rotting leaves folded over itself. Liquid dribbles from every available orifice on their bodies.

"Tenor! Tenor!" shouts Kronklich from somewhere in the darkness.

"Down here!" I shout back, driving Enivid through the forehead of another lecher.

He can't hear me.

With my torch nearly extinguished from the water, I watch the lechers stand awkwardly, recovering from their water-logged state. Slowly, they surround me with their numbers, ever moving forward, relentless with their intent.

Back against wall, Enivid at the ready, I hold the sputtering torch high above my head to see the reflection of blue-clouded eyes staring back at me. Hands reach for me as I begin slashing and stabbing, cutting off appendages as they come. One lecher, with no arms left to grab with, stumbles forward with its gaping mouth and presses its wet slimy body against mine as it snaps its jaws open and closed. The stink of its breath is horrendous as I jam one of the four blades of Enivid through its skull, severing the connection which allows it to live. As it falls to the floor, another takes its place.

Following the wall's jagged surface, I attempt escaping along its perimeter, creeping in small steps as I kick more lechers away and sever the head of another. Like so many times before, they are endless in their swarm. Keeping a pace like this will tire me, even while on the effect of Ebon root.

Hands burst through the wall, grabbing my shoulders, pinning me against its surface.

Is there no end to this madness?

Dirt and rock cascades over my hair and face as the lecher grinds its teeth close to my ear. I hear the moan rising in its throat, its body pressed close to mine. Rotten teeth chomping against one another. With Enivid still protruding from the head of a lecher in front of me, I jam one of my black blade daggers through its temple with my torch hand. Releasing it from my death stroke, I motion the same dagger forward, thrusting its metal and my fist through another lecher's brains.

"Can't you guys give me a break?" I say out aloud to the undead, reaching for one of the holy flasks on my belt. I know what I'm about to do is risky, but there is no choice. In a few moments, I will be overwhelmed by these walking flesh-eaters, and what good will that be for Dorian?

Aiming at the ceiling, I throw the flask high above their heads and the glass shatters, igniting on impact, bathing the lechers and the underground cave in a brilliant flash of fire.

I duck low to my hands and knees, avoiding the flames and scramble for my life, passing over the lecher's feet while using their bodies as shields from the heat.

Having dropped my torch, the only light to see with is the burning bodies of the lechers. Standing upright, I run for it, trying to get away from the light and into the darkness while the flaming masses uselessly shamble after me.

Again I hear Kronklich calling for me, "Tenor! Are you down there? T'is this way! Follow the echo of my voice!"

And I do exactly that.

Making a break for a nearby tunnel, the darkness is quick to encapsulate me. The lecher's moans fade, but the quality of my vision decreases. Entering into a hallow of a chamber, the subtle sounds of rushing water vibrating through the walls and below my feet bring me hope. Stumbling through the dark, I can't see beyond my hand.

Cupping my hands together, I shout for some kind of confirmation. "James! Councilor!"

Nothing.

The sound of rushing water intensifies as I start to hear voices. *Are they voices?* It's impossible to tell while traversing this terrain. Using my hands to guide myself between two giant roots, again I hear the sounds and this time realize I am not hearing voices, but a colony of bats rushing past me. They hit my face and strike my chest as they frenzy about my body, pulling my hair and tugging at my coat. Flailing my arms about me like a mad man, I shout in frustration, unable to control my anger. "Get away! Dammit!" Panting like a dog, I slash all about me, cutting down bats in the process, painting the roots red with blood. The swarm dies down a little and I make a blind charge through the dark, tripping over stones and splashing into a massive hole. The sudden change in elevation throws my balance off and again I find myself spinning into the muck, slipping down another jagged slope, and nearly spilling over a cliff.

Light approaches through my blurred vision. For a moment, I wonder if my sweet Diana is coming to my rescue, but the sharp rap against my ribs tells me otherwise.

"Grab on!" comes Councilor's frantic voice. The blunt end of his scythe is the one thing saving me from hurtling down into a chasm.

Dangling off the ledge, stones and rocks tumble deep into an abyss below. I look up to see Kronklich hovering over Councilor with a torch in his hand. His top hat and silly smirk are like the angels of God, which have come to watch over me.

"Well you certainly gave us a fright, Tenor!" calls Kronklich over Councilor's shoulder. "I do believe you are trying to give us all heart attacks. Not very noble, is it?" His smile is genuine, even with sweat and dirt smudging his face.

Heaving me over the side like a freshly caught salmon, Councilor gives only the slightest grunt in liberating me from an untimely death.

Rolling onto my back, gulping down breaths of air, I stammer out my concern as the moaning rises from the surrounding darkness. "Lechers. There's more of them that way." I point up the slope from which I tumbled. "We need to keep going unless you want to be their next meal. They won't relent and there are too many of them. Let's go."

Following the edge of the chasm for a while, the three of us eventually reach a natural land bridge made of twisted vines and roots, larger than any man-made bridge in any city I've been to. The structure is enormous and inspiring. As we race across its spongy surface, my thoughts linger on Dorian, the mental fuel that keeps me going.

With the sound of rushing water growing louder with every new step, I know we are approaching the aqueducts. The massive turbine water wheels can be heard in the distance, the squealing of their gears and the twisting cranking sound of winches spinning round and round.

"Not much further," shouts Councilor over his shoulder as he takes point along the narrowing passageway, his reason for being here, just as good as mine. Again I call to mind his undying dedication to find a cure for his daughter and yet, at the same time, clench my teeth in self-torment. I know he will never find a cure—for everything that is needed to know is right inside the book of Marcus Cornelius. The phrase repeats over and over in my head, the words flashing before my vision like the burned image of the sun… *there is no cure for vampires… there is no cure for vampires…*

Councilor runs up the slope with his scythe held low to his side, the two of us following him like sheep. He is Black Death ascending, maneuvering forward, his determination just as strong as mine and Kronklich's.

We come to a crest in the path, both sides narrowing us into a funnel of roots and dirt. At the top, we stop to admire the complicated waterworks of the underground cathedral. In itself, and of its own right, the aqueduct spreads before us like a maze, a spidery construct rising from the frantic tendrils of a raging river. Much larger and more complicated than Egleaseon's ruins, collections of water wheels, flumes, and sluices zig zag in every direction, gushing forth liquids like life blood passing through veins and arteries of the human body. It is massive and intense, and straight through the center of it all, a broken weathered path divides the phenomenon into two separate halves, one ascending into torch-filled archways, the other, descending into oblivion blackness.

"Well there's certainly no doubt which way we should be going," says Kronklich with the utmost beat, "sources point to the obvious, light versus darkness."

"Yes," I say. "Up into the light."

Before we have a chance to comment further, before we even think of exploring the aqueducts on a more personal level—the strangest sounds begin to creep into earshot as the three of us stand by looking around us, anticipating what it could possibly be.

From above and below, dark masses appear out of the shadowy parts of the cavernous chamber, skittering up and down the aqueduct mechanisms like ants. Dozens, no, hundreds of the masses converge. A maddening sea of golden glowing eyes. The horrific sight fills me with determination. Gripping Enivid tightly, I feel my body beginning to move naturally as sinewy arms and legs power the monstrosities before us. The horrible species known as bogarts is directly blocking our path.

CHAPTER
XXIV

"RUN," IS ALL I CAN say.

"What?"

"Run!"

Body already in motion, there is no need to explain further. The three of us run for our lives.

Hand over foot, we charge down the jagged path at back-breaking speed, leaping over crumbling cliffs and dashing along rusted railings. Large rocks break away into the rushing water below as the weight of our footfalls impact the foundation. The ground slick with condensation, a mist of churning water rises along either side of us as we descend into the valley of aqueducts.

"Don't stop!" I shout over the wailing noise of grinding metal and splashing water. The flumes and sluices channeling the water to unknown destinations rise like a forest of reeds as we begin panting. Legs burning, blood flowing, it's a matter of seconds before the first of the bogarts reaches us. With their one yellow eye set in a face full of razor-sharp teeth, these crossbreeds fall somewhere between a spider and a wildcat. The bogarts' humanoid frames are well designed for violence—climbing, leaping, and grappling—and their muscular grey bodies and long pointed nails have no trouble reaching us from any angle they choose.

The first one, screaming and howling like a banshee, descends on us with flailing arms. However, it doesn't take but one shot from Kronklich's crossbow to put it down. Then a pack of three hop along a sluice next to us, keeping pace with our movement, splashing copious amounts of water over the edge with each badgering pounce. Running and grunting, I see what they're about to do and switch my spot in the formation, falling behind Councilor as he takes lead as the wedge in our triangle. The bogarts leap from the sluice like greydon cats, claws and teeth first, only to meet with Councilor's scythe. Two of them are impaled at the same time in mid-air, while the third narrowly dodges Councilor. Kronklich with his repeater bow, fires a bolt into the next bogart's eye, sending it screeching as it tumbles away. While Kronklich exhales, he trains the crossbow above my head. I duck. He fires, striking the chest of another bogart. A simple nod from me and we continue on, huffing along the gravel path toward the divide.

"More approaching on the left!" yells Councilor as he cuts again through the air with his scythe, showering us in bogart blood.

They are gaining in numbers.

We aren't moving fast enough.

A pack of dark masses swarm up the side of the path and cross the raging river, running along the top of the water as if they weighed nothing. I throw Enivid without delay, sending its whirling blades in a deadly arc, cutting through limbs and severing throats until it returns to my hand, the blood and guts already cleaned from its flight through the misty air.

Up ahead, a large reservoir rises above us supported by long wooden pylons. And just beyond it, the divide. Many of the flumes gush their channels of water into its basin and at the bottom, a water wheel spins frantically, churning its metal turbine to produce electricity. The familiar hum of energy passes through conduits rising over the rushing water.

For a moment, the way seems clear as we continue sprinting, Kronklich training his crossbow on anything that moves, and Councilor focusing ahead. But aside from the wailing of the turbine spinning and the electricity pumping, the absence of growling creatures causes me to look behind us.

My heart beats faster.

An army of bogarts chases us. Hundreds of them. Clawed feet clacking against the floor. They are a massive shadow form working together for a common cause.

One by one, the bogarts in front pull away from the main pack, eager to sample our flesh and bone before the others. Their speed is godlike, and we can't outrun them.

Kronklich and I exchange attacks between crossbow and Enivid, filling the air with black missiles and flashing blades. The bogarts fall one after another, causing others to trip behind them. But this has no effect on the growing mass.

We pass under the reservoir, weaving in and out between the thick wooden poles until we clear the massive structure. Looking up, an idea crosses my mind.

Enivid leaves my hand in a furious windstorm, spinning away into the electrically charged atmosphere of conduits and rushing water. The first pylon pops, exploding into splintering wood and then Enivid hits the next, cutting straight through with precision. My blade continues forward, spinning round and round on its intimate path of destruction, cutting each of the support structures holding the reservoir up on one side. As Enivid returns to my hand, I feel the ground inclining, telling me we've reached the divide.

Within moments, the wood pylons groan in response and the reservoir lists drastically, spilling its contents down onto the swarm of bogarts, blasting them with water. A huge tidal wave crashes against everything, taking out bogarts, water wheels, sluices and flumes alike.

The sound is deafening as wood, metal, and bone crash into one another, breaking on impact and colliding with devastating force. The screams of bogarts wash down the side of the crevice and into the river as we continue our ascent.

"I must say, Tenor," shouts Kronklich while running, "That was strategically impressive!"

But our problems aren't over. Ahead of us, a new swarm forms. Bogarts run up the walls and leap from holes in the ground. Forced to rethink our strategy, I quickly devise a plan that hopefully will work. "Quick, Councilor, take right flank. I'll take the left."

Already understanding my intent, Councilor and Kronklich both nod and take up their positions. Kronklich readies his crossbow while Councilor rests his scythe behind his back, ready to lash out on a moment's notice. Having reached the stone archways lined with torches, the extra light brings on a whole new perspective.

We race forward, our new formation like a scythe all on its own. With confidence growing stronger, and our direction bolder, our spirit is rekindled. Kronklich fires away, destroying bogarts by the dozen. Defending our flank with Enivid, I slash through the air in large swooping X's, cutting through Bogart skin with ease. Enivid flares to life with every kill she makes. Dare I say my Diana is doing all the work. It is good to feel her alive and well.

Rushing forward in a maddening rage, Councilor's huge shadow presses the enemy with renewed vigor, as he throws one dagger after another. His deadly blades find every mark.

The slope soon turns to steps. I hear water rushing overhead across flumes running the length of the archways. Water drips from large cracks in the framework and onto our foreheads as we press on, passing each archway with caution.

I grab a new torch off the wall to replenish my dying one when a dark sinewy hand grabs my wrist, pulling me forward. It throws my balance off and my body slams against the archway. Struggling to be free, I come face to face with the hideous bogart, its mouth wide open, ready to strike.

Its teeth snap forward.

I tilt my head back.

"Kronklich!" I shout. Immediately, a bolt passes into its head and it flops to the floor.

Bogarts seem to fall from the sky, leaping from the tops of the archway and springing from behind pillars. For every one of us, four bogarts stand in our way.

Rows of teeth.

Growling.

I grin. The odds are still in our favor.

Producing a black wooden stake from within the folds of my coat, I ram its sharp point through the jaws of a bogart while slicing off the head of another with Enivid. Peering to my right, I see Kronklich fire another shot, slam a bogart in the face with his crossbow, and sling the weapon over his shoulder, drawing his cane sword at the same time with fluid like precision. In two blinks of my eye, his blade licks two bogarts back to back, each of them falling to the floor, blood gushing from their throats and torsos.

Councilor is surrounded. The bogarts are closer than anticipated and his scythe is too bulky for close combat. He is quickly overrun. They clamber over him, snapping jaws toward his face and cutting at his arms and legs with their claws.

Unable to release his cherished weapon, he draws a long dagger from his waist and rams the blade through one bogart's open maw, following all the way through with brute force. The backside of the bogart's head bursts open, ending in a spectacle of gore and bits.

Three remain.

Kronklich warns from behind and I duck just as his sword zips over my head. The blade pierces two bogarts at one time, pinning them to the floor in a death-like embrace. Kronklich races forward with the finesse of a cat, pulls his sword free and cuts the head off the final bogart just before sinking its teeth into Councilor's neck.

With a stab and two cuts, I finish off the bogarts in front of me before running to Councilor's aid. Helping him to stand, I see he is bloodied, but I'm unsure if it is all his own blood or that of the bogarts.

"Kronklich, get us out of here!" I say, helping Councilor to his feet.

He rises up without complaint but winces suddenly grabbing his side near his ribs. "Shit," he says, cursing under his breath. "Bastards got me."

Crossbow back at the ready, Kronklich continues peppering the enemy as we follow after him, he taking point as I force Councilor to stay in the middle.

Despite moving a few paces slower, our adrenalin continues to rage as we kill the relentless onslaught of bogarts. We ascend higher and higher, passing more archways, water seeping from cracks, running across stone steps. Slipping and recovering, flaying bogart after endless bogart, we finally reach the top of the stairs and pass through an open doorway with a portcullis embedded in the ceiling. My arms, sore from endless slashing, do all they can to keep the bogarts from passing beyond the threshold.

"Hurry! Close the gate!" I shout behind me. Kronklich, too busy defending our position, takes aim and fires past my head, sending two more bogarts tumbling down the staircase.

There is a loud bang somewhere in the distance and a chain rattles in response. Suddenly the ironbound portcullis rushes towards me and I dive backwards. The gate slams into the ground, skewering a bogart following after me. The creature squeals, flailing against the bars to escape, but can't go anywhere as the others slam into the gate one after another in a giant tidal wave of snarling teeth and flesh. They pile up against the bars, packing in every available space as I back away on hand and foot, my eye never leaving their sea of tiny yellow orbs.

But it's not their screaming or the possibility of them coming through that worries me at the moment. I turn to look at Councilor stumbling out of the portcullis room, holding his side from which blood is forcefully spouting. He has been bitten by a bogart. And although the bite is not as drastic as that of a vampire, I know, and Kronklich knows, in three days' time, Councilor will turn.

The three of us breathe heavily as we rest against the wall, sweat dripping down our faces. Shaking my head, I watch the bogart impaled by the gate struggle against its dying body.

"Well, you can't get any closer than that," comments Kronklich as he pulls a handkerchief from his coat pocket and pats down his forehead.

"Yeah," grunts Councilor. "You could say that." He grimaces while adding more bandages to the congealing wound at his side. "A little too close for comfort." He inhales deeply and exhales with a smirk. "Guess we have to find two cures now."

As I attempt to remain calm and composed, his thought overwhelms me.

CHAPTER XXV

"Release us... release us from our torment. Please sir... please help us..."

Voices in the dark.

I have a hard time discerning the sounds in the distance melding with the screeches of the bogarts nearby. I can't make any sense of them.

Sucking down a few more gulps of my water skin, I hand it to Councilor as I rise to investigate the mysterious plight from the shadows.

Am I hearing things?

A hand on my arm stops me suddenly.

"Don't trust it, Tenor. Could be a trap." There is a look of concern on Kronklich's face, but at the same time, we both know what must be done. He follows suit, holding his bow at eye level.

"Who's there?" I call out to the darkness.

Using a fresh torch to light the way, we inch our way forward slowly, weapons at the ready, sweat dripping into my eye.

"Oh the sounds... the sounds of those beasts are horrendous! Make them stop... make them stop!"

"Who's there? Show yourself!" I demand, but only see the faintest movement of white in the blackness.

"Only that if I could, I would," responds the voice.

A few more steps forward reveals a skeletal looking figure, withered down to nothing but taut skin over bone. It rests against the moldy wall. *A prisoner perhaps?* Kronklich and I move closer cautiously. Something isn't right. The sight is grotesque and unbelievable, something that shouldn't be.

What I thought to be a starved prisoner is more than just a man shackled to a wall.

The man *is* the wall.

A part of it.

Unable to move his head or any other part of his body, his eyes, dried and hollowed out, roll around in his skull, trying to get the best angle in which to see with.

"What... what the hell are you?" I ask, unable to fully comprehend what is before me.

The figure's eyes come to rest on me and his mouth moves. "I am a servant... an acolyte... to The Holy Order of Sunstone... much like the others... all around us."

I quickly pass the torch about realizing the skeleton is speaking the truth. There are more just like him. Dozens of them. But some of them aren't moving and some of them look fresh, with their skin and hair intact. Some are wearing clothes...

More cries for help echo from further down the hall.

"How is this possible?" I ask, moving closer to the acolyte embedded in the wall.

"As you can see… things have gone terribly wrong." The skeleton's eyes shift back and forth, left and right, before continuing. "Once, us being here was a good thing. Now it is not…"

More screeching from the bogarts echoes down the hall towards us.

"Make it stop, oh make it stop! Those terrible terrible sounds…"

Although I can't physically see the agony the acolyte is experiencing, his words are enough to stir action from within me. Stepping forward, I grip the skeleton by its ribcage and pull.

"No Tenor, don't!" cries Kronklich but my intent is quicker than his words.

The acolyte peels from the wall half way, tearing at the skin and breaking at the spinal column. Blood seeps from the cracks and the acolyte howls in pain.

Hands covered in blood, I back away with a horror I never knew. "What is this? *What the hell is this?*"

The voices surrounding us rise with excitement, my actions have somehow aroused them.

"You are kind," says the hallowed voice of the skeleton, a non-existent breath escapes its open mouth. "However I think our fate is sealed. It's good to know there are others like you. Others who would care about us."

"Others like me? What do you mean? Who else did you see?"

"A boy… no, a young man… who looked like you…"

My blood freezes.

I approach the acolyte, my bloody hands held before him but never touching. "When? Where?" I can barely contain my excitement. If I could, I would shake the answer out of this acolyte.

"Oh... it was quite some time ago I imagine... time here is something of the past..." The skeleton's eyes roll into the back of its head and cease to move.

"No! Wait!" I shout, gripping the skull in anger, tearing it from the wall. The skull breaks apart like sand, crumbling through my fingers. "No, no, nooo!" I drop to my knees, staring at the fine dust in my hands.

Councilor stands next to us now, surveying the scene with one hand staunching his wound, his eyebrows raised.

Kronklich places a hand on my shoulder and then whispers to Councilor, "We have a clue. Dorian came this way."

Councilor nods. He seems to stand taller and more attentive. "Ready when you are."

Kronklich nods the same and turns to face the wall where the skeleton was moments ago. "Right then. Gentlemen, I've come to the conclusion this place is *alive.*" His tone is solemn and dismayed. "T'is similar to Stellamane's fortress. Look at this..." He rubs his finger over the stone and mortar. "Blood is *inside* the walls... ."

What Kronklich is saying may be the reason why the tower has grown so high. If the Dark Cathedral was alive, who's to say the acolytes trapped in the walls weren't the ones serving as the building blocks to its existence? But the thought is fleeting and I don't care about Stellamane's fortress or this damn cathedral anymore. All I want is my son back and this acolyte just confirmed he's alive.

Rising from the floor, I turn to face the whispering darkness. "Let's go." I dash from the spot and become swallowed up by the darkness. There is no interjection from Kronklich or Councilor. They follow without question.

The long dark expanse of the hall is filled with echoing footfalls, a tunnel of metal bars and dried bones plastered into mortar and stone. There is no hope for those who are prisoners of this dungeon. Thieves, vagabonds, acolytes, all have been betrayed by the so-called Holy Order. Redemption and penance, these ideas seem petty now given the circumstances.

We move along at a fast clip, our weapons at the ready, waiting for something to lunge at us from the dark.

Searching for an exit, I wave my torch between bars as we investigate each prison cell along the way. In most of them, bones of the deceased lie dormant in piles of disjointed rubble. In some, shackles that once held prisoners remain open and free of any occupants. Where was everyone? Where were the vampires and the daver hounds and the caretakers with their glowing lanterns?

The sound of slurping travels up the corridor towards us, strong supping sounds as if someone were sucking the pulp from a fruit.

I motion Kronklich and Councilor to move to the far right wall. Advancing slower, it doesn't take long to witness the skinny hunched over figure on the opposite side of the tunnel, drawing the blood from the wrist of a corpse propped against the bars. At first it seems the creature doesn't notice us, but then, as it finishes slurping, it turns its gaze on us instinctively and sniffs the air. Eyes burn red in a gaunt trimmed face, it's facial features indiscernible in the low light of the dungeon. Panting heavily, it drops the drained wrist and wipes the blood from its fanged lips. Crouched low on hands and feet, the half-naked being looks at us as if sizing up its next meal.

I throw Enivid with a furious rage, hoping to gain the advantage of surprise. Its spinning blades skim the metal bars mid-flight, igniting the corridor with sparks. Kronklich drops to one knee and levels his crossbow, firing multiple shots in the process. The creature moves with unimaginable speed, faster than the naked eye, dodging Enivid and the flurry of arrows. Stopping on the ceiling upside down, the vampire hisses, exposes its fangs to us, and turns about, retreating down the hall in the opposite direction.

"After it!" I cry, sprinting forward. "It will warn the others!"

Kronklich and Councilor follow suit, giving chase down the dungeon hall with torches blazing.

The vampire, small in stature, is fast, almost too quick for me to determine which way it went. As the passage divides into two, I notice faint movement going left and so expectantly follow after it. With the blood of the hunter pumping through my veins, it feels good to be doing again what I was born to do. Hunting creatures of the night.

Our breath heaves heavily with erratic puffs of cold air as we slow to a trot, glancing left and right into the darkness beyond the prison cells.

"Where did it go?" asks Councilor, gripping his massive scythe timidly.

Councilor is a capable hunter of men, but when it comes to monsters, his lack of experience shows.

"Give it a minute," I say as Kronklich adjusts his stance and points his crossbow into the blackness.

There is a moan from somewhere in the deep and a fierce gust of wind blows through the dungeon corridor extinguishing our torches. Left in pitch darkness, a pair of red eyes appears in the distance. My nerves dance on edge as I ready Enivid, but then stop. Another pair of glowing eyes materializes. Then another. Then another...

"Kronklich!" I shout.

The sound of shattering glass fills the hall as a huge fiery inferno spreads across the ground. The darkness now obliterated into light, the vampires cower from its source, hissing and baring their fangs. Some of them are blinded from the sudden flash and so I use it to my advantage. I charge forward, slashing through the air with Enivid and stab one of the vampires through the chest, following through with a slice to its neck. Head lopped clean from its body, the vampire combusts into an effigy of fire and smoke.

A female vampire, angered by my actions, moves to engage, passing quicker than the wind. She lunges through the air, nails poised to pierce my body, but I sidestep her attack and use the momentum of her body to strike the shoulder, slamming her to the ground. Pinned and unable to escape, I draw a wooden stake and jam it into her heart, sending blood spraying across the floor. Mouth hissing in agony, her body writhes underneath me as she melts to smoldering ash.

A shout from Councilor grabs my attention. His large form faces off with one of the recovering vampires. He tries with all his might to reap the vampire with his scythe, but misses every time. Dressed in elegant clothing, the male vampire is behind Councilor before he realizes it and grips the back of his shoulders ready to bite. An arrow pierces the vampire's forehead, stunning him temporarily. He staggers back and reaches to pull the shaft from his face.

Another holy flask explodes behind us filling the dungeon with a brilliant light. The heat flares at my backside as Kronklich nods with a look of satisfaction. He slays two more vampires, teenagers by the looks of it, shooting them dead center in the heart.

Just as I think the situation is under control, Kronklich's face suddenly contorts. "Behind you!"

I feel a rush of wind.

Spinning on the spot, I drop to one knee and thrust upward with Enivid, piercing the vampire that was stunned through its neck. Ramming a stake through its heart, it bursts into flame and crumbles to dust.

"Come on!" I say frantically picking up the pace again, the immediate threat vanquished. A bright glowing yellow light flickers not far in the distance, an archway leading up to another part of the Dark Cathedral. I give a shout out with enthusiasm to my cohorts, "If there are vampires, then we're getting close!"

DAY TWENTY- SEVEN

CHAPTER
XXVI

DORIAN

THE SOUND OF ORGAN PIPES rattles deep from within the walls of the chamber. The music is low and resonating, reminding me of the hours I spent in church in Roland. The clergy master would play during and after sermons. So many times I found myself lost within those sounds. But now… now was not one of those times. Now… the music terrifies me.

The light seems dimmer as I struggle against my restraints for the thirteenth or fourteenth time; I've lost count. The rusted metal cuts deeper into my wrists and ankles. Given enough time, I would be happy severing a hand or foot if it meant my freedom. How bad I want to taste it. To be free of my chains. But the odds are irrationally impossible. I am a prisoner of vampires and evil priests.

How long has it been? How many days have passed since I was placed in here?

It seems ages ago when the Carnalreesee and Faeradon left me alone in this chamber. Where did they go? What is their intention now that I've been abandoned? There was supposed to be some sort of ritual taking place, but now all of that seems on hold.

My wish. My last dying hope is that somehow my father finds his way here. That at any moment he will come barging through those sealed doors at the end of the hall, his brilliant Bawaka in hand, his armor covered in blood. He could save me from this horrible nightmare. But there is none of that at the moment. No dreams to rest on. No happy thoughts of rescue. There is only silence and that horrible music. It's coming from somewhere—everywhere it seems, through the walls and floor, creeping slowly into my body like an invisible sickness.

Solitude.

My only companion.

Here I am again, the same as when I was in the dungeon. Cardinal Glass was there, be he friend or foe, it doesn't matter now. At least I was able to muster strength from his words of encouragement. At least there was something to *concentrate* on.

The lights in the laboratory flicker. Conduits running along the length of the walls lead to the electric lights on the ceiling which sputter and buzz like angry bees. I always wondered at the phenomenon of electricity, the great advancement of the ages. My father would tell me about it in stories, how the richest of cities were the only ones to carry such power. Light without fire. Never did I think it would be under these circumstances that I would finally get to see them. Of all places, it was here within this medieval place that electric power would be conducted. Such irony. How was it even possible to have electricity in our time? We are existing in a dark age. My father always said it was an ancient knowledge passed down from a time long forgotten. But why didn't anyone know more about electricity now?

One of the electric lights explodes exuding gas and shattered glass. Half the room goes dark while the air fills in an eerie static noise. Buzzing and humming and organ pipes in the distance…

I feel madness creeping into the dark places of my mind. Was this part of their plan? To drive me insane for whatever reasons they had?

"Uuhhg!" I growl into the empty room where no one is listening. "Let me out of here!" Sharp pain riddles my wrists as I struggle against the shackles one more time. *That makes fifteen.*

In the distant part of my mind, I hear the faintest of whispers reaching out from the depths of my sanity. Whether it is real, I am not sure, but I don't care. It is enough to occupy me. Accompany me. "Hello? Yes? I am here. Please speak to me. I am alone. So utterly alone." For a moment I analyze myself and come to the conclusion I am, in fact, alone, but it is a horrible conclusion. "Won't you stay with me? I could use the company. I have been alone for so long."

"You are not alone…" says a voice that first scares me half to death, but then, I am overjoyed at the prospect of it. I wait to hear more. I wait and wait and…

"You have never been alone…" comes the voice again and this time, I am all but too aware of its origin. The soft soothing sound of caramel. The voice of a noble lady. The sound that could only be produced by a loving mother. My mother.

An image of pure white begins to form in the darkness above me where the light shattered. It takes shape, twisting and curling in strands of glowing iridescent pearl. Never have I seen such beauty in such a dark place.

"Mother. Is that you?" I ask, part of me insane, part of me in denial.

The image lowers closer above me, hovering like a ghostly spirit. "Of course it is, my son." She smiles at me and for once my body warms in this damp cold cathedral. "Strength, Dorian. You need to show strength. You have done so well after all this time and now it is needed more than ever."

"Mother… I am bound and bleeding at my hands and feet. I am a prisoner. I have no strength." Tears well in my eyes.

"Do not cry, sweet Dorian. I know you are strong. I have seen it."

I shake my head back and forth. "No, no, no, mother. I am no such thing. I tried to be there for you. I wanted to save you, but I let you die. I was helpless. I couldn't stop the vampires. They took you right in front of me." I close my eyes as if to block the image from my memory, but it is clearer than the night it happened.

"No Dorian. It is I who failed you. I failed to protect you. I wasn't strong enough to save you." Her form floats even closer, a breath's distance from mine. I could touch her, kiss her, if my hands were free. "But things have changed. Things are different now."

"What do you mean, mother?"

"I will protect you from now until the end of time. This I promise."

I feel the words of impossibility forming on my lips. "But how? I don't even know if what I'm seeing right now is real. I must be going mad…"

"No Dorian. You are not mad…" Mother's image falters some, winking in and out for a brief moment. "Be strong, Dorian. We will be together. No matter what happens." Again her image wavers and for a moment disappears to re-appear in an instant.

"What's the matter? What's happening to you?"

Mother looks over her shoulder. "They are coming." She turns to look me in the eyes. "I love you with all my heart, Dorian. I will be with you in the darkest of times. I will protect you…"

And then, as if she never existed, her ghostly image vanishes in a puff of smoke, a trail of iridescent light dissipating into the atmosphere of the chamber.

Once again I am left in silence.

The thought of what I saw lingers along with the throbbing pain at the back of my head. With no water to drink, my throat is parched. I swallow back my saliva, so desperately waiting for nourishment, but it never comes. How can I be strong if I can't eat or drink? For the longest time, the Carnalreesee ensured I would eat and drink to my heart's content. But now… now they are withholding everything.

Faeradon mentioned wiping out the old Dorian. Was this how they were going to do it? To starve me to death? Force me into hallucinations?

Mother. My poor sweet mother. I'm so sorry. So, so sorry. I tried to be the man I should have been, the man father tried to make me. I couldn't save you… I couldn't save you… I couldn't… save… you.

CHAPTER XXVII

WOLFGANG

CLIMBING.

Endless steps.

The spiral staircase seems to go on forever.

Images play over in my head of what I will do to the Carnal-reesee when I find them. Violent images. Of maiming and breaking, bludgeoning and eviscerating.

My poor Dorian. What have they done to you? What terrible things will I find?

I know you are brave. Fear not my son, I am coming. Kronklich is here. Councilor is here. You will like Councilor, I promise.

Having escaped the aqueducts and dungeon with our lives, we carry on with new anxiety, pressing ever forward, ever upward.

My heart throbs in my ear as we reach the top of the stair landing. Drawing deep needed breaths, I place a hand on the cold stone wall, glancing back. The others are making their way up. Barely. Kronklich helps Councilor, his one thin arm tucked underneath Councilor's meaty shoulder, guiding him, encouraging him. "Not much further! That's it."

Nodding my appreciation, I turn on the spot and lower my torch, charging forward through the open archway, Enivid gleaming above my head like a scorpion's tail. With the Ebon root working its way through my system, I am an engine bursting with steam. Nothing will stop my progression...

There is movement beyond my circle of light. Strange sounds fill the spacious chamber as we stumble through the empty corridor. Sounds of rushing liquid, like draining water from a grate. Slowing my pace, I hold my arm out, signaling for Councilor and Kronklich to stop, but the warning is unnecessary. The horrific looks on their faces speak a thousand words.

A series of networking tubes dangle from the ceiling like tentacles of a squid. Curling and twisting at odd angles, the ends of the hoses terminate into male and female bodies lying supine about the room. Tubes jut from open mouths and open veins; they siphon copious amounts of bubbly red liquid into large metal vats, draining the life essence of these victims.

Half-naked, robes splayed open, the acolytes lie in trans-like states, staring into starless oblivion, their eyes black and glistening, their bodies shaking and convulsing. Some of them have already been transfixed into the walls, their skin bound and fused to the black stones of the cathedral like glue. The foundation is ever growing; the blood channels through cracks in the mortar. Some of the acolytes can barely speak while others hardly make a sound at all.

"Release... Please..."

The torment in their voices is unbearable. I want to do as they ask, but can't. There is no hope for them. Their hope was lost long ago. They are as good as dead…

A hand reaches for me.

"Release me. Please. Don't leave…" and I brush the hand away.

We cannot stop.

We will not stop.

I hear protest rising behind me. Councilor, most likely in disbelief, but it is Kronklich who makes sense for him. Good old Kronklich, always there for me. Always making sense for others that my actions never make.

Passing dozens of bodies, we disappear into a long narrow corridor, swooping past flickering candles and scurrying rats. The ground seems to elevate as the ground smooths out and in time another chamber appears before us.

It's strange being in this place. This place of death and disease. The air is alive with evil, as if drawing a breath would corrupt my insides, plaguing my lungs. But I know my nerves are conflicted. Why is that? Did it have to do with what I just saw? What the Carnalreesee are still capable of doing? Or was it seeing the images of those acolytes like seeing Dorian dozens of times over? A prisoner to these horrendous monsters. Tortured. His blood siphoned like the rest.

Rattling chains startle me and suddenly I am pushed back. Councilor's brute strength shoves me to the side as he groans a warning. "Careful, Tenor. Vampires. One of them almost got you."

An older woman, dressed in a commoner's dress, brown skirt and gray blouse lunges again, this time at Councilor. Hissing and baring gleaming white fangs, she fights tirelessly against the chains holding her to the wall, trying her hardest to get at the veins flexing on Councilor's neck.

"Whoa sister! Easy girl…" Councilor says, staying out of reach as he advances forward, avoiding others in a similar state. "Look at them all," says Councilor in disbelief. "It's a goddamn breeding ground."

Councilor's words couldn't be truer.

Throughout the chamber, victims, not that of acolytes, but citizens from Sunstone, line the walls of either side, chained at the arms and legs, preventing them the freedom to leave the room. Most fight against the restraints as we pass, trying with all their might to rend our flesh. But there are others who cower against the wall, shaking like drug addicts, vomiting blood and bile, over and over. Writhing in agony, they scream from the changes taking place inside their dying bodies. I know all too well this sight, the cursed changing process all newly initiated vampires go through.

The goddamn vampires are making an army.

Without another thought, I drive a stake through the closest vampire, piercing the heart in his chest, severing his head with Enivid. I feel nothing as I do this and move to the next one, meeting slight resistance as a vampire girl latches onto my arm bracer. I feel the teeth grind into the thick leather, but they will never penetrate it. It's the older ones that have the longer fangs.

I bring the blade up, forcing Enivid into her ribcage, and she cries in agony, the expression of pain on her face transforming to dust. Her chains rattle against the wall and floor, signaling Councilor and Kronklich to carry out the same actions. Within minutes, the vampires are destroyed, the room purged of evil and for a moment I feel sorry for the pale look in Councilor's face. He isn't accustomed to killing supernatural creatures. Though, for the first time, his resolve was resolute.

A nod of quick thanks to both of them and already I am leaving the chamber, the arched doorway flickering with more flames. As we meet more stairs to climb, a low resonating tone triggers something deep throughout my body. The sound is familiar yet I can't place it.

Up more steps and more climbing, we pass more skeletal walls of dead acolytes staring at our every move. Their eyes follow our every step, but I know it's the trick of the mind.

Again I hear the out of place tone and soon realize it is something I have come to know all my life, the sacred music of the church. The pipe organ. Low notes, drawn out blasts of air travel downward through the stairwell becoming louder with each ascending step. The music floods my memories of Albestan church and the courtyard and the gate where Nester did his damnedest to save the little boy Manson.

Lofty choir voices, not that of soprano, alto, or baritone, add to the ensemble of the deep-toned organ. Chills run the length of my arms as the choral music reaches my ears. Before I have a chance to say anything, it is Kronklich who expresses disbelief for the group. "Correct me if I am wrong, but is that children singing?"

Slowly, cautiously, we make it to the top of the stairs. Inching our way through the connecting corridor, we stop just within the archway, collecting ourselves for what awaits us on the other side. Peering around the corner, I am struck with disbelief. The insanity of what I see throws my reasoning to the wind.

Beyond the threshold stands a full choir of young boys. Dressed in white robes stained with splotches of reds and yellows, they hold burning candles and hymn from open books. The organist plays furiously behind them, his back to them, slaving over keys that connect to a set of steel pipes rising above them all like a great god.

Behind the pipe organ, a massive set of stained-glass windows in various colors of orange, purple and pink lie wide open. On the floor before us, long rows of polished pews run the length of the chamber. People's belongings—bags, clothes, and shoes rest on the benches up and down the aisles. What could they be but the belongings of citizens forced to leave behind their earthly possessions?

The three of us, now standing side by side, move into the chamber, weapons drawn, speechless.

The organist continues to play and the boys continue to sing as if we don't exist. Unable to contain my emotion, I move closer rapidly—too fast for either Councilor or Kronklich to stop me.

"What is this?" I shout over the music, but the boys' vocals become louder, more sinister. "Listen to me! Stop now! Answer me, damn it!" The organist plays a cacophonous cord.

Something approaches in the sky. Something fluttering. Bobbing up and down. A swarm of bats headed straight for us. The swarm splits into two and three bats pass through the stained glass windows with precision and ease.

Flapping about in a frenzy, the bats eventually maneuver to the music in sync, circling around one another in the center of the room. Neither the boys nor the organist seems distracted by their presence.

One by one, the bats land, transforming into human forms before our very eyes. All around us, the entry doors slam shut, their locks clicking into place, ensuring escape is impossible.

Realizing what's happening, my hand reflexively clenches Enivid, over and over, cutting the circulation off at the knuckles.

With the figures materialized before us, I can only assume who they are. A man dressed in blood red armor, long black hair flowing down the back, large sword at his side. A small thin man dressed in black, hair askew in a red storm of wind. And a tall lanky fellow dressed in a long white coat, black boots to his knees and blonde hair flowing over his shoulders. The Carnalreesee and Asher Vandrake.

The one with flaming red hair stares us down with his cold blue eyes. "Greetings vampire hunters. I don't think we've been properly introduced." The vampire steps forward gingerly, sizing us up like prey. "I am the one they call Martyr, and the big leering brute with the oversized kitchen knife is Vargus." Martyr chuckles to himself. "Sorry, Vargus. Couldn't help myself." Recomposing himself to a more serious tone, he continues. "I assume Asher Vandrake needs no introduction." He gestures to the man who tried to kill us, the self-proclaimed assistant to Marcus Cornelius. "He has come to us and told us everything that has happened."

I suddenly become very aware of the book under by breastplate.

"And so where does that leave us? Ah yes, the fact of who you are and what you are doing here in this most sacred of places."

"Most sacred of places? Are you kidding me?" asks Councilor coolly, looking about the make shift chapel as if it were some rundown playhouse for kids.

I notice Kronklich eyeing Martyr intently, an intensity in his brow I have not seen for a very long time. As if on cue, I hear him whisper under his breath. *"It's him…"*

The vampire's eyes sparkle with malice as they watch us, studying us.

"What?" I ask with a rasp, turning my head ever so slightly.

"It's him… the one who killed my parents."

A rush of memories hits me all at once as I recall the day Kronklich spoke of his parents' death to me. It was a sad day, watching a man's walls break down before you, as he explained what happened, the random attack in Porson, the vampire who came to his home and took everything precious from him. I glance at Kronklich with a look of concern, knowing very well what was going to happen next. He has talked about it since the first day I met him at the Five Cities Academy.

"I know it's him," says Kronklich more confidently now, his words louder, his actions drawing the attention of everyone. "I could never forget the image of the one who killed my parents. Red hair like fire. Sunken face of a skeleton. You sir..." shouts Kronklich defiantly; pointing at Martyr as if putting him on the stand to be judged, "... will die for the crimes against my family!" Kronklich draws his cane sword and swipes at the air in a figure eight. "Prepare thyself, vampire!" shouts Kronklich as the vampires stare on with empty faces.

"Are you serious?" laughs Martyr uncontrollably. He stumbles along the ground trying to balance himself. "He can't be serious." Martyr turns to look at Vargus for support. But before Vargus can answer, Kronklich charges forward with his face contorted in anger.

I knew this was going to happen and there is nothing I can do to stop it. The moment suspends us in time before all hell breaks loose.

CHAPTER XXVIII

WITH THE HYMN OF CHOIR boys rising and the organist blaring his chords, the music gives rise to the evil residing in this godforsaken place.

I follow Kronklich into the pit of vipers with Councilor right behind me.

Relentlessly, Kronklich attacks, slicing his sword in the direction of the three vampires.

Vargus, Martyr, and Asher disperse from the stage like birds, winging into separate directions dodging the blows. As if fated, we square off with equally matched foes, hunter with vampire. The two lumbering giants, Vargus and Councilor, Martyr with Kronklich, and Asher with me.

Our blades sing in conjunction with the music, clanging metal ringing in my ear, a dispersed grunt from Councilor as he is struck in his side, a cry from Martyr as Kronklich lands a slice to his arm.

Each of us is lost in the passion of mortal combat. Trading blow for blow, bruised limb for bloody face.

Carnage rages through the chapel.

Pews tear apart.

Candelabras fall to the ground.

A piece of wood soars over my head while Vargus hacks away at Councilor, every missed swing connecting with furniture.

A chair.

A bench.

The precision behind Vargus' intent is clear and deliberate, graceful and destructive.

Distracted, Asher lunges for me, wicked dagger in hand.

Teeth clenched, fangs jutting from red lips, spit flies from his mouth as he taunts me. "How about that book, Wolfgang? Give it to me! Oblige your new masters!"

He stabs at the air where my shoulder was and lashes again in a quick spinning counter. I block his blade with Enivid and force his attack to the floor, catching the dagger in the crook of the handles. Clenching his hair with my free hand, I drive my knee into his face, splattering blood from his nose and mouth.

He crashes to the floor in a daze and gazes up at me as I raise Enivid to severe his head. But he smiles at me instead of cowering, vanishing from the spot in a burst of speed.

Damn it.

Across the chamber, Martyr does all he can to avoid the sinister attacks of Kronklich's cane sword. With each stab, strike, and swipe, Martyr moves faster than Kronklich can swing, blurring from existence at the last moments, appearing next to him consecutively, attempting to pierce Kronklich with his long black nails.

Dangerously close, they move towards the ensemble of singing boys until suddenly Martyr appears behind a boy and grasps him by the neck. He shoves the boy before him, using him as a shield. Kronklich's blade stops inches from the boy's neck as the boy cries out in fright.

"Still have a conscious," growls Martyr, tossing the boy aside. In a graceful cat-like maneuver, Martyr vanishes from the spot, swooping around Kronklich's backside and appearing over his neck with fangs extended. Kronklich raises his sword, countering Martyr as he bites down on the blade, enamel ringing from the contact. The frustration resonates from Martyr's sunken gaze as Kronklich pulls the blade free, slicing through the dry papery skin.

Blood seeps from between Martyr's fingers as he holds his mouth, cursing Kronklich while retreating.

Another clang of metal rings behind me as Councilor and Vargus collide, their bodies like two great bulls of metal and leather, giant blades hacking away in the wavering candlelight. With overbearing power, Vargus raises Councilor from the floor, forcing him back in a great rush of speed. The act looks seamless as the motion propels them forward.

A loud crash shakes the foundation.

In the very space that the vampire and hunter occupied, now lies scattered splinters of wood, the large reinforced wooden doors, demolished.

"Councilor!" I shout, following after them through the newly created hole of destruction.

I enter the foyer, following the carnage of Vargus and Councilor's wake.

Tapestries ripped from walls. Rugs torn in half. Candelabras bent. The only thing left standing down the hallway are suits of armor, still as statues, those sentinels lying in wait for their command.

Shouts come from behind me as I turn to see Martyr burst from the chapel doorway with terrible speed, frantic in his maneuvers, Kronklich right behind him, assaulting with crossbow in hand. He fires continuous shots, grazing Martyr's shoulder and arm as they go.

In what seems a last attempt to escape, Martyr bursts through a stone wall and disappears beyond crumbling darkness. Kronklich's rage carries him forward, grabbing a torch from the wall and giving chase into the newly formed tunnel.

It is a game of cat and mouse.

"No Kronklich! Wait!" I warn, but the man does not hear me. He is lost to the hunt, his lifetime nemesis fleeing before him.

Dammit. How many times had he saved me from losing my own head? And now he's not listening to me.

Torn between following Kronklich or Councilor, I know Councilor is the one in need the most. He is outmatched by Vargus.

Looking down the hall, I see Councilor who has nowhere to go. He is the hunter now hunted, a wild boar trapped within man-made walls. Although his scythe is the size of Vargus, Vargus's sword is larger still.

I dash from the spot, charging forward to meet Vargus head on, but something lashes out in my direction, stopping me from advancing. Jumping back, a long metal poleaxe whizzes by my head. I back into a stone pillar as another axe comes soaring at my face. Ducking, I roll across red-carpeted floor and recover my stance with bated breath. It appears I have a new obstacle. The suits of armor have come to life.

Standing seven feet tall and made of full-plated steel, the suits groan and squeak with the slightest movement. Lethargic and bulky, they swing medieval weapons one at a time, attempting to pulverize the soft tissue of my body into doughy bread.

Are they ghost entities trapped inside golems, like the caretakers I've seen before, or something entirely different?

Behind them, I see Councilor struggling to match Vargus. They exchange blows, slamming each other into walls and demolishing tapestries until eventually, Councilor is thrown against the front doors of the cathedral, breaking open a large hole to the outside.

Gray sinewy hands reach through the gap trying to reach Councilor as he fights for his life. Yellow eyes—cyclop eyes—leer through the holes. Sharp teeth gnaw gashes in the wood. In a matter of seconds, bogarts shred apart the doors and pour through the threshold like ants, growling and drooling, willing to eviscerate anything in their path.

"Tenor!" yells Councilor as he pulls away from the door, a bogart's claws ripping the sleeve and flesh of his arm. He spins on the spot, swiping his black scythe up and severing the bogart's head.

Vargus brings his blade down again with ferocity, knocking Councilor to the floor like a child.

He's toying with him.

Tucking left, then right, two more poleaxes miss me, glancing off my leather armor as I race forward, a flask of holy fire in my hand. Lobbing it over their reach, it travels the length of the hall and smashes against the wall above the door, exploding into a twirling inferno of flame. Bogarts howl as the fire splashes over their skin, spreading across the floor, forming a temporary barrier between themselves and Councilor.

Startled by the sudden glare of light, Vargus appears more agitated by my actions and raises his sword to bring it down on Councilor once again.

Enivid leaves my hand, colliding with Vargus' sword mid-strike. The ricochet of metal rings loud as Enivid arcs its way back to me, landing in my palm just in time to dodge another suit of armor.

The distraction is enough.

Councilor connects his scythe with Vargus' leg, piercing it through the trunk of his thigh. The vampire hisses and howls like a wolf, gripping the blade with his hands, unable to pull it free. With no possible way to stop him, Vargus explodes into a frenzy of bats, scattering about the room in a dark mist.

Councilor falls forward from the sudden change in weight, flopping to the ground helplessly. I am unable to reach him in time as I watch him struggle, vulnerable and prone. Asher appears from the shadows, dagger in hand. With a sinister bloody grin, he thrusts the blade into Councilor's back.

There is nothing I can do. The moment unfolds in slow motion. I scream, unable to contain my emotion, the hatred I feel at this moment. A sharp pain ignites the side of my head as I am struck to the floor, a loud ringing in my ear growing louder and louder. Falling with a thud, metal suits of armor pin me down as I strain to see Councilor.

The effect is instantaneous.

Councilor's body spasms from the shock, the dagger protruding from his back.

No sooner does he react, does he stop shaking, crouching back onto his legs and swiping his scythe at Asher as he trips him, forcing Asher to the ground, Councilor rams the tip of his weapon through Asher's skull with a sickening crunch.

"It will take a lot more than your little knife to kill me," says Councilor, finishing off the vampire with a black stake to the heart.

Asher erupts into flame, squealing like a child.

Councilor staggers to his feet, bloody fingers slipping on the dagger he can't reach; falling to his hands and knees again, he pants aloud.

With ringing still in my ear and vision blurred, it's impossible for me to do anything except babble under my breath. "Councilor… Councilor, behind you…"

Somehow, someway, Councilor must hear me. I see him looking at me from the distance, blood seeping from his teeth, a stupid grin on his face. In a sudden burst of speed he turns on the spot, lashing out with his scythe firmly in hand.

But it is no match for Vargus. He is too strong. Too quick.

Now materialized into human form again, Vargus holds Councilor's scythe with one hand like a twig, lifting him off the ground like a snared rabbit. In a single motion, Vargus thrusts his sword through Councilor's chest, tearing open his back in an explosion of gore.

Councilor's eyes widen in shock as he gasps for his last breath.

CHAPTER XXIX

DORIAN

Iron breaks through flesh.

Iron breaks through bone.

I cry out in pain as my body begins to spasm.

I flinch at the sight of movement. Shadows pass alongside me moving with purpose.

Memory of it all is like the ticking hands of a clock. Something that takes your breath away. The plunging into an icy river head first…

How do I begin to describe the pain? How does one explain mutilation? Metal spikes ripping through your hands. Dulled tips of raw metal seeking the least path of resistance. One can't explain it really; I am doing it no justice.

I try to block the sound—the ringing in my ear—but as the next spike pierces my other hand, I can no longer hold it in.

Agony has taken me, so I scream.

It is a suffering I cannot explain.

The mighty pain I feel. Such terrible pain.

My vision wavers in and out of focus as I hear Faeradon's voice echoing through the chamber. Was this what he spoke of earlier? Purging the old Dorian?

Blood trickles down my hands and arms, pooling into puddles of crimson at the elbows. *They're going to drain all of my blood. Then what?*

Organ music hovers in the air. Its tones vibrate in the walls penetrating deep into my soul, caressing me, possessing me. I want the sinister music to stop, but at the same time I want it to continue. Is that choral music I hear? Children singing along with it? What sort of sad state had I reached? Delirium has taken me. *Oh dear God, keep me strong!*

"Mother!" I cry out on the table, choking back the dryness of my parched throat. "Mother!" I rasp again with less momentum, the energy draining from me, my lifeforce—my essence—seeping away from my self-awareness. Where will I go once I leave this place? Will my mother be waiting for me on the other side? So many questions. They are, at the moment, my only distraction, my only salvation.

"Mother—" My mouth is stuffed with sticky cloth before I can finish calling out to her.

"Oh would you quit your incessant whining!" comes Faeradon's voice. "It will soon be over, Dorian. Pain is just a temporary bliss, a nirvana sought after by far worse chosen ones other than yourself." Faeradon's face appears before mine. "Just think," he says, his rancid breath kissing my nostrils, "This entire tower was built off the backs of acolytes who would give everything they had for one more blessing from God. Dying in the name of

God, serving in the name of God! Bah!" Fareadon races across the room and grabs an edict by the robes. "This!" he shouts, waiting for my full attention, "is what it's all for!"

He shakes the edict violently, striking him in the face, and throwing him to the ground. Immediately the edict bows as if grateful for the thrashing. "Ha! You see, my dear boy, there it is… power. It is all around us for the taking!"

There is a burning fire in Faeradon's eyes. I try to scream again, but the cloth stuffed in my mouth forces me to choke. Instead, I whimper. Tears stream down my face and now Faeradon is back on me, wiping them away with his long fingers, scratching my skin in the process. He caresses me in a sick fatherly way.

"There, there, Dorian. No need to cry. Soon you will forget all of this like a bad dream to be tucked away forever. Soon you will have great power, great power like the rest of us. But we have to be patient, don't we, Dorian? That's a good lad."

Faeradon nods to an edict and suddenly I feel burning pain around my ankles.

"Let the ritual begin."

Chanting all around me fills my ears with both deep and high tones. My legs become taut, stretching and stretching more as if on a rack. Rope rubs the flesh raw at my feet and my impaled hands strain under the tension. If I strain or pull any harder, they will rip from the metal anchor.

The pain is unlike anything before. Unreal. I want to scream but can't. The rough texture of the gag in my mouth along with my own spit, chokes me.

My mother appears. Hovering above me like an angel of light. Her mouth is moving but I can't hear her. *Be strong Dorian.* The words form on her lips. *Be strong.*

I'm trying mother, whirls my thoughts, *but the pain! The pain is too great!*

My feet squirm uncontrollably.

"Hold him still," seethes Faeradon through parted lips.

A shorter figure moves past the vampire priest and grips my ankles aggressively, forcing my feet flat to the cold slab, one overlapping the other. Charles smiles back at me, his eyes wide in awe and fear, brown curls bouncing around his brow. "That's it, my lord. Don't fight it…"

What did he just call me?

Raising a hammer high, an edict drives an iron spike through my feet, spattering Charles' glowing face with blood. The sound is deafening, the pain, impossible. I am too weak to respond, too drained to react. I am arrested in pain. Chained with torment.

My mother's hand caresses my cheek. It brings warmth back to my cold dying face. *I love you, Dorian. Be strong.*

"Now it is time," says Faeradon, raising his hand before me and then above his head. "Blood of the father."

Something floats out of nowhere and lands in his hand. His gaze never leaves my naked body. A vial of some sort. A long needle protruding from the top. Down it goes into my chest. The impact takes away my sobbing breaths, replacing them with sharp gasps. The red vial drains. All of it goes into me. There is a rush, a surge of intensity.

Faeradon flicks the contraption away and places one hand on my chest while the other caresses my face. "Blood of the son." His smile reveals fangs beyond his parted lips.

Again he raises his hand as another vial lands in his palm. "Blood of those dead and gone." With a sharp intense look, Faeradon drives the needle into my chest a second time. The pain is quick and precise, forcing a gasp from me. This liquid is not warm like the last. This liquid is ice, piercing the depths of my soul.

My vision wavers again. I am in and out of consciousness.

Be strong.

Both of her hands are holding my face now.

I am strong, mother. I love you.

"And now for the stone that purifies all things." Faeradon beckons with a flick of his wrist. An edict appears beside him, goggles over his eyes to block the intense light emanating from the sun stone. Faeradon stares at it with a look of triumph on his face. With it clamped in both hands, the edict lowers the stone over my exposed stomach, the heat coming from it already burning my skin.

There is a pause as the edict gazes at the stone, then at me, then Faeradon.

"Do it!" shouts Faeradon. The manic look on his face is diabolic. Sinister. He strikes the edict in the back of the head, forcing him forward, driving the sun stone into my flesh.

The heat is unbearable as it burns my skin.

The cloth falls from my mouth and I scream.

I scream and I scream until the cords in my throat become raw. There is blood in my mouth and I scream again.

I sense the last of my thoughts and feelings—driven away.

Somewhere far away.

Another time, another place.

I watch the stone burn a hole into my stomach while Faeradon looks down upon me like a holy priest of God, hands raised before him, clutching the air, long fingers rigid like claws. And behind him, just beyond his shoulder, my mother, the white glow of her figure obvious, smiling as she always does, waiting, proud of her son who is supposed to be strong.

I am strong, mother. I am strong…

… and then I am gone. To another place. With them. The place where I grew up. The high walls of Wolfgang Manor. Corn and squash in the fields. Pumpkins on the stone walls. Cool summer nights where we picnicked under the stars, the cool stream in the distance trickling its song of tranquility.

Kronklich and Joachim.

Mother and Father.

Everything is as it should be and that is alright by me.

CHAPTER XXX

WOLFGANG

WORDS CANNOT EXPRESS THE EMPTY void in my heart.

Councilor.

My friend. My companion.

Now dead.

His lifeless eyes sparkle in the torchlight.

Then my thoughts dwell on Winter.

Poor Winter.

Fatherless. Alone in the cruel world. Already fated to a doom none could understand. The choice she never had.

Furry and passion fill me. It's here again, burning within me. Channeling through Enivid. Pulsating in my glowing hand.

Councilor was my savior and mentor. The one of darkness who showed me the light. The one who plucked me from the depths of the snow in that evil forest. Kronklich and I were left for dead, yet he saved us.

Councilor is gone from the world now. Brought into this vampire mess because of *me*. In the end it is I who brought his doom. Here in this terrible place of unholiness. This *Dark Cathedral.*

Now all I can do is set things right.

Fire rages inside me. Passion and hatred grows with each passing moment, each beating of the heart, my heart.

Straining my head back and forth, I watch Vargus as he approaches. His massive sword, the one used to kill Councilor now weighs through the air. A pendulum seeking a new victim.

Standing above my body, Vargus does not smile or grin, smirk or laugh.

No. There is something much deeper in those eyes. The stare that will burn a hole through your body.

Loyalty. Sense of duty. The Carnalreesee's ties go deeper than I could ever imagine.

The sword comes down and I summon love, passion, and revenge. I break free of the suit of armor's grasp, pulling its body over me, deflecting Vargus' attack. The blade penetrates the metal, piercing it through, stopping it short just enough to prevent the sword from reaching me.

In a furious rage, Vargus retracts the sword, snarling like a dog and brings the massive weapon down again wanting nothing more than to split me in half.

I roll away as the blade slams the ground. Sparks and chunks of stone scatter across the floor. Jumping back onto my haunches, I slice through one of the poleaxes with Enivid, breaking the shaft mid-way. Catching the broken end with my free hand, I drive the splintered piece into Vargus's shoulder with no effect, his red armor splintering the wood like fragile glass.

With a grunt, Vargus heaves his sword from the ground like a lumber jack and smashes through the suits of armor recklessly, attempting to cleave me in two. A brief moment warrants an opening and I strike, piercing his side with Enivid, right through his blood armor. He lets out a sound that almost sounds human and pulls away, gripping the newly formed hole with his hand, attempting to staunch the liquid fire pouring from it.

Eyes blazing red, teeth barred in hatred, he hisses at the air around him and transforms into a cloud of bats, passing from the room with great speed.

All at once, I collect myself, pushing pieces of armor and weapons from me as I navigate through the piles of junk scattered across the floor. *I can't let him escape.* I give chase, following the mass of bats from the foyer hall back into the chapel room, passing the giant hole where Kronklich went after Martyr.

Kronklich. Where is he? What has become of Martyr?

A loud crash from the other room forces me forward.

Kronklich is fine. I just know he is.

The chapel room is in chaos.

Music no longer plays from the choir and organ. The boys are scattering. The organist rises from his bench, disappearing down the back at the far end of the room. Having transformed to human again, Vargus staggers across the room, crashing through black wooden pews, casting the boys in his path out of the way.

He is weakening.

"Vargus!" I shout, leaping over upturned benches and fallen candelabras.

Sword dragging behind him, Vargus doesn't look back. It seems the slightest distraction will cost him. Smoldering blood trails behind him as he continues on, moving towards a hallway beyond the chapel, a hallway leading up.

Growls erupt from the deep. Up from the passageway we ascended when we first arrived in the chapel from the aqueducts and dungeons.

The bogarts. They have breached the portcullis.

I throw Enivid to slow Vargus' retreat, but the whirling blade deflects off Vargus' massive sword lifted behind him like a shield.

"Out of the way!" I plead as I push through the choir boys as if they were ants. Within seconds this place will be swarming with bogarts. "You need to get out of here! All of you! Now!" But my warning falls short. The boys do not hear me over the growls and screams pouring through the archway. They are distracted. The gray sinewy bogarts flood the chapel room. Yellow eyes and sharp teeth. They tear through the room, eviscerating the helpless young boys all the while to get to me. It is me they want. The intruder. The hunter.

I run after Vargus as the bogarts hone in on me. "All of you need to get out of here! Fight if you can! Live!"

A boy to my left is tackled as I cut the head off a bogart to my right. "Run, dammit!" I push one of the choir boys out of the way as a bogart slams into me, its claws tearing open the front side of my leather coat, exposing the leather plate underneath. With a jagged cut, I dig into the bogart's chest like a piece of meat. The creature falls to the floor in a dying gurgle as two more rush towards me.

All of us run in a group from the chapel. Reaching a set of stairs, we pass into the hall Vargus disappeared beyond. As I wait for the last of the children to run past me, I kill two more bogarts in the process, sweeping Enivid in a deadly arc, thrashing my surroundings with precision. "Go, go, go!" I continue shouting as the thickening mass of creatures gather at the base of the stairs.

Vargus is no longer in sight yet I cannot abandon the boys. Reaching for the last flask of holy fire on my belt, I hold it above my head with anticipation as Enivid returns to my hand.

Steady.

I stab a bogart to my left as it leaps for me.

Steady.

I sever a head and a leg to my right.

My body is heating up. I feel sweat underneath my armor collecting in pools at the small of my back. Heavy breathing. Muscles aching.

Now.

Lobbing the flask directly above me, I retreat from the spot, running as fast as I can, slicing through another bogart in my escape.

A huge fiery explosion ignites behind me as I turn to protect myself from the heat. My face aches and my hand tingles. The everlasting nightmare of fire will never leave me. I dive through the opening at the summit of the stairs as flames shoot through the archway. Bogarts squeal and burn as yellow light fills the previous hallway. Children running, Vargus ahead of them all.

No time to stop.

The children scatter in all directions seeking sanctuary as I continue pounding the ground, each footfall heavier than the last. I watch Vargus use anything and everything to his advantage, bouncing off of edicts in their red tunics and black boots, tossing them in my direction. "Stop him!" Vargus shouts, running past a massive stairwell that leads up into a circular dome.

Some of the edicts, confused and disoriented, run away like the children, while some live up to their master's desire. Sliding and ducking past an edict's axe midswing, I follow with a strike to the back, bringing the edict down in one mortal swoop. Another approaches from the distance and I throw, rage and disgust guiding Enivid into the edict's chest, painting the ground in bloody streaks. Pressing ever forward, Enivid lands back safely in my hand, and I notice the area before me is momentarily clear.

Stopping at the base of the great stairwell, I look up into the vast enormity that is the endless tower, the tower which rises into the clouds of the Dark Cathedral. I know at the top of the tower lies the ritual chamber, the place where Faeradon conducts his holy sermons. But I know those days are no longer, the rituals, now unholy and full of vampires. It, along with everything else in this place, is a lie.

Shouts and commotion come from another door across the great hall and so I follow, my only guess is that Vargus went this way.

In what seems a vast mess hall of long tables, chairs and plates, the room is full of edicts and boys dressed in white robes scattering about, dropping plates of food and running for the closest doors nearby. At the center of it all, Vargus tramps across the table tops, moving in the most direct line for the set of double doors at the far end of the chamber. Still holding onto his massive sword with one hand, with his other, he motions to his sides, sending edicts and boys alike sailing from the table. "Move you fools! Out of the way!" Daring a look over his shoulder, the sight of me puts him on edge and he begins flicking things my way. Plates. Chairs. Humans. It does not matter.

Following in the wake of his direct path, I too run across the tables, jumping from one to the next, sending bowls of porridge and plates of vegetables scattering through the air and across the floor. Leaping over two edicts, their hands up in defense, I hear Vargus grunt in frustration as he again flicks his hand aggressively. One of the tables, plates and all, lifts from the ground with unseen force and flies in my direction, nearly colliding with me just as I leap from my current table. Wood crashes into wood in a great exploding mess. Mass hysteria breaks out as the entire mess hall is filled with moving bodies like molecular atoms.

"Vargus!" I shout uselessly, trying to distract him anyway I can, but another edict comes at me, breaking me off from such an attempt. Some of them are still loyal, still trying to debilitate me, so I respond.

In seconds, I clear the hall with my face bloodied from the entrails of edicts.

"Vargus!" I scream again just as he reaches the base of a narrow spiral staircase.

Vargus holds onto the banister as if too weak to go on, but at the sound of my voice, his sharp eyes hone in on me like a vulture. Pushing himself off the railing with one hand, he uses his large sword to balance himself upright and separates into hundreds of bats once again.

"No!" I cry uselessly as the bats disperse up the stairs effortlessly. Reaching the base of the stairs, I have just enough time to watch the last of the bats vanish over the railing high above me.

There must be a hundred steps.

Panting, with sweat dripping down my face, I dig deep, pleading with my muscles.

Just a little more, Tenor. Just… a little more…

CHAPTER
XXXI

My muscles are on fire.

With my last step planted, I throw my momentum forward, plunging onto the landing riddled with boulders and rubble. A large expanse of wall, crumbled and fractured, opens into a chamber of brilliant light. Blood trails from the steps and passes through the opening, evidence Vargus went this way. It brings a smile to my face.

The bastard has nowhere to go now.

Sparks of electricity arc above as I enter a room that appears to be a laboratory of some sort. Metal conduits run along the ceiling while shelves of books line the walls. A stone dais lies in wait across the room like a lonely child waiting for attention. Beakers filled with discolored liquid rest on a table along another wall and it is here where my eye falls on Vargus propped up, resting. There is no doubt the bastard is dying. But it is not mercy or lack of conviction that stays my hand from finishing him off at the moment. It is the numerous black bolts scattered about the chamber that concern me.

From across the room, behind a shattered bookcase and broken table, Kronklich and Martyr rage in an unending exchange of furious blows. Kronklich's cane sword. Martyr's hideous nails. Black bolts protrude from Martyr's back like a pincushion while Kronklich's appearance is that of a bloody face and torn coat, as if shredded by a rabid cat.

"Ah, Tenor!" shouts Kronklich. "You made it! All is well here." He berates Martyr blow after blow. For now, it seems Kronklich has the upper hand, tormenting his long lost enemy with sword cuts to the face, chest and arms. But a sudden misstep on a loose book and Martyr gains the upper hand, parrying Kronklich's advance, slicing his shoulder in the process. "Nggghh!" groans Kronklich in pain.

Immediately I step forward to intervene, but jump back just as quick as a large sword passes in front of my face, nearly caving my head in. Vargus' blade is poised for the next strike. "Look around you, vampire hunter. You're too late." Vargus' deep voice chuckles. His lungs sound full of blood. "Time has run its course."

"Has it?" I say in response. His words are meaningless to me. A farce. Vampires are notorious liars and will say anything to gain the upper hand.

I lunge, grazing the red armor of his right shoulder. Vargus swings and I counter, parrying the flat of his blade before hitting the same spot again. Enivid glows with light as it penetrates the metal, burning through it like hot magma.

Vargus groans in pain as Enivid cuts deep, gouging another fiery hole into the vampire's body.

I follow through with a boot to his chest and send the giant skidding across the pebbled floor.

"Martyr," gurgles Vargus. He squirms about the floor, blood pooling from his mouth in a steady stream.

"Can't you see I'm a little busy?" responds Martyr, his tone, not the least bit concerned. He catches Kronklich's blade with his scissor-like nails and sends the weapon flying away. "Incredible, Vargus!" continues Martyr, "You couldn't ask for my help at the worst time, could you?" His hollow face turns to me and smiles. "No matter though. I've been waiting for my chance at the wolf for a *very... long... time.*"

"Watch out, Tenor!" warns Kronklich.

Martyr vanishes.

With pure instinct, I react, whirling Enivid defensively. Vampires that move this fast are unpredictable.

Martyr's shadow moves about the room, jumping from one spot to the next. His essence approaches and I parry. Sparks fly. He moves in again then retreats. It feels like he is all around me at one time and then suddenly his long nails are inches away from skewering my face. Holding my wooden stake just above his heart, it is the only thing preventing Martyr from killing me.

"You think you're so clever don't you?" Martyr hisses and vanishes again, lunging at me a second time. Silvery white blades spark against razor black talons. The contrast glints like treasure in the electric lights.

"So long I've wanted to kill you, Wolfgang," says Martyr, teasing with his steps, "But my master commanded me otherwise. There's always been such a big plan for you, waiting and waiting. Yet here we are, and you're still alive, and you've managed to kill all of the Carnalreesee. My brothers and sisters. Why is that?" He pushes his hand closer, forcing his nails and my blade to scrape even more. "I'll tell you why," he says tapping his forehead. "It's because I work with fucking idiots!"

Martyr shakes his red hair violently, forcing the waves to bounce about his shoulders like fire. He advances again, one step at a time. "No more waiting, Wolfgang! No more dancing! No more bullshit!"

Martyr crosses his arms and fans his nails, posing like a cobra. Just as he moves to strike, a bolt enters his throat. Confusion spreads across his face.

Blood spurts from Martyr's mouth as he tries to speak, but the words never come. He is shocked and dazed as he turns to Kronklich who is holding a black repeater crossbow.

Martyr begins shaking, his eyes flare red.

Kronklich doesn't wait. He fires over and over, sending three bolts into Martyr's chest. The vampire takes off with impossible speed, slamming into Kronklich with such a force, they hurl across the room crashing through wooden shelves, shattering beakers and glass tubes.

"Kronklich!" I move to help my friend, but a swift kick to my back sends me sprawling across the floor. Vargus comes at me again, hardly able to stand, steadying himself after every swing of the sword. He is relentless as he alternates his strikes from left to right, rotating it before him like a crazed barbarian. Each miss greets the floor with sparks and cracked stone. Each step is an attempt to cleave me in half. I try to avoid his direct path all together, but the amount of destruction in the room has left a wake of debris. I stumble over broken chairs and tables, landing on my back as Vargus's sword comes down. I twist to the side avoiding his deathblow and see an opening. I cut into both of Vargus's legs, bringing the giant beast down with a deafening crash.

Now standing over Vargus with Enivid in hand, the leather creaks as I squeeze the handle tightly. The vampire stares at me from the floor. His visage is cold and lifeless. No remorse for his actions. No regret for killing my friend. So much emotion has accumulated over these past weeks, I look down on him with hatred.

Channeling anger into Enivid is my salvation. Raising the holy weapon, I look upon Councilor's murderer one last time, "Die you son of a bitch," and drive the blade deep into Vargus' chest, piercing his armor and blackened heart, through and through.

The effect is instant. He ignites into burning flame and ash. All the years of his immortal life pass before my eye. His chiseled chin, his perfect cheeks, wither to wrinkles, then to bone, then to dust.

Pulling Enivid from pieces of bone and smoldering ash, I rush to Kronklich's aid. He struggles to collect himself from the debris.

"Where is he?" I ask Kronklich, helping him stand.

He is disoriented, wobbling on his legs as he tries to regain his balance. "Tenor, be careful... Martyr lurks somewhere close. Watch out..."

Kronklich pushes me out of the way just as Martyr appears, his eyes red with the vision of hunting. "Ahhhh!" cries Kronklich as Martyr's black talons pierce his arm.

Immediately I attack with Enivid, bringing the blade down over my head. Martyr catches my wrist with his grotesque fingers. Face to face, he smiles, blowing his bloody breath on me before head-butting my forehead.

A flash of light and I stagger back. Enivid falls from my hand as I am disoriented.

Martyr is on me before I have a chance to react, knocking me to the floor. Striking me with his fists, he attacks without mercy, pummeling me with ferocious strength. His nails gouge deep holes into the thick leather of my bracers. He bites down, clamping onto my arm with his fangs. The armor holds for now, but for how long, I'm not sure.

I bash Martyr on the side of the head with my fist until he releases. Exchanging blows, he does the same to me, beating me like a straw dummy. More stars. More flashes of light. I feel blood flowing off my face from all the lacerations as he continues his assault. I do all I can to keep myself conscious. His blows are like the iron hammers of a blacksmith.

"I'm going to mangle your brain into mush—" says Martyr, striking me again. He stops mid punch and opens his hand, smiling and pointing at me like a child, "—but first I'm going to give you scars to match the other side of your face."

His nails grow longer and thicker and soon I am staring down black talons ready to carve my skin. "Sorry, but this will hurt a lot—"

Blood sprays my face as Martyr's chest bursts open, a sharp blade jutting through it, red and raw. His hands freeze. His arms freeze. The look of absolute horror begets his face.

Enivid has pierced his heart.

I am in a state of shock myself as I watch Martyr attempt to remove the blade. But the blade is slippery and wet, and retracts quicker than he can recover.

In one quick motion, Kronklich severs Marytr's head, sending it tumbling to the floor. Kronklich stands over Martyr's burning remains holding Enivid before him in awe. A look of undeniable satisfaction fills his visage.

"We did it, Tenor. We avenged my parents. Retribution is served!"

CHAPTER XXXII

"James," I say, barely breathing. "What have you done?"

Standing before me, Kronklich braces Enivid firmly in his hands, a look of triumph on his face. Lowering the weapon, he looks to his wounded arm and shrugs his shoulder. "What, this? We've been through worse haven't we?"

But he has no idea. No clue to what I am referring to. How could he? I never told him about the book under my breastplate, the journal of Marcus Cornelius, the knowledge it possesses. A chilling thought possesses me. Kronklich may very well share the same fate as me now.

Immortality.

Although the notion is terrifying and horrific, it is also comforting at the same time. Maybe I won't be alone in this world after all, when all others have died.

"What, Tenor? What is it?" asks Kronklich.

"It's nothing, James."

Noise around us rises in great waves. Growls and screams. Sounds of the dying. Screeching bogarts. And yet another sound reverberates from across the chamber.

Banging from beyond the walls. Stone crumbles from a blasted wall.

I look around and come to understand more and more my surroundings, where we *really* are. And then all at once it dawns on me. The hidden laboratory, the secret place Councilor spoke of. There is the broken wall, the original entrance that was sealed to hide the forbidden practice. The place where we would find the cure to vampirism.

But there is no cure. This I now know.

"Tenor, where is Councilor?" asks Kronklich.

The question hits me like a ton of stones. I knew it was coming, but nothing could prepare me for it.

Thoughts of Councilor brings pain to my joints. I have no words to share that will do the great man justice. My look of silence says it all.

Numb. Empty. I stare at Kronklich shaking my head. There is no need for words. Kronklich will understand. He has to, no matter how devastating the news is. It's always been this way. Casualties of the job. But I see it affects him more than usual. I know it, because I feel the same.

"Here," says Kronklich, handing Enivid back to me. A solemn look has clouded his face. "There is still work to do."

"Indeed." I give him that look of knowing. That look that says, *I understand your pain.*

Glancing about the chamber, the carnage is all too real. Everything is destroyed, broken beyond usefulness. But as my gaze lands across the room, there is something I didn't notice before and my heart fills with dismay. Tucked away along a far wall near the dais, lays a stone table fitted with broken restraints and rope. Iron spikes protrude from the surface stained with blood. A stone the size of my hand, dull and devoid of any real color, rests at the center of the table.

"No," I say under my breath.

They were here. He was here!

"No, no, no!" I begin losing my grip on reality. "Dorian! Dorian!" My surroundings seem to close in on me and tunnel vision engulfs me like a sickness.

Kronklich is at my side. "What is it, Tenor?" but his question is answered with my gaze at the sacrificial table.

Banging ensues from across the room.

"Whatever is beyond that rubble has every intention of coming through," warns Kronklich glancing over his shoulder.

But his words are useless to me as I lean on the bloody table with both hands. The scent of metal lingers in the air.

All the Carnalreesee we've killed. Caesar, Constilla, Constable, Scepter, Vargus, Martyr. This insane hunt for my son. What was it all for? A waste. An absolute fucking waste. In the end, they got what they wanted. Faeradon got what he wanted. My boy. My poor boy. I have failed you and your mother. For that, I am a failure.

Kronklich shakes me from my tunnel vision. "Tenor! They're coming!"

I throw his arm off. "Let them come!"

Skeletal hands break through the cracks in the rubble.

"Our time is spent here, Tenor! We must go find Dorian!"

"No," I shout in his face. "It's over James! Dorian is gone! Dorian is *dead*!"

Wide-eyed and teeth clenched, Kronklich grabs me by the harness of my proofing and shakes me, harder than ever before. "No, Tenor! You mustn't give up! Not here, not now! We've come too *far*. Dorian is alive! You must believe it! If not for my sake, then for the sake of *DIANA*!" His finger lands on Enivid.

Diana. Her name brings me back.

Heat builds in the palm of my hand. Enivid begins to glow with power. *She is here. She is telling me something.*

Dorian. It must be Dorian. He is still alive.

Across the chamber, the landslide of rubble explodes into an array of projectiles as countless caretakers funnel through the narrow opening. Their hallowed screeches accompany the swaying of glowing lanterns, back and forth, back and forth. They animate stiffly towards us. The growls and screams of the bogarts have reached their climax and they too emerge into the laboratory chamber, fighting past one another, blending with caretakers alike, wanting the first chance to devour our flesh.

"Quickly, Tenor! This way!" shouts Kronklich over the deafening tones of demons and monsters.

Blindly, I follow after Kronklich putting all of my trust into the man. My energy is spent. My thoughts are fatigued. Anguish and dread fills my every step, but love and hope shape my reality. Ever onward. *Ever forward.* It is my family that gives me strength. It is what powers my death strokes while the monsters catch up to us as we run. One by one they fall, and we slay them as we navigate the hallways out of the laboratory and into a maze of corridors.

CHAPTER XXXIII

MY MIND IS A RAGING storm.

A blur of worry and guilt, and Dorian… only Dorian.

My boy. What have they done to you?

I must find him.

I must save him.

Kronklich is here with me—*James*, bringing up the rear, firing away with his repeater crossbow, landing shots in bogarts' and caretakers' heads as they give chase.

The only thing I can think of, the only place I know they might have taken Dorian to is the top of the grand staircase. The ritual chamber. Up that long-winded tunnel of a thousand steps.

But the way forward is no more.

The means to get there is lost.

The Dark Cathedral is changing. Much like Egleaseon's ruins. It is not just a place. It is a *thing*. Something *alive*. The walls keep moving. The way is forward for a moment, then, by the mere turn of a glance, the way is blocked.

We are stuck going in serpentine circles. Behind every corner, new foes greet us. Vampires have entered the fray. Young ones. Old ones. Some are wearing the white robes of the choir boys.

Some are wearing the red and black of edicts. What has Faeradon done? What other atrocities have been committed here.

Our situation seems doomed, but we never stop. How much time passes, I am not sure, but the maze seems to go on and on and on and…

Glowing eyes in the dark.

Creaking metal. Blue flames swaying back and forth.

Caretakers.

They are coming.

There is not much light to see with anymore. The embers of our torches are dying. Soon darkness will consume us.

Then what?

There are no windows. No doors. Only more turns. More corners.

Something drops from the ceiling and I shove Kronklich out of the way. It strikes me instead of him. Latching onto my shoulder like a spider, its claws scratch the leather plate of my proofing. Its fangs extend and—

I drive Enivid through its mouth. The vampire twitches from the steel and bronze, igniting on contact with the holy weapon.

Incineration allows enough glow to light the hallway. There, beyond the edges of darkness, the caretakers make progress towards us. Like a platoon of marching soldiers, they stamp their feet and clamp their jaws. Sentinels to keep the corridors free of debris.

"Quickly! This way," shouts Kronklich. We maneuver around another bend.

Encased in total blackness, my eye is unable to pick out any discernible light. We are as good as dead in this abyss.

"James, I can't see anything," I say, reaching with my hand in the dark. A breeze blows from somewhere ahead of us. "Have any candles left? Torches? There is an opening. I can feel wind."

"No, nothing, Tenor," replies Kronklich. "Seems we have a bit of a dilemma, doesn't it?"

I can't see his face, but I know he is smiling, even in this dismal moment of time.

My hand traces the outline of a smooth protruding orb fitted with sockets and immediately flinching, I step back into Kronklich.

"What is it?" he asks.

"It's—it's nothing. A skull in the wall." I reach through the dark, fingering a different part of the wall.

"A skull in the wall—that's it, Tenor! Quickly now. Help me."

I see blue eyes floating in the distance. "Shit, they're coming—Help you with what?"

"Search! There must be a mechanism of some sort. A secret passage…"

Of course. If this place is anything like Egleaseon's ruins, then it would be riddled with secrets. I recall my escape with Bronin from the caretakers.

"If only we had some damn light—" I say, straining my eye in the dark.

As if on command, Enivid begins to glow from my hip. A white light. Diana's light. The lighthouse on the rocky shore. For a moment it is blinding.

"She continues to watch over you," says Kronklich with a wink.

Our faces glow like ghosts in the surrounding darkness. The outline of skeletons appear in the distance.

"Hurry now. No time to waste!" Kronklich's much needed optimism brings new life to our search. Manically, we test the few remaining skulls jutting from the wall and there is a click, a groan, and a wall recedes into stone.

"Brilliant," I say to Kronklich as he begins firing bolts down the hall.

"Yes, yes, good show man. Quickly now! Almost out of bolts—" and just as he speaks, the casing holding the last bolt flings from the crossbow chamber.

A caretaker enters our circle of light and Kronklich uses the empty crossbow to bash the skeleton apart. "Go!"

The secret door opens into a narrow passageway large enough to fit one person at a time. I look inside to see a ventilation shaft. Beams of light shine through cracks in the framework high above.

Has that much time elapsed? Dawn is already here.

Metal rungs lead the way of ascension, hundreds of them in a straight line, rusted and aged with time. As I begin climbing, the tunnel fills with the echoing noise of Kronklich's attacks and groans. Looking below, I see him struggling to keep the caretakers at bay, his wounded shoulder is slowing him down.

332 | F.D. Gross

"Kronklich!"

He climbs the first few rungs of the ladder and clubs another caretaker, shattering the crossbow. Bones and lantern explode at the bottom of the steps in a show of brilliant blue light, only to be replaced by another caretaker.

Kronklich stops climbing and removes a black cylindrical weapon from his coat.

One of Nicholas's pistols, Last Resort. Pointing it at the caretaker climbing up, Kronklich looks at me and smiles. "I've been waiting to use this thing. Go, Tenor. This riff-raff doesn't stand a chance. Find your son!"

There is a flash, a loud bang, and the caretaker's skull explodes. Gray smoke fills the ventilation shaft forcing me to cough. Kronklich coughs as well, holding fast his position.

"What are you doing?" I yell at Kronklich.

More caretakers swarm the bottom of the shaft. One of them starts climbing.

"No, James, don't!" I shake my head. "You're coming with me! That's an order!"

But my words fall short. There is no reasoning with Kronklich. A caretaker grabs his leg.

"Farewell, Tenor. Save your son."

A lantern breaks across Kronklich's back, and the blue gaseous light inside seeps from its prison. Kronklich's eyes suddenly glow blue and his demeanor changes instantly.

"Kronklichhhhh! NO!"

With a blank expression, Kronklich stares at me one last time, emotionless and empty, and rips the rung from the wall.

Was that intentional?

The force causes stones to break away from the foundation. The effect is an avalanche. Kronklich, caretakers, and stone, fall down the shaft, exploding into a great cloud of mortar and dust.

CHAPTER
XXXIV

I CLIMB FOR MY LIFE now. For Dorian's life. For all the lives I couldn't save.

Tears stream my face. They are rivers of anguish.

Every rung higher is an encounter of extreme emotion, extreme conflict. Between Diana, Dorian, and now Kronklich, the choice to continue on is a harrowing one. My internal battle is endless it seems. A war I cannot win…

The last few seconds of Kronklich's death play over and over in my head.

Demon possession. Eyes fading to blue. Falling to his doom—I fear the image will never leave me. It will plague me until the end times.

Whenever they come…

I rub grit and grime from my eye. It is hard to see in the smoke-filled ventilation shaft, the after effect of Kronklich firing his pistol.

Saliva fills my throat, coating it not from irritation or dryness, but from realization and pain. It saturates my thoughts of nothing but my friend. His final act. His final sacrifice.

My body shudders on the metal rungs of the ladder. I feel like a child, unable to hold on properly. Weak. Cold. Depressed.

Suspended high above, somewhere between heaven and hell, I wonder if I'll ever see either one. Ancient mortar and stone surrounds me in the shaft like an airy tomb. A grave high in the sky. Beams of light escape through cracks in the framework. I see through to the other side of the wall. There are—*clouds…*

Cold and shaking, I realize where I am, and the predicament seems ironic yet lucky. It's a cylindrical extension of the Dark Cathedral tower. Just on the other side of the wall, the great staircase awaits.

Wind whistles by as I push through the misery. The warmth of Enivid at my side is not enough to replace the cold empty void in my heart, the bristling hairs on my neck.

I struggle more and my muscles are fatigued. Gulping breaths of thin air, I hear voices over the shifting breeze. Faint weathered voices, like far away specters from the cemetery. Voices pleading for help. Voices pleading for *God.*

What on earth…

They line the tower wall, one stacked over the next. All the way up as far as the eye can see.

Acolytes. Tons of them.

They are in the walls.

No.

They *are* the walls. They are the foundation holding everything up. Higher than ever before. Sacrificed for a cause, but what?

I ignore the pleas and cries. I dare not look at their over-extended arms petrified like stone. Their cold faraway eyes. Contorted bodies. Warped teeth. Were they vampires at one point? How did they not know their fate? What power would drive them to throw away their lives?

I climb another rung. A strong breeze buffets my face, pushing the loose strands of my hair from my filthy cheeks. A hole in the wall profits me a chance to view the inside of the cathedral. Spatially, I take mental notes, placing myself somewhere far from the bottom and closer to the top of the stairs. I have a grand view of candles lining the staircase, the hundreds of steps leading up and down, spiraling around the giant hole in the center. "The well" is what they used to call it. With the sun rising in the east, the long windows are closed tight. Extravagant red curtains block any chance of light entering the tower.

A commotion echoes from below but the curve in the stairs prevents me from seeing anything. I lose focus and my body slips a little, forcing me to adjust my footing. My muscles tense on the rung, I strain to look again through the small hole. A young man in pristine white clothes runs for his life. Sword sheathed at his side, a tuft of wavy blonde hair, much like mine, bounces around his head as he keeps looking over his shoulder.

"Dorian!" I cry out, but my voice sounds like broken glass. "Dorian," I try again but I know it will not reach him. He couldn't possibly hear me. I am too weak and he is too far.

Something chases him. A larger figure, thin and gangly, wearing the religious regalia of the holy order, white on white trimmed in gold. The hat on his head and the braid swaying behind his back makes it unmistakably Faeradon, the Arch-bishop. Two boys in the same white attire follow closely behind.

Frantically running and limping, Faeradon carries a bloody dagger in his hand, his intent very clear. He stops before Dorian and motions for the two boys to move in. They maneuver around Faeradon, engaging Dorian, moving faster than any human child should. But Dorian seems ready for them. As the servant boys attack, Dorian raises his arms to protect himself and shoves them back with a feat of incredible strength. One of them tumbles down the stairs, hitting his head on a stone step while the other tries to stop himself from flying over the edge. But the boy screams the whole way down while Faeradon stares, unable to do a thing. In a burst of rage, Faeradon lunges at Dorian, growling, dagger poised to stab, but Dorian easily evades him, stepping back into one of the curtains.

He grips the fabric with his pale hands and I notice they are immaculate. No blemishes, no scars, no blood. In fact his entire being seems radiant.

I watch with pride as Dorian pulls the curtain, ripping it from the metal rings holding it in place, allowing the morning sunlight to cascade through a multi-colored, multi-faceted, stained glass window. Reds. Oranges. Purples. They fill the ancient tower with their colorful pallet.

Faeradon screams.

Paralyzed within the sunlight, Faeradon is unable to move and begins to burn. As he continues to scream, Dorian stands back, watching in wide-eyed wonder, smiling at his accomplishment.

Good work, my son.

Faeradon ignites into a fireball and crumbles to the floor, reaching for Dorian one last time before all movement ceases. With a swift kick, Dorian sends what's left of Faeradon's remains over the edge.

I call Dorian's name again and this time, he seems to hear me. He looks in my direction and smiles. That face, so much like his mother's, those eyes, dark and foreboding—like his mother's.

In that brief moment of acknowledgement, with my boy standing there in the glistening light of a rainbow, everything seems to be alright. All the things we worked for, the pain and suffering, the sacrifice and death, now seems worth it. I begin to tear up again, doing all I can to choke back the sobs in my throat.

But as I wipe the wetness from my face, Dorian takes off suddenly and runs up the stairs.

"Dorian," I mouth. "Dorian!" I call out after him, but my effort is useless. My voice loses anchor in the wind. And then he is gone from my sight.

What the hell are you doing? But the realization hits me before I finish the thought. He must be headed for the ritual chamber at the top. He must know something I do not. Again I can't help but feel pride for my son. What he's been through, and still he is trying to help.

I resume climbing the metal rungs. I need to get to him. Help him. He is following in the footsteps of the Wolfgang House. He is being resourceful. He is going to make an excellent hunter one day.

I am climbing forever.

Nearly spent, my trembling hands find a ledge and I pull myself up. Lying on my back, I take in as much of the thin air I can. Directly behind me, an old decrepit wall seems to have fallen away from overexposure to the elements. Pushing through loose stones and brittle bones, I come to stand on a narrow ledge on the inside of the tower, high above the stairs leading to the set of double doors at the top of the staircase. The only place Dorian could have passed through. Jumping down would surely break my legs. The only way forward is to clear the small landings to the final one at the top.

Glancing over the edge, the world spins round and round, a giant spiral of doom lingering before me. Suddenly, I don't feel well. Normally, heights like this wouldn't bother me, but with everything I've been through, coupled with the thin air, I feel I could easily faint.

I take a moment to collect myself.

Staring at the three platforms and the door, I take a deep breath thinking—*Dorian needs me*—and I leap.

My body floats through the air and gravity pulls me down. My feet hit solid stone. I do it again and clear the second with ease, but it is on the third one my weight seems too much for the ancient stone. Some of the foundation breaks away, cracking under foot. My balance wavers. I bend and leap and the platform snaps from the wall. Down the platform goes, tumbling through the air, colliding with the wall and smashing onto the staircase below.

Taking a shuddering breath, I back away from the ledge, touching Enivid at my side. "That was close, my love."

Heart pounding with anticipation, I turn around. Just on the other side of these red doors is the only thing that matters to me anymore.

The time has come to reunite with my son.

And the feeling couldn't be sweeter...

CHAPTER XXXV

EGLEASEON

So long it has taken for my plan to work. The great long wait within the realm of darkness. Oblivion. Endless oblivion. A place to think. A daunting period of nothingness. Waiting on the plane between then and now. A place of purgatory to reflect. No one to talk to. Hearing only my inner thoughts.

All this time so much has happened, and yet here within the Dark Cathedral, I never thought events would turn out the way they have. Perfection really. My servants were able to carry out their mission within a period of sixteen years—not long of a wait when compared to my thousands of years of existence.

But sometimes, even the most perfect of plans can never be executed without complications. Sometimes, there are kinks in the chain and fractures in the wheel. Sometimes the broken wheel must be replaced.

Faeradon.

Never did I anticipate the betrayal of my own kin. To think, Faeradon, after all this time, hundreds of years maybe, wanted me dead, so he could rise as the new supreme terror of the night. He tried to stab me to death on that hideous stone table, right after the transformation. The coward. His plan all along was to transfer my spirit and absorb my power.

What a fool.

He could have had it all.

The Carnalreesee were to join me in this new brotherhood of eternal light as well. But like all power-hungry beings, they became bloated off the benefit of others.

And to think, they *all* could have walked in the daylight.

Fools they are.

Imbeciles really.

No matter.

My new body feels good. Standing here, warming myself in the rays of a new dawn. It wasn't always like this. I remember centuries before, when the sun would drain me into a bumbling fool, weakening me to the point of uselessness. How I hated those times. Of all things, I, Lord of the vampires, envied humans. Jealous because they could enjoy the day and the night. Walk free like free men do. But now… now all of it is behind me.

I take a deep *living* breath. The sights, the sounds. The morning birds chirping. The crisp breeze blowing against my fresh skin. The hair on my arms bristling with delight.

Dorian my boy. You did well.

You were the perfect sacrifice.

You were the perfect vessel.

The groan across the room alerts me to the arrival of the one solely responsible for my success. It is he whom I owe thanks.

Tenor Alvadine Wolfgang.

He thought I didn't hear him shouting out in the hallway. He thought I didn't see him crying for me. But I saw Tenor in that last moment, in his pathetic state. Our eyes locked. The way he looked on at his boy, Dorian, his only living heir to the Wolfgang House. I must admit, it tickles me so. The bittersweet feeling I have at the moment is exhilarating. Tenor has made the ultimate sacrifice and doesn't even know it.

The battle of ages is won, and a new era births.

The era of the *Vestige*.

The ones who walked the earth thousands of years ago. Before the dawn of man. Before the dusk of vampire. There is only one other who could understand what has happened here, this passage of fate and time.

Marcus Cornelius.

He is the last remaining Vestige roaming the earth. He has gone by many names. Hector, Romeo, Asmodeous, Fadonius, Alazante, a great many more. I wonder what he would say if he knew what has become of me. I wonder if he would turn around and flee, or accept me as his brother. I—now have joined the ranks of the Vestige, a segment of the supreme beings who will walk the earth again.

And it is all because of this—I look upon the great pulsating sun stone, the god stone that pierces the center of the tower like a great spear from heaven, bathing everything in its red aura. Even now its sound penetrates the air, electrically charging the molecules all around me. My hair stands on its ends.

Tenor makes his way toward me. One of his eyes has been mutilated. The other is big and round and his intention is even larger.

Hope.

Resolution.

I've seen that stare before. In the many wives I've taken. In the many children I've sired.

Stepping down from the windowsill, I move to greet him in the center of the chamber, the sun stone pillar humming nearby.

Tenor crumbles to his knees. "Dorian... my son... my boy..." He can barely speak. He can barely walk.

I move closer, holding my hand out as a kind gesture, and sigh inwardly to myself, wondering what it must mean to love so deeply. A love that can never be broken. Something that can only come from family, pride, or—blood.

"... I'm so sorry... Dorian." Tenor begins to cry, nearly sobbing as he attempts to collect himself. "I tried... I really, really, tried... and I failed."

Placing my hand on his shoulder, I feel the intensity of his blood pulsating through the rigidness of his armor. Energy transference. Heat conveyance. And yet his blood I do not crave. The urge to feed is—*gone.* What a strange feeling. So fresh, so—*new.*

"I know you're tried, Tenor," I begin, "You did what you had to do. Like any father would."

Wolfgang looks up. A glint of hope bleeds through his disparity.

I look into his crystal blue eye. "Tenor, you did not fail. In fact, you succeeded quite well."

"Yes, I—wait... what did you say?" Wolfgang's forehead wrinkles slightly as his eye twitches. "Why would you say that?"

I smile, playing a little longer with this charade. "Because, this is not the end, Tenor. I knew I would see you again. This thought I had sixteen years ago and it has finally come to fruition. We are just at the beginning stages, you and I…" I watch his reaction of disbelief at the mention of his name again. My words are of convolution and impossibility, something out of place. Words his son would never say.

"We have a chance at a new life in a way we've never seen before. A new utopia of peace and prosperity, a new Eden of the highest order."

Slowly, Wolfgang backs away allowing my hand to slip from his shoulder. The look of realization clouds his face like a menacing shadow. Terror I've witnessed on so many occasions before lingers within that realm of Wolfgang's battle-worn visage.

I realize for the first time how dirty he is, how unclean, unshaven his skin looks. He is a mess all unto himself. His mutilated cheek and eye socket speak evidence of struggle. He certainly has been through a lot. Scrutiny and doubt flows from his expression.

Then the moment comes.

I see his every thought and every move.

Wolfgang realizes his son is gone for good.

That Dorian is replaced with something *else.*

And that something else is me.

Yes my friend. I, Lord Egleaseon, have changed.

I am no longer a vampire, a cursed immortal of the night.

I am a Vestige, an immortal, dare I say *God*, keeper of *day* and *night*, and all the rest of the days to come.

And I cannot die.

CHAPTER XXXVI

WOLFGANG

"It's... not... possible."

"Oh, but it is, Tenor. *It... is.*"

I stare at the embodiment of Dorian before me. My own flesh and blood, speaking to me, cold and distant. Life-*less*.

My mind races with questions, a storm rages with impossibilities. Who is this imposter? What happened to my *son?*

"There is no answer, is there?" answers a voice inside my head.

I grip the sides of my face, shaking back and forth violently, trying to cast it out.

That voice. Deep and foreboding. Conniving and sarcastic.

I remember it from long ago.

Egleaseon.

The one who took the Hand of God so willingly and forced me to watch him die. I remember the smile. That look on his face. It's the same as Dorian's now.

He can't be alive.

"It's... not... possible," I stammer again, looking at the back of Dorian, his golden blond hair blowing in the breeze.

"But it is," says Egleaseon's voice in my head again. *"Through the power of light and darkness, all things are possible. We can learn to overcome our greatest weakness. Mortality."* Dorian turns to me, pointing at Enivid in my hand. "Even you have overcome this greatest burden."

It is Dorian's voice that physically speaks to me now. The feeling is horrible. Confusing. What am I to believe? What sort of reality was this? I don't even know how to address the thing before me. It *is* Dorian's perfect form. Strong and resolute. Pure. Clean. But in spirit, I—

Are you still in there Dorian?

I shake my head, swallowing back the dryness in my throat. "Defeating mortality is not something I did willingly. I did not know using Enivid would make me immortal. How did you know?"

The embodiment of Dorian smiles and turns away. He begins walking towards the red glowing crystal at the center of the ritual chamber. "Your thoughts, Tenor. I hear every word of them. One of the gifts of the Vestige's immortal power. All-knowing. All-seeing."

Dorian stops before the giant crystalline pillar with his hands and arms spread before it. "The era of God has ended, Tenor. Don't you see? He has placed all of his power within this stone and left it here for humankind to use." Dorian pauses a moment and glances in my direction. "But humankind is weak. Isn't it, Tenor? Surely you know this by now. All the weak people you've had to save so they could move on with their pathetic simple lives. You know what I know, Tenor. Don't play stupid. You've seen it. God, has lost interest in this world. He has smirked at its vast oceans and shitted upon its rocky shores. He's moved on. The sun stone is proof of that." Dorian waves his immaculate hand about him like a professor teaching his student.

I don't know what to say or how to act. My soul feels empty inside. I have come all this way for nothing. Nothing to show for my actions. And for every second that passes, the feeling gets worse and worse.

"You are not empty," says Egleaseon's voice inside my head. *"You just haven't learned how to harness the power of light and darkness like I have. I cannot die. I am forever. Let me help you, Tenor. Let me guide you to the path that has opened for us. Let light and darkness fill you up and make you whole again."*

Light and darkness. I know them all too well. Sure they are here, right now for the taking. But there's something more that Egleaseon, or Dorian, or whoever it is I'm speaking to doesn't know. What *I* really know. What I've come to learn over the course of these past grueling days.

My hand finds its way to Enivid at my side and squeezes tightly. Love.

Love for Diana. Love for Dorian. Love for Kronklich. Love for Councilor.

If a Vestige *is* the embodiment of all power, harnessing light and darkness, and cannot die, then it would also know that love is part of that all power too, for no greater power can exist without the manifestation of love.

And Egleaseon knows nothing of love.

Which means he is not a Vestige—*and can be killed.*

CHAPTER
XXXVII

EGLEASEON

W<small>HAT A FOOL.</small>

He actually aims to kill his own son? His only begotten blood child, birthed from the womb of Diana, his betrothed, his dead wife?

Ha! What insolence! What resilience! Fool indeed! Seems things never change no matter the length of time.

Wolfgang comes at me strong. Somehow his strength is renewed. Stronger than ever before. As if something were guiding him from the other side. And his thoughts are blocked from my sight. *Where are you Wolfgang? What sort of mask are you wearing?*

No matter.

Drawing on the forces of light and darkness, the energy surrounding the chamber comes to me in great undulations. Empowering me. Light coming through the windows and darkness from the corners of the room. Unsheathing the sword from my side, I poise my blade before me letting the point glint in the dawn of the sun.

Our blades collide.

Wolfgang's face is close to mine as he clenches his jaw, the vessels underneath the skin bulge with stress.

Pushing himself off, he comes back again and again, driving his forward momentum into my body. With Dorian's body still in its smaller adolescent stage, Wolfgang's mass is twice the size of mine. Normally a match in strength like this would overcome the weaker, but I am anything *but* weak.

With a great pulse of energy, I send Wolfgang sliding across the floor of the ritual chamber, tearing up stones in his wake. And I follow right after him, bringing my sword down with power and speed, with every intention of killing him. If he will not join me, then there is no need for hunters like him to live anymore. They are a dying breed. He will be the last of them.

Our blades collide again and there are sparks.

I lean over him, pushing down with the might of a Vestige, but he still holds, grunting with resolve. He forces our blades to the side and kicks me in the face as he back flips to an upright position.

I can't help but laugh.

Warm blood trickles from my lip, yet there is no pain. As a Vestige, there is very little that can hurt me. It will take more than a kick to the mouth to bring me down.

"Even after all these years you still want to kill me." I laugh again as my words penetrate his thoughts. *"I am a changed man, Wolfgang. No longer am I infinite darkness. No longer do I drink the blood of the innocent. I have embraced the light. And yet still,*

you want to kill me. I thought you would have grown over the last sixteen years, Wofgang. Where is your change?"

"I will never change!" screams Wolfgang as he slices through the air. His blade is different. It is smaller than the Bawaka and a crackling energy trails its every move.

"So the hunter in you will never go away then. Truly you must be cursed for such a fate. Maybe our destiny is that one of us continues on without the other." Concentrating my energy into one place, my body begins to elevate from the ground. *"At least I can say that I tried..."* And with a great burst of speed, I launch myself into his body, tackling him through a stone pillar. Brick and mortar breaks apart, exploding into great plumes of dust above our bodies as we tumble through the debris.

I raise my sword and drive it downward toward his hateful heart. But this new blade of his deflects it with ease. Again and again, I attack trying to skewer him like a fish, but he catches my blade within the crook of his handles and twists, prying my weapon away like a stick.

Springing backwards, I reach with my free hand, summoning a loose stone to me. My power is strong. I can control everything around me. The power of light and darkness emanates from the sun stone at the center of the chamber. Its red light pulsates, amplifying me with greater strength.

I grin. The stone flies from my hand.

Wolfgang dodges it with ease then dashes for me, holding his four-pointed blade like a shield.

I summon more debris and send each piece towards him in a furious waves.

Each piece he deflects. Each of my attempts he evades. *"Just die already!"*

"Raaaaghhh!" screams Wolfgang as he leaps towards me.

My hands stop him in mid-air. The power surging through me is great. Invisible and unmatched.

Holding him in place, although I can no longer see or hear his thoughts, the anguish on his face is pure determination. He truly wants to destroy me. He is still defiant even though he is out-matched. What is it that I'm missing? What power is driving this man, fueling him to burn with such tenacity?

And then realization dawns on me like rays of the sun outside.

Of course. I should have seen it, but this new power is so intoxicating, so distracting.

Lowering my hands to my side, I release Wolfgang from the energy prison and watch him drop to the floor. He rushes towards me, ready to give me the death blow he so willingly wants.

"No father, please!" I say in Dorian's voice and Wolfgang stops, inches away from piercing my heart. The expression on his face is that of doubt and hope.

Of course. Just as I suspected. The power that drives him is also his weakness. Love. What did love ever do for anyone, or anything? Weakness is the only discernable reality that stems from it for it lets the walls down. Just another reason to cast it out. What did it ever do for me?... except bring pain and suffering...

My face turns to anger.

Seizing Wolfgang's wrist, I pluck the holy weapon from his hand and it responds with white sparkling energy, sizzling in my hand. It does nothing to me as I drop the useless thing to the floor.

Over and over, I strike Wolfgang's abdomen, pulverizing the very life from his body. Every strike splatters my face with blood. His blood.

He is gasping now. Gasping for life. Gasping for air. Gasping for... *love.*

"Allow me to show you what love is, Wolfgang." My eyes burn with hatred. *"Me, removing you, the last of the Wolfgang House, from this world..."*

CHAPTER XXXVIII

WOLFGANG

WHAT IS PAIN IF THERE'S nothing to live for. Nothing to show for it.

I gasp for air, but it's replaced with blood.

I am choking. I am dying. So this is how it ends. Dorian beating me to death. Fitting for everything I've done and everything I haven't. Dying by the hands of my son.

"No, Tenor. Our son would never do such a thing. He loves you too much."

The voice. It's not Egleaseon. It's been so long since I've heard it. Is it her... could it be?

"Curse you Tenor, I will always love you. I will be with you until the very end."

Diana. She is here. I manage a bloody smile. Oh the heavens, she is here!

"The shell before you is not Dorian, Tenor... it's not our son!"

The dark eyes before me burn red.

Of course. There is no love inside this semblance of Dorian. Only that which I've battled and hunted all of my life. Anger and hatred. Egleaseon. After all this time, he came back for me, but in a different form. He used Dorian to get to me. And now Dorian is gone forever.

Reaching with my hand, Enivid comes willingly, sliding along the floor without question or doubt. Diana. Love is forever with me. And it will never leave...

As much as it pains me, I drive Enivid into the heart of my son.

Dorian cries out in agony as Enivid pierces his body through and through, tearing through skin and breaking through bone. *The body we sired, Diana, is now the body we destroy. Together. Forever.*

Light and darkness issue from Dorian's body in a horrific current. Howling wind and burning fire rise above as I cling onto Dorian with all that I have left. His body shakes violently and I feel the energy disperse from his being, his voice no longer his as he screams, but someone else's entirely.

"Nooooo!" shouts Egleaseon as the storm continues to rage. "Nnnyyaaahhh!"

"My boy! I'm so sorry!" I scream, holding onto Dorian's body as tightly as I can, trying to prevent his life from escaping. "I will never let you go!"

But as the last of the energy disperses, Dorian's empty shell goes limp in my arms. Gently I lay him down, caressing his face and hair, wondering if he has found peace once and for all.

But my answer is silence.

It fills the room with a great void. *Nothingness.* And the quiet tones of being alone harbor my guilt, and anything left of my self worth. Gone forever will be the days of self-pity, for there is no one left to give a damn.

All manner of sounds surface in the tower—the wind whistling through the cracks, the creaking of the foundation stones, the ceaseless humming of the red crystal, pulsating, beckoning me. It wants to challenge me. But I turn my back instead and walk to the open window.

Looking out over the horizon of a new day, all is as it should be. The clouds that covered the top of the tower have dispersed. Snow and rain no longer falls in its cold drifts. The great city of Sunstone spreads out below, spanning as far as the eye can see. The great evil that plagued this cathedral is now gone and all the tiny little people below can go back to their lives like before. Like nothing ever happened.

It's as simple as that, isn't it? The people have been saved, yet everything I loved has been taken from me.

I step out onto the ledge, bracing the window with my arms. The cool breeze mixed with the sun hitting my face is a nice feeling. Seldom do I experience moments like this. Comfort and warmth and reprieve. If only I could feel like this always. But I know inside I will never be the same. I could end it right now and all the worries in the world would melt away.

It makes sense.

If I were to stick around, the vampires would hunt me for my blood in order to resurrect their fallen. Marcus Cornelius mentioned it in his journal, that every vampire I kill transfers its power to me. Every vampire I kill makes me stronger. I have become death's immortal keeper.

But what would the world do if I were to leave? Who would be left to take up my place? Surely other hunters could rise to the occasion, but who am I fooling? They would be slaughtered. The vampires would prevail and then…

Shivering from the thought, I back away from the window and turn around.

Standing before me is Diana, in all her glory, in her white glistening gown, peonies wreathing her head and arms. She's astonishing and I am astonished.

For the first time since her death, we embrace.

She feels so real. I can smell her hair.

How is it possible? Is it the sun stone? The God stone? I still hear it humming in the distance.

"I can feel you. You're so *real*."

"Because I am real, Tenor. I never left you."

"How… why… how is it possible?"

"Love, Tenor. *Your love.* It's what's kept us together all this time. You, me, little Edmund, and now… Dorian." Her smile is sad, but genuine.

My boy, Dorian, stronger looking than ever, steps out from behind her, holding a baby boy in his arms. The tuft of dark hair on his head is so much like his mother.

"How is he here?" I ask, bewildered.

"It is how things would have been, how you would have seen him. He was a blessing all the same."

"Edmund. I like that name." But where my happiness would have been if our lives were different, only tears stream my face now. My entire world has vanished in the blink of an eye.

"Diana. Please don't go. I already lost you once. Now you must leave again? Please. Not again."

"I never left, Tenor."

I feel her body, her spirit begin to drift from me. The forces of the unseen working against me.

"Diana… please… I'm begging. You hold the keys to my kingdom."

"I will never leave you, Tenor. Always, am I, with you." She moves to stand with our children. Our ghost children. The ones that will never have the chance in this world ever again to live with me, to know their father one more day.

The three of them look at me. All of them smiling, strong, and resolute.

Again the sound of the God stone humming in the background makes me flinch. It's because of that red crystal my woe has overcome me. *It* has forced me into this life of eternal damnation.

How long will I have to suffer in this world for the sake of others?

The calling inside me pulls, and I must answer. It is my curse to bear and no one else's. The stone to me is a nuisance. A pestilence on the land. It is something that should not exist at all, to linger as it has done for centuries upon centuries.

With Enivid in hand, I look upon it again and understand now why Dora named it what he named it.

Divinity.

The Divine.

Diana is now the light that will vanquish the night.

Running up to the pulsating sun stone, the pillar of light coated in the blood of thousands of innocents, I cleave the God stone in half at the place of its most vulnerable weakness.

The single motion is enough. Resolve is the fulcrum of my intent.

The stone cracks, crumbles in on itself, and tumbles to the floor sending the upper half shattering into hundreds of sparkling rubies and diamonds.

Then the tower begins to shake.

CHAPTER XXXIX

I RUN FOR MY LIFE.

With the sun stone destroyed, the foundation, the power holding the tower together begins to crumble. I feel it beneath the soles of my boots. Deep cracks rising through the structure. Splitting up the walls and shattering supports throughout the cathedral.

A new urgency rises through me. Adrenaline reignites my body as I reach the stairs. Pieces of the grand staircase peel from the walls as I scamper down the steps, skipping two to three at a time, dodging falling debris and burning embers. A large boulder crashes before me, demolishing a section of the stairs. No thought, no second guessing, I leap, soaring through the air downward, hitting the other side of the platform and tumbling two flights of stairs.

Battered and disoriented, I recover, continuing my descent like a mad man. Large pieces of stone crack behind me, shaking the ground and sending me forward to my knees. Without looking back, I know the steps are gone.

Reaching the bottom of the stairwell, I slam into a wall stopping myself. I sprint as fast as I can shouting my warning to those who can hear me. "Run! Run!"

Choir boys and acolytes scatter as a great billowing cloud of dust and debris explodes behind me with a deafening roar. Innocents are crushed. Screams rise from the rubble and chaos.

A boy just ahead of me, trapped from a fallen stone, screams for help. Sliding to a halt beside him, I roll the rock from his leg as he cries out in more pain.

Bite marks run up and down his arms. Immediately, I flinch. My memory flashes and it all comes back to me. Manson, the little infant in the carriage at Albestan Church. Michael the vampire boy trapped in the fire at the Danbury Hovel. Jackson, the Cresthaven boy who tried to kill me in Cresthaven Manor.

All the ones I couldn't save.

My hand goes to the boy's neck, checking for signs, but there are no puncture wounds.

"It's alright, you're going to be alright."

His brown curls, matted down with sweat and blood, feels slick against my gloves. Bringing my shoulder up under his arm, his height for an adolescent reminds me of my son. "What's your name?" I ask as we navigate through the crumbling structure, dodging tilting pillars and falling stones. Already there are mass casualties. To my left and right, edicts lie scattered about like toys, smashed under piles of rocks and debris. One of their heads has exploded like a melon.

"Charles, sir. Thank you."

"Alright Charles, we're getting you out of here."

"But my parents. I was looking for my parents. They are somewhere in the cathedral. We have to save them!"

Shaking dust from my head, I already feel the guilt before saying the words. "There is no time, Charles. We can't stay. We have to go!"

"But my mother! My father!"

Charles struggles against me, but I know what waits for us if we linger any longer. Adjusting myself, I restrain Charles and force him along, even with him fighting against me the whole way.

We crash onto the grassy grove just outside the cathedral as the last of the building's skeleton caves in on itself. Rumbling and tremors shake the ground of the city Sunstone. Great plumes of dust and debris rise into the blue sky of the morning blocking out the sun.

Coughing from smoke, Charles and I collapse to the floor as the few remaining survivors do the same. Before I have a chance to recover, before I suck in my first breath of fresh air, a crowd begins to form on the edge of the demolished site. Citizens from the city, guards and townsfolk alike move closer. I hear their words of uncertainty and doubt.

"Who's in charge here?"

"What the devil happened?"

"Is that Lord Wolfgang?"

"Nah, it can't be. Rumor has it he's dead."

"Cardinal Glass. Arch Bishop Faeradon. Has anyone seen them?"

What birds could have been seen flying in the morning are now blotted out by the smoke screen creeping through the surrounding trees.

"Mother… father…" coughs Charles as he attempts to stand. He staggers a few feet and falls back down. There is a long gash in his leg, but he'll be able to walk. "Mother… father…"

"Charles, I'm sorry. Any second longer and we would—"

Charles looks back at me, his face flushed and red. "You! It's because of you they are dead!" Charles erupts into tears and staggers away, limping through the crowd and disappears.

Another voice, closer to me now speaks above the rest of the crowd. "Lord Wolfgang, is that really him? Lord Wolfgang! What in God's name happened?" The man, just a commoner among the townsfolk helps me to my feet as I dust off the debris from my tattered coat and scarred armor.

I turn to face the people, wiping away a smear of blood from my forehead. "Good people of Sunstone. A great evil has befallen this sacred city. Having infiltrated the holy order some years ago, this evil undermined the city's sanctity by robbing poor innocent souls of their free will to act upon their wicked desires. Know this! Today this great evil has fallen! The corrupted Holy Order is no more. Let not edicts or acolytes sway your motives any longer.

"You are now free to act and choose on your own without the tyrannical fear of the Holy Order. You must rebuild. Cast out the old ways and find a new path of life. Live your days free of corruption. Do not let evil have its chance to come back. Be strong. Be brave…"

Another man from the crowd steps forward. He is strong and capable, but his demeanor speaks of doubt and worry. "What about the vampires, sir?" he asks. "Won't they return? Surely is there nothing else that can be done?"

Through parting smoke, sunlight makes its way onto my face. A sign perhaps that even in the most dismal of times, if hope is strong, it produces results.

Shading my eyes from the morning light, I glare at the ruins, the people, and the sky. "Surely there is," I say to the man, placing a hand on his shoulder.

Without another word, I begin walking down the street. *There is still one more vampire to deal with.*

CHAPTER
XL

DESPITE THE SHINING SUN, THE streets of Sunstone are cold. Quite similar to the people living here. Wind howls through the sect portions of the city, cutting through back alleys and ripping tarpaulins from their foundations.

Despairing eyes stare at me as I limp along, covering my face as best I can with the fabric a good Samaritan provided me. At least one person views me as a hero.

Looks of scowls and fear seem to be the trend. I their savior and scapegoat, all the same. Now that the iconic tower of the cathedral is missing from the city horizon, uncertainty will be the talk of Sunstone in the months to come.

But really, their woes are hardly my concern at the moment. There are much bigger problems in the world. Ideas the common people can't possibly understand.

As I make the long trek through the streets, lost in thought, I think about the man's words from earlier, the same question that has plagued my family name for centuries. *"What about the vampires?"*

Yes. The vampires. What about them? We beat them didn't we? All of us.

I think about the ones who helped me defeat the Carnalree-see, Faeradon, and Egleaseon. Each of them sacrificing their lives in their own way and I am forever indebted to them.

Diana, your dark eyes. How they follow me everywhere I go. Your long strands of raven black hair flutter through the streets. I envision them everywhere I look, vanishing behind the merchants selling their wares in the street, disappearing within the branches of the birch trees.

I take a deep shuttering breath. The air is ice in my lungs, but renews me just the same.

Diana, my beauty of darkness. How I still long for you. I miss you. It started with *you* and without *you* I am nothing. Gone may be the days of our physical union—*I glance at Enivid on my hip*—but you are always with me.

Suddenly I find myself smiling, thinking of her father, Dora, and how much he wanted to kill me. How that man hated me. All the nights of sneaking in through her window to be with his daughter. We would try to stay as quiet as we could, giggling through the night between the sheets, but sometimes we failed—*I feel my cheeks burning*. And yet, I feel happiness and guilt at the same time. I may not have been able to save his grandson, but Dora played a crucial part in helping me slay the most powerful vampires in the world. The Bawaka. The Hand of God. Without his craftsmanship, Enivid would never have been created. Damn you old man. Thank you for coming through in the end. Your hammer was mighty and your soul was stronger than steel.

I wipe away tears as my mind falls silent. I feel physically ill, but the walk does me well. I turn around a corner and pass children playing in the street. At least they seem unaffected by what's happened in Sunstone. Children. So resilient even in the worst of times.

Two men dressed in black off load a cart as I pass. They remind me of Councilor. That big meaty oaf. If it weren't for him and his mangled bush of a beard, I would have never learned how to control my abilities. Still having bested me in knife throwing, I recall the days when everything was a competition. His growling laugh I could have sworn I heard on the wind just now. Half expecting a slap on my back, I still ponder the day he found Kronklich and I stranded in the Decameron Forest, frozen and near death. Despite his other intentions. Without a doubt the man was resourceful. He was Black Blade assassin to the root and yet his brusque mannerism was still salvageable in the ways of etiquette.

A chilly wind blows from the east but my mind is too occupied to think about the cold. How we were able to find our way out of those mountains, I'm still not sure, but Councilor did it. He promised he would get us to Sunstone even if it was his "secret way."

Waiting for a carriage to pass, I cross the street and make my way over to a vendor with a cozy cart. His horses, bundled up just as much as he is with rich blankets, snort and stamp the ground in disapproval of the snow.

"Well you certainly look like you've been through hell, Sir," says the man tilting his hat to me.

"One tin of Bergamot please," I reply absentmindedly.

The vendor smiles with big red cheeks and says, "Absolutely sir. That will be five copper dauntess."

At the mention of money, I suddenly realize I have none on me. "My apologies. My mind slipped. I have no coin with me." Shaking my head, cloudy and full of memories, I start to walk on, then hear the man calling behind me.

"Sir. Sir! Please…" says the man running up to meet me in the street. "Take it. I just realized who you are. You did this city a great service. It's the least I can do." He tilts his hat again and runs off to attend to his horses.

That was unexpected. I guess that makes two. I manage a smile as I hold the tin of Bergamot tea to my nose, sending me into a tailspin of morbid nostalgia.

Kronklich. What words do I have but—I'm sorry. Truly, undeniably, from the bottom of my miserable black heart. You were more than just a friend. We were companions. Brothers until the end. A brilliant coachmen. A capable doctor. An amazing tracker and undoubtedly one of the best swordsmen I have ever known. Your bow skills were top notch and goddammit—I can't stop the tears from dripping down my dirty face—your tea was fucking brilliant!

I duck into a nearby alley and try to stop myself from sobbing. But the pain racks my ribs, the hurt is unbearable. How does one continue on like this? Knowing your best friend sacrificed his life to ensure you would continue. It's not fair and God be damned, I should be the one who is dead, not him.

I stagger from the shadows of the alley, crunching through the thick snow and back onto the street. *Get a grip, Tenor. Focus.*

No sooner do I banish the thought of Kronklich from my mind, but a new thought replaces it. The whole reason we ended up here in the first place was to save my son, Dorian. I press on, trying to think only of the good times. The days and nights we spent together. I watched him grow into a strong capable boy. The hours we passed practicing with swords in the courtyard. The picnics where we played monsters and demons, running through cornstalks and tripping over vines. Seeing the smile on your mother's face every time you appeared in the room. She loved you so much, Dorian, and that in turn made me love you even more. I know you were brave, all the time locked up in that dark place, surrounded by vampires. I can't imagine what you went through but just know that your father did all he could in the end. I would have easily died for you if I had the chance. I know your mother watches over you and your brother now, the one I will never meet, Edmund. Tell him hello for me, even if he resents me.

Passing through another perimeter wall of the city—is it the fourth or fifth? I'm not sure—I know I am getting close. Soon I will reach the tunnel where the Elysium resides, the secret hideout of the Black Blade Society. But as a group of birds swoop down through a low-bearing archway, my attention is drawn to the north, and suddenly I find myself tracing the journal beneath my breastplate with my finger.

Marcus Cornelius. Still so many questions linger about that man. Just who the hell is he and *where* the hell is he? How did he know so much about the lineages in the vampire underworld?

How did he know about the Wolfgang House? The questions are mind boggling and there are no answers to them.

According to the journal, in his notes, it says the one who uses the ancient artifact, The Hand of God, will bear the gift of immortality. Was it such? Or was it really a curse as Constable mentioned? Am I really immortal? Egleaseon said he was a Vestige, and immortal, yet I was able to slay him in the end. So is it the same for me? The questions go on and on and my mind starts to spin to a bad place. I wonder if I should even worry about it anymore, for who would give me the answers I seek? According to Egleaseon's final words, Marcus Cornelius is the only Vestige left in the world, which means, if I can't find him, then I will never know.

Dogs run barking through the streets as I reach the tunnel, the entryway marking the location of the Elysium.

Whether I find out one day or not, only fate will tell, unless, of course, I die by some misfortune. A blade in my back. A vampire's bite. The list of ways I could die somehow comforts me.

I certainly have a morbid way of thinking.

Passing through the large wooden gate big enough to fit two horses side by side, I make my way down the long arched tunnel filled with torches. I count my steps for some reason, wondering what exactly will happen when I step through the doors, what decision I will make when it comes to it.

Pulling the handle to crack open the door, I pass beyond the threshold of the Black Blade's hideout and into the welcoming darkness of warmth.

All is as it should be.

Quiet inside. A ticking clock somewhere in the distance.

Dust flutters in rays of light; the source comes from the hidden drain grates in the ceiling. The fireplace smolders from a previous fire. The long war table with its maps lingers with no one in its chairs. The maddening walls of weaponry stand idly by, waiting for the next wave of implementers to use them willingly.

I hear Nicholas snoring in some far off room down one of the corridors. Good. It's still early morning. Better for him to rest for now. It's probably best he doesn't know I'm back just yet.

I make my way through the chamber recalling where Winter's resting place is, further down one of the back hallways, and to the right. Here in this bland room of empty walls sits a chair and table, and a single candle. It still flickers with life. Winter must have forgotten to extinguish it.

I sigh, letting the candle be for now.

Walking up to her coffin, I run my hand along its dusty surface while my other grazes over Enivid. Its warmth is comforting yet discerning at the same time. It knows the presence of vampires. Winter is no exception.

I snort to myself, shaking my head in self-revelation. In the end it all came back to this. The black box in the back of the cart. And to think I was so worried about it. Damn Councilor and his secrets. I remember the look of terror in his eyes when I discovered what Winter was.

But she proved herself didn't she? Provided food for us. Killed for us. Even found the secret entrance into the Dark Cathedral.

And then Councilor, you had to insist on coming with us into oblivion, to find the cure that would save your daughter. You thought somehow the key to her salvation resided within the blood of Cresthaven. But you were wrong. All the while I knew there wasn't one. The journal told me that.

In the end, I used you. We needed your brute strength, the strength of a Black Blade to *survive* and I am sorry for that. I'm sorry it has left your daughter fatherless.

Will Winter ever find an end to her vampire days? This I am not sure and I have no intention of telling her anytime soon. Not now, anyway.

"You and I are going to become very good friends," I say softly to Winter's coffin. Taking my hand off of Enivid, I sit down at the table and blow out the candle, allowing the room to become enveloped into darkness. As my mind begins to drift off from exhaustion, my body relaxes into the chair as I listen to the faint sound of Nicholas' snoring wafting down the hallway.

"The three of us have a lot of work to do."

EPILOGUE

I LOVE MY FAMILY. I would do anything for them. They are what keep me together in this hell of a world. They are my strength and reason for hunting and killing every last vampire until the end of time. They are why I do the things I do, seen the places I've seen, and speak of the horrors I now have come to know. I will continue to fight the hordes of darkness until I am struck down. This I swear, in their name. And only then, will I see them again, to rejoice in their bathing light and loving embrace…

END OF BOOK THREE

END OF THE WOLFGANG TRILOGY

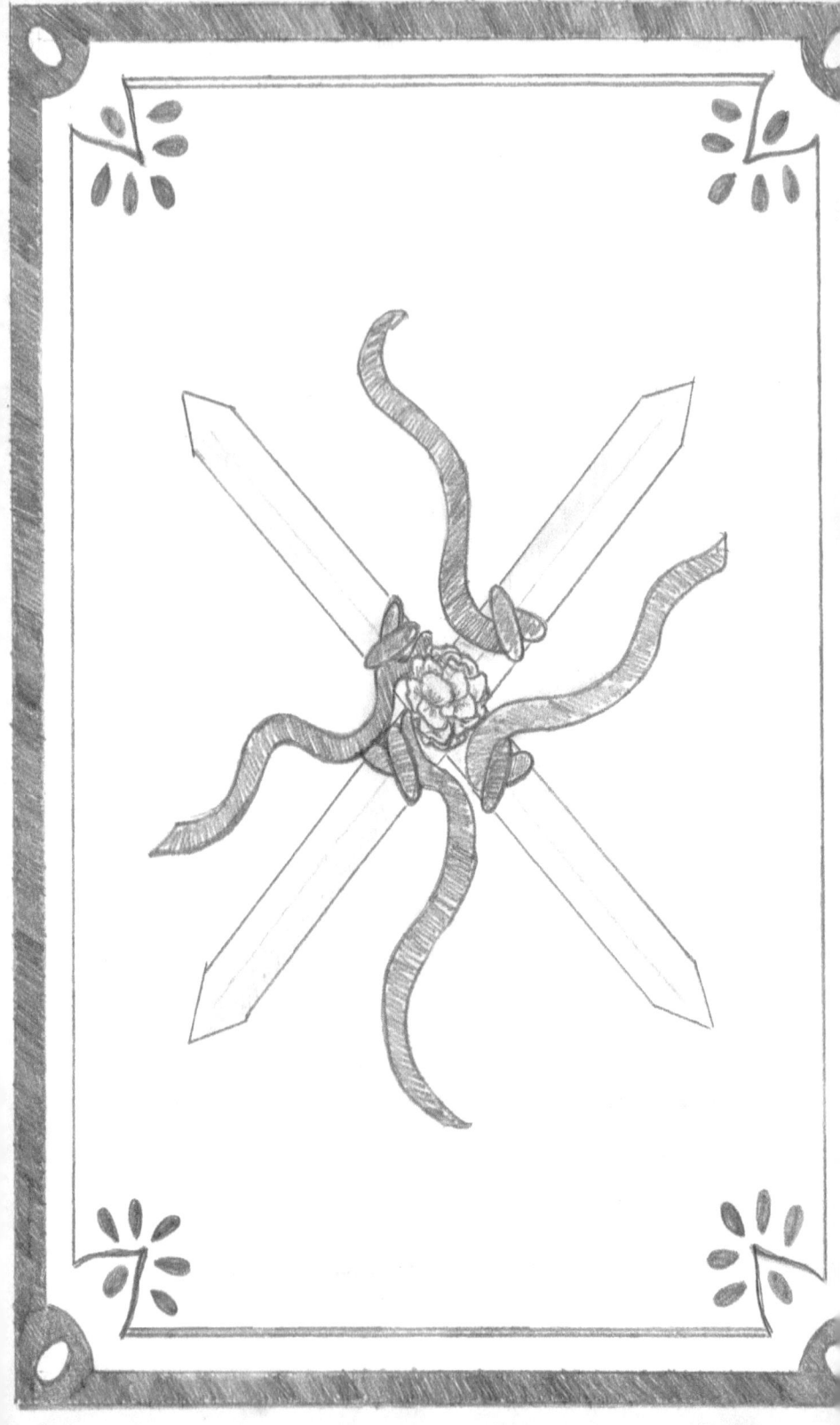

THE WOLFGANG TRILOGY
CAST OF CHARACTERS
IN ORDER OF APPEARANCES:

<u>Lord Egleaseon</u> - Lord of the vampires. Rumored to have existed more than a thousand years. Willingly destroyed himself with The Hand of God.

<u>Tenor Alvadine Wolfgang</u> - Vampire hunter. Lord of Wolfgang Manor. Son of Bealeon Tenor Wolfgang.

<u>Katrina Egleaseon</u> - Defiant vampire daughter of Egleaseon.

<u>Dorian Wolfgang</u> - Heir to Wolfgang Manor. Son of Tenor and Diana Wolfgang.

<u>Diana Wolfgang</u> - Lady of Wolfgang Manor. Wife to Tenor Wolfgang. Daughter of Dora Eddington.

<u>Joachim</u> - Butler/Servant to Wolfgang Manor. Suspected to have abducted Dorian from the Wolfgang House.

<u>James T. Kronklich</u> - Vampire Hunter. Advisor and best friend to Lord Wolfgang. Skilled in the art of all things.

<u>Nester</u> - Clergymen to Albestan Church. Organist and grounds keeper. Protector of innocents.

Bronin - Priest of Albestan Church. Trusted friend and advisor representing the Holy Order to Tenor.

Roul - Master Librarian. Resident vampire of Egleaseon Ruins. Torturer specialist. Advocate for Stellamane.

Caesar - One of the six Carnalreesee. Jester and scout of the vampire clan.

Madame Celeste - Gypsy woman of Widow. Provided the healing paste for Tenor's hand.

Scepter - One of the six Carnalreesee. The sarcastic and witty speaker of the vampire clan. Notorious for using a golden scepter used by kings as a form of persuasion.

Lord Mayor Tremont - The Mayor of Delore. Holds a long history of infatuation with Diana Wolfgang. Despises Lord Wolfgang.

Dora Eddington - Father of Diana Wolfgang. Blacksmith and Engineer of Delore. Known for his bronze work. Despises Tenor for marrying his daughter.

Belladonna - Mysterious woman resembling Diana in Delore. Tenor comes to learn about her dark secrets and inevitable destiny.

Constable - One of the Carnalreesee. Large in nature, serves as the muscle for the vampire clan. Notorious for using his black hook. Husband to Constilla.

Constilla - One of the Carnalreesee. She possesses the unique abilities of a spider. Some say her unquenchable thirst for fashion is stronger than blood. Wife to Constable.

Stellamane - The vampire king that was destroyed for abusing his power. Advocate of torture. His soul was banished to the Devil's Drain by Lord Egleaseon himself.

Councilor - a modern day assassin known as a Black Blade. A scythe enthusiast and expert in throwing knives. He and Tenor possess a long history of competition and rivalry.

Lord Cresthaven - Vampire lord of Westings. Oversees the commerce stability for the commonwealth. Possesses grand schemes of a new utopia.

Victoria Cresthaven - Vampire daughter of Lord Cresthaven. Possesses a high sense of maturity befitting the daughter of an aristocrat.

Jackson Cresthaven - Vampire son of Lord Cresthaven. Has learned to taunt his prey in the most unusual of ways.

Kathryn Cresthaven - Vampire wife to Lord Cresthaven. Lady of the Cresthaven estate.

Nicholas - Reyes the Baker. Bakery shop owner and retired Black Blade. Comes to befriend Tenor and joins the rank of vampire hunter.

Martyr - One of the Carnalreesee. Sadistic in nature, his whims can never be fully understood. He is a wildcard all on his own.

Vargus - One of the Carnalreesee. Being of old noble heritage, his ways are reminiscent of the knight. His red armor and sword serves as testimony to his stoically cold mannerisms.

Faeradon - Archbishop of the Holy Order. There is a long history coordinated between him, the Holy Order and the Carnalreesee. Corrupted the Holy Order for personal gain and was ultimately responsible for the deaths of so many.

Charles - A Balcony boy servant of the Dark Cathedral. Comes to befriend Dorian in the most dire of times.

Winter - Daughter to Councilor. Has succumbed to the vampires curse. She and her father seek a cure.

Asher Vandrake - Marcus Cornelius's attendant and estate caretaker. Ultimately wanted to join the vampire ranks by carrying out errands for Faeradon.

Marcus Cornelius - Doctor and philanthropist known by many. His research is rumored to be vast and his ideals even greater. Possibly a Vestige himself, he may be the last of his kind.

Cardinal Glass - The head of the Holy Order. Succumbed to imprisonment in the Dark Cathedral, formally known as the Grand Cathedral, for his suspicions of a corrupt Holy Order. He was made a vampire as punishment and used as an example to the people.

MONSTER COMPENDIUM

Caretakers - Lost souls condemned to walk the earth in search of new hosts. With their physical form consisting of a rotted walking skeleton, they may possess old articles on their bodies from previous lives. The most prominent feature however is the swaying lantern with blue flame. It is said that this is the heart of their existence. An individual struck by the blue fire is subject to possession, where the caretaker's souls then transmits to the new host and the old frame is left behind. It is said some caretakers have lived for hundreds of years, possibly a thousand, always roaming, searching for answers to their existence and the chance to move on.

Bogarts - Gray sinewy creatures that serve the vampires. Possessing a single yellowish eye in the center of their face, their compromised sight is made up in the sharpness of their teeth and claws. These ghoul-like monsters are derived from the spinal cords of humans, infused with the blood of a vampire. With their strong urge to proliferate, these fast moving monsters seek out human targets to pass on their disease. There is a three-day gestation period before the host that's bitten by a bogart molds into bogart. Bogarts can be killed just like any human can.

Lechers - Mindless undead corpses that walk the earth. With their origin unknown, rumors speculate their existence stems from the evil corruption plaguing the earth's soil. Driven by an insatiable hunger, they are known to "pop-up" unexpectedly and without warning, attacking and devouring anything that isn't already dead. Monster hunters say they are controlled by the undead, be it vampire or specter, but their is no real evidence of this. Lechers are very dangerous in large numbers and can only be killed by piercing what's left of their brain.

Eye Moss - Known to be the watchful eyes of the vampires, these brown and green mucous-like appendages extend from the earth in the most unusual places. The eye stalks watch for potential prey that will eventually fall one day. Even though they may not look mobile in nature, mucus glands allow them to slide across the ground similar to that of a snail, eventually engulfing carcasses to consume and grow. Similar to that of a mushroom, their habitat consists mainly of dark, wet places where time seems not to matter.

Willdermen - An ancient clan of werewolf-like beasts that proliferate in the forests across the world. With no real clues leading to their origin, some say it was a rabid wolf that bit a human on the brink of death after having been drained of blood by a vampire. Currently, the number of willdermen in existence is unknown, but it is known that their numbers are rising. They are able to take the form of man or wolf at will, while sometimes a cross between both. Terrifying rumors of willdermen ransacking villages in the night to increase their numbers is not unheard of. Some say their is a deep hatred between the willdermen and vampires. Although it is unclear wether or not silver effects a willdermen, dismemberment seems to be the most effective way to dispatch the beast.

Vampire - Undead creatures of the night possessing supernatural powers of sight, smell and speed. Although a majority of vampires show similar traits in their collective powers (ex: turning into bats or mist, elongating parts of their bodies for malicious intent, etc.), some have superseded their basic abilities of being able to resist more worldly harm than others. The Carnalreesee for instance can not be killed by conventional means. Only sunlight or holy relic can do the job. And their is only one vampire known to have resisted sunlight. Lord Egleaseon.

Vestige - Immortal beings said to be the predecessor of vampires and humans. Although the beginning of their existence is unknown, it said they have been around longer than the vampire. They are the physical and metaphysical manifestation of light, darkness, and love.

Daver Hound - A sickly-type of demon dog with fur-less skin that's serve the house of Egleaseon. Even in the death of their master's wake they continue to prowl the ruined corridors of the ancient castle, seeking out their next meal, regardless if its dead or alive. Daver Hounds run in packs, ensuring that if one of them is ever in trouble, others will be right around the corner to give aid. Their weeping skin which postulates blood and ooze serves as a way of marking territories, similar to that of a wild cat's spray.

Gellies - aquatic amphibious fish-frog creatures living within the waterways of the Faust and Carpella rivers. Mouths filled with razor sharp piranha teeth, instead of the mouth opening vertically, these unique creatures maws open horizontally, allowing them to confuse their prey with aquatic plants rather than a typical frog. With beady eyes set on each side of its face, it's a wonder how gellies are able to see their prey so well. Typical hunting habits consist of lying in wait at the bottom of the river bed among plants and rocks, waiting for movement from about the waters surface. Once convinced of worthy prey, they "spring" to life, propelling their bodies through the water and projecting themselves at targets through the air with their powerful legs. Their croaking sounds can be heard day or night.

Atters - Mutated corrupted squirrels that plague the Decameron Forest. Black fur-less skin stretches over their skeletal system giving them the appearance of starving bats. However wingless they are, the filmy white over their eyes allows them to see their prey from very long distances, filtering their colors and heat signatures through the densest thickets. Their unique skin, resilient to the acid rain, is a highly sought after material, particularly from the patrons of Widow. They are also hunted for their meat, however even the toughest of hunters label their catches "barely edible." And much like lechers, they are dangerous in numbers, often times working together in numbers and communicating with one another through various chirping sounds. They have been known to wipe out entire caravan parties in a single night.

Specters - Apparitions of the ghostly dead. Projected energy existing incorporeal on the earth plane. Also know as evil or malicious ghosts, they are the after effects of violent death victims. They go by other names as well: poltergeists, banshees, etc. Holding onto the earth by unforeseen circumstance, many vampires see such a fate if killed by their own kind. A sort of curse among an already defiant resolution. Specters have a deep rooted hatred for all things living and will seek them out to snuff their existence.

Ice Crows - Malicious, carnivorous birds of prey that live in the cold regions of the Cordova Mountains. Varying in colors of blue and white feathers, the distinguishing feature that betrays an ice crows identity is that of its red beak, stained from the blood of its victims. They have been known to follow potential victims for miles, watching them from the distant trees, waiting for them to slow down, weaken, until they were unable to defend themselves. Unlike the carrion vulture, ice crows kill their victims before they eat them.

THREE VAMPIRE LORDS
FIRST GENERATION

| FAERADON | EGLEASEON | STELLAMANE |

SECOND GENERATION

| CECIL | | KATRINA |

THE CRESTHAVENS

THE CARNALREESEE

VARGUS	SCEPTER	CONSTILLA
MARTYR	CONSTABLE	CAESAR
BOGARTS	DAVERHOUNDS	

THE HOLY ORDER OF SUNSTONE

CARDINAL GLASS

ARCHBISHOP FAERADON

VARGUS — EDICTS — MARTYR

PRIESTS — CLERGYMEN

ACOLYTES — ALTERBOYS — BALCONY BOYS

The Dark Cathedral

Chamber of the Cardinal

Heaven's Door

Quarters

Quarters

Hidden Laboratory

Library

Antechamber

Grove of Trees

Entry Hall

Chapel

Great Hall

Dining Hall

Dungeons

Aqueducts

Catacombs

Hidden Passage

ACKNOWLEDGEMENTS

Creating the Wolfgang Trilogy has been a long and arduous project for the last four years. But I can honestly say the journey was nothing short of wonderful, exhilarating, and exciting. Especially for those involved in seeing its completion a reality. And it is with great joy now that I thank those individuals for helping me in the last leg of the trilogy being complete. In a sense, we have all received Communion in one way or another. And the success of this series could not have happened without the following lovely souls:

A great eternal, undying thank you to my wife, Diana, for helping me in all things Communion-related. Between the revisions and artwork and feedback, she has been the one to pull me through the darkness before it swallowed me whole. Without her guiding light, the book would never be what it is today. Super huge thanks to my editor, Deborah DeNicola, for continuing to work on the Wolfgang Trilogy project and always providing sincere feedback with the utmost integrity. She has proven to be a willful and reliable ally. Chrissy Moon for serving as my link to the outside world. It is she who has guided me in the publicity world and continues to have faith in my work, passing the word along when and as much as she can. She understands public relations a whole lot better than myself and I thank her for her intuition. Janis Humpage for being one of my top peer reviewers. Your opinions and feedback has forced me to set the bar even higher for the next project. Thanks for always egging me on. Nick Reyes for your continued support and genuine interest in a fantasy world that otherwise wouldn't come across your lap. I'm glad I opened the door for you. My daughter London for your continued support and getting excited when I get excited for completing a milestone here, a chapter there. Also for your lovely support and belief in my artistic abilities. Eternal gratitude to Lori Colbeck, for your quick response time in production and completing the project. None of this would have come together as quick as it did. With so many more to thank, I couldn't possibly mention them here. So thank you to everyone else I didn't mention. You know who you are.

So many empty corridors I have walked. So many drops of my blood have I spilt. For this book and the ones before. I would do it all again, willingly. And so as my final thank you, I send it out to all of my fans, the ones who read my work and send me praise. You are the true life blood to all of this. You keep the spirit and enthusiasm alive, even in the deadest of nights! Who knows, perhaps there will be more blood to be shed. Actually, I am quite sure there is...

A CHAT WITH 'COMMUNION' AUTHOR F.D. GROSS

by Chrissy Moon

Chrissy Moon: *First of all, thank you for taking the time to talk to me. This is so exciting. First of all, congratulations for completing your beloved Wolfgang Trilogy! How does it feel?*

FD Gross: Thank you so much, Chrissy! It feels like the Titan finally lifted the boulder off of my shoulders after watching me from the distance for so long. Taunting me. Smiling its smirk of knowing and suffering.

I can finally breathe again and although it is over and stimulates feelings of sadness for me, I still feel a sense of accomplishment. A tale of a harrowing adventure that will be left behind long after I part from this world.

CM: *What a lovely way to express your feelings. Yes, this wonderful work of yours will absolutely live on.*

There is so much I'd like to ask you, so I suppose I'll just pick one question and go from there!

Let's focus on COMMUNION first, for obvious reasons. It's your newest book and the final trilogy installment. First off, I absolutely adored it. Even though WOLFGANG, INQUISITION, AND COMMUNION are all from the same story, each book has a subtly different feel to it. You've described INQUISITION as being survivalist. I might peg COMMUNION as being more adventurous; would you agree? How would you describe its overall feel?

FG: I would definitely say it has its moments of adventure, and that over all, its a culmination of Tenor Wolfgang truly finding himself. He now has all the tools necessary to conquer his foes. There's nothing holding him back.

Now he gets to focus on one thing and one thing alone. Getting Dorian back.

Although this has been the premise and main drive of the first two books, Communion is the metaphor for completion, becoming one, body and soul, quite literally in some cases for Dorian and Egleaseon's sake, the ending of the trilogy, Tenor accepting who he is, becoming a Vestige himself, and realizing there is still more to do in a world plagued by vampires and monsters.

So in one word, I would have to go with COMMUNION gives the sense of COMPLETION. Hence the tag line, "A new legend in vampire hunting is born."

CM: Perfectly said. Thank you!

And since you mentioned Dorian, I think we need to talk about him a little bit. I just have to say, I loved his character. He was so strong and quite a spitfire himself. I know this is not the most pleasant of topics, but I need to know: How did it feel to kill off Dorian? And while we're on the subject, how do you reconcile killing off beloved characters in your mind? Do you feel guilt, or do you have a more objective viewpoint about this?

FG: Although I like to think of myself as an emotionally charged individual, the world, in many ways, has desensitized me. It's possible that the very act might contribute to great story telling, but I could never fully admit that. What do we really know, right?

It felt terrible killing off Dorian, but at the same time I knew it was necessary that he was the one to be sacrificed. It was predetermined from the very beginning where his fate lied.

Dorian's death was essential for the development of Tenor further and to create this awesome vampire killing machine. Desensitize a man and make him suffer, and soon you've created something remarkably resilient and powerful. It's a scary concept for sure.

As whole, whether I feel resentment or guilt for killing off characters, I would say no. As a writer, I tend to stay objective with developments and continuously press forward, very rarely looking back with regrets. It is seldom my main objectives become de-railed by my character's whims. Don't get me wrong though. We do have arguments in my head about direction of the story sometimes, but this usually ends with me coming out on top. Ha!

CM: Ha! I'm glad you're... mostly in control. And who can argue with the results? This is magnificent work you've created. Truly.

It makes sense that his son's death was necessary for Tenor's growth. Seeing new sides of his personality was quite satisfying. Even at the end there, when he's thinking about all the people he lost on his journey, he's doing a little bit of internal teasing and joking. I even noticed a speck of snobiness earlier in the book! It was great.

My question to you, Frank, is whether or not all of Tenor's personality aspects were in place to begin with. As you wrote COMMUNION, did Tenor Wolfgang have a complete persona in your mind, or did you have to do a little more character constructing?

FG: Tenor's character traits were definitely in place during the first novel, WOLFGANG, whereas in the second book, INQUISITION, his demeanor sort of broke down. He was harmed in many ways, adding to from the first book, and so, I think what I'm trying to say is that his personality was depicted constantly by the actions he encountered.

His character was always cold, personality wise, but the people in his life, memories of Diana and having Kronklich around brought out the best in him. The caring side of him. And of course there were times he was uncomfortable around Councilor and Nicholas, since they were another breed of persona. And somewhat equals to him skill wise.

I think for COMMUNION, Tenor's overall presence was the most confident in knowing that he knew exactly where his son was, so even though he couldn't technically relax and kick back, there was still a sense of relief for him knowing a destination. He knew his inquisition was over. No more searching. No more guessing. Something tangible lies waiting for him on the horizon.

In this case, Dorian.

COMMUNION really showed his real self towards the end.

CM: I'd like to switch it up a little and talk about one of my favorite scenes in the book, which is the research scene in chapter 12.

I loved the descriptions of the library, as well as kind of seeing first-hand how the dynamics between the three men has changed since INQUISITION. Can I get a little insight into the enjoyment you must have had in creating this scene, and all that went into it?

FG: The library scene was more of a natural flow of writing when I got to this portion of the novel.

At this point, I had a feel for the three characters and how well they meshed with one another, despite their polar opposite personalities. Truly it was a fun experience, taking the reader through exploration and research in a grand library in an exquisite estate. I was trying to provide the feeling of how aristocrats would of interacted back in those times (such as the dinner scene), even though Tenor and Councilor were out of there element. It was Kronklich who really benefited to such a massive library.

The general idea of the library scene came from my past inspirations of movies and books, particularly Young Frankenstein (his father's secret library) and Sherlock Holmes. Not to mention the twenty billion fantasy novels where wizards go to research! So as you can see, adding such a scene was pure joy for me.

Relating to modern day, libraries are just as functional back then as they are now. And we seek them out to learn information, and in many cases, to unwind and relax (for some folks). So it worked out for the trio. That they could stop here, seek out answers, recover and rest, and without feeling the guilt that Dorian was still being held by the Carnalreesee. It was a task, managing Tenor's feelings about this.

CM: I think you did a fantastic job in handling Tenor's feelings during that scene. It's nice to know you enjoyed it and you know, while there were unique aspects of COMMUNION, there's also quite a bit of consistency in your writing, things your fans loved since DAY ONE.

For example, the horror aspect and the way you bring all kinds of scary creatures to life - personally, I like how your depiction of these creatures are neither traditional nor made up out of nowhere. It just feels really genuine to your craft and how you wanted to construct this world.

With this in mind, I just have to tell you that the gellies were terrifying to me for some reason. I can't explain exactly what it is, but man, what a great scene with them! And those haunted armors were a bit different from what Tenor has encountered previously during his journey. I also need to commend you for the genuine creepiness of the idea of using people as building-blocks. That was disturbing on so many levels, and as a horror fan, I loved it. What were some of your favorite horror scenes, both in COMMUNION and in the trilogy overall?

FG: Thanks for the kind words, Chrissy. I like to think there's something in the Wolfgang Trilogy for everyone.

Where do I begin with my favorite horror scenes? There are so many!

One of my favorite scenes in COMMUNION, although not entirely horrific in a sense, was when Dorian was in the catacombs and had a conversation with one of the acolytes in the wall. The talking skeleton. And then there shortly after his encounter with the caretakers. Those are one of my favorite monsters. Structurally and motivation wise. For Tenor, there were so many horrific scenes, I can't even count them all. But to go with one of them, I'd say the most that sticks out is the scene where he's forced to watch Councilor die. It was emotionally moving for me. Aside from Kronklich's final scene.

Traveling back in time now, revisiting the first novel, WOLFGANG, one of my favorite horror scenes there was hands down when Tenor and Bronin encountered the vampire master librarian, Roul. He was a sick, twisted individual. There was a lot of description and dialogue exchange during that encounter which also effectively lent details about Stellamane. And finally, overall for the entire trilogy, I'll take the scene in INQUISITION when Tenor has his eye plucked out from the ice crow. Gruesome. Painful. Gory. Yeah.

CM: Yes! That eye-plucking scene. You're right. There are so many great scenes throughout the trilogy.

I thought Constilla from INQUISITION was a badass, and a creepy one at that. You already know how much I adore Egleaseon and if I can't have him, I could see myself settling for Cresthaven.

I mean, we know you're a capable horror writer, but you've also proven yourself to be quite skilled in writing action. There were quite a number of engaging action scenes in COMMUNION - and there were so many times where you sort up upped the ante and put in some intrigue. Like, personally, all the scenes with holy fire just stole the show for me. Dorian had some breathtaking action scenes as well, so, great work!

Now, how are you able to combine action, horror, fantasy, and even literary fiction so seamlessly? If Wolfgang were a movie or a TV series, what genre would you classify it as?

FG: Is that so? Falling for the vampires I see! No worries, its completely acceptable these days.

Thanks for the compliment in action sequence writing. It's always been a thing of mine. Sometimes things need to be spruced up.

How I construct all the elements together as you described is sort of a blend method of creativity, passion, and practice. One exercise I always liked to do was write second person fantasy adventures. I did this a lot in my younger days, but over time, you start adding the bits and pieces of different genres. I won't lie, college classes and workshops helped me as well. To be critiqued by my peers, pointing out the senseless dribble of redundancy was a huge flaw of mine.

But at the same time I realized I really enjoyed audiences reading my work, giving me feed back, opinions, what they hated, what they loved. So over time it finally just clicked one day. And to add to that, I've always loved metaphors and play on words, word games, etc. So I found out that not only can you experiment with sentence structures and placements, but you could also experiment with the words themselves. Puzzles have always intrigued me. Maybe that's why I'm an avid gamer as well. Horror was always somewhere lingering in the background, waiting to surface, and I think my affinity with gothic architecture, schemes, moods, colors, was the gateway into that horrific realm.

If Wolfgang was ever made into a movie (crossing fingers) I would hate to label it myself. There are so many elements to it, you could effectively label it whatever you want. I have peace of mind knowing those types of decisions are left up to my readers.

CM: Beautiful answer about the genre and wow! Second-person fantasy! I don't even know where I would begin with that personally, so your expertise is starting to make a lot more sense to me.

There is a lot of symbolism in the whole trilogy, and oftentimes it's quite subtle. I think I may have to reread it all just to find things I've surely missed.

A lot of beauty is packed into this series. Countless poignant quotes, using music in analogies... you really give even the most critical reader something substantial and noteworthy to hold onto, I think.

There are times, especially when Tenor is narrating about his family, where the flow is just so smooth and lovely. Countless succinct opening lines in chapters. I could go on and on.

This part isn't really a question. I more wanted to tell you one of my favorite quotes in COMMUNION: "Suspended high above, somewhere between heaven and hell, I wonder if I'll ever see either one."

As you know, this is towards the end, and I find it not only useful for the sequence it's in, but also perfectly said and destined to be a world-famous quote.

It's one of those sayings that can make a reader have some introspective moments, inspire them to write something of their own, or even evaluate their own life. Magnificent. We don't have room to list every beautiful quote from the book, but they are plentiful and just waiting to be discovered.

FG: Introspect. Evaluation of their own lives. These are all great take-aways from reading the trilogy. My biggest wish for readers is to soak up the words and make sense of it in their own way. As mentioned before, there is something for everyone, and that's good enough for me.

CM: *Well, the ending is gorgeous. I see how you set it up for the end in the last few chapters and it is really poignant, uplifting, succinct.*

Aside from this I also want to talk about how, even though you left a couple open threads for new possible adventures - which everyone would love if you choose to do so - one really gets the feeling of closure. And it's not only because the storytelling itself was great; it's also because there are certain words and passages that you bring full circle.

So for example, we have Tenor's words about his family at COMMUNION'S end, which parallels his words before chapter one in WOLFGANG, which I thought was neat.

Also - you know I have to mention him again - but Egleaseon's COMMUNION chapters also kind of come full circle. I may or may not have memorized some of his words in his prologue in WOLFGANG, so him saying "What resilience!" about Tenor, really tickled me. It's like you're saying that you really know where your story hails from and what its original intention was, and you follow through with this purpose thoroughly. I respect that.

Thank you again for bringing Egleaseon back. Even though he's a fictional, evil, twice-destroyed vampire-vestige, I have faith that he will notice me one day.

In the meantime, I have to say that your instincts in telling this trilogy is so spot-on. It makes it even more bittersweet that it is over.

I know we've talked about this before and if I recall, last time we spoke you hinted at a story you were working on that is from the same universe as WOLFGANG. Any updates on this, and can you give us the scoop of anything else WOLFGANG-related in the foreseeable future?

FG: Rumor does have it that I am working on another piece that is in fact from the Wolfgang world. As it turns out, having left the ending to interpretation and with some open leads to go with it, there is a strong chance I could return to the Wolfgang lore. But currently I have no foreseeable time frame. I do have another project I am working on.

CM: Well, the literary world is waiting for your next project. We can't wait to see what you'll do next.

Before I let you go, can you talk to us a little about how you undoubtedly grew as a writer and creator, while writing each installment of this trilogy?

FG: I most certainly can. Writing the first book, WOLFGANG, was a huge learning process back in the day.

I knew I wanted to write a book and had all the necessary passion and support to move forward with it, but never new the enormity of the undertaking. Hours upon hours of proofreading, editing, revising, phone calls, rejections...the list goes on. Of course, as is for most authors, writing a book can be quite daunting to say the least. Becoming wrapped up in a world you are creating can sometimes force you to fade from the real world.

With that said, I had to learn how to shut it off during certain times of my life when I moved on to create the second book, INQUISITION. Writing this trilogy has taught me even more than what I already possess in the virtue of focus and patience.

By the time I got to writing COMMUNION, I was 150% vested in the story and very confident where everything would end. I would say to any aspiring writer the best thing you can do when writing prose or poetry is to keep WRITING without stopping to critique yourself. You will always have plenty of time to go back and fix things.

Since being in the author world, I have met many new people and all of them have been wonderful experiences. I'll take the time right now to say thank you to all of YOU. It's been an extraordinary journey. And of course, like all adventures, when one ends, another begins...

F. D. Gross is the creator and writer of The Wolfgang Trilogy series. A new legend in vampire hunting emerges with his works of literature. He writes many different types of fiction and experiences the world for inspiration. Traveling is a passion and resting in haunted places is another. Working in a haunted house happens to be one of his joys in life.

Aside from full-length novels, Frank has published various short stories ranging from dark twisted tales to open ended mysteries. He resides in South Florida with his wife, daughter, and three cats.

Website - https://www.wolfgangchronicles.com/

Goodreads - https://www.goodreads.com/author/show/15919155.F_D_Gross

Instagram - https://www.instagram.com/fd_gross/

Twitter - https://twitter.com/GrellDragon

Facebook - https://www.facebook.com/Wolfgang.Chronicles/

Youtube - https://www.youtube.com/channel/UCf-ODvSjF-pN-21nxe8kVnRw

Amazon - https://www.amazon.com/F.D.-Gross/e/B01LX-M86GO/ref=ntt_dp_epwbk_0

ALSO BY F.D. GROSS

THE WOLFGANG TRILOGY:
Wolfgang
Inquisition

SHORT STORY APPEARANCES IN
ANTHOLOGIES:

"Cords"
Demonic Household: See Owners Manual

"Cervantes the Puppet Master"
Demonic Carnival: First Ticket's Free

"The Locked Door"
At Deaths Door

WOLFGANG

Book One of the Wolfgang Trilogy

The book that started it all…

On the search for his missing son, Tenor Wolfgang must explore the depths of a ruined medieval castle while battling against the forces of darkness.

See what reviewers are saying about *Wolfgang*:

"Such a great book about hunting the evil in the night. An amazing story, with great character development and all killer, no filler content." – *Spencer Scott Holmes*

"Great story! A book that after you read it, you feel compelled to read it again to make sure you didn't miss anything." – *Nick Reyes*

"Captivating and page turning!" – *MolleeB*

"If you read "Wolfgang" now you will be hooked!" – *Lucile Arnusch*

"This book had me from the start. It got right to the point and it's pretty much non-stop action till the end." - *Kelsey*

"Any fan of the paranormal and vampires will find this book an absolute treat to read." – *Laura Furuta*

"Very cleverly written. 5 stars." – *Susan Angela Wallace*

INQUISITION
Book Two of the Wolfgang Trilogy

The journey continues with Tenor Wolfgang and James Kronklich as they race across a frozen gothic countryside in pursuit of Tenor's only son, Dorian. A runaway train. The Carnalreesee. Haunted forests. This chaotic ride of strife and suffering seems to have no end. Yet nothing will stop the band of vampire hunters in finding the answers they seek.

See what reviewers are saying about *Inquisition*:

"Inquisition was awesome. I think that's the perfect word to describe it. Awesome." – *Amazon Reviews*

"This book doesn't quite fit into one genre. It has some aspects of horror, fantasy, literary, and so much more. It's part of what makes it unique." – *Amazon reviews*

"What Gross does well, he does very, very well." – *Amazon Reviews*

"In Inquisition, you can immerse yourself in fast-paced action, strange forests, and characters at both ends of the spectrum of good and evil." – *Amazon Reviews*

"While I was reading this book I couldn't wait to get to the end to see what was going to happen. When I got to the end, I didn't want to stop reading!" – *Goodreads Reviews*

"This story is an interesting and excellent follow up to the first book in the series." – *Goodreads Reviews*

"This book is for you if you like: vampires & other gothic horror creatures, chase scenes & fight scenes, an "imperfect" main character, and a winding plot with varied settings, pace, and mood (as long as you can handle a little blood and guts along the way)." – *Goodreads Reviews*

www.ingramcontent.com/pod-product-compliance
Lightning Source LLC
Chambersburg PA
CBHW020235110726
47898CB00004B/1273